THE NYOGTHA
VARIATIONS

Novels by John Michael Greer

The Weird of Hali:

I – Innsmouth

II – Kingsport

III – Chorazin

IV – Dreamlands

V – Providence

VI – Red Hook

VII – Arkham

Ariel Moravec Occult Mysteries:

The Witch of Criswell

The Book of Haatan

Others:

The Fires of Shalsha

Star's Reach

Twilight's Last Gleaming

Retrotopia

The Shoggoth Concerto

The Nyogtha Variations

A Voyage to Hyperborea

The Seal of Yueh Lao

Journey Star

THE NYOGTHA
VARIATIONS

A Fantasy with Pseudopods

John Michael Greer

AEON

Published in 2024 by
Aeon Books

Copyright © 2020, 2024 by John Michael Greer

The right of John Michael Greer to be identified as the author of this work has been asserted in accordance with §§ 77 and 78 of the Copyright Design and Patents Act 1988.

British Library Cataloguing in Publication Data

A C.I.P. for this book is available from the British Library

ISBN-13: 978-1-91595-203-5

Cover art by Margaux Carpio
Typeset by Medlar Publishing Solutions Pvt Ltd, India

www.aeonbooks.co.uk

CONTENTS

CHAPTER 1

UNQUIET DREAMS

Still in her nightgown, Brecken Kendall climbed the stairs as quietly as the elderly wooden steps would let her, opened the door and slipped into the second floor apartment. Pale light of an autumn morning splashed through the windows onto familiar shapes: a low table in the middle of the parlor, a sofa against one wall, a well-aged upright piano against the facing wall with sheet music stacked all anyhow atop it. She pushed the door behind her until the latch clicked softly shut, started for the kitchen.

An instant later six shapeless black things came bounding toward her from the far end of the room, calling in high piping voices, "Mama Brecken! Mama Brecken!"

"Hush," she said, smiling down at them. "You'll wake your mother." Then, changing from English to a whistled language of musical notes: ♪*Let me see to breakfast, and then we can tell each other our names today and talk about our dreams.*♪

They quieted, watched her with an assortment of luminous greenish eyes as she went to the big slow cooker in the kitchen, made sure the Scotch oats she'd set to cook the night before were ready. When at rest, which wasn't often, they resembled iridescent black beachballs half inflated, sprouting pseudopods of varying shapes. Their half-transparent mantles looked gelatinous but were actually cool and dry, and the

1

masses inside resembled clustered black bubbles, from which eyes emerged at intervals and then sank back down again. Hideous? Brecken had thought so the first time she'd seen a shoggoth—had that been only five years back?—but time and certain intimacies had changed that assessment. Now they were as essential a part of her life as the instruments she played and the music she composed.

Once she'd checked the oatmeal, she went back into the parlor and sat on the floor near the table, folding her legs underneath her. The habits of a gawky adolescence had mostly fallen into her past. She'd discarded the gaudy colors she favored back then for tones that didn't clash quite so grievously with the light brown of her skin, and taken to tying back her hair—long, black, somewhere between curly and wavy—so it didn't incessantly fall forward into her face. Other changes, subtler, set her apart from the nervous young woman whose photo hung on the wall over the piano, a silver flute in her hand.

The moment she settled, six shoggoth broodlings slid over and heaped themselves in and around her lap, looking up expectantly through varying numbers of temporary eyes, giving off a scent a little like ripe Brie cheese: a sign of ordinary calm, that last, one of many scents that marked shoggoth emotions. ♪My name today is Dreams Of Watching,♪ she whistled in the shoggoth language, ♪and I'll tell you why in a little while. Now tell me your names.♪

She had given all of them names in the human fashion, names that would stay with them for more than a single day. The names humans used for themselves felt wrong, though, and so she'd settled on terms from music, assigned according to their habits of movement and speech and the lasting alliances that formed among them in their first weeks of life. Presto, Allegro, and Adagio ran together, and were respectively quick, forceful, and calm in their speech and actions. Vivace and Andante rarely left each other's presence, though one was lively and the other leisurely. Then there was Fermata, who was smaller than the others and quieter; she thought before saying or doing much of anything, and sought out Brecken's or her mother's company more often than that of her broodmates.

♪*My name today is Rises Up,*♪ piped Presto. Before she had finished speaking, Vivace said, ♪*Mine is Patch Of Moonlight.*♪ The others spoke in turn, names tumbling over one another— they were not quite three years old, but shoggoths matured faster than humans and their language was inborn, so they could speak like seven- or eight-year-old children.

At last only Fermata was left. ♪*I have the same name as yesterday,*♪ she said after a little while. ♪*Into A Quiet Place.*♪

♪*You're not supposed to do that,*♪ said Allegro, who had a bossy streak.

♪*Is that true?*♪ Brecken asked her.

Allegro opened three more eyes in surprise. ♪*Can you really do that?*♪

♪*If you feel exactly the same way today as yesterday, yes,*♪ Brecken told her. ♪*You know what you should do now, don't you?*♪

Allegro huddled down a little in embarrassment, but slid over to Fermata and with the formality of the young said, ♪*I take back my words, Into A Quiet Place. You can choose whatever name you want.*♪

♪*So can you,*♪ said Fermata. The two of them flowed up against each other—a shoggoth hug, as Brecken thought of it—and then Allegro slid back to Adagio and Presto. With that settled, Brecken got them talking about their dreams, and described two of hers, including the one where she'd watched their mother and so gotten her name for that day: an ordinary social habit among shoggoths, one of many she'd taken up since they came into her life.

They'd just finished discussing their dreams when another shoggoth flowed out through the gap under the bedroom door. Full-grown by the standards of her kin, the smallest of the shoggoth kinds, she would have been some four feet across if she'd drawn herself into a sphere. As it was, she moved in a subtle architecture of pseudopods and flowing curves spread across six feet or so of floor. Pale eyes blinked open and a speech-orifice formed, said "Good morning." Her voice sounded unnervingly like Brecken's—she'd learned to speak English in adulthood, and so never went past the habit of mimicry to find a voice of her own, as her broodlings had.

"Good morning," Brecken said with a smile. The broodlings all bounded over to the newcomer, calling out variously "Mama!" in English and ♪*Broodmother!*♪ in the shoggoth language, and she scooped them up in an assortment of pseudopods, tasted their surfaces to be sure they were in good health, squeezed and patted them and replied to their greetings with affectionate trills and pipings of her own.

Sho, Brecken thought. My improbable darling. She reached out, and Sho flowed into her embrace, wrapped pseudopods around her, raised part of herself close to Brecken's mouth to receive a kiss.

♪*It is well with you?*♪ Brecken asked.

♪*Yes and no. My name today is Unquiet Dreams. And with you?*♪

♪*Yes. My name today is Dreams of Watching. Do you wish to tell me your dreams?*♪

♪*Later, I think.*♪ Changing languages: "How is June?"

"Fine. I've been down to check on her already. If she just gets enough rest—"

A ripple of amusement ran through Sho. "Humans aren't good at that." Brecken laughed, but didn't argue the point.

Later, when breakfast had been served and eaten, when Sho was in the kitchen teaching Vivace and Andante how to take care of dishes and the other broodlings were sweeping up dust from the floor with more enthusiasm than efficiency, Brecken picked up her composition notebook and went looking for a mechanical pencil. Once she'd found it, she turned, looked across the parlor at the iridescent black shapes doing ordinary chores in their far from ordinary way. Unquiet dreams, she thought, and wondered why the words troubled her so much.

She had too much work to do to linger over the thought. The old sofa creaked as she sat on it, creaked again as she shifted to get the notebook. She had opened it to a nearly blank page of staff paper when a whistle came from below: ♪May I?♪

It was Fermata, as she guessed at once. ♪Of course,♪ she replied. A moment later the broodling was on the couch, and in another moment she nestled into Brecken's lap. Brecken stroked her for a little while, and Fermata quivered and emitted a scent like freshly washed mushrooms, then closed most of her eyes and slipped over onto the dreaming-side.

Unquiet dreams. Brecken pushed the thought aside, concentrated on the quartet for recorders she was writing.

* * *

"You made the New York *Times* this morning," said June Satterlee. Brecken, who was pouring coffee, gave her a dubious look, and the old woman laughed. "Exactly. No better than the last time, I'm sorry to say."

Morning sunlight poured in through the windows of the first floor parlor, glowed on the bindings of old books on the shelves, the sofa on which June sat, the varnish of the grand piano that filled a good quarter of the room. It glowed likewise on the dark brown of June's skin, rose flannel of her bathrobe, neat silver braids of her hair. Her right hand rested in her lap, fingers half-clenched, and the right side of her face sagged noticeably.

Brecken finished pouring the coffee. "Do you need a straw?"

"No, I'm fine." The right arm shifted and strained as she tried to reach with it, and the hand slid along her thigh, reached its limit about halfway to the cup: most of an inch further, Brecken judged, than the last time she'd tried. June sighed, reached with her left hand, took the cup. When she drank, it was with the left side of her mouth.

Brecken took the coffee pot back to the kitchen, set it on the stove, returned and sat on the couch with a grace she couldn't have managed when she'd first come to live in June's house. "The *Times* article," she said then. "Let me guess. Quentin Crombie?"

Half of June's face smiled; the other half tried to. "Of course." She sipped coffee.

Brecken rolled her eyes, but reached for the bulky newspaper on the coffee table, glanced over headlines about a sudden downturn in the stock market and bad news from the Antarctic ice cap, found the right section after a moment's fumbling. The article claimed to survey the latest trends in music—meaning, since it was Quentin Crombie, the latest trends in those corners of avant-garde art music he happened to favor, or at least wanted to discuss—and she had to follow it to an inside page before she found the brief waspish paragraph that gave dismissive mentions to her and her Cantata in E flat. Of course he called it the Rainbow Cantata, a nickname she disliked but knew she'd probably have to live with, and of course he referred to her as "the reclusive neoclassical composer," which she disliked even more, and which she knew she'd probably have to live with too.

She finished the article, put the newspaper section back on the table, and only then noticed the cup of coffee she'd neglected. She picked it up and sipped at it, made a face as she realized she'd put in the cream but left out the sugar, busied herself getting the coffee the way she liked it. She'd just finished that process when the phone rang.

Answering it was another of Brecken's chores, and she flung herself to her feet, went to the land line in the kitchen, picked it up. "Hello? Satterlee residence."

The voice on the other end, male, was dimly familiar. "Brecken? Is that you?"

"Yes," she said, suddenly wary.

"Don't worry, I'm not trying to sell you power washing," the voice said. "It's Mark Tanabe. Do you have a minute?"

"Sure," Brecken said. Mark had been a classmate of hers a few years back, taking courses in conducting to fill out his degree in theater while Brecken took the same courses to fill out her degree in composition. She recalled that Mark had gone on to pursue a master's degree, a luxury she hadn't been able to afford.

"Thank you," said Mark. "I'm in a real bind and I hope you can help me out. I don't know if you've heard, but I'm doing a production of *The Magic Flute* this semester."

"I've got a ticket," Brecken said. It was true, too; the moment she'd seen the story in the Arkham *Advertiser*, she'd considered what she'd have to do without to pay for a good seat, and headed down to Miskatonic's theater department the next morning. The tickets were available online, but there were good reasons for her to buy the ticket in person and pay cash.

"Thanks for the vote of confidence. You may not need the ticket, though. You know Gwyneth Elwood, right?"

The name conjured up memories of friendly but lively competition in the Miskatonic University music department. "Of course."

"She was in a car accident yesterday." Brecken let out a little cry, and Mark went on in a hurry: "She's fine—well, mostly. Her right arm is in a cast for the next two months, and that's a huge problem, because she's first flute and opening night's in six days. It's just four performances—" He rattled off the dates. "—but I've got to find a flautist who knows *The Magic Flute* inside and out. Maybe there's somebody else local who qualifies, but ..." He let the sentence trail away into silence.

There might also be good reasons why she should beg off, Brecken knew that, but none of them stopped her from saying, "When are the rehearsals?"

"Whenever you can fit them in. I've spent the last hour on the phone with the other musicians and they're ready to do whatever they have to."

"Okay," Brecken said. "I can do that."

"Oh my God. Thank you, Brecken. Are you free this afternoon or evening?"

They settled the details, Mark babbled his thanks, and then Brecken hung up. From the far side of the room, June regarded her with a bland inscrutable look. "So what was that about?"

"Do you want a ticket to *The Magic Flute* Saturday after next?"

The inscrutable look went away in a hurry. "You're not going?"

"I'll be playing in the orchestra."

"Okay, that makes a little more sense. I was trying to parse the idea of you giving up a seat at a Mozart opera, and not getting very far."

"Oh, I know—and especially that one. But would you like to go? I'm sure we can find someone to get you there and back."

June pondered that for a moment. "Please. Miriam can take me, and I think I can probably handle that now."

"Of course you can," said Brecken, smiling. She knew perfectly well that there was no "of course" about it. June's stroke had left the old woman bedridden for most of a year, and brought a sudden stop to a distinguished academic career. So simple a task as walking from bedroom to parlor remained a challenge, even with a walker. She's come so far already, Brecken reminded herself. Aloud: "You'll have a great time."

June smiled in response and sipped her coffee.

* * *

The first rehearsal was at four o'clock that afternoon. By three-fifteen, when Brecken slipped out the kitchen door with her flute in a sturdy shoulderbag, she'd made time to do the chores she'd taken on as June's caregiver, get dinner going in the two big crock pots in the downstairs kitchen, spend time with Sho and the broodlings, and put an hour into practicing the tougher parts in the score for the opera. That last had been a review, nothing more, for she knew the music for *The Magic Flute* inside and out, had adored it since she'd attended a Sunday matinee with her grandparents at the age of seven. Bits of melody from the score swirled in her mind as she started for campus.

Autumn sunlight streamed down from a sky dotted with clouds, made the cyclopean university buildings stand out against the sagging gambrel roofs of old Arkham and the dim hills beyond, showed signs of deferred maintenance every-where and the occasional telltale board in place of a window. Fall semester was under way. Though enrollment was down again that year and APARTMENT FOR RENT signs lingered in more windows than usual, the little shops and takeout res-taurants that catered to Miskatonic's students had their usual quota of tent signs out on the sidewalks, and plenty of students hurried about as Brecken neared the campus.

Upton Hall, Miskatonic's performing arts center, rose north of the main cluster of university buildings. It was a stark rectangular mass of red brick with few windows and fewer outward signs of life, but two years studying at Miskatonic, mostly in that same building, had taught Brecken most of its secrets. Clocks in the hallways showed three-thirty when she tried the doors of Upton Hall's auditorium, found one that was unlocked, and made her way down to the space in front of the stage where half a dozen musicians had already gathered.

"Brecken!" Mark Tanabe, short and wiry and full of energy, with black unruly hair and black-framed glasses, came trotting over the moment she appeared. "Thank you, thank you, thank you. Did I say thank you?" Laughing, Brecken let herself be introduced to the other musicians. Most of them responded to her name with the same blank friendly look she gave them in response, but one—a cellist named Mike Ellison, a tall young black man with an unexpectedly deep voice—gave Brecken a startled look and said, "Brecken Kendall? I heard you were a composer."

"Well, yes," said Brecken. "But I started out as a flautist."

"Last I checked you still are one," Mark said. "Here." He handed a copy of the flute score to Brecken, hurried away. Brecken went to her chair, assembled her flute, got the score settled on her music stand, and warmed up with a few quick scales and then, from memory, the long *presto* passage at the end of the first act's finale.

By the time she was done the rest of the musicians had arrived: sixteen in all, around the same number that would have played *The Magic Flute* in Mozart's day but a small fraction of the orchestras that usually played the same opera more recently. Hurried introductions, brief aimless talk, half-random noises as everyone warmed up: it was all utterly familiar to Brecken. The conductor, who had ghost-pale skin and flaming red hair and was named Sean something, arrived at ten to four, shook Brecken's hand distractedly, and hurried up to the podium, where he got busy with the score. Brecken chatted a little with the second flute, a tall brown-haired senior named Melinda Kress, but kept one eye on the conductor.

A minute past four o'clock, Sean looked up and blinked, as though he was startled to find himself surrounded by musicians. "From the top," he said, lilt of an Irish accent in his voice. "If everyone's ready?" His gaze lingered a little longer on Brecken than on the others; Brecken smiled, got a little answering nod. The baton went up, hovered. His left hand rose also, poised, and then the baton came down, calling up the first great swelling chord of the overture.

From there the familiar music unfolded. It helped that Sean had a good clear style with the baton; he didn't flap like a deranged seagull, as Brecken's high school band director had, or make little tentative movements behind the podium, as the conductor of the university orchestra did. Even so, matching the pace and sound of the other players, who'd had weeks to learn to play as one, took hard work. By the time the last majestic chord of the first act finale faded to silence, she felt as though she'd run a race and crossed the finish line well after the other runners.

"That will do nicely," Sean said then. He mopped his forehead with a handkerchief. "Thank you, all of you, for working so hard. Ms. Kendall—"

"Brecken," she said. "Please."

The conductor gave her an owlish look, but nodded. "Brecken, then. Thank you for stepping in on no notice. I'll want to talk to you about a few things but you'll definitely do."

Brecken blushed. "Thank you. I'll do my best."

Sean nodded. "Fifteen minutes, maybe? Then we'll go onto the second act."

* * *

"You're sure you'll be okay," said Brecken.

June gave her a cool glance, softened it with a half-smile. "Of course. I got everything settled with Miriam last night." She made a shooing gesture toward the door. Brecken laughed, picked up her shoulderbag, and headed out into the muted light of the morning.

Eleven days had passed since Mark's phone call, and Brecken had spent a good part of five of them in rehearsals and much of three more in performances. She'd fumbled more than once the first time the singers had rehearsed with the orchestra, because Mark hadn't mentioned that the production used an English libretto. Brecken had been too intent on the music to notice the English words of the first few arias, but having the birdman Papageno come on stage singing "I am a man of widespread fame, and Papageno is my name" instead of *"Der Vogelfänger bin ich ja, stets lustig, heisa hopsasa!"** startled her enough that she lost her place in the music and had to scramble to find it again. Still, she'd recovered well enough

---

* "The birdcatcher, yes I am, always jolly, hip hooray!"

in the second act, and played the rehearsal the next night with relentless focus.

The last evening before opening night had been a full dress rehearsal, with lights, scene changes, and all the other complications of an actual performance, including a small audience—friends and family members of the cast and the musicians, mostly, and a dozen or so elderly regulars who showed up for every Miskatonic production come hell or high water. The rehearsal wasn't quite bad enough to be a total failure but it barely managed to avoid that. Brecken reminded herself of the old theatrical adage that a bad dress rehearsal promised a good opening, and also reminded herself that the success of the entire production didn't rest on her. Even so, she slept poorly that night, and the dreams she described to Sho the next morning were splintered images shot through with pointless dread.

The adage turned out wiser than Brecken's fears, though. Opening night hadn't been flawless but it was far from a flop. In the two performances that followed, all the moving parts of that maddeningly complex thing called an opera finally found their shared rhythm. Brecken had seen better productions of *The Magic Flute* but she'd seen many worse, and even though the fussy electronic sets never quite worked as intended, the singer who played Pamina didn't have a voice strong enough for the part, and one of the oboes squeaked occasionally on high notes, the applause at the end was considerably more than polite.

One matinee and then back to her normal routine: that was the thought that circled in Brecken's mind as she walked through familiar streets. The North Side Branch of the Arkham Public Library, a bleak brick building on Hyde Street a block from June's house, reminded her that she hadn't checked her email there in days, and the little postal station on Curwen Street murmured a similar message about her post office box. I can get them tomorrow, she thought, then remembered that the next day was Sunday and let out an annoyed sigh.

Upton Hall rose up before her at last, and she hurried through the big double doors, turned the wrong way, caught herself and reached the green rooms in plenty of time. Mark had done everyone the favor of taping little cards to four of the doors with labels in his neat angular hand; Brecken went in through the one labeled ♀ MUSICIANS, said the usual things to the four other women already there, found a space by the big wall-length counter with mirrors above it and got changed into the sober black dress with cap sleeves she'd chosen for the occasion.

That took a certain amount of caution, for she wore a pendant most people couldn't be allowed to see. Fortunately the others were busy enough that she had no trouble keeping it out of sight. Fixing her hair and freshening her makeup took only a little while; she was ready to head for her chair by the time the last of the women in the orchestra had gotten to the green room.

Muted lights and low sounds of the first members of the audience taking their places met Brecken as she crossed to her place and sat. Both violinists and the bassoon player were already warming up and the cornet player was assembling his horn; Brecken's flute, a fine old silver Powell, gleamed as she put it together. She played a G major scale, adjusted the angle of the mouthpiece slightly, and then rejoined the rising cacophony, playing three more scales and then a series of the quick dancing flurries of notes that represented Papageno's panpipes.

A familiar pandemonium rose in crescendo as the rest of the orchestra took their seats and warmed up, sank down again to let Brecken hear the muffled sounds of the audience on the way to their seats. June had arranged to come early, and Brecken knew exactly where she would be sitting, but the music demanded her concentration. Melinda Kress finished her warmup and gave Brecken a questioning glance. Brecken nodded and smiled.

Then Sean walked over to the podium, and the house lights dimmed. A ragged silence replaced the bustle and murmur of the audience. The baton rose and fell, and the music began.

After twelve years playing the flute, Brecken could perform any number of pieces with her mind on something else, but *The Magic Flute* wasn't one of them. Even where the flute wasn't needed, she followed the score measure by measure, and when she had something to play her focus narrowed to phrase by phrase and note by note, with no attention to spare for anything else. In that way the opera went by. The intermission between the two acts hurried past—Brecken got through the line at the women's restroom in time to flop in a chair, catch her breath, sip some water, and then bolt back out to get in place before the second act started.

Then Sean brought the baton down again, and Brecken and the others launched into the bright solemnity of the March of the Priests at the beginning of the second act. From there on she had few chances to rest, since her playing had to provide the voice for the Magic Flute in Tamino's hands and also keep up a part in the music more generally. By the time the triumphant allegro passage at the end resolved in a glorious final cadence, she felt again as though she'd run a race, but this time she'd reached the finish line along with everyone else.

Applause swelled, faded, swelled again as one curtain call gave way to another. Brecken sat back in her chair and tried to relax. The singer who'd played the Queen of the Night, who'd managed the appallingly difficult high notes with only occasional signs of struggle, got a solid ovation; so did the big barrel-chested senior whose rich bass had given the High Priest Sarastro a good first draft of the serene power the role needed; but even the run-of-the-mill singers got enough applause to leave them beaming as they rose from their bows. Mark came out with a portable microphone in one hand, once everyone in the cast had taken bows, and introduced himself and the others who'd labored backstage. Then came the reason Brecken couldn't relax.

"And a special thank you to Brecken Kendall," Mark said, "who stepped in as first flute on a week's notice and did a stellar job." Brecken sent an imploring look up onto the stage, met Mark's unyielding smile. A few moments later, flute in hand, she came onstage just as Mark was saying something about Gwyneth Elwood. She crossed to the middle of the stage, curtseyed, blushed, and went back offstage as quickly as she could without seeming rude.

The applause died down eventually, and the house lights came up. Brecken took her flute apart, gave it a quick cleaning, and put it in its case. She'd just finished when Mark came bustling out from backstage saying, "Don't forget the reception! Room 301, Billington Hall on the old campus. Things'll be starting there in about half an hour. You've all told your friends and family, right?" Brecken put on a bland expression, hoping Mark wouldn't notice her—parties were among her least favorite activities—but that turned out to be a forlorn hope. Mark made a beeline for her and said, "Brecken, don't you dare slink off. You saved my butt, the least you can do is come have a good time."

Brecken tried to parse his logic and failed, but nodded anyway. "I can probably spare an hour or so," she told Mark.

"Oh, come on." Brecken didn't answer, simply met his gaze with an uncompromising look of her own, and after a moment Mark said, "Okay, I suppose that's better than nothing. Let me get things settled here and I'll give you a ride."

Getting things settled backstage took less time than Brecken expected, but even so the parking lot behind Upton Hall was mostly empty by the time the two of them crossed to Mark's bright red Volvo. Neither of them said much as Mark turned onto Federal Street and, once south of the campus, veered through the university neighborhood to the West Street bridge. Maybe that was why Brecken noticed no fewer than three rental trucks parked by buildings that had sported APARTMENT FOR RENT signs a few days earlier, disgorging boxes and small items of furniture. It was odd to see that when the quarter was well under way, and odder still that in each case the men who were hauling things up to their newly rented apartments were in their late twenties or thirties, too old to be students.

CHAPTER 2

BROKEN SILENCES

Back before the Second World War, when Miskatonic was a small Ivy League university best known for a first-rate medical school and a habit of sponsoring polar expeditions, the old campus downtown around its central quad had been more than adequate for its needs. That sense of scale didn't survive the mania for metastatic growth that seized the United States in the postwar era. Once the new campus rose north of the river and new departments began popping up like mushrooms after a spring rain, the fine brick buildings of the old campus were condemned to decades of malign neglect, used only by a few tag-ends of campus bureaucracy. The one upside of that policy was that such spaces as the bureaucrats didn't want were readily available to Miskatonic students who had or could invent a plausible excuse to use them.

That didn't seem like much of an advantage to Brecken as Mark's car pulled into a parking place on West Street, a block past the grimy brick facade of Billington Hall. Except for the university buildings and two rundown bars, every door and window in sight was boarded up. Still, Brecken had been to the old campus often enough since June's stroke, getting pension and benefit forms or returning them, that the air of urban blight didn't startle her. She got out of the car, pulled her shoulderbag after her, and closed the door.

"I can lock that in the trunk," Mark said as he came around the car, indicating the shoulderbag and the flute inside it. Brecken gave him a wry look, letting him know they both knew what he had in mind, and Mark laughed and led the way back to Billington Hall's front doors. Inside, cracked plaster and worn linoleum added to the feeling of decrepitude. A big age-darkened portrait of Alijah Billington, whose bequest to the university the hall's name celebrated, gazed down at the entry hall with an air of inexpressible weariness.

An equally weary elevator let them out on the third floor, and Mark led the way across the hall and through a pair of ornate wooden doors. The big open room on the other side was noticeably less dismal. Oak wainscoting rose to waist level on the walls. Windows framed in the same wood hid behind curtains that screened out the ragged roofscape outside. Gilt brass fixtures glowed overhead, and portraits of nineteenth-century university presidents on the walls added a hint of unexpected elegance. Along one wall, tables strained under a burden of refreshments; a makeshift bar with two drama students as bartenders stood in one corner; elsewhere, comfortable chairs and sofas gathered in clusters. The room was already crowded.

"This is really nice," Brecken said, looking around.

Mark grinned. "Isn't it? This isn't your common or garden variety cast party, you know. We got some serious grant money for the production, so the department paid for a reception to try to get more donors interested."

"Grant money?" said Brecken. "I'm impressed."

"Couldn't have done the production without it—you know what the department budget's like these days." He steered her over to the bar. "One of my profs put me in touch with the Chaudronnier Foundation. Heard of it?" When Brecken shook her head: "The Chaudronniers are old money from Kingsport, richer than God, and they donate a lot to the arts. I bet Martin Chaudronnier shows; if he does, I'll introduce you."

"I've already met him," Brecken said. To Mark's sudden startled look: "The summer I moved to Arkham I played my Concerto in B flat for a few people. It was mostly professors from the composition program but he was there, too."

"Smart." Mark turned to the bartender and ordered a complicated drink; Brecken decided it sounded like a hangover in a glass. "That could really boost your career."

"I'm not holding my breath," said Brecken. She asked the bartender for a glass of white wine, got it, tried to pay for it but didn't protest when Mark waved her efforts aside and paid instead. Even with free rent and the paycheck she got as June's caregiver, her budget didn't stretch far, not with six hungry broodlings to feed.

Mark gave her an amused look and started to say something, then stopped, looking past Brecken. "Give me just a moment," he said. "I'll be right back."

Brecken recalled his habits well enough to guess that "just a moment" could be half an hour. As Mark aimed effusive greetings at someone in an ornate dress, Brecken wove her way through the crowd, and reached one of a cluster of empty chairs in an out-of-the-way corner of the room. The thought of slipping away from the reception and heading home to Sho tempted her, but she reminded herself that she'd agreed to stay for an hour or so, and settled into the chair instead. A good swallow of the wine took the edge off her nerves. She tucked her shoulderbag behind her calves, let herself sink into the cushions.

* * *

Minutes passed. Bursts of laughter and loud voices rose over the background hum of conversation. After a little while, feeling the strain of more than two hours of hard playing, Brecken clenched her eyes shut, opened them again, and tried to get the muscles of her shoulders to unknot themselves. That task kept her sufficiently occupied that she didn't notice another of the attendees walk past, notice her, and turn.

"Brecken?" The voice was familiar, though she didn't recognize it at first. "I hope you won't mind if I join you."

She glanced up, and her guarded expression went away in a hurry. Dumpling-shaped and fussily dressed, with a pink complexion and a mop of irrepressible gray hair, Dr. Michael Peaslee had taught two classes she'd taken at Miskatonic for her general studies requirements, and his fondness for Baroque music made him a regular part of the audience whenever she performed. She motioned toward the nearest chair, said, "I hope you liked it."

"Very much." He settled into place, balancing his drink. "It would have been respectable for a professional company. For a college production—" He raised his glass. "First rate. I didn't have to shut my eyes *or* my ears even once."

Brecken laughed. "That's really high praise."

"It's not always true," said Peaslee. "Did you go to last year's *Ring* cycle at the Met?" When she nodded after a moment's hesitation, he went on. "Not exactly a triumph."

"The singers were really good," Brecken protested, "and so was the orchestra." Then, admitting defeat: "The rest of the production didn't do much for me, though."

Peaslee's mordant expression told her he'd heard everything she hadn't said. "Too few people these days realize that there's only room for one monumental ego in a Wagner production, and Wagner owns that role." He glanced past Brecken, said, "Hi, Miriam. Care to join us? We're discussing the sins of the New York Met." To Brecken: "I don't know if you two know each other."

Brecken half turned in her chair, saw a silver-haired woman, lean as a heron, in a black dress and white sweater. "Of course," she said. "Hi, Dr. Akeley." She turned to Peaslee. "I'm June Satterlee's caregiver these days, and Dr. Akeley comes to visit all the time."

Miriam Akeley settled in another of the chairs. "June's home," she said to Brecken. "She said to tell you to stay as long as you want and not to worry about her." She met Brecken's dubious expression with a smile. "You're discussing last year's *Ring* cycle, I imagine. Did they really dress all the characters as those little marshmallow animals?"

"Yes," Brecken admitted. "Wotan was a bright yellow rabbit with one ear bitten off."

"An extended metaphor," Peaslee said in a high-pitched, plummy voice, "for the cultural-political function of opera as a nexus of conspicuous consumption." Then, sourly, in his own baritone: "*Sic.* Sick as a dog, to quote Dorothy Parker."

Akeley laughed with the others. "Granted. I'm not about to defend the more extreme end of what goes on in the arts these days—"

"I'm delighted to hear that," said another voice off behind Brecken: male, elderly, mordantly precise. "Surprised, mind you, but delighted."

"Good afternoon, Elias," Akeley said. "I should have known you'd be here."

"But of course." A short balding man with a neatly trimmed white beard made his way over to the last empty chair in the circle. "May I?" He had a stout knob-handled walking stick in one hand and a glass full of scotch in the other.

"You haven't met, have you?" Peaslee said. "Dr. Elias van Kauran, professor emeritus—Brecken Kendall, one of our graduates."

Before Brecken could say anything, van Kauran's bushy eyebrows rose sharply. "Brecken Kendall, the modern Baroque composer?"

Brecken's face lit up. "Yes, and thank you."

He took his seat. "How you tolerate being lumped in with the neoclassicists, I don't pretend to know." To Akeley: "No doubt you've rather have had the music today played on kazoos by schoolchildren. How very relevant!"

Akeley met the gibe with a smile. "A straw man already? Elias, you're slipping."

Brecken gave Peaslee a worried look, and was partly startled and partly relieved to see him grin in response. He turned to Brecken and said, "As a composer, you've got to have your own take on the sort of thing the Met did."

Put on the spot, she froze, made herself go on. "Well, yes," she said. "Most productions these days are trying so hard to be original that they've forgotten how to be any good."

That got immediate attention from both of the contending forces. "Fair," Akeley said. "You're suggesting that von Neumann's game theory applies here, and it's only possible to maximize one variable at a time."

Brecken got a glazed look on her face as she tried to remember whether she'd heard of von Neumann. Fortunately, van Kauran spared her the need to answer. "Excessive complexity is the besetting sin of your discipline, Miriam," he said. "Is it really necessary to invoke an outré branch of twentieth century mathematics to make so simple a point?"

Akeley's smile didn't waver. "Excessive narrowness is the besetting sin of yours, Elias. I'm far from certain the point is as simple as you seem to think."

"I don't know about von Neumann," said Brecken. She rarely spoke of her ideas about music—it was much better, she thought, to let her compositions do the talking—but wine and weariness conspired to loosen her tongue. "But there are things that work and things that don't. That's just the way the world is, and if you have to do something original every time, sooner or later you run out of things that work. If the sets have to be original, eventually you're stuck with bad sets, because you've run through all the good ones. If the costumes have to be original, you run out of good costumes and dress Wotan as a marshmallow rabbit—"

"God in Heaven!" van Kauran said, with a look of horror. "I trust that's a joke."

"I wish," said Peaslee. "The Met did it in last year's *Ring*."

"As I said," Akeley noted, "I'm not about to defend the more extreme end of what goes on in the arts these days, but—"

Within moments she and van Kauran were arguing again. Brecken gave Peaslee an uneasy look, and he grinned at her again and winked.

* * *

"That's what it is," Brecken said then, and then stopped in surprise: she'd been deep in thought and hadn't meant to say the words aloud.

"What what is?" Peaslee asked. Akeley and van Kauran both turned toward her.

"The problem with Wotan the marshmallow rabbit," she said, flustered.

"Simple absurdity isn't enough?" van Kauran asked.

"It's more than that," said Brecken. "Most opera companies these days are so busy making statements and trying to be original that they've forgotten about the opera." Searching for an example: "Let's say Mark does *The Magic Flute* again but decides to do it as a metaphor for the argument you two have been having. So it's not just Sarastro, it's Sarastro as Dr. van Kauran as the voice of tradition, and it's not just the Queen of the Night, it's the Queen of the Night as Dr. Akeley as the voice of innovation."

"In that case," said Peaslee, grinning, "I insist on being Papageno as the voice of absurdity." He broke into song: "*Der Akademik bin ich ja, stets muffig, heisa hopsasa!*"*

That got a general laugh. Faces turned toward them. "Okay," Brecken said, joining in the laughter. "You've got the part. But every time they pile another meaning or metaphor on top of the production, every time they bring in the artist's statements

---

* "The academic, yes I am, always fusty, hip hooray!"

and the irrelevant sets and the marshmallow rabbits and the rest of it, the production gets further and further away from—from the opera itself, and whatever the opera itself is trying to say."

"Are you by any chance familiar with Count Algarotti's *Essay on Opera*?" van Kauran asked. Brecken shook her head, and he went on: "A fine piece of eighteenth century criticism. One of his comments is more than usually apposite here: 'As with machines, so with opera—the more complex they are, the more likely they are to go out of order.'"

"Yes, exactly!" Brecken said. "If you're going to play baroque music, you don't dress the musicians up in funny costumes and you don't make the stage look like, oh, a merry-go-round or something, to try to make a point the composer didn't intend to make. You play the music and let the music make its own point. For opera, you need costumes and sets and singers who can act, sure, but why not keep all the other things simple enough that they don't get in the way?"

"That's been done more times than I can count," said Peaslee. "A college production, or a workshop, or Bayreuth after the Second World War, does an opera with no scenery but lights and a few curtains, minimal costumes, minimal props. The performance is great, the budget's modest, the audience loves it—and then ten minutes later everyone's forgotten about it and we're back to chasing complexity for its own sake."

"Back in the postwar years," Akeley said, "that kind of radical simplicity was considered the last word in modernism." Van Kauran gave her an unsanitary look, but she went on "That's an interesting point about opera. I wonder if it could be taken further. You've talked about sets, costumes and staging. What would happen if you applied the same logic to the music?"

"The first opera ever performed," said van Kauran, "was scored for five instruments."

"*Five* instruments?" said Akeley.

Van Kauran nodded. "Harpsichord, lute, archlute, viol, and triple flute."

"Monteverdi used a larger orchestra than that," Brecken ventured.

"This was before Monteverdi," the old man informed her, a little tartly. Then, relenting: "This was *Dafne*, score by Jacopo Peri, libretto by Ottavio Rinuccini. The libretto's survived but I'm sorry to say most of the music hasn't."

"Good heavens," said Peaslee. "I wonder what it sounded like."

"So do I," Brecken said then, staring at nothing in particular. She could imagine the five Renaissance instruments easily enough, the harpsichord blending with the lute and archlute, all three of them with the distinctive tone of plucked strings, and then the viol and the triple flute adding their own voices. She could just as easily imagine their modern not-really-equivalents, piano, guitar, bass guitar, violin, and flute, and taste the difference in the result. But the possibilities that a simpler orchestration opened up, each instrument standing alone the way the voices of the soloists did, not blending into broad shapes of sound like voices in a chorus—she'd explored those any number of times in her compositions, but never with instruments and voices at the same time. The prospect hovered in her imagination, enticing.

"Thank you," she said. "I didn't know that, about Peri's opera."

"You're welcome," said van Kauran, smiling as though he'd proved a point.

Just then Miriam Akeley rose from her chair. Brecken realized an instant later that she was looking off past Peaslee, into the crowd. "I hope you'll excuse me," she said, and headed toward the middle of the room. Van Kauran watched her go, then considered the empty glass in his hand and said, "A world that turns Wotan into a marshmallow rabbit is unbearable without good scotch. Michael, Ms. Kendall—" He hauled himself to his feet and headed for the bar.

"Do they often fight like that?" Brecken asked Peaslee once he was out of earshot.

He grinned. "Those two," he said, "are dear friends, and if you see them together and they're not arguing, make sure they both have a pulse." Then: "I have to agree with Elias, though. Can I get you another—what is that, white wine? Excellent."

* * *

Left to herself for the moment, Brecken watched the milling crowd for a little while. Mark Tanabe was standing not far away, in animated conversation with a man in his forties Brecken was sure she didn't know—someone from Miskatonic University, maybe? Further off, a little clutch of professors from the university's music department stood talking earnestly. She recognized all of them and had taken classes from two, but none of them had become close friends, and the music professor she would have wanted there more than anyone else—Paul Czanek, her composition teacher—was on sabbatical in Budapest that year.

A few minutes passed, and then Michael Peaslee pried himself loose from a conversation and returned to his seat. "Here you go," he said, handing Brecken a glass of wine. "You'd think that an event like this would focus on opera, wouldn't you? I had no fewer than four people from Miskatonic stop me on the way back from the bar, wanting to talk about the financial mess the University's in." With a little bleak laugh: "I suppose that's not so far from opera after all. We're almost as far in the red as the Met is."

"I read something about that," said Brecken. "How deep in debt are they?"

"Close to sixty million dollars," Peaslee said. "And it's their own fault. They kept on producing modern operas that nobody wants to listen to, and then did a really expensive *Ring* cycle the critics adored and nobody else could stand."

"The singers and the orchestra were really good," Brecken protested.

"It doesn't matter how well a marshmallow rabbit sings," retorted Peaslee. Brecken choked back a laugh, sipped wine.

She had just lowered the glass when Miriam Akeley rejoined them. "Brecken? I don't know if you remember Martin Chaudronnier."

Brecken got to her feet. "Of course." She'd already recognized the stocky figure behind Akeley, though the hair and neatly trimmed moustache were grayer than they'd been when he'd listened attentively to her concerto five years back. They shook hands, and as she sat, he settled into the chair that Elias van Kauran had occupied. Then, unexpectedly, a brown-haired girl maybe eight years old in an elegant white dress came over and stood by him, staring at Brecken with a solemn pleading look.

"I hope you won't find this question inappropriate, Ms. Kendall," Chaudronnier said then, "but do you teach flute to beginning students?"

All at once Brecken understood the child's expression. "I don't have a music education degree," she said.

"So noted. That wasn't my question, though."

Flustered, she nodded. "Yes, I've taught beginners."

"Excellent. My granddaughter Emily—" A motion of his head and a smile indicated the girl. "—has been deciding what instrument she wants to learn, and today's opera settled that for her. Miriam suggested that you might be available to teach her."

Brecken nodded again, turned to the child. "Emily, if you want to learn how to play the flute, that's going to take a lot of hard work. You'll have to practice every single day."

The child met her gaze squarely. "I know. Mama plays the piano every morning."

"Good," said Brecken. "So do I." She drew in a breath, and to Chaudronnier said, "Yes, I'd be happy to do that."

"Excellent," he said again. He pulled a card from a pocket inside his jacket and handed it to her: a business card on fine cream-colored paper marked with the heraldic crest of a cauldron and three serpents, the name Martin E. Chaudronnier in fine Renaissance script, and in a less ornate font, his address, phone, and other contact information. "Perhaps you can give me a call sometime in the next few days and we can settle the details."

Brecken made some kind of appropriate noise; he stood, and so did she; he shook her hand again, and then headed off into the crowd, Emily trotting alongside him like an undersized shadow. Miriam, who'd risen as well, turned to Brecken and said, "Thank you."

"You're welcome," Brecken said, "and thank you."

Miriam went elsewhere a moment later, leaving Brecken first to stare after her and then to sit back down in her chair. Old dreams and old fears contended with one another in the unquiet air around her. Peaslee got to his feet, raised his glass in salute, and headed off in another direction, through a crowd that looked noticeably thinner than it had a quarter hour before. Brecken, glancing at the clock on the far wall, gathered her strength for the walk home.

Melinda Kress forestalled her, approaching out of the crowd. "Oh, hi, Brecken," she said. "Do you need a ride back to your place?"

Brecken thanked her, and moments later she was following Melinda out the double doors to wait for the tired elevator. Alijah Billington's portrait watched them mournfully as they went out into the evening, headed toward Melinda's well-aged Volvo. Three turns to manage one-way streets got them to Garrison Street and headed for the bridge across the Miskatonic River.

"Tired?" Melinda said as the bridge rattled beneath them.

Brecken blinked, realized she hadn't said a word since they'd gotten into the car. "Well, yes," she admitted. "But mostly thinking about a piece of music I want to write." Melinda gave her a startled look, kept driving.

It wasn't quite true, but only because the stirrings in the deep places of Brecken's mind hadn't yet drawn together into musical form. The five years since she'd begun composing had taught her to recognize the movements of her own creativity, the gathering tension that told her a piece of music was taking shape, the subtle prompts that would tell her where to look for inspiration if she paid attention to them. Those familiar patterns showed themselves to her then, though what they heralded was still hidden.

"Well, I hope it works out," said Melinda, and turned onto Hyde Street. She pulled over a few blocks later. "This is the place?"

Brecken made an agreeable noise, got out of the car in front of June's gray Victorian house, waved goodbye, veered up the driveway, and let herself in the kitchen door.

* * *

"What do I need to know about the Chaudronnier family?" Brecken asked. She and June were sitting by themselves in the parlor downstairs as evening gathered in the bay window and the lights of Arkham flickered on one by one. From above, a faint murmur brought Sho's voice; she was teaching the broodlings one of the scores of songs that young shoggoths learned by rote in the course of their education.

"That depends on why you want to know," said June, with a fractional smile.

"Martin Chaudronnier asked me today to teach his granddaughter to play the flute."

The old woman took that in. "That could be very fortunate for you, or—" She left the rest of the sentence unsaid, and Brecken saw no need to complete it. The murmur from above shifted as the broodlings began to sing the passage they'd learned.

"The Chaudronniers are an old Kingsport family," June said then. "French originally, aristocrats back before the Revolution. They've got a mansion down in Kingsport, and for the last ten years or so they've been buying up abandoned farmland all over the lower Miskatonic valley to lease out to people who want to get into farming."

"Wasn't there something about that in the *Advertiser*?" Brecken asked.

"A couple of months ago, yes." Half of June's face frowned. Glancing up: "That's very nearly as much as I know. They've got a reputation for eccentricity, but that's true of all the old families in Kingsport. They give a lot of money to the university and to local arts groups. There's a community theater in Bolton that basically survives on Chaudronnier donations, and I think they also cover a lot of the upkeep for that tall ship in Kingsport harbor."

"The *Miskatonic*."

"That's the one. Did he say what they'll be paying you?"

Brecken shook her head. "I'm supposed to call in a few days. I'll have to go online and find out what the standard fee is these days—it's been almost a year and a half since I've had students, and with everything that's happened to the economy since then—"

"Don't worry about that. Just let him name a figure. It'll be more than you'd ask for." To Brecken's look of surprise: "You haven't dealt with old money much, have you? He'll offer you what he thinks you're worth, not what you think you're worth."

Brecken nodded after a moment. "Okay."

"That's the good side," said June. She leaned forward, suddenly intent. "Here's the bad side. When New England gossips say a family's eccentric, tolerably often that means they dabble in the old lore. If that's what's going on with the Chaudronniers, they might be on our side, but more likely they're in it for whatever they can get, and it's also possible that they're working for the other side. So you'll want to be very careful."

That warning followed Brecken through the evening. It circled through her thoughts as she practiced her flute, waited at a distance as she finished the rest of her evening routine—an archaic ritual called the Vach-Viraj invocation to protect them all, prayers to the uncanny being the old books named Nyogtha—and returned as she settled down to sleep in the big four-poster bed with Sho's cool shapelessness pressed close against her, warm quilts over them both, and the broodlings nestled together in a comfortable heap, cradled in a big soft-sided dog bed in one corner of the room. It was still waiting for her, patient and cold, as she got up in the gray dawn and went down the stairs to check on June.

The other side—who were they? What did they want? For five years those half-answered questions had challenged her. What Brecken knew about them came partly from a few glimpses she'd caught in Partridgeville, helicopters circling in the night, indistinct faces driving gray SUVs, people fishing for information under false pretenses. The rest had come from a flurry of scattered clues: Sho's recollections of the terrible end of her people, a few hints June had dropped from time to time, a few more hints from a nameless man who belonged to the Fellowship of the Yellow Sign, and one brief conversation with the living darkness called Nyogtha, the Dweller in Darkness, The Thing That Should Not Be.

It didn't amount to much. Somewhere out there were people who wanted the world to belong to humanity alone, who talked about man's conquest of nature and meant those words literally, who hated and feared shoggoths and every other creature of the elder world, who defied the Great Old Ones and, for reasons Brecken didn't pretend to understand, had the power to make that defiance mean something. They belonged to an organization called the Radiance, though it had other names in the past. They had plenty of money and plenty of influence, armed men in uniform and agents who served them in secret—and five years back, they had blasted their way into a colony of shoggoths under Hob's Hill near Partridgeville, and turned flamethrowers and incendiary grenades on the inhabitants, killing all but one.

Back upstairs in the apartment, she greeted the broodlings as they came bounding over to her, checked the big crock pot where breakfast was cooking, then sat on the floor to talk to the broodlings and to Sho. The thought that there were people out there who could only see shoggoths as monsters to be destroyed sat cold and heavy in her deep places.

CHAPTER 3

TUNES FOR WINTER

Two days later Brecken left June's house after an early dinner. She stopped at the post office, the library, and the little storefront branch of her bank before heading to the bus station on Dyer Street. The big white MBTA buses had stopped coming to Arkham nearly two years back, after yet another round of budget cuts, but the county bus system still kept a dozen routes limping along somehow and the station was busier than usual. GAS PRICES HIT NEW HIGH, the Arkham *Advertiser*'s headline yelled from every vending box she passed, explaining why. As a bus bound for Kingsport rolled out of the station, Brecken ducked through the crowd and joined a group of a dozen or so waiting by a sign with the number 7 on it.

She'd timed her arrival well. Only a few minutes slipped past before a bus rolled up, 7 IPSWICH VIA BOLTON on the sign above the windscreen. She boarded along with the others, settled into a seat as the driver pulled out of the station and turned west onto Derby Street. Fading university buildings and rundown condominiums slid by as the street curved along the flank of Meadow Hill, gave way to a more varied landscape: on one side, empty warehouses and abandoned shops turned their backs to the autumnal colors of the hill; on the other, an abandoned railway the state had never gotten around to converting into a bike trail followed the green serpentine arc of the Miskatonic River; beyond the river, the rumpled countryside of northeastern Massachusets stretched away into the middle distance, crisscrossed by old stone walls and half overgrown with pines. Off to the north, the great ragged shape of Briggs' Hill loomed up against scattered clouds.

Though the scenery had sparked one of Brecken's compositions—the North Coast Sonata in E, originally for string quartet and then for recorder consort—she didn't seek inspiration from it that evening. Instead, as the bus crossed the Miskatonic on a gray concrete bridge and turned onto Aylesbury Pike, she pulled her mail out of her shoulderbag and sorted through it. She'd already opened everything, and deposited three modest checks for musical scores: more and more often, people paid her by check or money order, now that credit card theft online had become so pandemic. The mail also included a letter from her Aunt Mary down in New Jersey, four letters about gigs in Arkham and the towns close around it, and one more from another address she knew all too well.

She distracted herself from the last of those by copying down the details from the three music orders into a spiral notebook, so she could send them the scores once the checks cleared. Unsurprisingly, all three were for recorder scores. The recorder, that durable Renaissance instrument, was in the middle of one of its occasional surges of popularity, but few composers wrote new pieces for recorder and even fewer were willing to work up recorder arrangements of classic and Baroque standards. Brecken did both, and the modest income that brought her was equally beneficial to her self-confidence and her bank account.

The same page of the notebook had notes on the emails she'd read on one of the library's public computers. Using those instead of an internet connection of her own was a way to save money, but there was more to it than that. "Cellphones can be tracked," June had said, one day not long after Brecken moved in; that was before the stroke, when every movement

June made was precise and imperious. "So can anything that's connected to the web. That's why the only phone I use is a land line and I'm only on the internet when my job requires it. You might want to think about doing that, since—" A motion of her head indicated the upstairs apartment and the shoggoth who lived there. Brecken had agreed, of course. It wasn't as convenient as carrying a smartphone, but she'd gotten used to it, the way she'd gotten used to so many of the burdens of her divided life.

The letter from Aunt Mary was full of gossip about her cousin's divorce and good news about Uncle Jim, who'd had a heart attack but was recovering well. Two of the letters from nearby addresses asked whether she was available for weddings in April and June respectively—she had flyers up in every wedding-related business in the area, and those brought in another steady trickle of income. The other two were answers to letters she'd sent out months back offering to play at local venues. One was a vaguely polite thanks-but-no-thanks, but the other invited her to play at a holiday charity bazaar at the Kingsport Senior Center. Those never paid much, she knew, but the exposure was worth it. She reached for her spiral notebook again, added the date and a reminder to get another box of business cards.

Then, finally, she opened the last letter, the one she dreaded. The return address was a post office box in New Jersey, and the letterhead read REV. LOUISE CONINGTON, CHAPLAIN and nothing else, but the moment Brecken had seen the envelope, images surged out of memory: the great silent mass of the penitentiary behind a double fence topped with razor wire, the haggard and sullen woman on the far side of the visiting room's glass windows. More than a decade had passed since Brecken's mother had begun her life term there, and Brecken had gone to see her only a few times during that interval, but every detail hovered in her memory when the quarterly letter from the prison chaplain arrived.

Fortunately the latest letter had nothing out of the ordinary to relate. Her mother had been sent to solitary again for picking a fight with another inmate, but that had happened every few months since the beginning of her term. The chaplain assured her that her mother's health was still good and that she looked forward to each of Brecken's letters, and that was all.

By the time she finished reading the letter, Briggs' Hill loomed dark above the road and the first lights of Bolton glimmered up ahead. Brecken put everything back in her shoulderbag, sat back while the bus made a sharp turn onto Central Avenue and rolled past the old National Guard armory. That had been sold off and boarded up a long time ago, and so had the Bolton Worsted Mills, for more than a century Bolton's largest employer, now a vast ruinous shape of brick and rusting iron frequented only by pigeons and feral cats.

The end of that shape was her signal to pull the bell cord. Once the bus rolled to a halt she climbed down to the cracked and tilted sidewalk, went back half a block through gathering dusk, turned onto Pond Street. Rundown cottages huddled in narrow lots to either side, and half the streetlights had been turned off by the town council to save money. Still, she walked the four blocks to the end of Pond Street without incident, climbed the stair to the front door of a cottage sitting well away from its neighbors, and knocked.

The door opened. "Hi, Brecken," said the young woman who'd pulled it open: lean as a runner, dressed in sweat pants and a tee shirt, her wavy brown hair tied back. A grin creased her face. "I hope you've got something for us. Matt's impossible to live with when he doesn't have anything new to practice."

"Hi, Hannah," said Brecken, laughing. "Yes, I've got a couple of things."

"Any Dowland? He's really good."

"Not this time, but I'll see what I can do." Brecken extracted a small instrument case and a folder full of printouts before handing over her shoulderbag, and then gave Hannah her coat. Both went on a wooden peg on one wall of the entry, and then Brecken followed Hannah into the parlor where the others waited.

* * *

The parlor was a cozy room with a wood stove in one corner and an assortment of secondhand furniture ringing the walls. Three people looked up as Brecken entered; two of them greeted her cheerfully, and the third smiled. Brecken greeted them back, settled in the usual chair, and handed the music to Hannah, who passed copies to everyone.

They called themselves the Bolton Recorder Consort, and they'd introduced themselves to her after a performance of hers two years back. Since then they'd become friends of hers, as close as the requirements of her divided life allowed. Matthew and Sarah Waite were husband and wife, twenty-six and twenty-three years old. Hannah Gilman was Sarah's sister, nineteen, and Daniel Marsh, eighteen, was a cousin of Sarah and Hannah. Dark eyes, brown hair, and skin color between brown and olive spoke of an ancestry even more varied than Brecken's, and the family resemblances were hard to miss, too. Sarah and Hannah looked like sisters, even though Hannah was lean and muscular and Sarah soft and plump, and Danny looked like a thinner male version of the same plan. Matt was the odd one out, big and broad-chested—you could tell at a glance that some of his ancestors had been New England fishermen and others had been sailors in the tall-ship days, when crews from the four corners of the world worked together on the ships that called New England home.

"I'm sorry I had to miss last week," said Brecken then. Matt said "Don't worry about it" and Sarah said "Oh, that's fine" and Hannah rolled her eyes and made a dismissive noise in her throat, all at the same time. They looked at each other and laughed, and Brecken laughed with them. Danny settled back into his corner of the sofa and smiled a little half-smile, which Brecken knew was as close to a laugh as he ever went. He never spoke, either; "mute" was the term Brecken had learned growing up, though the internet preferred "nonvocal" just then.

While Brecken assembled her recorder, she and the others talked about upcoming gigs, a lecture in Arkham the next evening, and *The Magic Flute*. Brecken blushed pointlessly when Sarah told her that a neighbor named Mrs. Eliot had gone to the Friday night performance and spoken highly of it. After a quarter hour or so of talk, Sarah said, "We should probably get started," and a few minutes later they launched into a familiar piece, Brecken's Bourrée in B flat.

The Bolton Recorder Consort wasn't simply four people with the soprano recorders most amateurs used. Sarah played a soprano, but Danny had an alto, Hannah a tenor as long as her forearm with keys on the lower end, and Matt a mighty double bass the size of a bassoon, with a metal tube arching in a graceful gooseneck curve to get his breath to the upper end and silver keys to stop holes too widely spaced for anybody's fingertips. Quality instruments, all of them, and wood rather than plastic: the relative who'd spotted the set somewhere up past Ipswich, in a charity shop that had no idea what they were or how much they were worth, had done the Consort a very good turn. Brecken, whose pleasant little pearwood soprano recorder had come to her courtesy of an Arkham yard sale, kept watching similar venues for the smaller and higher-pitched sopranino she coveted, but so far the gods of blind chance hadn't smiled on her.

Instruments well spaced across the musical staff made the bourrée's harmonies come alive. It helped, too, that Brecken had worked up an arrangement for the piece that played to the strengths of each member of the Bolton Recorder Consort, and deftly avoided anything each of them found too difficult. That degree of care wasn't an accident; the bourrée was the first piece of music she'd ever composed, and its theme was the first sentence in the shoggoth language she'd ever whistled to Sho. By the time the last notes finished she was beaming.

They played half a dozen more pieces, all of them Brecken's arrangements and half of them her compositions, then stopped to rest fingers and lungs and sip tea.

"We'll have to skip two weeks from now," Matt said, after downing a mouthful from his cup. "A cousin of ours is getting married in Maine on the Saturday, and Sarah's older sister in Stillwater, up in Vermont, just had a baby and we're going to visit them on the way back."

It wasn't the first time he'd mentioned relatives in various corners of the region. Brecken, feeling a certain amount of envy, said, "You've got family all over New England, don't you?"

"Pretty much," Matt said. "And some way over in the western end of New York State. The Waites got around back in the day."

"Do you have family locally?" Sarah asked Brecken. "If you don't mind my asking."

"Not really. An aunt and uncle down in New Jersey, and a cousin in Arizona." Brecken busied herself with the sheet music, tried not to think about her mother. "We talk on the phone sometimes, and Aunt Mary sends me letters all the time."

"Be glad that's all you got," said Hannah. "I've got family all over Essex County, and it's kind of a pain in the ass." Sarah gave her a hard look, and she went on, grinning: "Present company excepted, of course."

"Time for a tune," Matt said, before either of them could say more. "'Westron Wind,' maybe?" Everyone but Danny voiced their agreement, and he nodded. A pause to pick up instruments, and they began playing the Elizabethan tune. They went through it twice, and then Sarah and Hannah lowered their recorders and began to sing—

> "Westron wind, when wilt thou blow
> The small rain, come down rain,
> O that my love were in mine arms
> And I in my bed again."

—while Brecken, Danny and Matt played accompaniment. The two women had pleasant voices if not professionally trained ones, with hints of the old Massachusetts accent adding something nicely archaic to the singing. It sounded at moments as though the parlor had broken loose in time and drifted back to the seventeenth century.

The two of them finished the verse, then raised their recorders again and joined in. One more pass through the tune and then a little coda, and it was done. "Wow," said Matt. "That's *seriously* good." To Brecken: "Any chance you're up to playing with us in some of our gigs? That second soprano part of yours makes all the difference."

"I'll have to check my schedule," Brecken said, blushing, "but if I can, sure."

"I want to try this new piece of yours," Hannah said then. "'Dances for Winter.'"

"I thought it was Matt who wanted something new," Brecken said, teasing her. Hannah laughed, and picked up her recorder.

* * *

Matt always walked her to the bus stop when they'd finished playing, a courtesy Brecken appreciated. Bolton wasn't a high-crime area but it wasn't exactly the opposite, and the bus stop was halfway between the ruins of the Bolton Worsted Mills and the near end of Preston Street, where half of Bolton's taverns huddled behind garish neon signs. The two of them talked about music and upcoming gigs and the compositions she meant to work on next, until the county bus rolled up and she thanked him and climbed aboard.

The bus grumbled into motion and pulled away from the stop. Ahead, the Aylesbury Pike reached away into unseen distances, a tunnel carved out of the darkness by headlights. Brecken tried and failed to distract herself with a Bach fugue she was arranging for recorders—one more thing she could sell online and bring in a little money. Her thoughts kept circling back to Sarah's offhand question about her family. That stung, because Brecken had one good reason to keep her distance from her relatives when she'd graduated from Miskatonic. Now she had six more, and all those reasons were iridescent black.

You chose that, she reminded herself. Don't cry about it. That was true, too. One afternoon in her sophomore year, she'd returned from a campus visit to Miskatonic to find her apartment a shambles and Sho nowhere to be seen, and the moment of terror and imagined loss before Sho answered her frantic whistle had taught her how much she'd come to need the shoggoth. She'd made promises to Sho after that, and repeated those promises to the infinite darkness that was Nyogtha: freely and with her whole heart, too, and she knew herself well enough to know she'd make them again without a moment's hesitation. That didn't stop her from feeling a stab of envy when she listened to Sarah and Matt talk about their relatives, or from wincing from time to time when she had to shore up the barrier she'd raised across the middle of her life, with Sho and the broodlings on one side and everyone but June on the other.

The lights of Arkham came into sight ahead, around the darkness that was Meadow Hill. The words of "Westron Wind" played in her thoughts: *O that my love were in mine arms and I in my bed again.* Brecken made herself smile: her love would be in her arms soon enough, and the two of them would be in their bed again once the last tasks of the day were done with. That held troubling thoughts at bay until Brecken got off the bus and walked the two blocks home.

June was still up when she came through the kitchen into the parlor: curled a little awkwardly on the sofa, propped on pillows. She had her reading glasses on, a book open in her lap and a glass of bourbon and water in easy reach of her left hand.

Brecken met her gaze with a bright smile. "I ought to nag you about getting to bed."

"Oh, probably." Then: "Another half hour won't hurt me, and I want to finish this."

"What is it?"

By way of answer June held the book up: a slender hard-back with a dust jacket long since gone yellow with age. The cover, a piece of classic Art Nouveau—Aubrey Beardsley's work, Brecken guessed, recalling something from an art survey course—showed a crowned figure in scalloped and tattered robes, with an abstract mask covering its face and long white hair swirling in the wind. *The King in Yellow*, the title read; below it was *J.-B. Castaigne*, and below that, *translated by Oscar Wilde.*

"Have you read it?" the old woman asked. When Brecken shook her head: "You might like it. It caused quite the scandal back in the day."

"That sounds promising," said Brecken. Then, all at once, she realized what the title implied. "*That* King in Yellow?"

"I like to think of it as family history," June said with a little bland smile.

Brecken nodded. "I'll be down in half an hour," she said, and headed for the stairs.

The lights were out in her apartment—no surprise, since shoggoths had senses she didn't, and could see with perfect clarity in pitch darkness. As she closed the door behind her, though, the lamp beside the sofa clicked on. ♪*It is well with you, broodsister?*♪ Sho whistled, drawing back the pseudopod that had turned the switch.

The endearment scattered the last of Brecken's dour mood. ♪*You are here, broodsister,*♪ she replied, ♪*and so it is well with me.*♪ She shed coat and shoulderbag, went to the couch, slumped against Sho's shapeless curves. Two pseudopods flowed up to embrace her, and she let out a long ragged breath, turned to kiss Sho's mantle, and caught a scent like freshly washed mushrooms rising from the shoggoth, the sign of happiness.

Thereafter, as the quiet chores and ordinary pleasures of the day's end went past in their usual order, with an hour of flute practice to round things out, Brecken managed to keep her thoughts in check. It helped that when the two of them went to bed, Sho flowed up against her tentatively in a way she recognized at once, and she murmured something agreeable, wriggled out of her nightgown, and reached for the shoggoth.

Five years before, once their friendship had turned into what Brecken called love and Sho named with a complex pattern of notes neither of them could figure out how to put into English, they'd fumbled their way to something that bridged the gap between human sexuality and shoggoth ♪*sharing-of-moisture.*♪ The white-hot passion of those days had mellowed, but they'd learned more about each other's bodies since then, and Brecken's mouth and fingers and Sho's pseudopods knew exactly where to go and what to do. By the time the shudders of her last climax faded out, Brecken felt drowsy and sated, and she could feel the faint pulsing in the shoggoth that told her Sho was already slipping over onto the dreaming-side in simple delight.

That mood lingered into the morning, and didn't break until an hour or so before noon. That was when Brecken, looking for a volume of Bach harpsichord music she'd misplaced, spotted Martin Chaudronnier's business card on the corner of the piano where she put things she wanted to remember. June's warning had lost none of its force, and Brecken stood there looking at the thing for a long moment before she made herself pick it up. Then, bracing herself, she whistled a quick explanation to Sho, and headed down the stairs to make the call.

The phone conversation went well: pleasant and professional, and the fee that Martin Chaudronnier offered her for giving Emily one hour-long lesson a week was so far beyond what she usually charged for teaching that she nearly dropped the phone. She wouldn't be out bus fare, either—he offered to send a car for her, as though it was the most ordinary thing in the world. Perhaps, she thought, for him it was.

That was promising, but June's caution circled in her memory, warning her that there might be more to it than a rich family's generosity. There's no way they could have found out about Sho, Brecken told herself, but she knew better than to be too confident of that.

* * *

That evening the Miskatonic Valley Early Music Society had a meeting and lecture on campus: the same event she'd discussed with her friends in Bolton the previous night, though it took a stray glance at the calendar on the wall of her apartment to remind her of that. She had to make a few changes in half-formed plans to make room for the event, but she managed those. On a sudden impulse she left most of an hour early, stopped at the post office and the bank, and spent the time she had left at the North Side Branch of the Arkham public library.

A garish mural in the entry showed the long mournful face of H.P. Lovecraft gazing morosely down above the main doors, with a lumpy, bright green image of Cthulhu on one side of him and a blobby black thing she guessed was supposed to be a shoggoth on the other. Brecken gave the paintings a reproachful look, hurried on past. The bulletin board beside the door merited an equally cursory glance; it had a new flyer on it about a chess club, but Brecken paid little attention to that. Moments later she was settled in the main room of the little library with a hefty volume from the North Coast History Collection titled *Kingsport: A Tercentenary History, 1639–1939.*

The book was library use only and she had just forty minutes before the library closed, but it was enough, because she wanted to know what the book said about the Chaudronnier family, and that didn't take forty minutes to find out. The first Chaudronnier in Kingsport had arrived in 1838. The private secretary to an exiled French nobleman named Marc d'Ursuras, he'd married his employer's daughter, and inherited the d'Ursuras mansion in Kingsport when the old man died in 1866. After that the Chaudronniers had been one of the little seaport's wealthy families, one step below the prolific and fabulously rich Ambervilles and one step above the even more prolific but not quite so wealthy Greniers: local dignitaries, patrons of the arts, honorary chairpersons of worthy causes, filling all the usual roles assigned to big fish in small ponds. What lay behind that facade Brecken couldn't begin to guess.

She tried to put the question out of her mind as she hurried beneath a darkening sky to Upton Hall and the Miskatonic Valley Early Music Society. The effort didn't accomplish much, because the Chaudronnier name came up again minutes after she got to the meeting. She had time to hurry into the bleak concrete-walled classroom, find a seat next to her friends from Bolton, exchange quick greetings with them and a few others. Then that year's president of the Society went to the podium, made a few forgettable comments, introduced the evening's speaker, and thanked the Chaudronnier Foundation for the donation that paid the speaker's fee.

The speaker, an adjunct professor at a school of music somewhere in Pennsylvania, was a plump balding man in his forties with a round brown face and a broad mustache; he wore broad suspenders and had a long and elegant Hispanic name which Brecken made an effort to remember and so promptly forgot. She'd spent most of the afternoon trying to recall what the lecture was about; a flyer had come in the mail, she'd put it somewhere she'd been sure she would recall, and so of course she had never been able to find it again. Thus it was maybe ten minutes into a highly informative talk about late sixteenth century Italian music that she realized that the subject was the origins of opera.

That would have been more than enough to hold Brecken's attention, for the speaker knew his subject and discussed it with genuine passion. Another five minutes into the talk, though, in the middle of a discussion of *recitar cantando*—"singing recitation," the musical innovation that launched opera on its way— he grinned suddenly. "Let me show you," he said, drew in a breath, and sang a passage from one of the first operas in a crisp tenor voice.

Brecken listened, entranced. She'd half expected the flowery all-over-the-place recitative of grand opera, but this was different, spare and understated, as much speaking as singing. All at once she remembered what Elias van Kauran had said about the orchestration of the first operas, and her hand drifted up to her face, curled around her chin, as her thoughts leapt from the lecturer's voice to the imagined instruments that might accompany it, and from there to the productions Michael Peaslee had described, spare and simple enough that the music and the story couldn't be elbowed out of the way by marshmallow rabbits.

She had to wrestle her attention back to the lecture when the lecturer stopped singing and launched into his talk again. It was worth the effort, though. He spoke of the Florentine Camerata, the little group of amateur musicians who dreamed opera into being, and Claudio Monteverdi, the composer who took their tentative creation and turned it into the most wildly popular art form of the age. He sang again: a few scraps of *Dafne*, the opera Professor van Kauran had mentioned, and then an aria out of Monteverdi's *Orfeo*, the first really great opera. By the time he finished, fielded a few questions, and stood there smiling as the audience applauded, Brecken was gazing abstractedly at nothing anyone else in the room could see.

All at once she realized that most of the audience had already left their seats. Her friends from Bolton were standing over to one side of the room, giving her amused looks, while others moved past toward the tables in back where coffee and snack foods waited. She sent a rueful look toward the Bolton Recorder Consort, got up and went to join them.

"You're working on something," Sarah said as soon as they'd gotten coffee.

Brecken blinked, had to take a moment to put the words together. "No, not really," she said. "Just thinking about the lecture." Sarah's wry expression told her what she thought of that, but Brecken had too much on her mind to want to argue the point.

"You ought to write an opera," said Hannah, grinning. Sarah turned toward her with a quelling look, but the younger woman met the look with rolled eyes and went on: "The kind of good old-fashioned opera Mozart liked to watch. Or listen to. Or whatever."

"Whatever," said Matthew. "Definitely whatever."

A moment passed while Brecken sipped coffee and the others bantered briefly, and then a half-familiar voice said, "I'm inclined, Ms. Kendall, to agree with your young friend."

It was Elias van Kauran, she'd known that the moment he'd spoken. She turned toward him and covered her embarrassment with introductions. "A recorder consort?" van Kauran said in response, bushy eyebrows rising. "I'm glad to hear that. A well-played recorder is worth hearing." Then, with a slightly pained look: "I trust that Italian madrigals don't feature too heavily in your repertoire."

Matthew took that in. "Not a fan?"

"They can be overdone," said the professor, "and usually are."

"Do you like John Dowland?" Hannah asked him, and reddened under the bland tolerance of his gaze. "In moderation," van Kauran said, and turned to Brecken. "I meant what I said," he told her. "I believe your style would be suited to opera, and I hope you'll consider writing one."

"Thank you," said Brecken. "I'm not sure there's much point to it, though. With all the financial problems we were talking about the other day, I doubt there's an opera company anywhere that would put on something as unfashionable as a modern baroque opera."

Before he could reply, Sarah said, "Maybe you should try a chamber opera."

"That," said van Kauran, "is a capital idea." When Brecken gave them both puzzled looks: "You're not familiar with the form? Think of the difference between chamber music and a symphony. Chamber operas have one or two acts, a very small orchestra, no chorus, nothing that couldn't be done in a good-sized parlor if it came to that. Critics have been saying for years now that chamber opera's the music of the future, but so far—" He made a little shrug. "The composers who've tried it have all been on the far end of the avant-garde."

"Postspectralist?" Brecken asked, naming the fashionable cutting-edge musical style.

"Unlistenable, certainly." He raised the end of his walking stick in salute. "You could do much better. Just a thought."

He headed back into the dwindling crowd. Brecken watched him go, considered the possibility of writing a chamber opera, and dismissed it. She had plenty of other projects to keep her busy, she reminded herself. Her friends from Bolton made one convenient set of distractions, a dozen other friends and acquaintances provided others. By the time Brecken left Upton Hall, walked to the bus station with her friends, and then went home through Arkham's narrow streets, she had chased the idea entirely out of her mind.

CHAPTER 4

KINGDOMS AT WAR

Brecken slid the white king's pawn forward, beginning the game. Pale sunlight spilled through the window onto the kitchen table. From above, faint but audible, came the familiar sound of broodlings repeating a song they'd learned.

June smiled, and moved the black king's pawn to block it. Brecken considered her options. Another pawn, king's bishop, or one of the knights? King's knight, she decided. The knight leapt past the protective screen of pawns to put June's advanced pawn in peril.

"Why?" June asked, still very much the teacher.

"I want to castle as soon as I can," Brecken admitted.

The old woman nodded. "Don't be too obvious about it." She brought her queen's knight out to guard the pawn. Brecken studied the board for a moment and then brought out her king's bishop, clearing the way for the castling move that would get her king safely behind a wall of pawns and free up one of the rooks to guard him.

She'd known next to nothing about chess when she arrived in Arkham—a few beginner's lessons in Camp Fire Girls back in Harrisonville, New Jersey were the extent of her education in the game, just enough to teach her the names and moves of the pieces—and she'd had no time to learn more during the two years after the move, as she finished her music composition degree under Paul Czanek's demanding tutelage. Then she graduated and June had her stroke, and Brecken, flailing around for something to help the bleak bitter moods that dogged the old woman thereafter, asked her to teach her to play. She'd meant it simply as a distraction, and it filled that role well enough, but she'd come to enjoy the game as well. Something about its formalities reminded Brecken of the fugues and canons of Baroque music, made the same kind of sense to her. More than a year had passed since June stopped going easy on her and started playing for blood. Brecken still lost many more games than she won, but the ratio slipped a little further toward the breakeven point with each passing month.

June brought out her other knight, countering the threat of Brecken's bishop, and said, "So what's the latest composition?"

It was a transparent attempt to distract her, a common bit of trickery in casual chess games, but Brecken didn't mind. After so many years playing piano, she could keep up a conversation and a chess game the same way she could play melody with one hand and harmony with the other. "I'm not sure yet. I've got some recorder arrangements to work out first—a recorder group out in Kentucky needed a bunch of hymn tunes in a hurry and paid up front."

That earned her a raised left eyebrow. "Coming down in the world, I see."

Brecken castled, moving king and rook. "Don't you dare tell me you never sang something you didn't like for a big tip."

"Hush." June tried to give her a quelling look, but the effect was spoiled by a half-smile she couldn't suppress. She advanced a second pawn.

It wasn't coming down in the world to arrange hymn tunes, Brecken wanted to say, but knew better. June had her prejudices, and anything belonging to the religion her mother had abandoned stirred one of them. That wasn't Brecken's religion either, but she'd played the organ for a few short months in a Partridgeville church the year Sho had entered her life, and the simple dignity of the hymn tunes left musical memories that still surfaced now and then in the small hours of the night.

"You're going to the physical therapist Wednesday, right?" she asked, and moved her bishop to threaten June's pawn and the more potent pieces behind it.

June made an amused noise in her throat, and moved another of her pieces. "Yes, Wednesday at one o'clock." Gesturing at the board: "What am I setting up?"

The sudden swerve from competition to instruction didn't startle Brecken. She pondered the board, tried to gauge what June had in mind. "A trap for my bishop," she guessed.

June nodded. "Good. Stop me."

There were half a dozen ways to do that, Brecken knew, but most of them risked more than she was willing to lose that early in the game. After a moment, she moved a knight so that June could take the bishop only by losing control of the center of the board.

"Good," June repeated, and moved one of her bishops to counter Brecken's knight.

Just then the phone rang. Brecken got up from the kitchen table, went to the phone. "Hello? Satterlee residence." She listened to the recorded message—it was from Miskatonic's pension office, reminding June to send in forms Brecken had taken to the pension office most of a week before—and then hung up and went back to the table.

Something was wrong. She realized that immediately, though it took a moment for her to notice that one of June's bishops had slid two squares to one side, a move the rules didn't allow. She gave June an uneasy look, and said, "I think you moved a piece."

June glanced up at her, nodded, moved the bishop back. "Excellent. You can't assume that the other player will follow the rules."

"Do chess players actually do that?" Brecken asked.

"Some, when they think they can get away with it."

Brecken sat, pondered the board, and moved a pawn forward, freeing more of her pieces. "That seems so pointless," she said then. "It just spoils the game."

"You think it's a game?" June asked. When Brecken gave her a puzzled look: "Chess is war." Her left hand jabbed toward the board, with its knights and castles. "Kingdoms at war."

* * *

The following Saturday, Brecken went onto the porch at ten-thirty sharp, and glanced both ways along Hyde Street. Her flute and a half dozen pages of basic exercises she'd printed out were tucked into her shoulderbag. She'd donned the nicest of her dresses and taken more time than usual with her makeup and her hair, all the little rituals that helped her deal with worry, but she still felt unsure of herself. Wind darted down the street in unsteady gusts, sending stray leaves and litter tumbling by.

A moment after the door clicked shut behind her, a Cadillac turned onto Hyde Street. It was an old model, Brecken guessed, venerable enough that it might have left the factory when June Satterlee was a girl. It stopped in front of June's house, and the driver got out: a short man in a black suit of old-fashioned cut, with hair the color of polished steel combed straight back from a pale and oddly expressionless face. She went down to the sidewalk to meet him.

"Miss Kendall?" he asked. When she nodded, he turned without another word and opened one of the rear doors of the Cadillac. The interior was opulent without calling attention to that fact, with far more legroom than Brecken needed and butter-soft seats of maroon leather. Brecken climbed in and got settled. The driver closed her door. Moments later he was in the driver's seat, setting the engine purring.

She tried to think of something to say as they pulled away from the curb, and failed. The college district moved smoothly past; the Cadillac turned right onto Peabody Avenue and crossed the river; downtown Arkham slid by, a desolation of mostly empty buildings, and then Peabody Avenue became Old Kingsport Road and climbed up out of the Miskatonic Valley. The remains of an abandoned shopping mall rose out of brush and saplings, and further on a few ruined barns and farmhouses interrupted the forest. After that the road wound through silent hills thick with gnarled willows and shore pines, looking so wild and desolate that Brecken found herself wondering if anyone had ever lived there, or ever would.

Finally the Cadillac crested one last rise and began to descend, and the silver line of the sea spread out across the southern horizon. To the left, gray cliffs soared skyward, rising one behind another to the mighty bastion of Kingsport Head. Below the cliffs, pale sunlight glinted on the huddled roofs of Kingsport. The Cadillac drove past half-ruined condos and a fringe of mostly empty luxury housing from recent decades, pierced the ring of postwar sprawl further in, and then veered onto a narrow street lined with ancient trees, fieldstone walls, and tall clapboard-covered houses, topped with a panoply of peaks and gables against the crisp blue of the sky.

A left turn onto another street—Green Lane, the sign told her—sent the car rolling slowly over cobblestones. At length the Cadillac turned through an open wrought iron gate into a driveway. The house beside it rose up in a symphony of red brick and white trim. June hadn't exaggerated, Brecken realized, when she'd spoken of the Chaudronnier mansion. A sprawling Georgian structure, it reeked of inherited wealth.

The Cadillac stopped under the carriage port, and the driver got out and opened the door for her. Brecken climbed out, nerved herself up for what might be an ordeal. "If you'll go in," said the driver, "one of the maids will take you to Madame and Miss Emily."

"Madame" sounded daunting, but Brecken thanked him and went to the carriage port door, while the driver climbed back into the Cadillac and drove back toward the garage.

As she reached the door a woman in a maid's uniform, dark-haired and dark-eyed, opened it and motioned her in. "Good morning, Ms. Kendall. May I take your coat?"

Brecken surrendered her coat, waited while the maid took it into a cloakroom and returned, and then followed, feeling utterly out of place, along a corridor that seemed to run from end to end of the mansion. Carpet silenced their footsteps, and oil paintings in ornate frames kept dignified watch from the walls. They passed a grand staircase leading up. Not far beyond it the maid led her to a door and opened it. "Madame? Ms. Kendall."

"Thank you, Henrietta." The voice wasn't at all what Brecken expected from someone servants called "Madame": a quiet voice, edged with something that sounded like shyness.

Henrietta motioned her to the door. Brecken braced herself and went into the room.

That it was the mansion's music room she knew at a glance. A gorgeous Steinway grand piano filled one end of the room, a floor harp occupied another corner, and two large wooden cabinets sheltered smaller instruments. Green wallpaper in an elegant pattern of stylized leaves covered the walls, and the vaulted ceiling was lined with one of the better grades of sound-absorbent tile. Emily stood by the Steinway in a bright blue dress, holding a child-sized silver flute in both hands as though it was a living thing and she was afraid of hurting it. Near her, sitting on the piano bench, was a woman in her early thirties who looked far too much like Emily to be anything but her mother. She had brown hair and a pleasant face, and the style of dress she wore and the full curve of her belly beneath it showed plainly enough that Emily would have a sibling within a month or two.

The woman reached out a hand. "Ms. Kendall? I'm Charlotte d'Ursuras, Emily's mother." They shook hands. "My husband Alain wanted to be here to meet you, but he had to go to France on business. I hope the trip down from Arkham wasn't too much of an inconvenience."

Brecken said something appropriate. "I should let you and Emily get to work," Charlotte said then. She smiled, rose heavily, and left the music room.

Once they were alone, Brecken inspected her pupil's flute—a good student model, less demanding and more forgiving than her own silver Powell—and then walked Emily through the first things she'd need to learn: how to hold the flute, how to work the keys, and a first pass through the tricks of breathing and embouchure that would eventually coax music out of the play of metal and wind. Emily's first notes were rough, though Brecken had heard far worse, and with some hard work a first breathy approximation of the proper tone started to show itself. Then it was on to a slow and fumbling attempt at the first three notes of the C major scale, and finally the first line of "Au Clair de la Lune," which used those notes and no others. Brecken still remembered the first time she'd played that beginner's piece smoothly, the sudden shivering delight in making music that had seized her then, and hoped the same delight would help Emily on her way to becoming a musician.

The hour went past quickly, and Brecken didn't have to use any of the little games and distractions she'd prepared to keep the interest of a bored child. Emily wanted to learn, that was clear to Brecken already, and she guessed that the child wouldn't balk even if the lessons ran long. Once Emily cleaned her flute and put it away under Brecken's careful tutelage, she led Brecken out of the music room and down the hall to reclaim Brecken's coat, and then to the door by the carriage port. The Cadillac was already waiting, and so was the driver with the pale expressionless face. Emily thanked her profusely, promised to practice every single day, and then made off. Brecken went to the car, said something polite to the driver, and settled into the back seat as he closed the door.

* * *

She shut her eyes for a few moments as the engine woke and the car headed out the driveway and down Green Lane. Though Emily was a pleasant child and her enthusiasm for music cheered Brecken, the mansion, the servants, and the Cadillac all left her feeling deeply uncomfortable. You need the money, she told herself, and it was true: her monthly stipend as June's caregiver and the very modest income from her music sales and performances covered her bills for the moment, but she had a future to prepare for.

That thought led in directions she didn't want to follow just then, and she stared out the car window, tried to lose herself in the desolate scenery of the hills. What came to mind instead was a memory from many years back: her middle school music teacher, Mrs. Macallan, telling Brecken one rainy Friday afternoon why she loved to teach music to children. Brecken had listened enraptured, and on the way home through the streets of suburban Woodfield later that same day, she'd daydreamed of being a music teacher, sharing the same gift with other children that Mrs. Macallan had shared with her.

Reality got in the way of that dream, as it did with so many others. You could hardly find a high school with a music program any more, much less anything for younger students, and nearly all the schools that still taught music had embraced the latest fashionable theory of music education, which Brecken had seen in action her second year in college and couldn't bear the thought of inflicting on anyone, least of all on children beginning to learn music. That left her the occasional private student at most, and there were two established flute teachers and half a dozen piano teachers in the Arkham area already, typical where the local university had a good music program.

She was still brooding over that when the Cadillac stopped in front of June's house, and the driver came around to open the door. Brecken thanked him and hoped that he didn't expect a tip. His bow communicated nothing. A few moments later the car pulled away from the curb and Brecken went up the driveway to the kitchen door. Inside, she let out a long uneven sigh.

The parlor felt hushed, though Brecken could hear Sho's faint piping from upstairs, and a moment later the ragged voices of the broodlings in chorus. They weren't busy at a lesson this time. Shoggoths, all shoggoths, performed rites for Nyogtha, commemorating the ancient pact with The Thing That Should Not Be, celebrating the help he had given them in winning their freedom from the Elder Things in ages long past, giving him life and strength in return. Sho had explained to her years back, apologetically but firmly, that those rites were for shoggoths alone. There were supposed to be human worshipers of Nyogtha, but no one seemed to know where, and so Brecken had to content herself with offering up her gratitude to the Dweller in Darkness with clasped hands beside the bed each night.

A glance at the clock warned Brecken that Sho and the broodlings would be busy for another hour yet. A glance into June's room found the old woman comfortably asleep atop the covers of her bed, with a crocheted throw over her for warmth. Brecken pulled the bedroom door shut slowly, so the hinges made no noise, then went back over to the sofa. Half a dozen chores called her, but none of them were urgent, none of them appealed to her, and none of them offered a refuge from the thoughts that troubled her.

That was when she saw the book on the sofa's arm.

She picked it up idly, saw the crowned and masked figure on the cover, recognized it: *The King in Yellow*, the play by J.-B. Castaigne June had been reading earlier that week. She opened it at random, found lines of verse labeled *Cassilda's Song*:

> Along the shore the cloud waves break,
> The two suns sink beneath the lake,
> The shadows lengthen
>   In Carcosa.

> Strange is the night where black stars rise,
> And strange moons circle through the skies,
> But stranger still is
>   Lost Carcosa.
>
> Songs that the Hyades shall sing,
> Where flap the tatters of the King,
> Must die unheard in
>   Dim Carcosa.
>
> Song of my soul, my song is dead,
> Die thou unsung, as tears unshed
> Shall dry and die in
>   Lost Carcosa.

The mood of the words matched her own troubled feelings so well that she flopped on the sofa, turned back to the title page, and started reading.

Three or four times in the first act she nearly put the book aside. It was one more standard nineteenth-century melodrama, she thought, with every box checked—faux-medieval setting, star-crossed lovers threatened by jealous rivals, a scheming and ambitious high priest, even a madwoman. Each time she was about to close the volume, though, a whisper of profound irony or a hint of something truly strange behind the too familiar happenings kept her reading. The most unnerving thing was that each time, it felt as though Castaigne had anticipated her reaction, had lured her into just that feeling of bored disgust, and then deliberately dropped that hint of something deeper to draw her further in.

The predictable catastrophe ensued, the stranger from Carcosa died on Thale's poisoned blade, the princess Cassilda turned the same blade on herself and died calling on the King in Yellow, her sister Camilla shrieked in horror and ran through the streets of Alar, and the first act ended. Brecken paused, but June had not stirred yet, shoggoth-voices still piped dimly from the floor above, and she turned the page.

The first words of the second act made her draw in a sudden sharp breath. From that point on, the idea of putting the book aside would have seemed absurd if she'd thought of it at all. A gentle push from Castaigne's hand sent the apparent melodrama of the first act spinning away into nothingness and recast the whole tale in the stark and terrible light of a lengthening afternoon, as the Pallid Mask gazed with blind eyes on the end of the kingdom of Alar and the whole tale unraveled into a vision of human folly in the face of an indifferent cosmos.

By the final scene, as the King in Yellow turned away from the open tomb of Aldones the last king to gaze across the long-ruined city of Alar, and the black stars of Carcosa began to glitter in the sky, tears tracked down Brecken's cheeks. They weren't tears of grief, or for that matter of delight, but of a kind of homecoming. In the last weeks before she'd left Partridgeville for Arkham, as the tangled web of danger and tragedy that surrounded her there finally unraveled, she'd found her own way to the same clear vision Castaigne had woven into his play: the knowledge, at once terrifying and liberating, that nothing she could possibly do or leave undone would ever matter to the universe. Meeting that vision in the play was like encountering an old friend who'd changed much over the years, or discovering that a strange town was actually the childhood home she'd more than half forgotten.

She squeezed her eyes shut, opened them again. The shoggoth-voices from upstairs had fallen silent, and afternoon glowed golden on the westward windows, reminding her suddenly of the shadows lengthening over Alar. She got up, blinked again, glanced at the clock, and hurried up the stairs to get dinner going for Sho and the broodlings.

She was most of the way to her apartment before her mind began to clear. When that happened, the first thing to move through her thoughts was a slow strange melody. It wasn't until she opened the door that she realized that the melody had words, and they were the words of Cassilda's song, the verses she'd read when she first opened the play.

* * *

By the time she woke the next morning, scraps of melody and harmony darted through her mind the way sparrows did through the trees outside. Off in the middle distance, church bells sounded: voices of Sunday, Brecken's quiet day. Even in wedding season, when she played as many paying gigs as she could get, she left Sundays unscheduled when she could, and devoted such of the day as chores didn't occupy to reading, playing and composing music, spending time with Sho and the broodlings, and writing her weekly letter to her mother.

That Sunday turned out to be quieter than most, and she was grateful for it. She managed to sleep in for a change, and once she'd taken care of breakfast and written a cheerful description of the more ordinary part of her life for her mother, she spent most of the remaining morning reading a Mexican cookbook she'd checked out from the library, trying to distract herself from the building pressure of the music taking shape in her. Meanwhile Sho softly whistled the song she meant to teach to the broodlings next, making sure she had every note correct, and the broodlings wore themselves out playing tag around the parlor and then settled down to a game that involved piling oddly shaped pebbles into heaps one stone at a time. Sho had tried to explain the game to her, and so had the broodlings, but Brecken still had only the vaguest idea of how it was played: one more reminder of the gap that separated her from the shoggoths in her life, a gap her heart had long since leapt but her mind could not.

All the while, the scraps of melody she'd heard in her mind the evening before kept circling, insistent and patient. She knew her own creative moods well enough to recognize what that meant, and had thought of the obvious problem by the time she went downstairs for the second time to help June up for the day.

"Do you mind if we talk a little?" she asked as soon as June settled on the sofa.

"Not at all." The old woman gestured for her to sit. "What's on your mind?"

"It's the play you were reading the other night."

"*The King in Yellow*."

"Yes. I read it yesterday, and—" She made a little helpless gesture. "I can hear the music that goes with the words. I think it wants to be written."

June regarded her for a long moment. "That play's got quite a reputation," she said, "and now and then deserves it. People have strange reactions to it—but you're the first person I've ever heard of who wanted to put it to music." With half a smile: "Well, other than Erik Satie, who wrote the music for the original performance."

Brecken gave her a startled look. "I had no idea."

"I don't think anyone knows what happened to the score." Her shrug was not quite as one-sided as usual. "What are you thinking of doing?"

"I think," Brecken said slowly, "it should be an opera." The conversations she'd had at the reception and after the lecture pushed their way into her thoughts. "A chamber opera. And that's the problem, because I really don't know whether it would be safe to do that."

June considered her. "You're worried about the other side."

Brecken nodded. "I don't want to draw their attention to you, or—" A glance upward indicated Sho and the broodlings.

"That's a real risk," the old woman said. "And it's not the only one. What did it feel like to you when you read it?"

Brecken considered that. Tentatively: "Like I've been living someplace where people speak a foreign language, and suddenly someone talked to me in the language I grew up with."

June regarded her for a long moment. "When I first read it," she said, "it was like somebody threw a bucket of water in my face and woke me up for the first time in my life. It wasn't an easy awakening—not for me, and not for others. I know three people who read it, quit their jobs, and went on to do the most amazing things with their lives—but I know two others who ended up in mental wards." She paused, met Brecken's shocked look. "All in all, it may not be something you want to mess with."

Brecken nodded again. "Okay," she said. "I can just do something else, then."

"I hope so," said June. "It's a play, but it's also an emanation—from Carcosa." In a low voice: "From my father."

June's father, Brecken thought. Even after five years, even after a childhood fascinated by old myths where gods and goddesses mated with human beings, it still took an effort for her to fit her mind around the idea that one of the core themes of the old mythologies was a simple fact. The Great Old Ones coupled with human beings now and then, and sired or bore children by them: it was as straightforward as that, and June was one of those children.

She'd told Brecken the details a few months after the move from Partridgeville, on a cold day during winter break when she and Brecken and Sho were all curled up on the big down-stairs sofa sipping hot chocolate. The story belonged in a book of myths, Brecken decided on the spot: the passion for secret lore that sent June's mother in search of forbidden books; the ritual that opened a gateway between her world and the world where the city of Carcosa rose, its black pyramids stark against a blind white sky dotted with sable stars; the consequences of the ritual, and the child that resulted; then, when the child was nineteen and well into a career as a singer, the unexpected fare-well, for Nora Satterlee had found a way back to Carcosa and would not be returning to the Earth her daughter knew.

"Can you ask him?" Brecken asked then.

June gave her a look she couldn't read at all. "I could call whoever the Fellowship has watching over me right now, ask for the question to be taken to Carcosa—" Another uneven shrug dismissed the possibility. "There won't be an answer. There never is." She paused. "I'd say set the play aside and do something else. Anything at all."

There was an edge to her voice Brecken hadn't heard often, though she recognized it at once. There were human beings who sought the attention of the King in Yellow—June's mother and those who set out to join the Fellowship of the Yellow Sign among them—but most of those who knew anything at all about the old lore feared the terrible silent gaze of the greatest of Earth's ancient gods. The thought that the Pallid Mask might find some reason to turn toward her sent a chill down Brecken's spine that the efforts of the furnace couldn't erase. "I'll do that," she said aloud.

CHAPTER 5

ARTIFICIAL WORLDS

The attempt didn't get far. For the rest of that day Brecken fumbled her way through the things on her get-to list, managed only distracted answers to questions sent her way, barely noticed the ripple of amusement in Sho's mantle as she whistled to her broodlings, ♪*Your foster-mother does not hear you. She is making a song.*♪ Chores gave her something to distract her for a time, but once Sho began teaching the broodlings another of the songs they needed to learn, Brecken went downstairs with a bleak expression on her face.

June glanced up at her as she came down the stair. "No, I didn't think you could."

Brecken shook her head. "The music just won't leave me alone."

"Fair enough. Keep in mind that it doesn't have to go straight to performance."

"That's true," Brecken said, her expression brightening. "Did Wilde's translation get performed right away after he finished it?"

"No, not even in his lifetime. The first production I know of was in 1911 in London. There were riots the first night it played, and some of the members of the audience had to be carried out of the theater after the performance."

"Did any of them end up in—in a mental ward?"

"Oh, probably." June sipped coffee, imperturbable. "Life does that to people all the time, you know." Brecken gave her an unfriendly look. June smiled fractionally and turned her attention back to her coffee.

"The other thing I have to figure out," Brecken said then, "is the text. I don't have a libretto and I don't know how to write one."

"You could just use the play as is," June said.

"But—" Brecken gave her a startled look. "Is that even an option?"

Wry amusement showed on the old woman's face. "These days? Nothing *isn't* an option. But using a play straight out of the book as the libretto for an opera, that's not even new. Debussy used a play by Maeterlinck as the libretto for *Pelléas et Mélisande*, Strauss used an Oscar Wilde play for *Salome*. If that's what you decide on, nobody's going to bat an eye."

"Nobody but Quentin Crombie," said Brecken, with a sudden smile.

June laughed. "Granted." Then, fixing her with a hard look: "And if you have to do this and that's what the music wants, then screw Quentin Crombie. Do it."

Brecken took that in. June motioned toward the nearest bookshelf, and Brecken got up, found *The King in Yellow* there, and brought it back with her. A quick movement opened it at random. Act I, scene ii, the heading said; the first thing she noticed was a bit of dialogue:

CAMILLA: *You, sir, should unmask.*
STRANGER: *Indeed?*
CAMILLA: *Indeed it's time. We all have laid aside disguise but you.*
STRANGER: *I wear no mask.*
CAMILLA: (terrified, aside to Cassilda) *No mask? No mask!*

Brecken bit her lip, caught herself trying to force the words into musical form, made herself stop and listen to the music of the words themselves. That first line—"You, sir, should unmask"—the rhythm and tone of the words flowed effortlessly into recitative, not the flowery recitative of grand opera but the spare *recitar cantando* of Monteverdi and the Florentine Camerata. The repeated words—"Indeed? Indeed," "no mask. No mask? No mask!"—those called for careful ornamentation, so that Camilla's and the Stranger's voices could dance around each other in performance as they did in Brecken's mind.

She went to get paper and a pencil, started to write down notes. A few minutes later she had the melody line worked out, and a few of the harmonies sketched in as well.

June watched her the whole time. "It knows what it wants," the old woman said.

"I'm not sure if it's that, or—" She shrugged. "But I can do this."

"Of course you can," June said, with the faintest of smiles.

Brecken blushed, turned her attention back to the music. It took her only a few minutes to write the whole thing out, while June watched her with an amused look. "Would you like to play that?" the old woman said then.

Brecken considered the idea, got up. "Yes. Yes, I would."

The grand piano waited. Once she got the lid propped up, she sat down on the bench, uncovered the keys. A few notes into the melody she stopped, because the music felt mutilated without at least one singing voice to make it whole. She started again, singing the words as she played. Camilla's part was a little high for her natural range and the Stranger's was decidedly low, but she managed it somehow. Even as she sang it she could feel the music's incompleteness, sense the hovering ghosts of the orchestration that would give it its body and the precise vocal technique that would give it its soul, but that could wait for later.

She covered the keyboard again, turned. June was watching with her left hand cupping her chin and something strange and intent in her gaze. "That's really rather odd," she said. When Brecken gave her a questioning look: "Every time I've seen the play produced, that's a seriously spooky moment. The Stranger's got a mask on like the rest of them, and yet there he is, saying it's not a mask."

"That's not how I read it at all," Brecken said, puzzled. "The Stranger's saying, look, this isn't a mask or a pose, it's who I am. He's trying to tell Cassilda that what he said about love isn't a mask or a pose either."

June considered that. "Okay," she said after a moment. "Why is Camilla terrified?"

"Because the whole kingdom of Alar is nothing but masks and poses," Brecken said after a moment. "Because she knows, they all know, that there's no kingdom any more, just a handful of people in a half-ruined palace in an empty city, and if she lets herself accept what the Stranger's said she has to stop pretending and deal with what's real."

After another moment, June nodded. "Interesting. I don't think I've ever run across anyone else who took it that way, but—" A half-smile creased her face. "If you made a good case for that in a term paper, I'd have given you an A for originality."

Brecken brooded over that later in the day, as she went down the stair into the basement to take care of the laundry, the one cleaning chore shoggoths couldn't do. The single bare bulb that lit the basement sent long shadows across the fieldstone walls, made the furnace and water heater stand out against the dim angular shapes of cobweb-draped boxes and the blackness beyond them. It occurred to her, as she loaded clothes into the washer, that her take on the play might be as arbitrary as dressing Wotan as a marshmallow rabbit. Once the washer was running, she went back upstairs, where *The King in Yellow* waited in its place on the bookshelf.

She had other things she needed to do, but none of them were urgent enough to prevent her from sitting down with the play then and there. The second reading reassured her in one sense, left her more uneasy in another. Her understanding of the play hadn't changed at all; it wasn't spooky, just realistic, to point out that all human pretensions were as empty as the masks and poses of the court of Alar, just as it was common sense that something didn't have to matter to the universe to matter to Cassilda, or the Stranger, or anyone else. ♪*The world has no eyes*♪, shoggoth tradition put it, ♪*but we have eyes*♪—it seemed so obvious, phrased that way.

Why, though, did what communicated so clearly to her fail to do the same thing to June, or to other people? She shook her head, put the play back on the shelf.

* * *

She expected to sit down that evening and launch straight into writing the opera, the way she would have written a fugue or a Baroque dance suite. By the time she nestled down next to Sho for the night, though, her first attempts at sketching out passages had run up against enough unknowns that she knew she needed to know more about how operas worked. The next morning right after breakfast she went to the university and headed for Orne Library, where her alumni card gave her borrowing privileges.

The third floor, where books on music, literature, and the arts had their home, was even more empty than usual, and the marks of deferred maintenance and inadequate funding were even more visible than they'd been the last time Brecken had visited. A few grad students huddled there over stacks of old books, but none of them paid her the least attention. Images of the nine muses gazed down appraisingly from stained glass windows framed in Gothic stone arches as she carried a hefty armload of books to a scarred oaken table, settled in a chair and began to read.

Those same stained glass images were most of the company she had for the next three hours, as she buried herself in librettos and scores from chamber operas and took copious notes in a spiral notebook she'd brought along. Orne Library had fallen into the fashionable habit of purging old books from its collections and replacing them with shallow modern substitutes, but it still had a fair number of books from the late nineteenth and early twentieth century, when opera was still one of the most popular art forms in Europe and America. Scraps of information the authors let fall gave her some clues about what had changed since then, and what she might need to do and leave undone in her chamber opera to change things back.

She also found three books that discussed *The King in Yellow*, and one thin volume published by a small university press in the 1960s that gathered all that anyone knew about the playwright. All of them took it for granted that *The King in Yellow* was the most brilliant and poisonous product of the Decadent movement, a book that would have been fit only for burning if it wasn't such a work of genius. While it violated no definite principles, promulgated no doctrine, outraged no one's convictions in any obvious way, they seemed to think that it deserved all the heated denunciations that had been heaped onto it, though none of them ever quite got around to explaining why.

The play's creator was just as enigmatic. Jean-Baptiste Castaigne, she learned, had been born in the provincial town of Ximes in 1869. His father hadn't come home from the Franco-Prussian war two years later, his mother died of tuberculosis when he was nine, and he spent the rest of his childhood in an orphanage. He won a place at a famous school in nearby Vyones by sheer talent, graduated, and moved to Paris to embark on a career as a writer and poet, penning poems that shocked the polite society of the day. *Le Roi en Jaune* finished the process of endearing him to the extreme end of the Decadent movement and outraging everyone else.

A chapter on his life after the play's one performance dropped dozens of names Brecken didn't know and a few she remembered from classes at Miskatonic. Like his friend Erik

Satie, Castaigne had been a close associate of that strange figure the Sâr Péladan, whose lush novels of sex and sorcery had caused a sensation in their day. He'd had an affair with the painter Suzanne Valadon and another with the novelist Rachilde, and had his portrait sketched in charcoal by Renoir; the book reproduced the image, a strange hollow-cheeked face with deep-set eyes and a shock of unruly hair. *Le Roi en Jaune* was his only venture into drama, but he'd written a dozen novels with titles Brecken couldn't translate, as many volumes of poetry, and a great many essays in strange periodicals before dying in the influenza epidemic of 1918.

None of that helped Brecken make sense of *The King in Yellow*. After she finished reading the book, she turned back to the Renoir portrait and brooded over it for a while, thinking: you went through the same things I did—losing your parents, finding your talent, trying to say something with your work that most other people don't want to hear. Is that why what you say makes so much sense to me?

The portrait offered her no answers. After another few moments, she closed the book, set it aside, and reached for the score of a chamber opera she'd found in the music section.

* * *

Noon saw Brecken hurrying back from campus to June's house with half a dozen books on opera she'd checked out. Those occupied her free hours during the afternoon, but as the cold blue glory of the evening sky spread over Arkham she'd worked out most of the details of her chamber opera. The play had eight speaking parts and two silent ones—Jasht, the acolyte of the High Priest Naotalba, was mute and so had no lines, and Castaigne had given none to the King in Yellow either. That gave Brecken her singing parts, though it took some time for her to assign each of them a vocal range, Cassilda to soprano, King Aldones to bass, the others to the musical space in between.

The question of which instruments should accompany the singers kept her staring into space for a while, too. She wanted something not much bigger than a chamber music group, she knew that already, close to what the Florentine Camerata had used for its first operas. Eight musicians, she decided after half an hour or so of thinking through the options: two violins, viola, cello, flute, oboe, bassoon—that much was clear to her, but there would need to be one more, something that could provide the quiet background the recitatives needed. Piano, she thought, or harpsichord, or—

Memories of a vanished friendship settled the matter. Harp, she decided. Harp it would be, a big floor harp if she could find a musician who had one and could play it.

The opera filled her thoughts as she went to the bus stop that evening and headed for Bolton. Stars gazed down blindly from a hard clear sky as she huddled in an inadequate coat and hurried down Pond Street to the cottage. Inside, warmth poured from the wood stove, and Hannah went to the kitchen and returned moments later to press a mug of steaming hot chocolate into Brecken's hands. "Got the milk heating at ten 'til," she said, grinning. "We can't have our favorite composer catching a chill." Brecken blushed.

Once the hot chocolate was inside her and she'd rinsed her mouth, the recorders came out, and they worked through a dozen of their standards. "Anything new?" Matt asked then.

"There he goes again," said Hannah, rolling her eyes. "We're doomed."

"Yes, you are," Brecken agreed, and reached for her shoulderbag. "And it's your fault, too. You were the one who talked about how much you like John Dowland."

Hannah's face lit up, and then she caught herself and tried to suppress the reaction, without much success. Meanwhile

Brecken extracted a sheaf of sheet music from her shoulderbag and began handing the pages out.

"Now here's one I agree with," Hannah said, grinning. She brandished the sheet music for a Dowland piece, "Away With These Self-Loving Lads," and then made a rude motion with her other hand. Brecken choked, Matt laughed aloud, and even Sarah chuckled, though she made herself frown a moment later. Danny made no more noise than usual, but smiled.

"That's not actually what it's about," Brecken protested. She tried to think of a way to explain Dowland's lines, and could think of nothing better to do than sing the first verse:

"Away with these self-loving lads
Whom Cupid's arrow never glads.
Away poor souls who sigh and weep
For love of them who lie in sleep,
For Cupid is a meadow god,
And forceth none to kiss the rod."

Hannah grinned again at the last line, but before she could say anything—and Brecken had no trouble guessing what she was about to say—Sarah fixed her with a baleful look. Hannah rolled her eyes, but left the comment unmade.

"I'd like to see you two sing that verse, the same way you do with 'Westron Wind'," Matthew said to the two of them. "Okay," said Hannah, and Sarah: "It would be even better as a three-part round. Brecken, would you like to join in?"

Brecken let herself be talked into it, and the five of them raised their recorders and played the melody through twice. Then, on Sarah's nod, the three women lowered their instruments, and Sarah began the first lines with a fine contemptuous toss of her head as Matthew and Daniel carried the melody. Hannah came in as Sarah began the third line and Brecken as she reached the fifth. Sarah and Hannah fell silent as they each finished the last line, and when Brecken did the same, they raised their instruments and joined with the men for one more pass through the tune.

A moment's silence went by when the music was done. Then Matt said "That's really good" and Sarah said "Oh my" and Hannah said "Wow," all at once. They looked at each other and laughed, and Brecken laughed with them. Danny settled back into his corner of the sofa and smiled his little half-smile.

"I'd love to do that on Black Friday," said Sarah. "That and 'Westron Wind' both. Are you free that afternoon, Brecken? That's Bolton's holiday bash. There's always a big crowd."

"It's a busking gig," Matt added, "and a good one. We usually do pretty well, and some people we know throw a big dinner for everyone that evening. You've got to come."

If the date in question had been Thanksgiving, Brecken would have found an excuse—to her, that day and Christmas Day were sacrosanct, for reasons that had nothing to do with the usual holiday celebrations—but the Friday following Thanksgiving had no such importance to her, and money, publicity, and a big meal on somebody else's nickel were powerful incentives. "I think I'm free that day," she said. "I'll be able to tell you for certain next week." Matt gave her a look she recognized at once, and she blinked. "That's right, you'll be gone then."

"Two weeks from now is fine," said Sarah. "Or give us a call."

* * *

The rest of the week went past in a blur that blended ordinary chores and fragments of an unborn opera in roughly equal parts. The first rush of creative absorption faded as it usually did, leaving Brecken a little less drawn into herself than before. That was helpful, for a glance back over what she'd written so far showed plenty of passages that she'd made so difficult that only a first-rate singer or musician could perform them.

Too many composers paid no attention to such things, but it was a minor vanity of hers to make her pieces as playable as she could, and she spent long sessions at the piano reworking those passages until they could be sung or played well by those with ordinary skill.

She had other things to distract her that week. The visiting nurse, a big furry bear of a man with little round glasses, came by to check on June that Wednesday. He brought a four-footed cane for June and gave her instructions on how to use it, and made a cheery comment about how clean the house always was. Brecken smiled, thanked him, and thought about what he would say if she told him what it was that slid along the floors and shelves and counters every day or two, ingesting every last grain of tasty dust.

She spent much of the week wondering, too, whether Emily d'Ursuras would practice the exercises she'd been given. That was the one thing that mattered in a music student, Brecken knew well, the line that divided those who would go on to become musicians from those who wouldn't. Too often, she'd seen all the advantages of talent, enthusiasm, and instruction go to waste because a student wasn't willing to face up to the inescapable labor of scales, drills, études, familiar tunes endlessly repeated, all the hard work that was needed to burn the essentials of making music into a novice musician's mind and hands.

Her worries were pointless, but she had no way of knowing that until the Cadillac pulled up into the carriage port. As the driver opened the car door, Emily came pelting out to wish her an excited good morning, then took her hand and all but dragged her to the music room, talking all the while about what her mother and her father and her little sister Sylvia had said about her playing. Once there the child assembled her flute, offered it to Brecken for her approval, then reclaimed it and picked her way through the first line of "Au Clair de la Lune" that showed the hours of work she'd put into practice.

Brecken praised her, then went on to correct Emily's mistakes, and was delighted to discover that her pupil didn't mind the corrections and did her best to respond to them.

An hour later, Emily had learned two more notes and she'd begun work on "Merrily We Roll Along." A few sheets of paper in one of Brecken's notebooks sketched out the course of study she'd planned for Emily, and she'd already amended that after working with the girl and getting a first tentative sense of her strengths and weaknesses. A bitter memory stirred more than once as she pondered the lessons she meant to teach: the one class on music education she'd taken at Partridgeville State University in New Jersey, during her sophomore year, where she'd been taught to force mechanical obedience to mindless exercises on every student. Learning music was hard enough, she'd decided, without making it more miserable than it had to be.

Had the people who designed that program meant to make it miserable? She'd wondered about that much more than once, thinking about the systematic way that schools had purged their curriculums of music, art, and everything else that didn't require mechanical conformity to some set of rules of other. She shook her head, guessing she would never know the answers.

As Emily led her toward the carriage port, Brecken spotted Charlotte d'Ursuras sitting in one of the parlors. Brecken smiled; Charlotte smiled in return and looked as though she was about to say something, then visibly caught herself and looked away. Brecken wondered how to take that, but the austere silence of the mansion offered her no guidance, and Emily led her on.

On the ride back to Arkham, she let herself sink into the music she was composing, and pieced together a few fragmentary passages, first in her head and then in the pages of a notebook she'd remembered to put in her shoulderbag. At first, as she'd done now and again since beginning the opera, she wondered whether her reading of the play was as improbable as June seemed to think it was, but once the process of composition took over, such thoughts wandered away and lost themselves. All that remained was the music and the story it meant to tell, and she let it take its own shape as her pen darted across the page.

She had barely enough presence of mind to thank the driver when he opened the door for her in front of June's house. As she headed for the kitchen door, though, scraps of music circled around half-remembered passages from *The King in Yellow*, and she had to struggle to keep her thoughts on anything else. June was napping when Brecken crossed the parlor, and no sounds came from above; when she came up the stair and went into the apartment Sho and the broodlings were settled on the sofa, over onto the dreaming-side, the way they spent so much of the cold days.

That managed to dispel the music for a moment, and Sho completed the process by blinking two eyes open and reaching out with a drowsy pseudopod. Brecken, once she'd shed her coat and put down her shoulderbag, settled gratefully next to her, put her arms around the shoggoth, and let herself slump against the familiar shapeless darkness.

♪I am glad you are back,♪ Sho piped after a few moments. ♪When the air is this cold it is too easy for me to remember and be afraid.♪

♪I understand,♪ Brecken replied, and turned her head to kiss the shoggoth's mantle. No more had to be said. Brecken recalled vividly, and knew that Sho did too, the cold autumn night when the rest of Sho's people had died.

Time passed. Finally Brecken gave Sho a squeeze and whistled, ♪We should speak of food for when the light fades.♪ Changing languages, since there were no shoggoth words for the dishes she had in mind: "I was thinking of mac and cheese earlier, but now—cheese polenta?"

That summoned a sudden burst of the washed-mushroom scent that was the shoggoth equivalent of a smile. "Please," Sho said. "That would be very good."

Two of the broodlings, Presto and Vivace, had blinked awake at the sound of the words and looked up at Brecken expectantly. She laughed and said, "You're on. I can get some cookies baking, too, just in case somebody's hungry before then."

* * *

By the time the cookies were cooling on the rack, though, the weather had turned gray and damp, and so did Brecken's mood. She thought about joining Sho and the broodlings on the sofa, but a restless mood was on her, and she crossed to the window, looked out at the broken pavement of Hyde Street and the rundown houses on the other side. A fog had come creeping up from the river, turning the porches across the street into dim blurred shapes and bleeding the life out of everything.

I've built a little artificial world, Brecken thought, inside the walls of this house. Here I have Sho to adore, her broodlings to love and raise, June to take care of, music to play, music to compose, an opera to write even though it won't be produced in my lifetime. And out there ...

Out there: headlines from the news and memories from a bitter childhood flowed together into the phrase. Out there, past the fog, moved forces and facts that could shatter everything she cared about in an instant and never even notice what they'd done. She thought again of Mrs. Macallan, who'd built her entire life around teaching music to children, and slit her wrists one fine summer day after the school district decided that giving the district administrator yet another lavish raise mattered more than her life's work.

I'm just as vulnerable as she was, Brecken reminded herself. It was true, too: if the vagaries of fashion that had given life to the neoclassical revival turned and went the other way; if June had another stroke and died or had to go into a nursing home, leaving Brecken and Sho without their safe haven; if any whisper of Sho's existence found its way outside the walls of June's house; more hideous still, if those who'd killed the rest of the shoggoths of Hob's Hill finally succeeded in tracking down the one survivor of that dreadful night, and turned their destroying flames on Sho and her broodlings; if any of a hundred other things happened—what then? Would there be anything left for her except a futile scrabbling for existence in the void left behind by failed and empty dreams?

She left the window, crossed to the sofa, settled next to Sho and pressed her face against cool shapeless softness, clenching her eyes shut in a futile attempt to keep tears at bay. After a little while, a pseudopod flowed around her shoulders, comforting.

♪*Broodsister,*♪ said Sho in a quiet whistle. ♪*You are sad.*♪

♪*I'm scared,*♪ Brecken admitted.

♪*Of what?*♪

♪*The world.*♪

♪*I understand,*♪ said Sho.

Brecken managed an unsteady smile, opened her eyes to see one of Sho's temporary eyes regarding her face from a few inches away. ♪*I know you do,*♪ she said. She put her arms around the shoggoth, felt pseudopods flow around her in response, took what fragile comfort she could from their closeness.

Later, though, when Sho had slipped back over onto the dreaming-side, Brecken got up from the couch as gently as she could, pulled a crocheted throw over Sho and the broodlings to make them feel more sheltered, and went back to the window. The fog had grown oppressively thick, turning the houses across Hyde Street into vague spectral presences. The rest of Arkham lay drowned in a white blankness that left her thinking irresistibly of the waves upon the cloud lake beside black Carcosa. The colder side of the insight Castaigne had woven into his play, the knowledge that the universe never noticed the countless things it broke and cast aside, surged up in her again, but this time it took a form she could face squarely: a sequence of notes, measured and mournful, tracing out a bass line that seemed to contain all the world's empty misery. It would be perfect, she decided, for the overture to the second act.

She went to the coffee table by the sofa, found her composing notebook and a pencil, took those to the green chair by the window and sat. The sequence of notes played themselves over in her mind, and she paused, pencil in hand, trying to find the rhythm and the harmonies that would give them the power to say what they needed to say.

Another sound broke in on her thoughts just then, the soft plop of a shoggoth broodling dropping from sofa to floor. She glanced up, saw a small black shape sliding across the floor toward her chair. A glance at the slow uneven pace of its movements told her it was Fermata.

♪May I?♪ she asked when she'd reached the foot of the chair. Then, in English: "I don't feel so good."

"Of course," Brecken told her, and reached down to help her onto the chair. Fermata stretched, flowed, nestled down between Brecken and the arm of the chair. The broodling had an unfamiliar scent about her, a little like ammonia, and that made Brecken stare at her for a long worried moment. It occurred to her for the first time that Fermata's slow growth and unsteady movements might be signs of something serious, some illness the broodling wouldn't simply outgrow. The thought troubled her, and she tried to shove it aside.

That futile effort, in turn, cleared away the last barriers to the music.

Sometimes, when a theme took shape in her mind and she went to work turning those bare bones into the living body of a piece of music, voices and harmonies tumbled into being so fast she had to struggle to keep up with them and get them onto paper before they fled. At first, this was not one of those times, and the theme's funereal rhythm set the pace of her musical imagination. The notes appeared to her one by one, moving with the leaden formality of the servants in Castaigne's play, curtseying to her as she sent them to their places in the score. The flute darted in sudden flurries of high quick notes and then sank down exhausted; the oboe sang its threnody in the middle ranges, with the bassoon repeating the theme with slow sullen tones and the harp echoing it in patient shimmering glissandos, and then—oh, of course, she thought, seeing exactly where the strings would come in, pianissimo at first and then swelling, taking the theme from the bassoon and then changing it into ... into ... she sat there floundering for a while, trying to figure out what the theme would become, but caught herself, stopped, listened.

An inner silence opened up. In it, a fragment of the motif she'd chosen for the King in Yellow sounded, first on the cello, then on the viola, while the violins and the flute trembled in fearful agitated flurries of fast triplets. A second fragment followed, and all at once the whole motif thundered, repeated itself a fourth lower, then again a fourth lower still.

Then she was writing with frantic speed, using quick jagged marks across the staff to indicate bursts of notes she could fill in later, jumping from instrument to instrument as melodies and harmonies came crashing into her mind. The rest of it came together in what seemed like minutes, rising up to a harsh crescendo, then cascading back down to a recapitulation of the first bleak and patient theme before the final cadence brought it to a harsh end.

She sat there staring blankly at the notebook for a time after she'd written the last notes, and only then thought to wonder why she could barely see the paper in her lap. A glance up at the window showed that the fog had faded from white to dark gray; a glance over at the clock told her that evening had arrived, and she'd spent more than three hours composing.

She shifted, winced, let out a little yelp; her muscles ached as though she'd run a race. Fermata opened four eyes, and asked, ♪*Is it well with you, foster-mother?*♪

She patted the broodling. ♪*It is well. I have been still too long, and it is past time to make food for us all.*♪ Fermata pressed herself against the arm of the chair, and Brecken hauled herself to her feet, set the notebook and pencil aside for the time being, and headed for the kitchen to get the cheese polenta cooking.

CHAPTER 6

BIRTHS AND BUDDINGS

"Happy birthday," Brecken said, sitting on the floor next to Sho. The broodlings clustered around the two of them, squirming and expectant. Weeks had passed since she'd begun work on the chamber opera, and most of her spare time still went into the unfamiliar effort of fitting voices and instruments to the words of a libretto. Still, this day was important.

Celebrating birthdays wasn't a shoggoth habit. Lacking even the concept of numbers, they had no calendar and didn't count the years of their lives. Even after Sho had grasped what numbers meant, a mental leap Brecken guessed was like the one she herself would need to understand Einstein's theory of relativity, it took the two of them several long conversations to figure out that Sho had been budded in the late summer and was probably half a year younger than Brecken. When the broodlings were almost a year old, though, Brecken had suggested a birthday party, and once Sho understood the concept, she'd been delighted by it.

♪Sing the human-song, little ones,♪ Sho whistled, and the broodlings responded in chorus with the familiar birthday song. Brecken joined in for the third and fourth lines: "Happy birthday, dear broodlings, happy birthday to you." When they were done, she said, "And how many years old are you?" She watched them wrestle with the concept, then raised one finger, a second, a third, and beamed as they counted "One, two, three!" together. It was a little thing, she knew, but learning to count might help them get by in the unknown future that waited for them, and Brecken enjoyed the chance to teach.

Then she reached onto the table and brought down a plate with six frosted cupcakes on it. There would be no candles—though more than five years had passed since that terrible night inside Hob's Hill, the sight of flame still left Sho trembling with dread—and no decorations; Brecken had hung crepe paper streamers for that first birthday party, only to have Presto eat one and become queasy from the dye. Still, the broodlings each engulfed a cupcake. As they signaled their delight with a burst of washed-mushroom odor, she was content.

There was a present, too, and Sho brought it out from within herself as soon as the broodlings had their cupcakes entirely ingested: a Chinese checkers board with colored marbles. ♪*This is a game,*♪ said Sho, ♪*one that human broodlings play. It is strange but pleasant, and your foster-mother will teach you to play it.*♪

Of course that meant the board had to be set up at once and the broodlings coached through the opening moves. Once they'd grasped the rules and the game was well under way, Brecken got up, checked the two big spaghetti casseroles in the oven, came back into the parlor to answer a question about jumping one marble over another, then went downstairs to make sure June was fine. She was up again a few minutes later—June was ensconced on the sofa with a newly published history of early jazz, and needed nothing but solitude—to find the broodlings huddled around the board, so intent on the game they spoke only in occasional whistles.

Brecken watched them for a while, then settled on the sofa. After a moment Sho flowed over and joined her, and Brecken put an arm around the shoggoth.

♪*It is a good gift,*♪ said Sho. ♪*I am happy that it pleases them.*♪

♪*And I am happy that you are happy,*♪ Brecken said, smiling. Then, considering the shoggoth: ♪*Does something trouble you?*♪

♪*Yes. No. I am remembering*—♪ Brecken could nearly see her work out the number in her mind. ♪*Three years ago.*♪

♪*I remember also.*♪ She gave Sho a comforting squeeze.

It hadn't helped at all that budding wasn't preceded by nine months of pregnancy, just by a week or so when Sho had been sluggish and unusually hungry. Then, in the pitch blackness of the night's small hours, Sho's sudden terrified whistle: ♪*Brood-sister, broodsister, something is happening, something is—I—I—*♪ All in a rush: ♪*I think I am budding—*♪

It had taken Brecken some minutes to get Sho calm enough to find out what she needed, and by then six swellings had begun to bulge from her mantle. What she needed was food and comfort, plenty of both, and those kept Brecken hurrying from bedroom to kitchen and back again for a solid hour. Once the swellings drew up into spheres nine inches across and separated from Sho, the newly budded broodlings had to be fed, and rolled in a fluid that oozed from the wounds in Sho's mantle to keep them from eating one another in their first blind hunger. Brecken rubbed the same fluid on her hands and forearms, and when one of the broodlings tried to engulf her toes and another made several valiant attempts to ingest part of her nightgown, she pulled off the garment and smeared herself with the fluid from head to foot.

The sun was well up before Sho and her broodlings, limp with exhaustion and lumpy with undigested food, finally slipped over to the dreaming-side. Then Brecken wriggled back into her nightgown and headed downstairs to check on June, who was only a few months back from the hospital. The old woman had given her an incredulous look and started to laugh, the first laugh she'd managed since the stroke, and Brecken had to glance in the mirror on the closet door to see why: the fluid she'd daubed on herself looked like greenish-black paint and, half dried, had transformed her hair into a fright wig almost two feet across.

♪*You are thinking,*♪ Sho said then.

♪*Remembering how frightened we both were, and how everything still ended well.*♪

♪*You did so much, for me, for the little ones.*♪

♪*Broodsister,*♪ said Brecken. ♪*How could I do anything else?*♪

A scent like freshly baked bread rose from Sho. Brecken bent and kissed Sho's mantle, and then pressed the side of her face against the shoggoth. A few moments later, Presto whistled a question about the game, and Brecken laughed, kissed Sho again, extracted herself from the sofa and went to the game board and the broodlings to help sort out their perplexities.

All in all, it was a pleasant evening. The only thing that troubled Brecken, as she nestled down in bed that night next to Sho, was that Fermata lost her appetite after ingesting the cupcake, and only wanted a few spoonsful of spaghetti casserole for her dinner.

* * *

Toward the middle of that week, the neighborhood around June's house went silent as most of Miskatonic's students headed home for Thanksgiving. Brecken spent a good part of her spare time that week getting ready for the holiday dinner. That involved a trip to the old First National grocery up on Walnut Street—one of the few survivors of that venerable chain, so the local newspaper said, though she'd shopped at another down in Partridgeville during her time there—and a trip home in a taxi. She didn't like spending the taxi fare, even though the money was June's, but she habitually got a pair of twenty-pound turkeys to provide leftovers and soup stock for the rest of the holiday season, and that plus the other things she needed for the meal was more than she could haul a dozen blocks home on foot.

The trip to the store was on Tuesday, and the streets went quiet on Wednesday. Brecken went to the library and the post office that day, got eleven emails at the first of those and a vacuous letter from Aunt Mary at the second—she'd worried for weeks that Aunt Mary would send some of her famously inedible zucchini bread, and breathed a sigh of relief when that didn't happen. The bulletin board in the entry of the library had the same chess club flyer as before, and Brecken stopped to read it, noted that the Arkham Chess Club had moved to new quarters in the library's event room. The thought of playing against someone other than June enticed her, though for some reason it also made her feel uncomfortable, and she took a moment to note down the club meetings, 6 pm on Tuesdays.

Thursday morning Brecken plunged into cooking, shuttling back and forth between the upstairs and downstairs kitchens, keeping both ovens going all day. Five years back she and Sho had spent their first Thanksgiving together, and looking back, she'd sensed that it was then that her friendship with Sho had begun to ripen into love. Since then, Thanksgiving had been one of their special days. They'd made room for June and the broodlings, but every Thanksgiving there were moments when Brecken felt the years dissolve and she and Sho were young and frightened and lonely again, fumbling their way toward the improbable life they'd made together.

This Thanksgiving, Brecken pulled out all the stops. While the turkeys filled the air downstairs with mouthwatering scents, she baked a brace each of pumpkin and apple pies upstairs, then put a huge casserole dish of stuffing to bake there and hurried downstairs to make a salad and get it in the refrigerator. Cooking for others, whether the others in question were human or not, set someting warm and trembling in her deep places, and she needed that, needed the pleased look she got from June, the whistles of delight from the broodlings, the pressure of one of Sho's pseudopods curving around her in an affectionate embrace.

By the time the meal was over, five of the broodlings had gorged themselves until they strained to surround their undigested meals. Sho looked distinctly lumpy, June leaned back in her armchair and let out a contented sigh, and Brecken helped herself to another half slice of apple pie and then let herself slump against her broodsister. Only after she and the shoggoths had climbed the stairs and settled back into the apartment, leaving June to doze comfortably below, did she let herself think about the way that Fermata had taken only a little of each dish.

A glance at the far end of the sofa, where the broodlings lay digesting in a comfortable heap, gave her more cause to worry. Fermata stood out, faintly but definitely, among her sisters. The mantles of the others were the iridescent, half-transparent black of a healthy shoggoth, but Fermata's was noticeably duller and more opaque.

The shapelessness that embraced Brecken shifted. She glanced down to see that Sho was also looking at Fermata. A pale greenish eye glanced up at her, then sank back into blackness.

Later still, when the broodlings were far over onto the dreaming-side and Brecken and Sho had slipped under the covers of their bed, they talked about Fermata. ♪I am afraid,♪ Sho whistled: quietly, so the broodlings would not hear.

Brecken gave her an uneasy look.

♪There was a thing that happened sometimes,♪ the shoggoth went on, ♪with the little ones. Something was wrong with certain of them from the time they were budded. They would live and grow for a time, though they would never be wholly well and they would never be as large as their broodmates. Then their mantles would become dull, and they would begin to lose the wish to feed. The black color would give way to gray. Pale streaks would show in their mantles, and when that happened it was time to speak words of farewell, for they would not live long after that. I am afraid that Watches the Moon is one of those.♪

Brecken tried to speak, failed, tried again. ♪Was there nothing that could be done?♪

♪*A few could be healed,*♪ said Sho. ♪*They would be treated over and over again with certain moistures, though it was painful for them, until something gray came out of them and they were well for a time. Maybe there is another way to do that, but the broodmothers did not speak of it, I never saw it, and those others did not concern themselves with such things.*♪

That got an involuntary wince from Brecken. She'd learned from Sho long before that the creators of the shoggoths, the alien creatures Friedrich von Junzt called Elder Things and shoggoths called simply "those others," treated their manufactured slaves as disposable objects, and a shoggoth who showed the least sign of illness or injury was simply put to death.

♪*None of my broodmates were ill in that way,*♪ Sho said then, ♪*nor my broodmother's broodmates. I did not think it would appear in my broodlings. I have been so very lucky—*♪

Brecken put her arms around the shoggoth, felt pseudopods flow in response and cling to her. ♪*Maybe it is not that,*♪ she whistled to Sho. ♪*Or maybe Watches the Moon can be healed in the way you have said. Or maybe something else can be found.*♪

♪*Broodsister,*♪ said Sho in response. ♪*You are so very kind to me.*♪

Brecken winced again, catching the implication. Lacking any other answer, she kissed Sho's mantle. One of the shoggoth's pseudopods brushed her cheek a moment later, but the fresh-bread scent of affection in the moisture it left there was tinged with the bitter note of grief.

* * *

The next day the county buses ran only at long intervals. Brecken got to the station early, huddled in her thin coat and tried to convince herself that she didn't mind the chill. Her conversation with Sho the night before still haunted her.

The number 7 bus came almost half an hour late, but Brecken had expected that. Once she settled into a seat and the bus rolled out of the station toward the Aylesbury Pike, she fixed her gaze resolutely on the autumn landscape and did her best to push worries about Fermata out of her mind. Two difficult passages in Act II, scene 2 of *The King in Yellow* made that easier than it might otherwise have been, but she didn't manage it entirely until the bus turned onto Central Avenue and passed the old National Guard armory. To her surprise, the weathered plywood had been taken off the windows, and a rental trailer in the parking lot spoke of renovations under way. She pondered the old building until it was well behind her, then almost pulled the bell cord out of habit but caught herself in time. Six blocks further into Bolton than she usually went, she pulled the cord and stood up as the bus grumbled to a stop.

She grabbed her shoulderbag and hurried down the stair to the sidewalk. As the bus pulled away, cold sunlight untangled itself from scattered clouds to stream aimlessly past Briggs' Hill onto Bolton's Victorian brickwork. Banners splashed with bells, holly, and other bland secular imagery sagged motionless in the cold damp air. Beneath them, children bundled against the cold scampered about, making excited noises, while their parents and grandparents plodded from store to store hauling shopping bags. The sound of a choir belting out holiday carols with more energy than skill reached Brecken's ears through the hubbub. She found her bearings, wove her way through the crowds toward the music.

"Brecken!" Hannah's voice cut through the babble of the crowd. Brecken turned, spotted her friend, wove through the press toward her. Hannah motioned with her head and led Brecken to where the other members of the Bolton Recorder Consort stood waiting, next to a brick wall festooned with cheap plastic snowflakes three feet across. They wore thin jackets and no scarves or hats—scant comfort, Brecken thought, against the raw weather, but they seemed perfectly comfortable. She wondered whether most native New Englanders were that used to cold.

She and they said the usual things, waited while the choir struggled with "O Holy Night," found their rhythm again with "O Come All Ye Faithful," and then finished up with a respectable performance of "The First Noel." Applause rose above the background noise for a few moments, faded again. Matt checked the time—he had an old-fashioned pocket watch on a chain, the only one Brecken had ever seen outside of a museum—then cocked an ear to listen to the nasal voice that spoke briefly over the PA system, and motioned: go.

They went. A sinuous route, single file, brought them across a small brick plaza to a low portable stage draped along three sides with bedraggled red and green tinsel. Folding chairs in ragged rows faced it from the street side, most of them empty, the others offering a brief respite to weary parents and grandparents who looked as though silence was the music they most craved. Brecken, who had played for plenty of less promising audiences, glanced over them and decided that she'd count the day a success if half the chairs were filled by the time the fifty minutes allotted to the Bolton Recorder Consort were up.

While Matt opened an old fiddle case, set it on the front of the stage for money from the audience, and put a stack of flyers next to it, Brecken got her recorder put together, then waited while a tired-looking volunteer set up a microphone for each of them. A quick adjustment made her recorder match the note struck by Danny's pitch pipe. She gave the others a glance and a quick smile. Sarah met the glance with a smile of her own, nodded one, two, three, and all five of them came in at the same moment with the opening notes of "The Coventry Carol."

The medieval harmonies Brecken had used for the arrangement, so unexpected to modern ears, got sudden startled looks from some of the passersby. "Christmas Lamentations," the fine old sixteenth-century piece that followed, got more of the same. By the time they reached "Westron Wind" and Sarah and Hannah lowered their recorders and sang the plaintive words that went with the tune, they had a small but attentive crowd gathered around the stage.

The fifty minutes were up sooner than Brecken expected. "Away With These Self-Loving Lads" turned out to be the high point of the set, to judge by the applause, and they ended with "Hey, Ho, Nobody Home," another piece with a three-part round in the middle. Well over half the chairs were filled by the time the last haunting minor chord fell silent, so Brecken felt satisfied by the performance. She also felt tired and chilled to the bone, and tried to nerve herself up for the wait at the bus stop and the ride back to Arkham.

"Come on," Sarah said once they'd left the stage and gotten their instruments put away, and Matt had reclaimed the fiddle case and the leftover flyers. To Brecken: "You look like you could use a nice hot bowl of chowder." Brecken tried to parse that, then remembered that Matt had said something about dinner. The thought of hot soup was appealing enough that she didn't bother with questions, and simply motioned for them to lead the way.

The sounds of holiday crowds faded promptly as soon as they left Bolton's business area behind. Half a dozen blocks, through streets lined with old clapboard-sided houses, brought them to a long two-story building with a peaked roof that reminded Brecken of a Grange hall where she'd played for wedding receptions back in Harrisonville. Sure enough, the familiar wheat-sheaf logo and the word BOLTON GRANGE stood watch above the doors, and beside the entry an old-fashioned announcement board, with white letters on fake-velvet backing, read:

BOLTON GRANGE #89   1ST TUES 6PM
UNITY IOOF #126   4TH THURS 730PM
MISKATONIC EOD #11   2ND & 4TH SAT 4PM
SPACE FOR RENT CALL 839 187 2004

IOOF meant the Odd Fellows, Brecken knew—the Harrisonville Odd Fellows Lodge was another rental space where she'd played more than once before going away to college—but EOD rang no bells. Some other lodge, she guessed, and shrugged mentally.

Inside, on the ground floor of the building, a long room with little windows high up on either side stretched away to doors that opened onto glimpses of a kitchen. The walls were decorated with old lithographs in frames; near one end was an ornate banner in a glass case, with symbols all over it she thought she'd seen in the Odd Fellows hall in Harrisonville. Little clusters of people sat at long tables, talking; scents of fish chowder and fried oysters made Brecken's mouth water. Matt and Sarah veered off in separate directions and Danny slipped away a moment later, but Hannah took charge of her, introduced her to a dozen people whose names Brecken promptly forgot, got her parked at a table and fetched a cup of coffee. "Hang on," Hannah said then. "I'll be right back."

* * *

A basket of sugar packets and creamer made a welcome distraction. Brecken got her coffee fixed and sipped at it. That first sip helped clear the cobwebs from her mind; another did more along the same lines, and so did the chance to sit quietly and rest after the noise of the crowds and the effort of the performance.

"You're Brecken Kendall, aren't you?" said a voice she didn't recognize. She looked up to find an old woman with thick glasses standing on the far side of the table. Before Brecken could figure out how to respond, the old woman laughed. "No, we haven't met. I went to *The Magic Flute*, and saw your curtain call. You didn't look too happy about that."

"Well, no," Brecken admitted, blushing. "It was kind of embarrassing."

She pulled out a chair, sat. "I bet. I'm Susannah Eliot, by the way."

Brecken said something polite, considered her. Susannah Eliot had the muscular build of a woman who'd worked with her hands all her life, gray hair pulled back into a braid that went well down her back, a face well lined with wrinkles. She wore a sturdy sweater over a plain practical dress, the sort of thing any elderly Bolton housewife might have on, but Brecken doubted that many Bolton housewives could muster the air of serene authority that surrounded the old woman. It didn't help that her expression suggested that she knew exactly what Brecken was thinking and found that mildly amusing.

Before she could say anything more, Hannah returned with a tray loaded with two bowls of chowder. She stopped just short of the table, did a doubletake, and then said in a voice far more subdued than Brecken had ever heard from her: "Hi, Mrs. Eliot."

The old woman smiled up at her. "Hello, Hannah."

"Can I get you—"

"No, I'm fine."

Hannah set a bowl in front of Brecken, another at the place next to her, settled into the latter and murmured something Brecken couldn't make out over the chowder: grace, Brecken guessed, and dipped her head respectfully. That done, Hannah pulled over a box of oyster crackers, offered them to Brecken, then poured out a good helping into her bowl and tucked into the chowder. Brecken picked up her spoon, gave Mrs. Eliot an uncertain glance, and the old woman smiled and motioned for her to eat.

If it wasn't the finest chowder she'd ever tasted, Brecken decided, it was very close. She finished it off in a matter of minutes while Mrs. Eliot asked Hannah about the Bolton Recorder Consort and Hannah answered without the least trace of her usual attitude. The moment Brecken's bowl was empty, Hannah got up, scooped up the bowl and carried it off.

"A talented young lady," Mrs. Eliot said then, watching her go. "Once she stops trying so hard to be annoying, I think she'll go very far."

Brecken choked. "I think it's her age," she managed to say.

That got her a raised eyebrow. "Were you like that at nineteen?"

The thought of explaining why she'd been silent and troubled at nineteen made Brecken quail. "Well, kind of," she said. "And I had a friend who really was."

The old woman's expression suggested that she'd heard everything Brecken hadn't said. She changed the subject effortlessly, and by the time Hannah came back they were in the middle of a conversation about the local music scene. The second bowl of chowder was as welcome as the first, and it came with a platter of breaded fried oysters tasty enough that when Brecken ate the first of them, she couldn't repress a sigh of sheer delight.

"That," said Mrs. Eliot, "is the kind of applause the cooks hope to get." She got to her feet. "Brecken, it's been a pleasure to talk with you. I hope we'll see you here again."

She headed off toward another part of the hall, which was filling up with people. Brecken watched her go, then turned to Hannah and said, "Who is she?"

Hannah gave her a look she didn't know how to read. "Mrs. Eliot? She's—she's an old friend of my family. She's known me since I was in diapers."

There was more to it than that, Brecken sensed, but she decided not to push; besides, the rest of the oysters and the chowder waited. By the time she'd finished them, Danny and Sarah reappeared, and settled down across the table from Brecken. The moment they showed up, Hannah headed off and returned with another round of oysters for everyone. Matt showed up a little after that with a tray of his own, plopped down in a chair, then pulled an envelope out of a pocket and handed it to Brecken. "Here you go," he said. Brecken thanked him, and he grinned and tucked into a robust meal.

Conversations swirled about Brecken. Time passed, people talked, various tasty things put in an appearance at intervals, and finally Brecken noticed the clock on the wall and let out a yelp: the last bus back to Arkham would leave Bolton in twenty minutes. Matt and Sarah were both somewhere else just then, but as she scrambled to her feet, Danny got up as well, touched Brecken's arm to catch her attention, and motioned toward the door.

Once she'd pulled on her coat and scooped up her shoulderbag, Danny led her back through the silent streets to her usual bus stop. Brecken spent a little while wishing that Matthew had been free to walk her to the stop, so she could have asked him about the people who'd put on the dinner. Most of them seemed to know each other, and something about the way they talked and teased each other reminded her more than a little of the members of the Grange and the Odd Fellows lodge she'd met back in Harrisonville. Danny's little half-smile communicated nothing.

The bus came a few minutes late, to judge from the distant tolling of church bells. Brecken thanked Danny, who smiled again and made off, and climbed aboard. The bus was mostly empty, and nobody else sat close to the seat she chose. After a few minutes, as the bus sped around the shoulder of Briggs' Hill, she took a calculated risk, pulled the envelope from Matt out of her shoulderbag, and counted the money.

It was a considerable sum, much more than she'd expected to make, and all in cash. That cheered her. She had a modest amount of cash tucked away in hiding places, in case she and Sho and the broodlings needed to flee June's house without warning, and what she'd just made could be added to that.

It was a small thing, maybe, but it made her feel a little less vulnerable. She put the envelope back in her shoulderbag, got out one of her notebooks, and got to work on the violin parts for the last dozen bars of Act II.

* * *

The day after that, when Michaelmas let her off at the carriage port and Emily came trotting out to greet her with a bright dancing look in her face, she could sense at once that something had happened. Henrietta met them inside the door as usual and took her coat, and she considered asking the maid, but old insecurities argued against it. Instead, she smiled, said something inoffensive, and let Emily lead her to the music room. After they'd reached the room Brecken said, "So tell me what you're all excited about."

Emily beamed. "Sylvia and I have a brand new baby brother. His name is Geoffrey."

Brecken congratulated her and asked for the details, knowing the girl wouldn't be able to think about anything else until that was out of the way. She got more details than she expected—someone named Martha Price, who (from Emily's few words of description) didn't sound like a doctor, had delivered the baby, and put Emily to work straight through the labor and the hours that followed it. The thought of having an eight-year-old run errands during labor startled Brecken, but after a moment's reflection she decided that it sounded like a good idea.

Once Emily had told her story and Brecken congratulated her again, they went to work on the flute. Emily played two tunes, not too raggedly, then picked her way through a simple étude over and over again, trying to achieve a steady flow of breath, while Brecken accompanied her on the piano. By the time they were finished Emily looked tired but elated, and with good reason. Her last pass through the étude had been well played for a beginner, music rather than vaguely melodic noise.

The two of them discussed the next week's assignments while Emily cleaned her flute and put it away. They'd just finished that process when the door opened. Brecken looked up, expecting Henrietta or perhaps Michaelmas, but the woman who looked in had a thin plain face framed in a mop of mouse-colored hair.

Emily sprang up with an inarticulate cry, ran over and flung her arms around the newcomer. "Aunt Jenny! Oh, I hoped you'd come home."

"Well, of course," the newcomer told her. "I want to see your new brother." Then, glancing up with a smile at Brecken: "Good afternoon. I'm Jenny Chaudronnier. You're Emily's music teacher, aren't you? Charlotte's written about you."

Brecken went over and introduced herself, and they shook hands. Aunt Jenny was in her mid-thirties, and so short that the top of her head barely came to Brecken's chin; she wore a baggy Oregon State University sweatshirt and jeans that had seen better days. Her rumpled look spoke of long hours on crowded airliners.

"Mama's sleeping," Emily was saying to the newcomer. "Geoffrey's in the nursery, of course. Papa and Grandpa are in Boston on business, and Sylvia's got her nose in a book but she'll come looking for you as soon as she hears. I bet you haven't had lunch yet, have you? I'll go tell Fern you're home and we can all have lunch with Mom when she wakes up."

Brecken smiled at them both and made for the door. "Please give my best to your mother," she said to Emily, and to Jenny: "Pleased to meet you."

"Likewise," Jenny said, with a matching smile, and stepped out of the way.

Henrietta was in the hall outside, beaming; Brecken gathered that the Chaudronnier family weren't the only people in the mansion who were glad to see Jenny. The maid walked with her to the carriage port and handed her her coat with every sign of friendliness, and Michaelmas was unfailingly polite as always, but Brecken ended up feeling as she so often did, standing outside a circle of warmth and affection she could never enter.

I've got my own family, she reminded herself tartly as the Cadillac turned onto Green Lane. Thinking about Sho and the broodlings helped, though it also called to mind her worries about Fermata. She pulled a notebook out of her shoulderbag, turned her attention to the music for the masked ball in her chamber opera.

* * *

June slid the white king's pawn forward to begin the game. Brecken, black this time, took the queen's bishop's pawn and moved it two squares forward.

"Sicilian defense," June said, considering the move with narrowed eyes. "Why?"

"Wednesday you said my playing was too predictable," Brecken replied amiably. "So I decided to be less predictable."

The old woman made a skeptical sound in her throat. "Meaning you've watched me mess you over with that opening often enough that you think you can return the favor." She brought out one of her knights. Brecken said nothing, advanced her queen's pawn a single square to guard the pawn she'd moved first.

Outside the parlor, snow drifted down onto Hyde Street and turned Arkham's roofs into blurred shapes against featureless white. A deep hush swallowed every distant sound, made nearby sounds seem preternaturally acute. Schools and government offices were closed, or so the radio announced when Brecken turned it on after breakfast; the county bus routes had shut down until snowplows could clear the roads, and that month's meeting of the Miskatonic Valley Early Music Sociey had been cancelled. It was a good day to stay indoors, she'd decided, and the fridges and cupboards were full enough that she felt no need to do anything else.

June moved another piece, trying to draw her out. Brecken responded with another careful move, strengthening her position.

"How's the opera coming?" June asked her then.

Brecken smiled, as much because her work was proceeding well as because she knew that June was trying to distract her.

"Most of the way done," she said. "Act I just needs a little polishing, and the first scene of Act II's almost as far along. All I really have to do now is a few bits of the last scene, and then the finale." As she'd guessed, while she was talking, June brought out one of her bishops to threaten Brecken's defense. It was one of June's habitual moves, and Brecken had a knight waiting to deal with it.

June glanced up from the board as Brecken's knight moved into its place. "One of us," she observed, "is playing very predictably."

"I'm sure it's me," Brecken said cheerfully. June made a little bleak noise down in her throat and moved a pawn, shoring up a position that had suddenly become much less secure.

Half an hour later, maybe, June laid her king down on its side, conceding. "*Le Roi est mort*," she told Brecken. "You've been paying attention."

Brecken blushed as she gathered up the pieces. "I've got a good teacher," she said.

June gave her a wry look. "There are things you can teach and things you can't," she said. "You've said that yourself about the d'Ursuras girl." Brecken nodded, and June went on. "That's one of the things I like about *The King in Yellow*. Castaigne got that. The things that might have saved Alar were things none of them could learn, except for Cassilda, and she was too busy falling in love and then dying." She considered Brecken. "In a way, the play's like the endgame of a chess match. All the choices that matter have already been made, and it's just a matter of following them out until you finally see what was implied by them all along."

Brecken thought about that later that afternoon, when June was napping, Sho and the broodlings lay sprawled on the sofa in a somnolent heap after hours of schooling, and Brecken herself sat half curled up in an armchair near the window filling in the orchestral parts for a portion of Act II, scene 2. June was right, she decided; Castaigne's play really was like the last moves of a chess game. Alar's side had its king, Aldones; one bishop, the high priest Naotalba; two knights, Thale and Uoht; one rook, the citadel of Alar itself; and at least four pawns, the madwoman, the high priest's acolyte Jasht, and the princesses Camilla and Cassilda. Carcosa's side—that was where the metaphor fell apart, for alongside one knight, the Stranger, and one rook, Carcosa itself, it had a piece with no equivalent in chess, the King in Yellow, who could touch every square of the chessboard at once without moving from his place.

That wasn't just a dramatic convenience for Castaigne's play, Brecken knew. Tucked in the bottom drawer of her dresser were two old volumes she'd brought up from New Jersey, *The Book of Nameless Cults* by Friedrich von Junzt and *The Secret Watcher* by Halpin Chalmers. Both were full of shoggoth-lore she'd long since confirmed in conversations with Sho, and both also spoke of the King in Yellow, mightiest among the Great Old Ones while Cthulhu lay dead yet dreaming in lost R'lyeh, whose cold six-fingered hands had flung down planets from their orbits, and who knew even the unborn thoughts of mere human beings.

Hastur, Brecken thought. You didn't say the name aloud, not unless you wanted the Pallid Mask to turn your way and incalculable consequences to follow. For all his daring, Castaigne hadn't broken that taboo. The words Cassilda spoke before she died appeared in the play as "O King," though the myth he'd gotten from von Junzt and used as subject matter for his play had her call on the King by name. Thinking of that, Brecken shuddered. She was glad, and not for the first time, that it was Nyogtha rather than one of the far more ancient and terrible Great Old Ones who had taken an interest in her and in Sho.

CHAPTER 7

LENGTHENING SHADOWS

A few days later she went to the bus station and climbed aboard an unfamiliar bus—13 TO SALEM VIA KINGSPORT, the sign in the front window said. Her flute, a music stand, and an assortment of sheet music for tunes she already knew by heart sat in her shoulderbag, along with a sheet of notepaper on which she'd written directions to the Kingsport Senior Center. It was an ordinary trip, she told herself, to an ordinary solo gig, no different from all the others she'd played in Arkham and the towns nearby over the past five years. The effort didn't accomplish much, and Brecken wasn't sure why.

The bus lumbered into motion, headed for Peabody Avenue and the route Michaelmas drove each Saturday. From her place by the window a few seats back from the driver, Brecken had a better view of Arkham's downtown district than usual, but that simply meant a clearer look at a ragged landscape of urban decay only slightly veiled by half-melted snow. The big brick building on the corner of Peabody and Pickman with K OF P HALL on the cornice, empty since long before Brecken came to Arkham, had a few lights on inside and a few people visible in the windows, but that was the only unexpected sign of life she spotted. The rest of the town seemed to crouch beneath iron-colored clouds like a wounded animal.

Half a dozen blocks further, Arkham dwindled into a scattering of outlying businesses and homes and then gave way to woodland and scattered farms. Old Kingsport Road rose up out of the Miskatonic valley, passed the ruins of the old shopping mall, and then plunged into the barren hills between Arkham and Kingsport, where gaunt willows clawed at the sky and the sparse and fading traces of past human settlement were hidden under the snow.

In due time the bus broke from beneath bare trees and headed down the slope to Kingsport, passing a scattering of farms with lights in the windows. The outer belt of abandoned condos and empty luxury homes slipped past, the half-empty ring of postwar tract housing followed, and then all at once the bus hurtled through the dark heart of old Kingsport, past gnarled trees, old fieldstone walls, and gable-roofed houses that loomed over the streets, gazing down from small-paned windows behind which anything might lurk.

The Kingsport waterfront sped by, with its marina and its tall ship for tourists, and when the bus turned back onto High Street Brecken pulled the bell cord. Moments later she stepped onto the sidewalk, breathing cold salt-scented air. The bus briefly replaced the scent with diesel fumes as it growled into motion. Brecken checked her directions and found her way through narrow streets to the white clapboard building that housed the Kingsport Senior Center.

Inside, an old man with round glasses and thinning gray hair was all smiles when she went to the front desk and introduced herself. She let him lead her to another room, where a bevy of old women were busy stocking tables with assorted handicrafts for the charity bazaar, then excused herself and spent a few minutes in the restroom making sure her hair, her makeup, and her blouse and skirt were neat enough for the occasion. Her nerves always got to her before a solo performance, and the little rituals of preparation helped. It helped, too, that when she returned to the meeting room, went to the

corner they'd set aside for her, set up her music stand and busied herself getting ready for the performance, nobody seemed
to notice her at all.

The handful of chairs set out for listeners were untenanted
when Brecken glanced at the clock up on the wall, raised
her flute, and launched into one of her own flute pieces, the
Partita in G. She'd chosen that because it had a gentle melody
she'd used more than once to lull cranky broodlings onto the
dreaming-side. It didn't have quite the same effect on the old
women behind the tables or the people of all ages who began
to trickle into the room, but that didn't trouble her. There in the
corner of the room, with her flute in her hands, she could let
herself sink into one of the two things in her life that always
made sense to her, and watch the delighted looks as people
who had braced themselves for the mindless cacophony of pop
music or the all too intellectual cacophony of art music got to
hear something that made sense to them instead.

She was just finishing the Partita when familiar faces peered
in through the door: Emily and a girl of five or so who had
to be her sister Sylvia, with their aunt Jenny following. Emily
trotted over to the chairs facing Brecken and perched in the
closest. Jenny and Sylvia did the rounds of the tables and then
stood listening for a while, before Sylvia took her aunt's hand
and pulled her out of the room. Brecken played while people
came and went, finished up the set with a flute arrangement of
her Bourrée in B flat, and sank gratefully into the chair they'd
left for her.

The man from the front desk brought her a bottle of water,
smiled, vanished again. Brecken sipped water, asked Emily
about her mother and Geoffrey, listened to the reply, and then
got to her feet when a middle-aged woman approached dif-
fidently to ask whether she might be available to play for a
wedding. Brecken put on her best professional smile for that,
noted down a date and an email address and handed over a
business card. She had just settled back in the chair when a

couple in their twenties came up to her and the same sequence repeated itself.

That was the way the afternoon went: three forty-minute sets with twenty-minute breaks between them, playing for the bored, the harassed, and the attentive, while the bazaar filled up and then slowly emptied out again. She handed out five business cards to people who asked about hiring her, thanked eight more who praised her playing, and beamed at a harried young woman about her own age whose fussy infant quieted, nursed, and went to sleep when rocked to the sound of Brecken's flute. Emily listened with an entranced look while Brecken played, talked excitedly during the breaks. That was all that happened until a few minutes before the end of the last set, when Brecken's friends from Bolton walked through the door, glanced her way, did a double-take and then worked their way around the tables.

* * *

As soon as Brecken finished her set, they made a beeline for her corner. "Fancy meeting you here," said Matt, grinning. "We came down to visit some friends, Sarah spotted a poster on a telephone pole, and when we got here, there you were."

"I'm a sucker for charity bazaars," said Sarah. "You get the best things there. Ever tried doing dishes with a crocheted cotton dishcloth? You'll never want to use a sponge again."

Brecken made agreeable noises and hoped Sarah wouldn't press the issue, since there was no easy way she could explain why she didn't need either sponges or dishcloths for cleaning purposes, not with seven shoggoths at home. Fortunately Emily was there, and made a suitable distraction. Brecken introduced them, then got her flute disassembled and cleaned while the child peppered them with questions about recorders and the music they played. Just as the flute slid into her shoulderbag and Brecken started taking apart her music stand, Emily's aunt showed up with Sylvia in tow and said, "Hi, Brecken. I hope the performance went well."

Hannah glanced toward the newcomer and started back like a scalded cat. The others didn't respond quite so obviously, but their reaction wasn't that different—as though a celebrity had suddenly shown up, Brecken thought.

"Pretty much," she said to Jenny. "And I had a very attentive audience."

Jenny laughed. "I bet." Then, to Emily: "Ready?" Emily scrambled to her feet and said good-bye to Brecken and the others; Sylvia watched them all with a solemn look. Brecken said the usual things, Jenny smiled and replied and took Emily's hand, and the three of them left.

"Can we offer you a ride?" Sarah asked then. "We brought the car."

"Please," said Brecken. "And thank you." She got everything stashed in her shoulderbag, deftly sidestepped a question from Hannah about something one of the vendors at the bazaar had been selling. On the way out she stopped at the front desk. The old man talked effusively about how wonderful live music was, and followed it with the more tangible applause of a check. Brecken thanked him, assured him that she'd be delighted to play at any other function the senior center had in mind, and followed her friends out into the cold brisk air of a winter evening.

They had to walk four blocks through Kingsport's narrow streets to the car, a station wagon that looked decades older than any of them, with fake wooden sidewalls and absurd little tail fins over the rear lights. The engine rumbled to life readily enough, though, and Matt extracted them from Kingsport's maze of cobbled streets. Once he turned onto Old Kingsport Road and old houses began to give way to postwar tract housing, Sarah turned to Brecken and said, "I didn't know you knew Jenny Chaudronnier."

Brecken glanced toward her, tried to read her expression in the orange glow from passing streetlamps, didn't get far.

On the other end of the seat, Hannah watched with an equally uncommunicative look "Emily introduced us," Brecken said. "I'm at the Chaudronnier's every Saturday morning these days, remember." Then: "Is she famous or something? You looked really surprised when she showed up."

"Well, kind of," said Sarah. "She's got a doctorate from Miskatonic, you know, and she travels all around the world. I heard she was in Laos over the summer. It's mostly just that you don't expect to see people that rich popping up at charity bazaars in senior centers."

"I think the only reason she showed up was so Emily could hear me play. Emily's mother just had a baby boy, and I don't think she's going out yet."

Hannah laughed. "Your fan club is growing, Brecken."

That stirred bittersweet memories. "When I was first learning the flute," Brecken said, "whenever my teacher played somewhere and I could get there at all, I'd go listen even if I had to walk the whole way." With a little laugh: "One time I caught the county bus to this little church outside of Woodfield where she was playing for an evening wedding, and by the time it was over the last bus had gone and I had to walk six miles home by myself in the dark. I was scared out of my wits, but I did it."

"How did your mother handle that?" asked Sarah, startled.

"She was out when I got home," Brecken said with a shrug. "That happened a lot in those days. I don't think she ever found out."

Later, when the conversation flagged for a while and the station wagon hurtled through a darkness edged with gaunt gray trees, Brecken winced inwardly at the half-truth. She'd never told her Bolton friends much about her mother, hadn't hinted that "out" might not mean her mother had gone somewhere else for the evening. The image came up all at once: light from the kitchen slanting across a parlor otherwise dark, her mother sprawled motionless on the sofa with eyes rolled back in a blank vacant face and an empty bottle by one limp hand, faint movements of her chest the only sign of life, reek of spilled vodka tainting the air. Brecken had fixed mac and cheese for dinner, left her mother's share in the fridge and put a note on the table before slipping up to her room and letting herself sink exhausted into bed. The note and the mac and cheese were both gone in the morning, but her mother never mentioned either of them.

The station wagon passed out from under the trees, and the lights of Arkham glinted below. "You look sad," Sarah said to her.

Brecken forced a smile into place. "Remembering some things that happened when I was little. It wasn't a very good time."

Sarah nodded, uncertain. The car hurtled through the night toward Arkham.

Not long afterward, she waved to her friends, watched them drive away, headed indoors. The house on Hyde Street embraced her protectively; a short time later, so did Sho, and the familiar comforts of serving and sharing dinner kept other concerns at bay for a while. Later that evening, though, when she went downstairs again to help June get ready for bed, she asked, "Do you know anything about a Dr. Jenny Chaudronnier?"

That got her a sudden measuring look. "Why?"

"I've met her," Brecken said, "and some friends of mine looked kind of surprised and kind of uneasy when she showed up at the bazaar today."

June took that in. "She's a Miskatonic graduate," she said then, "history of ideas, used to be one of Miriam Akeley's grad students. Miriam's still in contact with her. She didn't go for an academic position—I'm not sure what she's doing with her degree."

"Traveling around the world," said Brecken. "That's what my friends told me. They said she was in Laos last summer."

"Laos," June said. "You're sure that's what they said." When Brecken nodded, June leaned forward. "Remember what I told you about the Chaudronniers? Double and triple it. Laos gets a few tourists and a few scholars from Western countries, but if somebody interested in the old lore goes there they've got something else in mind. Do you know what's north of Laos?"

"I probably should," Brecken admitted.

"The plateau of Leng."

Brecken took that in. "Von Junzt talks about that, doesn't he?"

"He went there. You could get there from the Chinese side in his time, or from Myanmar—Burma is what they called it in his day. I don't recommend trying that now." Then: "If they've got family members going to Leng, they're not just dabbling in the old lore, they're in it up to their eyeballs—and there's still no way to tell which side they're on."

* * *

The next week was finals week at Miskatonic, and the student district north of the river took on the discordant tone Brecken remembered well from her own college days, the frantic tension of last-minute cramming for exams jarring against the relief of those who'd finished theirs or had no reason to fear them. The balance shifted as the week went on; by Friday night the tension had trickled away, and so had most of the students. The night was so hushed that when a trio of young men staggered drunkenly down Hyde Street, belting out the old Miskatonic drinking song "Shagged by the Shoggoth from Shaggai," Brecken could hear every word from inside the apartment despite closed windows and drawn curtains.

Sho could hear the song just as clearly. Once the voices had faded into the background murmur of the night, she gave Brecken a puzzled look and whistled, ♪*Do they not know that there are no shoggoths on Shaggai?*♪

♪*They don't know that there are shoggoths anywhere,*♪ Brecken reminded her. ♪*Besides, they're drunk.*♪

Sho had tried alcohol precisely once. The experience had left her huddled and queasy, and she could not be convinced thereafter that humans responded to it any differently. ♪*Then I pity them. Why do they do that to themselves?*♪

♪*They are young and silly,*♪ Brecken whistled, ♪*even for humans.*♪ Then, as the question occurred to her: ♪*Where is Shaggai?*♪

♪*Very far from the sun,*♪ said Sho. ♪*If you could fly through the Great Deep as those others did, and went outward past the little worlds of stone and the great worlds of gas to the little worlds of ice, you would come to Shaggai in time. My people knew little about it, for those others could not go there and live.*♪ In a low whistle: ♪*One of the old songs says that in the times of times when we were slaves of those others, my people used to wish that they could go to Shaggai and dwell there, where those others could not be. That was before the Dweller in Darkness taught us how we could be free of those others without leaving this world.*♪

♪*I'm glad you didn't go,*♪ Brecken replied. ♪*It would have been hard for me to get out there and find you.*♪

♪*Broodsister,*♪ said Sho, with an affectionate look, and nestled up to her.

The winter break, always fraught with memories for Brecken, proceeded in its usual fashion. Arkham went silent; even with enrollment down as far as it was, more than half the town's usual population consisted of students at the university, and their absence left a sense of spreading desolation. Most of the businesses in the student district shut down until the new semester started. Brecken's trips to the library, the post office, and the grocery took her through mostly empty streets, and she was always glad to return to the familiar warmth of June's house and the embraces of her shoggoth family. Her two trips each to Bolton and Kingsport helped, for Emily d'Ursuras and her Bolton friends were as warm and enthusiastic as ever, but the feeling of isolation that gripped Brecken as she returned to Arkham left her nerves frayed.

On Christmas Eve, Brecken didn't go out at all. June gave her a wry smile and waved her upstairs as soon as Brecken had finished the few things she needed to do. The broodlings slid downstairs after dinner to nestle down comfortably in a heap on one of June's armchairs and slip over onto the dreaming-side, and for once, Brecken and Sho had the evening to themselves. Brecken made thumbprint cookies filed with apricot jam, another commemoration, and they sat together on the sofa, ate cookies, and talked quietly as night deepened outside.

♪Sometimes it feels like only a little time since I came to you,♪ Sho whistled after a long pause. ♪And sometimes it feels like an age of ages.♪ All at once she huddled against Brecken. ♪Broodsister, broodsister, you have been so good to me!♪

Brecken put her arms around the shoggoth and kissed her. ♪Is it well with you, broodsister? You sound—♪ She fumbled for the right shoggoth-word. ♪Worried.♪

Two pale eyes opened, gazed up at her. ♪A little. They are old fears, and will pass.♪

♪I hope so. I wish I could make all your fears go away.♪ She bent, kissed the shoggoth again between the two temporary eyes. In response, paired pseudopods flowed up to cradle her head and stroke down the sides of her face, leaving lines of wetness behind. Brecken sighed and kissed Sho again, and things proceeded from there.

Morning's first dim light found the two of them in their bed, all atangle under the quilts, Brecken's head pillowed on one of Sho's pseudopods, one arm and leg draped across the shoggoth's cool shapelessness. Brecken blinked awake to find Sho still far over on the dreaming-side. Once she was sure she wouldn't get back to sleep, she kissed the shoggoth's mantle—gently, to avoid rousing her—and slipped out of bed. Nightgown, bathrobe, and slippers helped fend off the cold. It was far too early for her to check on June or to play music, so she went out into the parlor, closed the door silently behind her, walked to the nearest window and stared out at the bleak silence of the sleeping town.

The same sense of vulnerability that had inspired the overture for her chamber opera's second act haunted her again, made each dim moving presence on distant streets seem to whisper a half-heard threat. Was it the worry she'd felt in Sho the night before, or something else? She could not tell. All she knew was how fragile the barriers were that she'd raised across her divided life, how little it would take to expose Sho and the broodlings to the baffled horror of Arkham's other residents or the destroying flames of the Radiance.

She had a fair amount of cash tucked away in well-hidden envelopes; she had two big duffels with wheels on one end, and knew that Sho could fit in one and the broodlings in the other; she'd noted the locations of abandoned houses in half a dozen communities within a short bus ride of Arkham where she and the shoggoths could hide while she tried to figure out their options. The thought of putting those plans into effect terrified her, not least because she knew that doing it would mean the end of her career as a performer and composer—but if it came to a choice between that and losing Sho, she knew she would accept it.

Feeling wretched, she slipped back into the bedroom, shed everything but the nightgown and nestled back against the shoggoth. She didn't expect to fall asleep, but it happened anyway, and when she woke two hours later the only trace left of her troubled mood was a fragment of a dream in which something she couldn't see watched her out of the darkness.

* * *

Though the calendar insisted it was Christmas, the day that followed was perfectly ordinary, or as ordinary as a day could be with six shoggoth broodlings and their broodmother in it.

Brecken fixed a lavish breakfast for everyone, beamed when Fermata ate more than a little, tried not to notice that even so she'd engulfed less than half as much as the other broodlings. With one thing and another, it was well into the afternoon before June settled down for her nap and Sho and the broodlings got busy with lessons, leaving Brecken at loose ends.

The weather was no less gray and bleak than it had been early on, though Brecken could see less of it from the ground floor windows. After a while she picked up the notebook she'd all but filled with the opera score, flipped through the pages looking for a part not yet finished. It took her most of ten minutes to find a dozen measures in Camilla's final aria in Act II, scene 2 that needed the instrumental scores filled in. She got the notes written down, walked over to the grand piano, and played through the piece, making sure that the passage would work.

Once that was done, she flipped through the score again, looking for the next passage that needed to be written, and found none.

It's finished, she told herself. The words seemed to hang in the cold silent air, incomprehensible. It's actually finished.

She got up after a few minutes and wandered over to the kitchen, feeling vaguely lost. A flurry of sleet hammered against the windows. An odd disquiet edged her mood, made her feel as though she'd left something incomplete, but the clock told her that she still had plenty of time before June needed her, and still more time still before she had to start work on dinner. After a few moments of uncertainty, she went after a cookbook she'd checked out from the library a week before, paged through it, found a recipe for a casserole bread she'd wanted to try, and made sure that it would neatly fill the rest of the afternoon.

A half hour or so of pleasant distraction followed as she chopped and measured, let familiar scents and labors keep her mind from things she didn't want to think about. She was stirring green onions and cheese into the batter when June came out of her room, made her patient way to the kitchen door, and asked, "So what is it?" Brecken described the casserole bread in enthusiastic tones, and the old woman shook her head, amused. "I don't think I've ever heard of a musician who likes to cook the way you do. The ones I toured with back in the day thought leftover fried chicken and waffles was as good as food got."

"Liberace liked to cook," Brecken said.

That fielded her a startled look. "Most people your age haven't even heard of Liberace."

"My grandfather liked him." The batter went into a casserole dish. "Not really as a pianist, but he said he'd never met anybody else who was that good at working an audience."

"True enough." June allowed a sly smile. "So when will you start wearing rhinestones and fur capes? Or are you dreaming of having seven dining rooms in your future mansion?"

Brecken blushed, laughing, and said, "Two's enough for me." The oven door groaned open, closed again. She started toward the sink to wash bits of batter from her hands, remembered to set the timer, finished the interrupted trip. As the water splashed over her hands: "They've got a cookbook by Liberace at the library, you know. It looks pretty good." June made an amused noise in her throat, went back into the parlor.

Working on another set of recorder arrangements gave Brecken something else to hold her attention while the casserole bread baked. Making and then serving dinner provided a further distraction, and Fermata helped, too, by eating a little more than she'd done at breakfast. The ordinary rhythms of a household part human and part shoggoth filled the rest of the evening. When Brecken slipped under the covers and nestled down next to Sho, she felt nearly at peace.

She spent most of the night in dreamless sleep, as far as she could recall. Toward dawn, though, she rose up out of oblivion into a dream more vivid than any she'd had in years. She was standing in a walled garden, looking down at a pool where pale nenuphars blossomed in the water, shedding a subtle scent. The water was a strange color, and moments passed before she realized it was reflecting that color from the sky. She looked up, stared uncomprehending at a blind white sky dotted with black stars that glittered like polished jet.

Moments passed, and then she realized she was not alone in the garden.

She knew, even in the dream, that she didn't want to see the one who stood there, but the dream left her no choice, moved her head for her. He stood on the far side of the garden, looking away from her, but that was the only consolation. He was many times her height and gaunt as winter, and white hair flowed down in a torrent from beneath a crown she guessed was made of improbably reddish gold, or perhaps of motionless flame. His heavy robes of stiff yellow brocade were tattered and scalloped at the hems. The hand she could see had fingers long and angular as a spider's legs, and there were six of them.

He was facing away from her. She clung to that detail, even as she saw the pallid line that traced the limit of the unseen face and knew that it was the edge of a mask. She knew also in the same moment that the figure knew she was there, that only a deliberate act of forbearance kept him from turning what he had instead of a face toward her—

And then she was blinking awake in her bed in Arkham, with two of Sho's pseudopods embracing her and a third rising up so that a temporary eye could see her. ♪*Broodsister,*♪ the shoggoth said, ♪*is it well with you? You cried out.*♪

Brecken squeezed her eyes shut, opened them again. A winter dawn tinged the bedroom curtains. Everything was as it should be, except for the image that hovered behind her eyes. ♪*I had a dream that troubled me,*♪ she admitted. ♪*A dream about the One in Yellow.*♪

Sho's stiffening reminded her of a sharp indrawn breath. ♪*Did he look upon you?*♪

♪*No,*♪ Brecken said, reassuring her. ♪*No, he didn't.*♪

♪*I am glad,*♪ Sho whistled, and slumped in relief. Brecken tried to drown her fears in the same feeling, but she'd known from the moment she awoke why the Pallid Mask had not turned toward her, and what its wearer demanded in return.

* * *

"You're sure of that," said June.

"No." Brecken sat huddled in a corner of the sofa, a coffee cup in both hands. "But that's what was going through my mind when I woke up."

The gray weather of the days just past had given way to ice-blue skies and pale sunlight, and a raw wind that felt more like the beginning of February than the end of December rattled and bumped against the old house. Brecken had fled into the morning's chores for refuge, but with those done and Sho busy teaching the broodlings part of another ancient song, she'd nerved herself up to speak to June about her dream.

"Tell me this," June said then. "Could you bring the score down here and give it to me, so I could lock it away in one of my filing cabinets?"

Brecken opened her mouth to say yes, and stopped. It wasn't that the words refused to come. It wasn't even that some barrier stood in the way of doing as June suggested. The world simply didn't contain the possibility of locking the score away. She could feel the flow of events, quiet and inexorable, bending every choice of hers toward the thing she feared.

The blood drained out of her face, and she turned wide eyes toward June. "I know," the old woman said. "I've had the sense that things were moving this way since you told me you read the play." With a little shrug: "I've never done anything with sorcery, but I'm my father's child, and I can feel things sometimes."

"Do you have any idea—" Brecken started, then read the answer in June's eyes.

"Why? No." She leaned back, considered Brecken. "Friedrich von Junzt says that humans have about as much chance of understanding the minds of the Great Old Ones as the dust mites in Mozart's wig had of understanding his music. I don't know for sure that he's right, but I've never found any reason to doubt it."

"Then I guess I have to figure out what to do," Brecken said.

That wasn't true, and she knew it the moment she finished speaking the words. She knew exactly what she had to do, but June didn't seem to notice.

Later that day, brooding over what June had said, she went into her bedroom and got out Friedrich von Junzt's *Book of Nameless Cults* from its place in the bottom drawer of the dresser. Afternoon lengthened outside the windows, reminding her of the second act of *The King in Yellow*, as she left the bedroom for the parlor. Five of the broodlings played Chinese checkers while Fermata and her mother lay on the sofa, well over on the dreaming-side. Brecken smiled, then went to an armchair, curled up in it, and started reading. The index was worse than useless, and finally she gave up and started turning the pages. Instead of the passage about Mozart's wig, though, she spotted the words "Nyogtha" and, on the line below them, "witch-cult."

She stared at the words for a little while, then remembered seeing the same words five years back. After a moment, she paged back, found the beginning of the chapter and began to read a passage where von Junzt talked about his journeys around the globe in search of strange cults. He'd arrived in New York City in 1822 from Hamburg, and after a few months talking with Dutch sorcerers in Brooklyn and an eerie journey through underground tunnels to meet a naked, phosphorescent being of whom he said little, he took a stagecoach to somewhere in Massachusetts he didn't name. There he settled into a rooming house and began studying books on strange lore. He also bedded a local woman—if his book told the truth, which Brecken more than occasionally doubted, that happened nearly everywhere he went—and she introduced him to a strange cult of which von Junzt had previously heard only rumors. He wrote:

> Joanna brought me to a house I will not describe, and there I spoke for the first time with worshipers of Nyogtha, whom the old books call The Thing That Should Not Be. They answered few of my questions about themselves but spoke freely concerning Nyogtha, and much of what they said I later found repeated in archaic writings in Lhasa and Damascus. They told me …

She turned the page, then another and a third—some other time, she told herself, she could read again what von Junzt had to say about The Thing That Should Not Be—and finally reached the passage where he got back to the witch-cult. Its members claimed that their founders had come from Germany in the seventeenth century, and that Abigail Prinn, the notorious witch of Salem, had been a member of their cult. Names she didn't recognize—Abaddon Corey, his daughter Judith, and a Dutch sorcerer from New York State named Dirck van der Heyl—wove in and out of the story. Then von Junzt described a symbol she knew well: a disk of polished black stone set into the floor in a basement room, surrounded by a circle of mosaic work in blue, green, and purple.

A quick movement of one finger caught on a silver chain around her neck, extracted the pendant she always wore, and she glanced down at it. It bore the same symbol in miniature, the circle of polished black stone, the delicate mosaic work around it framed in silver. Memory brought back the face of the strange old bookseller who'd given her the pendant just before she'd left Partridgeville, the one glimpse she'd had of human worshipers of The Thing That Should Not Be. If the pendant had any special power or purpose, it hadn't revealed that to Brecken, and she wore it as much as a memento of her one encounter with Nyogtha as for any other reason.

After a moment she slipped the pendant back inside her blouse and turned the page, hoping to find more about the witch-cult, but von Junzt talked instead about his romance with Joanna Orne. Another page or so, and he described sailing to Newfoundland to meet a strange old man who claimed that people had come there from Europe before Columbus, and gone west to perform a strange rite with terrible consequences; other names out of ancient lore filled those pages, but Nyogtha's was absent. She paged further, found nothing.

She closed the book, wondered why she'd never heard of any of the cults that von Junzt seemed to find so readily. A moment's thought gave her a bleak answer, for the Radiance didn't just hunt down shoggoths and other creatures of the elder world. They'd whipped up mobs against the worshipers of the Great Old Ones many times, von Junzt said, or sent in armed men when mobs weren't enough. She knew better than to think she could expect any more mercy from them than they'd given to Sho's people.

That night, as she did every night, she knelt at the side of her bed before joining Sho under the quilts, clasped her hands the way she'd done in her childhood prayers, and called to Nyogtha. Dweller in Darkness, she thought at the deep places of the world. Thing That Should Not Be. You told me once that you would ask me to do something for you, for saving my life, for saving Sho. If what the King in Yellow wants from me won't let me repay you—

The thought dissolved into nothing before she could finish it. Subtle and wise as Nyogtha was, he was no Great Old One, and if the King in Yellow had marked her for a different fate there was precisely nothing the Dweller in Darkness could do about it. She crept into bed after a few more minutes, lay awake for a long while before sleep came.

The next day, she went to the public library and sent an email to Mark Tanabe, letting him know that she'd written a chamber opera and asking if he'd like to look at it.

CHAPTER 8

EVENINGS IN CARCOSA

S leet came down from torn gray clouds the next Saturday, and a gusty wind flung bursts of droplets against the windows of the Chaudronnier's music room. Emily worked hard on two simple études and a breath control exercise, building some of the skills she'd need to play well. As a reward, Brecken had worked out an easy version of the melody of Beethoven's "Ode to Joy," which was one of Emily's favorite pieces, and walked her through it a few times. "Now," Brecken said, "let's do it for real." She sat down at the Steinway, counted "one, two, three, four," and played a basic accompaniment of chords, slowly, while Emily played the melody.

By the third note Emily's face was alight, and so was Brecken's. She knew what it meant to a beginning musician to have the chance now and then to set aside the scales and exercises and take part in playing real music, music worth hearing. Emily's fingering was stiff, her tone breathy and uneven, and her long notes tended to trickle away as she ran out of wind, but with only a few months of practice behind her that was the best that could be expected. The briefest glance at the child's look of delight proved that none of it mattered.

"Again," Brecken said when they finished, and Emily drew in a deep breath and started over. Brecken added a moving bass line and made the harmonies a little richer. "One more time?" she asked as they finished, and Emily nodded frantically and started a third time. This time Brecken let herself go, improvising the kind of intricate accompaniment she liked to use in her compositions, and beamed as Emily's eyes went wide with delight. A fourth time would be too many, she sensed, and used a standard cadence to bring the piece to a close.

When they finished, Emily lowered her flute, tried to say something, failed. Brecken stepped smoothly into the moment. "That was really good, Emily."

"It was, wasn't it?" said Charlotte d'Ursuras.

Brecken, startled, glanced toward the door to find it open and Charlotte standing there. "I didn't want to interrupt," Charlotte went on, "but that bit of Beethoven's an old favorite of mine, and I enjoyed hearing the two of you play it."

Emily blushed hard, tried to speak again, gave up, and went to give her mother a hug. Brecken got up from the piano, noticing signs of tiredness on Charlotte's face she was used to seeing on June's. "Can I get you a chair?" she asked.

That got her a grateful look. "Please. I haven't been back on my feet that long."

By then Brecken was already fetching the chair. Charlotte settled onto it, thanked Brecken, and said, "Please don't let me interrupt the lesson."

"We're almost finished," said Brecken. While Emily cleaned and disassembled her flute, Brecken talked with her about the week ahead and the études and exercises she needed to work on next. The whole time she could sense Charlotte listening, attentive. That's right, she reminded herself. She's a pianist—isn't that what Emily said?

Charlotte confirmed it a few minutes later, when the lesson was over. "Would it be useful," she said, "for me to accompany Emily now and then? I've had to take a few weeks off, of course, but I've played the piano since I was her age, and I've always liked duets."

Emily's eyes went round again; the thought that she might someday play duets with her mother had apparently not yet occurred to her. As she turned a pleading glance toward her teacher, Brecken said, "That would be really helpful. Would you like me to leave the piano parts for the tunes and études she'll be practicing?"

That earned her two grateful looks. "Please," Charlotte said at once. Then: "I should probably look at them before promising anything, though."

Brecken extracted them from her shoulderbag and handed them over. Charlotte examined them one at a time, nodding. "I can certainly do these," she said. "If I were to put in a little ornamentation, would it be a problem if it was more toward the Romantic end of things?"

"Not at all," said Brecken. "You prefer the Romantics?"

"The first piece of Brahms I ever played was practically a religious experience." Charlotte considered her, then visibly gathered up her courage and asked: "Would you terribly mind if I offered you tea, and maybe a little lunch? These days I don't have a lot of chances to talk music with people who know anything about it. Alain's a perfect sweetheart, but he doesn't have a musical bone in his body, and it's been months since I've been able to go out."

There were good reasons why she should refuse, Brecken knew, but those didn't stop her from saying, "I wouldn't mind at all. I should call home, though, and I don't have a cell phone."

"I'll have the maid call," said Charlotte, and turned to her daughter. "Emily, can you have Henrietta come here? And let Fern know I have a guest for lunch."

Emily beamed, and trotted out of the room. Once she was gone, Charlotte turned to Brecken and asked, "I hope she's a good student."

"She's eager to practice," Brecken said, "and she doesn't get upset when she's corrected. I don't know of anything more important."

"I'm glad. It took me a long time to learn either one." Glancing at Brecken: "She's very strong-willed. If she wants to do something, she'll spend hours at it. If not—" A little shrug. "We've had to work on that." She essayed a smile, and Brecken answered with one of her own.

* * *

Close to two hours passed before Brecken settled back against the leather seat of the Cadillac and watched Kingsport's architecture give way to the high bleak hills between Kingsport and Arkham. Her thoughts were a jumble the whole trip home, so much so that she didn't even get out the score of her opera to make some of the dozens of minor revisions it still needed. She and Charlotte had spent the entire time over lunch and tea talking about music: Charlotte's favorite Romantic composers, Brecken's favorite Baroque composers, and the reasons why the two of them favored the composers they did.

As though we're friends, Brecken thought, and pondered that for some minutes as the Cadillac sped past stark gray hills. She liked Charlotte, that was certain, and Charlotte seemed to return the feeling. She tried to tell herself that it made no sense—Charlotte belonged to the second richest family in Kingsport, with relatives in France who were counts and barons, and could have her pick of talented musicians and conversationalists—but the effort didn't get far. Charlotte was shy, and there were griefs in her past, Brecken was sure of it; music meant very nearly as much to her as it did to Brecken. It made all the sense in the world that she would want to talk music with her daughter's flute teacher.

Was that really what was behind it, though? She knew she had no way of telling, and wished that Charlotte d'Ursuras had been much less pleasant. It would have been so easy, she thought, to confide in Charlotte the way that Charlotte had confided in her. It stung that those confidences might have been intended to lure her into saying something she needed not to say. You've got Sho to talk to, Brecken told herself, and tried to believe that it was enough.

June was awake when she got home, settled on the living room sofa with a book open in her lap. "No, I didn't feel like a nap," the old woman said. "For a change." Then, leaning forward in something like her old imperious style: "I got the message the Chaudronniers' maid left. What happened? Tell me everything."

As soon as Brecken had shed coat and shoulderbag, she sat on the couch and complied. June listened with the same bland expression she put on during chess games. When Brecken finished, she nodded and said, "And she didn't bring up anything but music and her daughter."

"She mentioned both her younger children."

A gesture of June's left hand dismissed that. "But nothing related to the old lore. That could mean one of three things." She held up one finger. "She could be exactly what she looks like, a rich man's daughter who's delighted that she's found someone congenial to talk to." A second finger rose. "She could be exactly that, but her family is using her for purposes they haven't told her about." A third finger joined the first two. "She could be a capable actress who spotted your vulnerabilities and knows how to play on them. And we have no way of knowing which of those is true."

"What do you think I should do?" Brecken asked.

"Go on as though none of this has ever occurred to you," June told her. "As though you're a perfectly ordinary flute teacher who doesn't have a thing to hide, and who's flattered that Mrs. d'Ursuras wants to talk to you. Anything else might reveal too much. If they've got their own agenda in all this, sooner or later they have to make a move that'll reveal it."

An unwilling smile bent Brecken's lips. "What you're saying is that sooner or later the opening's over and the middle game begins."

That got her a considering glance and then a nod. "More or less. The main difference is that in chess you know what the other player's pieces are, and in this game you don't. Have you ever played poker?" When Brecken shook her head: "Pity. Chess teaches you strategy, but poker teaches you how to bluff, and how to know when the other person's bluffing."

"I suppose I could learn," said Brecken.

June made a little rough laugh in her throat. "One game at a time."

I wish, Brecken thought. Just then it felt as though she and Sho were pawns of one color on a board she couldn't see clearly, and what color the knights, rooks, and bishops elsewhere on the board might be was hidden from them both.

* * *

More than a week passed before she heard back from Mark Tanabe. That came as no surprise, for she guessed he'd left Arkham for the winter break, and his eventual email confirmed it with a cheerful comment about skiing in Vermont. The email suggested meeting for coffee a few days later at a place downtown called Café Yian—not the former location on College Street, he stressed, the new one on the corner of Garrison and Pickman. Brecken had never heard of either one, but she wrote down the address as well as the date and time.

She got to Café Yian a few minutes early. It was a big comfortable place, cheaply decorated but clean, in an old brick building Brecken guessed had probably held many other restaurants before it. Red tablecloths covered the tables; scroll paintings in black ink hung from plastered walls—landscapes full of high stark mountains and broad plains, mostly, done in an Asian style she didn't recognize. A brown-haired waitress with a round smiling face came out to greet her, led her to a table with a view of the door, took her order for coffee, and made off. She was back a minute later with the coffee, made a little conversation, and went down a corridor from which low voices could be heard. A back room? Brecken guessed so.

Once she'd sipped her coffee she pulled out a notebook and started working on a pleasant little partita for solo flute she'd started a few days before. It took the sudden harsh noise of a chair being pulled out across the tile floor to jolt her out of her concentration. Mark was standing there, grinning. She blushed, greeted him, endured the minutes of polite conversation that had to be gotten out of the way, and then handed over a photocopy of the play festooned with notes she'd written on it, followed by a printout of the score. That took more of an effort than she'd expected. She found herself thinking of the way June had reacted to the first few lines of music she'd written for the opera, and wondered whether Mark would find equal fault with her interpretation of the libretto.

The waitress came back to get Mark's order. Mark grinned up at her and said, "Hi, Patty," and ordered "the usual," whatever that meant; Patty laughed, and returned to set down a coffee cup full of something that looked and smelled a little like a hot milkshake. As soon as she went away again Brecken said, "You're a regular here."

"Pretty much." He grinned. "Only place in town I can get decent Asian food. I found the little hole in the wall place on College Street my sophomore year, I think it was. It gets kind of an odd crowd, but that never bothers me."

He gulped some of his coffee, then, and turned all his attention to the opera. Narrowed eyes flicked back and forth from score to libretto and back, sudden and sharp as knives. Watching, Brecken tried to convince herself that she should feel relieved. Every shift in his expression made her more certain that he would finish reading, slap the score and the photocopy down on the table, and tell her he wasn't interested.

He finished reading, slapped the score and the photocopy down on the table, and said, "This is really good. The libretto's a good honest melodrama, the music's solid Baroque stuff, and you've made it really playable, which is a major plus. You want the usual fee for a production, right? Good. I want to produce it."

She managed to stumble through words of thanks, then asked, "You don't think it's too spooky or anything?"

That fielded her a blank look, then: "You mean the stuff at the end about how nothing means anything to Carcosa's stars? Nah, lots of nineteenth century plays and operas have that kind of stuff in them. For audiences these days, it's water off a duck's butt."

Brecken was still processing that when he went on. "Okay, let's go on. You've got all kinds of notes here about how this or that scene ought to be handled. What's behind those? What's your vision for how you want this produced?"

She'd rehearsed half a dozen explanations in the days since she'd emailed him, but all of them dissolved now that she had to explain it in person. She drew in a breath, said: "People forget that an opera's some singers and musicians telling a story. That's all it is. It's not, oh, I don't know, a political statement, or a chance to show off how much you can spend on costumes and sets, or whatever. It's a play where the actors sing, or a concert where the singers act."

"That's been done," Mark said.

"So?" She went on before he could break in: "Mozart's *Eine Kleine Nachtmusik*'s been done. Same notes, same instruments, same tuxedos and black dresses. Audiences keep showing up for it." Then, remembering a detail she'd read at the Orne Library: "Opera used to be like that. The New York Met used to put on the same productions with the same costumes and sets over and over again, and filled every seat six days a week. They started losing money when they stopped doing that—when they started trying to be original instead of trying to be good."

Mark took that in, leaned forward, and nearly put one of his elbows in his coffee. He gave the cup a blank look, then picked it up, downed half the contents, set it down further away from him. "Okay," he said. "That's doable, and it's certainly going to cost a hell of a lot less than a standard production. But there's no way we can do it at the university."

The word "we" sounded promising, but the rest of the last sentence jarred. "Why not?"

"Because too many people won't have anything to do." He downed more of his coffee. "At Miskatonic everybody wants a piece of the action. The set design people want to design fancy sets, because that's what they do; the dramaturgy people want to turn everything into a statement about something or other, because that's what they do; the costumers—well, you can fill in the blanks yourself. If you don't give them something to do they get pissy, and they can make things really tough for you if they decide to go to the department chair or the dean."

Brecken nodded, understanding a little more about marshmallow rabbits. "So you can't do it."

"I didn't say that." Mark shrugged. "At this point in my MFA program I should do something outside the university system anyway—if I prove that I can cope with the real world, I've got a better chance of landing on my feet when I graduate next June and start doing this stuff for real. Since this thing's going to be dirt cheap to produce, all we need is some fairly modest funding, and a performance space with decent acoustics."

"I don't know how to get either of those," Brecken admitted.

That got her a startled look. "That's not your problem," said Mark. "That's the producer's problem. My problem, if you'll let me at it."

"Will you do the production the way I want it?"

"Are you kidding? Of course." He grinned. "The critics'll call this the New Minimalism, or some dumbass label like that. They'll think it's a gimmick, and they love gimmicks."

"It's not a gimmick," Brecken said.

"Of course not." The grin vanished. "It might just be the salvation of opera. Do you have any idea how far the New York Met has run itself into the red?"

For once, her memory behaved itself. "The figure I heard was close to sixty million."

Mark shook his head. "Upwards of seventy at this point. They gambled big this fall on a new opera by some postspectralist composer, I forget who, and the critics were the only people who could stand it." He gestured at the opera score. "A solid libretto, music that people can relate to, and production costs a goddamn community theater could cover any day of the week—those are big incentives. *Big* incentives."

All at once he leaned back and folded his arms. "So. Do I get the job?"

She should have been terrified, Brecken knew. She should have been thinking about how certain it was that having her chamber opera produced would catch the attention of the Radiance and bring down disaster on everyone she cared about. Something held those thoughts at bay, though, so a sudden uprush of giddy dancing delight could take their place. Was it the same thing that had pushed her to email Mark in the first place? She could not tell.

"Yes," she told him. "You get the job."

His face lit up. "Thank you, Brecken. Seriously—thank you."

* * *

Five days later she went down to Kingsport for Emily's lesson, and again was invited to lunch in the lilac parlor afterwards by Emily's mother. They had already made the transition by then from Mrs. d'Ursuras and Ms. Kendall to Charlotte and Brecken, and spent most of an hour over tea and sandwiches talking about Chopin, Wagner, and Debussy. Just as the talk turned to Liszt, the door opened and Martin Chaudronnier came in.

"I hoped you'd still be here, Ms. Kendall," he said. "Please—" His gesture urged her to sit back down. "The Chaudronnier Foundation has fielded a really remarkable query," he went on.

"Have you really written an opera based on Castaigne's *Le Roi en Jaune*?"

Charlotte turned a look of pure astonishment on Brecken, who drew in a breath and tried to look professional. "Yes—yes, I have. Did Mark Tanabe contact you about it?"

"He did indeed. We helped fund his production of *The Magic Flute* last fall, of course." He settled in an armchair, facing her. "What made the query a surprise is that the family's had a connection with that play for quite a long time."

All June's words of caution came flooding back into Brecken's memory just then. The opening is over, she thought, and here comes the middle game. She fixed a smile on her face, braced herself for whatever the next move might be, and said, "That's really interesting. What kind of connection?"

"You probably know," Martin went on, "that Erik Satie wrote the music for the original Paris production." Brecken nodded. "One of my three times great-uncles was a good friend of his, and played the piano at the one performance that production had. Five other relatives of ours were in the audience. So—" He smiled. "*Le Roi en Jaune* is in our blood, you might say."

It wasn't a move Brecken had anticipated, and she found herself wondering if his words had some meaning other than the obvious one. She nodded again, uncertain.

"So the Foundation's potentially interested in funding the production. I wondered, though, if you might be willing to play some of the music for me, perhaps in a week or two."

That put Brecken back all at once in familiar territory. She'd long since lost count of the number of times her willingness to play on a moment's notice had earned her a paying gig. "I could do that right now if you like," she said. "I've got the score with me."

Martin considered that, nodded. "Certainly, if you don't mind. Shall we?"

They went to the music room, and Martin motioned at the Steinway, inviting. Brecken raised the lid and uncovered the keys while the others found seats, then perched on the bench and got out her handwritten copy of the score. "This is the overture," she said, and began.

For all its versatility, the piano couldn't give the opening bars of the same subtle texture she would get from harp and bassoon, but the music still worked. The theme of Alar gave way to other melodies, until Cassilda's theme rose up over chords that started out gentle and shifted note by note until they radiated a chill foreboding. Then the terrible discords that announced the King in Yellow rang out in three different octaves, and the overture rose to its climax, descended again into the theme of Alar and the bridge to the first scene.

"The Masked Ball," she said then. She'd written that as an abbreviated Baroque dance suite, the strings playing the dances earnestly while oboe and bassoon added troubling harmonies that suggested frantic gaiety in the gavotte, gathering weariness in the bourrée, uneasiness turning a little at a time to stark terror in the allemande. Then a harsh chord broke the rhythm, descended in a flurry of notes that slowed and fell silent.

"That must have been the Stranger's death," said Martin.

Brecken nodded, pleased. "Yes. And this is Cassilda's song."

She hadn't planned on singing anything at all when she sat down at the piano, but the words needed to be sung just then, she could feel that with a clarity that ached. The intricate harmonies she'd assigned to flute and harp shimmered under her hands, and she waited for the right moment and began to sing. Her voice wasn't professionally trained and the tricks of operatic technique were beyond her, but her listeners weren't judging her on the quality of her singing and she knew it. She sang the whole song, improvised a closing cadence on the piano—in the opera, the song blended in seamlessly with the following recitative, but it needed some more definite conclusion this time—and then turned to face the others.

Charlotte's face was luminous, but Martin regarded her with a look she couldn't read. "That's very good," he said, "but surprising, in a way. Many people find *Le Roi en Jaune* troubling. I gather from the music that you don't."

"Well, no," said Brecken. "When I first read *The King in Yellow*, it was like talking to a stranger for the first time and finding out he understood everything I wanted to say. It makes that kind of sense to me. I know it's got a reputation, but—" She let a shrug finish the sentence. She wanted to say more, but the secret of her divided life hovered between them, and she backed away from anything that might risk revealing it.

Martin nodded, as though her words had confirmed a guess. "I'll have some questions for Mr. Tanabe," he said, "but the Foundation will encourage him to put in a full application." Brecken stumbled through something more or less gracious, and Martin nodded and said, "Well, I won't keep you." He got to his feet. "Charlotte, you might show her Satie's scores."

He was out the door before Brecken processed that. When she did, she blinked, turned to Charlotte in astonishment. "The scores for the original production?"

"Yes, we have five of the pieces he wrote—the *Prelude*, the *Sonnerie d'Aldones* and the *Sonnerie du Fantôme de Vérité*, the *Valse Masqué*, and *Le Chant de Cassilda*. Would you like to see them?" That got settled promptly, and Charlotte went to a cabinet near the piano.

"Can I ask a question?" Brecken asked as a drawer slid open. Charlotte glanced back at her. "Of course."

"Do you think *The King in Yellow* is—troubling?"

"No, not really." She gave Brecken a quick glance, then turned away to a chest of drawers, extracted a sheaf of yellowing papers covered with spidery script, handed them to Brecken. "Here you are."

Brecken took them and paged through them gingerly, reading the notes and pondering the ways Satie had woven the words into his music, so different from the ways she'd done the same thing. There was a vast distance between their two styles, hers inspired by the bright morning of the classical tradition, his belonging to its last flickering dusk, but the differences went deeper than that. The *Fanfare for the Phantom of Truth* marshalled precise discords to hint at the looming disaster to come; the equivalent passage in her chamber opera, eight bars just before the Stranger appeared, moved from somber minor chords to a quiet melody in B flat major, like waking from troubled dreams into daylight. Comparing the two left Brecken wondering about marshmallow rabbits again, and questioning her own sense of the play.

Just below the final bars of the *Sonnerie*, though, a curious scrawl brought her thoughts to a sudden halt. It looked a little like a Chinese character and a little like a word in Arabic, but she had seen it before, worked in gold on a black pendant. She knew its name, too: the Yellow Sign.

Abruptly she realized that Charlotte was watching her. With ordinary curiosity, or with something more? She could not tell. She turned the page, and the moment passed.

* * *

Two days later she boarded the bus to Bolton beneath winter stars. Now that the opera was finished and in Mark Tanabe's hands, a certain sense of pressure she'd felt since reading the play had vanished, and once she'd sorted and read her mail, she sat back in the bus seat, watched the night move past the window and left her composing notebooks in her shoulderbag. She had more reason for that than the completion of the chamber opera, too, for her post office box had contained three checks for recorder scores and a piece of unexpected good news: the music director of a tolerably well known chamber music group from Baltimore wrote to say they were adding her Concerto in B flat to the group's repertoire, and brought up in diffident tones the possibility of recording it on their next album.

Placing her music with respected players was one breakthrough she'd hoped to achieve for years, getting at least a few of her pieces recorded was another, and having both of them in a single letter had her thoughts in such a whirl that it took the sharp turn onto Central Avenue in Bolton to break her out of it. A glance out the window showed still more construction in and around the old National Guard armory. The building had been surrounded with chainlink fencing, the windows had all been replaced with new glass, and antennas that didn't look like they were for cell phones rose above one corner of the roof. She watched the building slip past, wondered who was remodeling the building and why no signage answered that question.

Her friends in the cottage on Pond Street had no idea either, and they settled down together to an evening of recorder practice. "Something new?" Hannah said as Brecken pulled sheet music out of her shoulderbag. "Oh, good."

"I thought Matt was the one who always wanted new music," Brecken said, teasing.

"This'll keep him from being impossible to live with," Hannah said without missing a beat. "For a week, maybe." She took the sheaf of music from Brecken, glanced at it—another John Dowland piece—and handed it out.

"I'm glad to see this," said Matt then. "And not just for the obvious reason. When you didn't bring anything over the winter, I was worried you were working yourself too hard."

"Thank you," said Brecken, blushing. "I just had some other things to take care of."

"I know what it was," said Hannah. "You were doing the opera I said you should write."

Brecken's blush deepened. "Actually, I did end up writing a chamber opera."

That earned her four startled looks. "Seriously?" Sarah asked. When Brecken nodded: "That's really good to hear. What's your libretto?"

"A French play from the 1890s," said Brecken. "The title's *The King in Yellow.*"

The parlor went so silent that Brecken could hear the flames crackling in the wood stove in the corner. Then Matt said "Okay" and Sarah said "Seriously?" again, and Hannah opened her mouth and closed it again. They looked at each other, but no one laughed. Brecken gave them an uncertain look and said, "You've heard of it."

"Yeah," said Matt. "It's got quite a reputation."

"I know," Brecken said. A shrug expressed indifference she didn't feel. "I don't always get to choose what inspires me, and I thought it was a really good play."

"I want to see what you've done with it," Hannah said. "Seriously. You've got to get it produced."

"I've got a producer looking at it," admitted Brecken. "The same one who did *The Magic Flute* at the university last fall. I'm waiting to see if anything comes of that."

Hannah grinned and Matt and Sarah said encouraging things, and thereafter they discussed the new Dowland piece and how to fit it into the repertoire of the Bolton Recorder Consort, as though nothing had interrupted the ordinary flow of conversation. Brecken happened to glance up at Danny a moment later, though. He was watching her with a solemn look, as though he knew some of what she hadn't said.

The rest of the practice session went past without disturbing incidents. The opera came up only once more, and that was just before Brecken boarded the bus to head home. Matt walked her to the stop as usual, and they stood talking about gigs and tunes and his job prospects—he was getting ready to apply for a teaching position at a parochial school in the area, he said, and accepted her good wishes with a broad smile. Only when the bus pulled up did he give her a glance she didn't know how to interpret, and say, "*The King in Yellow*. Wow." The doors of the bus opened and he turned away, leaving Brecken to climb aboard, find a seat in the mostly empty bus, and brood over his reaction most of the way home.

CHAPTER 9

ARCHAIC RITES

"This is Henry Blakeney," Mark said. "The best stage manager in town." The man next to him gave Mark a wry look and made a dismissive noise in his throat.

The three of them sat in Café Yian while a gray damp afternoon unfolded outside the windows. Three cups sat on the red tablecloth: coffee with cream and sugar for Brecken, some kind of complicated espresso drink for Mark, and black coffee without compromise for the stage manager, a lean long-limbed man with a square resolute face and gray eyes. Brecken tried to assess him without letting him notice that that was what she was doing.

"So what does a stage manager do?" she asked.

"Manage," said Henry. She raised an eyebrow, and he broke into a smile and said, "I'm not joking. My job is to take care of all the annoying little details so you and Mark and the others don't have to. I used to be in business, so management comes easy, and I took early retirement once I made a pile and found other things to do with my time. Theater, mostly."

"I met him at the Bolton Community Theater," Mark said then. "I directed *Jesus Christ Superstar* when they produced that last spring. He was a really first-rate prop manager, and I did the smart thing and recruited him as stage manager for my summer stock production of *The Pirates of Penzance*. He did a great job with that and also with *The Magic Flute*."

A memory surfaced. "You were at the reception afterwards, weren't you?" she asked.

He gave her a startled look. "Yeah. I don't think I saw you anywhere."

"I was over in a corner talking to some professors," Brecken admitted.

"Sensible of you," said Henry. "I showed up, had one drink, thanked everybody I hadn't had time to thank earlier, and got out of there before any of the amateurs who'd composed operas or musicals could pin me down and try to get me to talk Mark into producing their latest work."

"He's not kidding," said Mark. "I had to listen to six of them." He shuddered.

"You're producing mine," Brecken reminded them both.

Mark opened his mouth, closed it again. Unexpectedly, Henry laughed. "Good," he said. "But there are three differences. One, you used a libretto by someone who actually knew how to write. Two, it's a famous play—"

"Infamous," Brecken said with a smile.

"I won't argue." He smiled in response. "But people know about it, so you can count on an audience. Three, you really went out of your way to make it cheap to produce, and that's not something your amateur dramatist thinks about."

"That wasn't what I was thinking about," said Brecken. "I was trying to get back to the sort of simple approach opera had back in its early days."

"Works out to the same thing," Mark interjected. "But there's a fourth reason—the music. I found videos of some other chamber operas. I know what the composers were trying to do, but these were all the latest avant-garde stuff, and just painful to listen to. Yours isn't."

Blakeney shrugged. "I don't read music, so I'll take your word for it." To Brecken: "What's your musical style?"

"Modern baroque," she replied. He aimed a quizzical look at her, but said nothing.

They spent the next hour talking over the details of the opera. More precisely, Mark asked one probing question after another, Brecken answered as best she could, and Henry took down copious notes on a smartphone. "Okay," Mark said finally, when Brecken felt as though her brain had been wrung out like a wet towel. To Henry: "Can you do the financials?"

"Easy. I can have them to you—" He paused. "Day after tomorrow."

"Great." Mark turned to Brecken. "I've already started looking for a venue—I'll want you to take a look at the prospects, to make sure they'll work with your vision—and I'll get the grant proposal put together pronto. We'll make this happen."

He got to his feet, went to the cash register to pay their tab. Once Mark was out of earshot, Henry turned to her and asked, "Any chance you're free to have coffee sometime?"

Brecken's two years at Miskatonic had included a procession of young men, and some young women, who wanted to ask her out on dates, so she'd had plenty of chances to practice her response. "Thank you," she said, "but not really."

That got her a sidelong glance. "Somebody else?" She nodded, and he smiled his ready smile and said, "Fair enough. I figured it was worth asking. You know what they say— familiarity breeds attempt."

She stifled a laugh. "One hour counts as familiarity?"

"You're interesting," said Henry. "You're not just following trends, doing what everyone else is doing. You've got your own ideas, your own vision, and it's actually your own, not just something you borrowed from somebody else."

"Not at all," she said. "I borrowed it from a man named Wolfgang Amadeus Mozart."

Mark came back from the cash register then. Hands got shaken, and then Mark and Henry went out the door, Mark talking and waving his hands while Henry listened and took down more notes on his smartphone. Brecken waited a spare minute or two before she went out the door. A glance both ways told her which route the two of them had taken, and she went the other way, even though it meant a slightly more round-about way home. She wanted solitude, and Henry's question had her hackles up. I wish I dared to wear a wedding ring, she thought, and smiled, imagining Sho sliding down a church aisle beside her while bells rang.

The bells of Christ Church, sounding two o'clock, matched her thoughts so precisely that she laughed aloud. Shaking her head, she turned onto Peabody Avenue and crossed the Miskatonic on the old steel bridge, passing two men who looked like soldiers in civilian dress. A left turn onto Hyde Street would have taken her home, but she went a block fur-ther, ducked into the post office to get her mail, then veered back down to Hyde Street and the public library. Fifteen min-utes on one of the library computers emptied her email inbox and brought her an inquiry about playing for a May wedding; she sent back a cheerful response, noted down the date, logged out and headed for the door.

The flyer from the Arkham Chess Club was still on the bulletin board. She stopped, read it. Meetings were on Tuesdays at six, it said, and people interested in playing chess could simply drop in whenever they liked. She pondered that for a few moments, wondering why the thought of going to the club made her feel uneasy, then wrote down the details and left the library.

* * *

"I hope I haven't landed you in too much trouble," Charlotte said as they sat in the lilac parlor. Mixed rain and snow drummed on the windows. The steam radiators that kept the Chaudronnier mansion comfortable clanked and hissed.

"Oh?" Brecken asked.

"It's Mrs. Amberville," Charlotte went on, as though that explained everything. When a glance at Brecken showed her that it hadn't, she said, "Mrs. Leticia Amberville. She's the oldest of the Mrs. Ambervilles in Kingsport, and richer than any three of the others put together."

Brecken gave her an uncertain look. "What kind of trouble am I in?"

"It's a little complex. Last Sunday one of her nieces got married. She went, of course, for the sake of the family, even though it was a same-sex wedding and Mrs. Amberville's old-fashioned and disapproves of those. But she came to tea Tuesday and told me that the one thing that made it tolerable was a fine Baroque cantata by some modern composer named Brecken Kendall. I made the mistake of mentioning that you're teaching Emily, and now she wants to commission a piece for the wedding of her oldest grandson."

Brecken's face lit up. "Thank you. That's really good news."

"You haven't met Mrs. Amberville," Charlotte said. "She can be—difficult. I tried to hint that she should talk to you next week, so I could warn you, but she doesn't take hints. Maybe with the weather this bad—"

Just then the door opened noiselessly and Henrietta looked in. "Ma'am," she said, "Mrs. Amberville's arrived and she's asking for you. Should I fetch tea for three?"

"Please," Charlotte said in a weak tone. Brecken drew in a deep breath, braced herself.

A few moments later Michaelmas ushered Mrs. Amberville into the room: a stout old woman with fussily dressed hair and a face like a bulldog, wearing a morning dress that might have suited her thirty years before. Brecken got to her feet at once. Mrs. Amberville said, "My dear, for heaven's sake, you don't have to stand," but Brecken knew the words were purely for show. She sat down only after the old woman had pressed Charlotte's hand and then hers, and settled into an armchair almost as overstuffed as her clothing.

A little aimless conversation followed until Henrietta arrived with tea. After the maid left, Mrs. Amberville came to the point of her visit. "Charlotte tells me that you wrote the cantata I heard last Sunday. Do you often compose in the Baroque style?"

"Thank you," said Brecken, pleased. "Yes. In fact that's all I do."

The old woman nodded once, a quick hard motion. "I'm pleased to hear that. So many young composers these days insist on turning out the most appalling sort of atonal trash."

She fixed Brecken with a baleful look, as though expecting her to argue. Instead, Brecken said, "Oh, I know. I spent my first two years at college at a school that only taught the latest avant-garde styles. I had to transfer to Miskatonic to study the kind of music I love."

"You're a Miskatonic graduate?" When Brecken nodded: "Who did you study with?"

"Dr. Czanek was my composition teacher."

"I know Paul Czanek. I've told him more than once that if he was a murderer rather than a musician, none of us would be safe." Brecken put a hand to her mouth to stifle the laugh. Mrs. Amberville fixed her with the same baleful look and said, "You find that amusing?"

"Because you're right," Brecken said, trying with limited success not to smile. "He's so meticulous, he'd commit one perfect crime after another."

The old woman's gaze did not soften, but Brecken caught the faint upward twist at one corner of the bulldog mouth. "Doubtless," she said. "Tell me about your compositions."

Brecken complied, sketching out her career as a composer— the first tentative pieces, the concerto in B flat for flute and piano she considered her first serious work, the requiem in D, the cantata in E flat, and the four concertos, two sonatas, two partitas, and eleven Baroque dance suites she'd composed since settling in Arkham—and finished up by saying, "And I've just written a chamber opera. The libretto is Oscar Wilde's translation of *The King in Yellow*."

The old woman's eyebrows jolted up, and every trace of amusement vanished from her face. "You've turned *Le Roi en Jaune* into an *opera*?" When Brecken nodded, she muttered something that sounded like *say crapo*, then put on a serene expression with a visible effort and asked, "Do you think you'll be able to have it performed?"

"I don't know," Brecken said. "I've got a producer lined up, and the Chaudronnier Foundation's considering funding it."

Mrs. Amberville glanced at Charlotte, and though Charlotte said nothing, some scrap of communication passed between them. "Well," the old woman said. "That makes a certain degree of sense, and Sa—and heaven knows it'll set the cat among the pigeons in some circles that desperately deserve it." Brecken choked, and the baleful look fixed her again. After another silence, Mrs. Amberville said, "In the meantime, I have a grandson who'll be married in June. I want an original piece for the wedding—instrumental, not vocal."

"I'd be delighted to do that," said Brecken at once. "Do you have instruments in mind?"

That got her a long hard look. "Most composers don't ask such questions."

"Baroque composers did," Brecken said, smiling, sure she'd taken the old woman's measure. "I always thought it was the polite thing to do."

Amusement trickled back into the look the old woman aimed at her. "Flute," Mrs. Amberville said. "With piano, harp, harpsichord—suit yourself."

Brecken extracted a notebook from her shoulderbag, noted down the details. "When will the wedding be?" The old woman named a date in June, and Brecken copied that down too. "If it would be helpful at all," she said then, "I play the flute."

"I'm well aware of that," Mrs. Amberville said tartly. "You aren't teaching little Emily to play kettledrums." Then, relenting: "Perhaps you can keep the date free."

They settled the financial side of the transaction— Mrs. Amberville offered a sum that took Brecken's breath away, but she managed to recover quickly enough to sound grateful but not stunned—and then the old woman exchanged a little more gossip with Charlotte, finished her tea, extracted herself from the armchair, and went her way.

Once she was gone, Charlotte allowed a quiet laugh and said, "I'm impressed. Most people have a much harder time handling her."

"How many brides on their wedding days have you had to cope with?"

Charlotte covered her mouth with one hand. Then, blushing: "Just one. Me."

"I'm sure you were meek as a lamb at your wedding," Brecken reassured her.

"I was terrified that I'd do something to embarrass the family," Charlotte admitted. "It took Father and my cousin Jenny and my great-aunts Sylvia and Claire I don't know how long to calm me down. Then I started down the aisle and saw Alain, and the rest was easy."

They talked for another hour or so before Brecken said her goodbyes and went to the carriage port. All the way home, she brooded over the conversation. Charlotte had shared any number of intimate details about her feelings and her relationship with her husband, and it stung that Brecken couldn't respond by telling her about Sho. You knew what you were getting into back in Partridgeville, she told herself. While that was true, it didn't help much.

* * *

Sunday was another quiet day with a letter to write and music to practice, Monday took her to Bolton and another recorder session with her friends there, but Brecken wasn't able to relax either day, because she'd decided to go to the chess club meeting on Tuesday. She could think of no reason why that could possibly be a problem—June was doing well enough that she could easily spare Brecken for longer than the hour and a half the chess club meeting would last, and Sho and the broodlings would probably be on the dreaming-side the whole time, the weather was that bitter—but a cold sick feeling stirred in her when she thought about going. She tried to talk herself into thinking that it was intuition, warning her of some danger, but that notion didn't survive a long hour of brooding late Monday night as stars burnt cold in the night over Arkham.

I want to do something just for me, she thought, staring out the window at the silent town. Why does that scare me? The night offered her no answers.

Despite her nerves, she got to the library right at six o'clock the next evening. Inside she saw no sign of chess players at first, then remembered that the meeting was in the library's event room. The door stood open, and a glance through showed maybe a dozen people and more than half that many chessboards. One last burst of pointless terror, and then she was through the door, glancing uncertainly at the people already there.

A stocky, pink-faced, middle-aged man in a loud flannel shirt and worn jeans came over to greet her. "Hi. Let me guess, first time here? Welcome to the Arkham Chess Club. I'm Dave Coty. President Dave Coty, and that and five bucks will get you a cup of coffee."

Despite herself, Brecken laughed and then introduced herself, and they shook hands. "You know how to play?" he went on at once "Great. Do you have a rating?" Her uncertain look was as much answer as he needed. "Don't worry about it. This isn't your formal kind of club. The way we do things is you show up and play chess. So—" He glanced around, and so did Brecken. To one side, two beginners were being coached by an old woman in an improbable strawberry blonde wig; everyone else seemed to have settled down to play in the focused silence she'd learned from June. "Shall we?" he finished.

"Sure," said Brecken, and they found an unused board. He motioned for her to set up the pieces, and then said, "Why don't you go ahead and play white," making her take the lead. Both of those were tests she'd expected, and so were the gambits he tried in the first dozen moves or so, to see if she'd fall into obvious traps. The third of those cost him a knight, and he laughed good-naturedly and settled down to play in earnest.

He was a considerably better chess player than she was. Brecken was certain of that by the time the middle game began, and well before it ended she knew that he was going to win the game—she'd lost too many pieces and too many of her options to prevent that. Still, she set out to make him work for the inevitable checkmate, and succeeded. By the time she laid her king down on its side, conceding, most of the other games in the room were over and four of the other players had come over to watch the endgame.

"Not half bad," Dave said, with his broad smile. "How long have you been playing?"

"Only about three years," Brecken admitted.

That clearly startled him. "Wow. Who taught you?"

"A retired professor from the university. She had a stroke and I take care of her. Chess was one of the few things she could do even when she was bedridden."

"Professor Satterlee," said one of the onlookers. Brecken looked up, startled. She didn't recognize the man who'd spoken—lean and a little stooped, with dark brown skin, a shaved head, rumpled clothes that didn't quite fit him.

"Yes," she said. "How did you know?"

"I heard about her stroke." He turned to Dave. "June Satterlee studied with Bogdan Gurevich at Fordham. She handed me my ass the one time we played."

"Jesus," said Dave. To Brecken: "If she can get out of the house we'd love to see her here. If she can't, hey, I'd be happy to stop by some time and play. Nothing teaches you better than getting your butt handed to you by somebody who really knows the game."

"I know," said Brecken, smiling.

Dave grinned and shook his head. "Nah, you didn't do half bad. More time with more players, that's all you need." Then: "I hope we'll see you here next week."

"I'll have to check my schedule," Brecken confessed, "but sometime soon."

The last games wound down, the librarian came in to remind them all that the library would be closing soon, and the meeting broke up. Before she left, the lean man who'd recognized the reference to June said, "Tell Professor Satterlee that Seth Ames said hi." He wouldn't meet her gaze and didn't offer a handshake, but Brecken had met enough people with Asperger's syndrome that she didn't find that upsetting.

The walk back to June's house was less difficult than the trip out, though she breathed a sigh of relief when she found June napping. She didn't mention the chess club that night, and it took her an effort to mention it the next morning. The old woman seemed unconcerned, until the mention of Seth Ames made her eyebrows go up.

"Dr. Ames teaches physics at Miskatonic," she said when Brecken gave her a questioning look. "I knew him slightly, and yes, I gave him a good hard flogging the one time we played chess. Like a lot of social chess players, he knew less than he thought he did, and like a lot of very smart people, he thought he could think his way around anything anyone else could throw at him. I'm glad to hear he's going to chess club meetings. It'll be good for him."

"I hope it'll be good for me," Brecken said.

That got her an assessing look. "Probably. Especially now that I can do more—" Her shrug moved both shoulders. "You might as well put some time into other things." Then, after a long silence: "I'll pass on having them drop by here, but I'd like to go myself once I can get out again. I want to see if I can wipe the smile off Ames' face the way I did seven years ago."

* * *

The rest of that week went placidly enough, though she fielded three phone calls from Mark Tanabe and spent another afternoon at Café Yian going over the libretto with him and discussing what the performance space would need. Saturday, though, she got back from her weekly trip to Kingsport to find the broodlings silent and Sho gathered up in something close to a sphere on the sofa, radiating an astringent scent Brecken had rarely caught from her. ♪Is it not well with you, broodsister?♪ she whistled as soon as she came in sight of the shoggoth.

♪It is well with me,♪ said Sho in response, ♪but it is not well among the broodlings. We will have to offer judgment.♪ Something Brecken recognized as exasperation tinged her piping.

Brecken got her coat and shoulderbag put away and sat in the middle of the floor. Sho slid down and joined her, while Brecken frantically tried to remember the details of a tradition of justice that had already been hoary with age when the first dinosaurs were young. At Sho's signal—a gentle pressure on one leg, substituting for the senses shoggoths had and humans lacked—she drew in a breath and whistled in an ancient form of the shoggoth language, ♪Let all come forth that judgment may be offered.♪ One by one the broodlings slid over to join them in a circle: Fermata moving more slowly than before, Adagio visibly upset, Allegro and Vivace just as visibly angry, Andante and Presto silent and sullen.

Once they had arrived, Brecken repeated a few more formalities, then fell silent and gave Sho a sidelong look; the hint of freshly washed mushrooms she got in return reassured her that she'd remembered the words correctly. In a shoggoth colony, one of the younger shoggoths would gather the others for judgment, and the elders would ask questions, discuss the matter, and decide. In the little colony in the apartment, Sho was as close to an elder as there was, and so Brecken had taken the other role until one of the broodlings was old enough to replace her.

Once everyone had gathered, it was Sho's job to ask questions and Brecken's to make sure everyone behaved as they ought. That latter was easy enough, for the broodlings always seemed overawed by the formalities of judgment, and a sharp look from Brecken or the brief pressure of a hand on a broodling's mantle were enough to stop any misbehavior. Over the quarter hour that followed, as question followed question, Brecken figured out what the difficulty was: Andante had picked a quarrel with Adagio over some detail in a game of stone-piling, Presto had rushed in to defend Adagio, and she and Andante had ended up in a full-blown fight, slapping each other with pseudopods until they'd bruised each other's mantles.

There were customary punishments for broodlings who fought, and Presto and Andante both huddled down when Sho told them they would go without their dinners that night. What to do about Andante's role in the original quarrel was another matter.

♪I think she should go without food longer,♪ Allegro whistled, still angry. ♪Rain On The Roof♪—that was Andante's name that day—♪was really mean.♪

Brecken turned a reproving glance toward her, and the broodling huddled down, embarrassed. ♪When someone is hurt,♪ said Sho, ♪who knows what is enough to heal the hurt?♪

♪The one who is hurt,♪ Allegro admitted—that was something like a shoggoth proverb or something like a law, Brecken had never been sure which.

Everyone but Andante looked at Adagio, who tensed visibly—she had the right to name a punishment, but if the others found it unreasonable, they had the traditional right to impose the same penalty on her as well. ♪I just want Rain On The Roof to leave me alone,♪ she said after a moment. ♪I don't want her to talk to me or come near me until it's dark and then light again.♪

A flicker of approval passed from shoggoth to shoggoth, and Sho asked Brecken whether she approved as well. When that was settled and a few details worked out, Brecken whistled the words of dismissal, and Andante crept to the bedroom, where she'd be spending the day. Once she'd slid under the door, Vivace went over to Adagio and piped, ♪May I go with her?♪

♪I didn't say I wanted her to be all alone,♪ Adagio replied in a fretful tone. ♪Just that I don't want her to come near me.♪ Vivace flowed up tentatively against her, then slid off to the bedroom in Andante's wake. Presto and Allegro went off to play a game of stone-piling, Fermata found a warm place and slipped over onto the dreaming-side, and Adagio went over to watch the stone-piling for a while and then joined Fermata, putting a comforting pseudopod over her.

"Adagio will be the elder and teacher," Sho said in a quiet voice. Half an hour or so had passed, and she and Brecken were curled up together on the sofa. "Vivace and Andante will be broodsisters once they're old enough, I'm sure of that now, and I think so will Allegro and Presto. I hope so—they'll each help the other when budding time comes, and Adagio will help all of them and they'll all help her."

"You don't think she'll be anyone's broodsister," said Brecken.

A pale eye glanced up at her. "No. Allegro and Presto, Andante and Vivace—when they're troubled, they seek each other, as broodsisters do." A pseudopod curved around Brecken, who smiled and moved a little closer to Sho. "Look at Adagio. She doesn't look for comfort, she thinks of comforting Fermata instead."

Brecken nodded, but said nothing. She hadn't missed the fact that Sho had said nothing about Fermata's future.

* * *

Later still, Sho went over to the dreaming-side with four broodlings nestled around her, and Brecken sat by the window finishing up a recorder arrangement for Mozart's *Eine Kleine Nachtmusik* that gave the most difficult bits to the alto part—another request, this one from a new customer in Omaha.

Rain drummed hard on the windows near her. After a while, Adagio slid off the sofa, crossed the parlor to Brecken's chair, and asked, "Mama Brecken, is it okay if I bother you?"

"You aren't bothering me," Brecken said, set the music aside, and patted her lap. It didn't surprise her that Adagio had used English. The broodling knew the language better than any of her sisters, and used it by preference with Brecken and June.

Adagio let out a little puff of washed-mushroom scent, flowed up onto the lap and settled down, then went on, still in English: "Was it fair for me to want Andante to leave me alone?"

"Of course it was." She considered pointing out that the others hadn't assigned her the same punishment, then realized what that would have meant. "You took the same punishment you wanted her to have, you know."

Four eyes blinked open on the broodling's upper surface. "That's true," Adagio said after a moment. "I didn't think of that."

They talked for a while about fairness. When the conversation wound down, Brecken decided to ask a question that had been bothering her since she'd gotten home from Kingsport. "Do you know why Andante was so cross? That's not like her."

Adagio huddled down on her lap. In a low voice. "It's Fermata. She's not okay, is she?"

Brecken tried to keep her reaction off her face, failed. "No," she said. "No, she's not."

"Do you know what's wrong?"

"Your mother and I aren't sure," Brecken admitted. "But it might be really bad."

"I know," said Adagio.

Brecken took that in, said nothing.

"We all know," the broodling went on. "She can't feed well and she can't breathe well. I'm scared for her. We're all scared for her. I think Andante was mean because she's scared." All her eyes closed, and she huddled down further.

"I'm scared for Fermata too," Brecken admitted. "I wish there was something I could do." She stroked Adagio's mantle, felt the broodling shudder and then relax a little.

Time passed. Eventually Brecken glanced up at the clock, set aside her notebook, and scooped up Adagio, who was well over on the dreaming-side by then. She set the broodling on the sofa next to her broodmother, then slipped out of the apartment and went down the stairs to check on June and see to dinner. She had just reached the parlor when the phone rang.

"Brecken?" said a familiar voice. "It's Mark. I've got some great news."

"Okay," Brecken said. "What's up?"

"Two things. First of all, I've probably got the funding. I told you that the Chaudronnier Foundation gave me a grant for *The Magic Flute*, right?" She made the appropriate noises, and he went on. "I queried them, got the go-ahead to submit a proposal, sent it in and got a really positive response. Any idea how they might have heard some of your music for the opera?"

"Well, yes," Brecken admitted. "I played some of it for Martin Chaudronnier." He let out a squawk, and she went on. "I'm his granddaughter's flute teacher these days, you know."

"No kidding," he said tonelessly. Then, rallying: "Okay, great. The second thing is I may have found us a space. Ever been to the old East Church downtown?"

"No. Why?"

"Yesterday I talked to a guy who did a performance art piece there last fall. There's just a handful of old people in the congregation these days, so they rent the place out. Ray said it's cheap, the seats are okay, the acoustics are decent, it's got everything we need. He even had a floor plan, so I know we're good. Do you want to go there and check it out, or should I just call and make the arrangements?"

Maybe, Brecken thought. Maybe this is going to work out after all. Her heart was pounding, more slowly but more forcefully than the rain on the windows. "No," she said. "No, I think I probably ought to go see it first."

* * *

Church Street had been the heart of Arkham's business district back in the nineteenth century, and brick buildings five and six stories tall still framed the view west toward the low tree-crowned shape of Hangman's Hill. A few of the storefronts at street level had tenants—as she hurried down the slush-covered sidewalk, Brecken passed two pawnshops, an antique mall with irregular hours, and an off-brand dollar store—while other spaces stood bare except for well-aged FOR LEASE signs. Christ Church still raised the gray solemn mass of its Norman bell tower above the corner of Church and Garrison Streets, but the next block east was almost completely desolate, a mass of Victorian commercial buildings remodeled to fit the worst excesses of late twentieth century modernism and then aban-doned to the elements. Beyond that was Peabody Avenue, run-ning with meltwater and busy enough that she had to wait for the light to cross, and beyond that was the squat brown shape of Arkham's East Church.

Brecken looked up at it, and her heart sank. A grimy brick edifice with all the elegance of a packing crate, it turned one blank wall to the Peabody Avenue sidewalk—splotches of vaguely brick-colored paint showed where the caretaker had fought his most recent battles with graffiti artists—and another to Church Street. She backtracked, went around the north end of the church and found a double door with an unhelpful sign on it that read EMERGENCY EXIT ONLY. A little further, a walk led inward between neglected landscaping on one side and a recently closed auto parts store on the other, to a smaller

door. Next to the door was a wooden sign with paint starting
to peel. She glanced at it casually, then stopped and read again:

OLD EAST CHURCH
Founded 1698—Rebuilt 1877
FREE BAPTIST CHURCH OF ARKHAM
Member, Old Independent Liberal
Baptist Convention of Massachusetts

Below that was the word *Services*, and a piece of cardboard
taped over what had once said *Sundays 10:00 AM* or the like.
On the cardboard, under waterproof tape, someone had written *Call for Times*, but there was no phone number to help anybody follow that advice.

She considered the sign for a moment, and shook her head.
Back in Partridgeville, the gorgeous old First Baptist Church
atop Angell Hill had belonged to the Old Independent Liberal
Baptist Convention of New Jersey. Though she'd played
the organ there on Sundays for several months, she'd never
figured out what distinguished that particular flavor of Baptist
religion from any other, and shelved the question as unanswerable when she'd moved to Arkham.

That Massachusetts had a local version of the same idio-
syncratic denomination amused her, but the contrast between
the Georgian magnificence of the church in Partridgeville and
the bleak Victorian squalor of its Arkham equivalent left her
dispirited. She considered giving up on what looked like a bad
prospect, but made herself take the last few steps to the door.
There was no bell. After a moment, she knocked.

A minute or two passed. Cars splashed their way up and
down Peabody Avenue, and a trio of crows flew overhead,
calling in harsh voices. Then the click of the lock brought
Brecken's attention back to the door. It opened a few inches,
revealing part of a haggard and unsmiling face and one pale
blue eye. "Yes?"

"I'm Brecken Kendall," she said. "I called about renting your hall."

The door closed, and Brecken thought for a moment that the man inside had latched it, but heard the rattle of a chain being unfastened. The door swung open again. "Please come in," said the man inside, as though he doubted she would.

Inside was a vestibule with coatracks to either side. Brecken shed her wet coat and directed an apologetic smile at the man who'd let her in, hoping he wouldn't mind puddles on the floor. He waited in silence, watching her. He was tall and slightly stooped, with white hair that probably hadn't been much darker when he'd been young, a long angular face, and pale blue eyes. Woolen slacks, a cardigan, and a shirt and fussily knotted tie gave him an antique look. Only on a second glance did she realize that his left sleeve was empty, and had been neatly pinned so that its end rested in the cardigan's pocket.

"Pistorius," he said once she'd left the coat on a hanger. "Leo Pistorius." Hints of an accent in his voice made her wonder if he'd grown up speaking another language.

"Pleased to meet you." She shook his hand.

He considered her, then turned. "Come with me."

CHAPTER 10

UNEXPECTED VOICES

B eyond the vestibule, gray light filtered through two narrow windows as they passed through a space not much larger than Brecken's apartment. Six long pews faced a wooden altar and a lectern that looked as though it had been borrowed from a classroom a century back. The far wall was bare, though it had a heavy nail in it, of the kind that might support a large wooden cross. "The east chapel," said Leo Pistorius, and turned right, toward an archway.

That let them into a dim echoing space filled with rows of pews, lit from above by narrow clerestory windows. To one side, a choir loft slanted up into shadows; to the other, the pews gave way to a low platform, another wooden altar, and a simple pulpit. A door off to one side of the platform looked as though it might lead to a storage room. "The worship hall," the old man said then. "The space we offer for rent. The pews and other furnishings can be moved."

"Okay," said Brecken, looking around uneasily. The pews had padded seats, and faint echoes in the stillness hinted at good acoustics, but would those be enough? She didn't know.

Pistorius faced her. "You spoke of a musical performance."

"A chamber opera."

"You'll have to put in a temporary stage, then, and make room for an orchestra. We cannot permit other changes to the structure."

154

"Of course not," said Brecken. "It's going to have really minimal staging."

He nodded, turned and went toward the altar. "Which opera?"

"It's new," Brecken said, following. "The title's *The King in Yellow*."

He turned to look at her. It wasn't a quick motion; it was precise, measured, formal, and only the widening of his eyes revealed how surprised he was. "I wasn't aware," he said, "that Castaigne's play had ever been made into an opera."

Startled, she regarded him. "I've written the music," she admitted.

Pistorius nodded after a moment. "How large an orchestra?"

"Just eight musicians." When his expression did not change: "One of the things that inspired me is the simple orchestration the earliest operas used."

"The Florentine Camerata."

"Yes, exactly!" Brecken said, beaming. "You're familiar with them."

"I played a great deal of Monteverdi before—" A slight shrug of his left shoulder made discreet reference to the absent arm.

"I'm really sorry," said Brecken.

"I survived. That was by no means certain at the time." Pistorius turned toward the altar, glanced back over his shoulder at her. "It occurs to me that you may find this of interest."

He started walking up the nave, and Brecken followed. They were most of the way to the east end before the dark presence filling one corner resolved itself into a church organ, with varnished wood below and tall pipes of golden metal rising above. Her breath caught.

Pistorius glanced back at her again. "Do you play the organ?"

"It's been almost five years," said Brecken, "but I used to play for a church in New Jersey." A sudden impulse made her go on. "That was a Baptist church, too—part of the Old Independent Liberal Baptist Convention of New Jersey."

His face barely shifted, but she knew she'd startled him again. "Where was this?"

"Partridgeville. The First Baptist Church of Partridgeville."

"Ah." Whole worlds of meaning concealed from her circled in that monosyllable, she was sure of it, but Pistorius simply turned and walked the rest of the way to the organ. Brecken followed. Once they stood beside the instrument, Pistorius glanced at her and motioned at the instrument, inviting; when she hesitated, he said, "Please."

Since she wanted nothing more at that moment than to try out the organ, she didn't argue. Two keyboards—manuals, she reminded herself, on an organ they're called manuals—and a row of long slender pedals waited for her. She settled onto the bench and found the switch that turned on the blowers. White porcelain knobs stood in ranks to either side of the manuals, half-familiar inscriptions on them: 8' Diapason, 8' Dulciana, 4' Flute, 4' Violina, 16' Bourdon, and more. She pulled the ones she wanted while the organ woke. In place of the broad swell pedal she'd learned to use at the First Baptist Church, the organ before her had a narrow iron pedal shaped like the sole of a shoe; she adjusted it, then brought her fingers down on the keys.

A D major chord filled the space around her. She closed her eyes, listening to the chord as it filled the hall, followed with a few bridging notes and then an A major chord, noting the hall's acoustics. Next she returned to D, and then launched into one of the hymn tunes she'd played regularly in Partridgeville. Measure by measure, the melody paced with simple dignity over a landscape of chords, settled down finally to rest.

"This is a really beautiful instrument," she said once the echoes faded away.

"Hook and Hastings built it in 1903," said Pistorius. "The largest organ firm in the United States then. This was one of their smaller models. We've arranged to keep it in good repair." Then, turning to face her: "How many performances of your opera?"

"We're planning on four," said Brecken.

"We'll rent you this hall for a nonrefundable deposit of one thousand dollars and one quarter of the proceeds from your ticket sales."

It was a much better deal than she'd expected. "Thank you. That's generous of you."

"The building is being sold," Pistorius said. "We've accepted an offer, so our financial needs are modest. Your performances will need to take place by the end of June, however."

"That's fine," said Brecken. "Is it going to be any problem for us to have rehearsals here and build the set and everything?"

"Not at all." His shrug this time involved both shoulders and didn't emphasize the empty sleeve. "For the last eight years our services have been held in the east chapel. We don't have enough members these days to fill anything larger."

"I'm sorry," Brecken said, and he nodded, acknowledging.

She turned off the blowers and got up from the bench, and just then a possibility came to mind. "I wonder," she said. "Do you think there might be a way I could come here sometimes and play this? I really miss the organ, and—" Something she'd been told by Carl Knecht, the music director in Partridgeville, surfaced then. "I think this organ misses being played."

His look offered her no hint of his reaction. "I'll have to discuss that with Mrs. Hirsland. I have your phone number. Once the contract is ready, I'll contact you. We can settle other matters then." With that, she had to be content.

* * *

She spent half an hour on the phone once she got back to the house on Hyde Street. Most of that time went into a conversation with Mark, letting him know all the details about the space, but the last five minutes went into a call to Martin Chaudronnier. His response was exactly the measured approval Brecken had hoped for. "The Foundation can certainly cover the advance," he said. "Before we can go beyond that, though, I'll need to see a budget for the production." Brecken's knowledge of theatrical economics was more or less on a par with her knowledge of preglacial Hyperborean grammar, but she promised to see to it, thanked him, wrote a quick note to herself, and stood there for a long while staring blankly out the kitchen window at the rain.

At Café Yian the next day, when she brought up Martin's comment, Mark gave her a quizzical look. "You don't have to worry about budgets," he told her. "That's not the composer's job, that's the producer's job." He waved the waitress over, ordered his third double espresso of the afternoon. "Henry got the financials worked out weeks ago, and now that we know what the venue's going to cost us, he can do the final budget and I can get it to the Chaudronnier Foundation right away." He cocked his head to one side. "You really aren't used to working with other people, are you?"

"I work with other musicians all the time," she protested.

"Let me guess," he said, fixing her with a wry look. "You're the one who arranges the tunes, coaches the others, and frets for a week before every performance because maybe it won't come out right." He was square on target, and she knew it, but before she could figure out what to say in response he went on. "You can do that with music gigs, sure, but you can't do that with opera. I bet you want to play the flute part, too." He was right about that, too, but once again he went on before she could reply. "Don't even think about it. Your job as composer is to sit in the best seat in the house on opening night and watch the rest of us make your opera happen. My job as producer is to sit backstage on opening night and tear my hair out and try to get other people make your opera happen. The conductor, the stage manager, the singers, the musicians, the stage hands, they're the ones who make it happen—" He leaned forward, suddenly intent, eyes wide. "And you have to let go and let them make it happen. If you won't do that we're wasting our time. I mean that."

A frozen moment passed. "Okay," Brecken said then.

"Seriously," said Mark. "I've got some sense of how much this thing means to you. I hang with playwrights a lot. But if you want it to live you've got to let it have its own life, and that means letting the rest of us take care of it for you."

"Okay," Brecken said again. Then: "Does that mean you want me to hand you the score and just walk away from the whole thing?"

He started back as though she'd kicked him under the table. "No!" Recovering: "Not at all. I just need to be sure you can let the rest of us do our jobs, and not try to do our jobs for us."

"Yes," she said after another silence. "Yes, I can do that."

Mark waved Patty over again, asked for a menu, and when it arrived, handed it to Brecken. "Order anything," he said. "Absolutely anything at all."

She stared at him, realized he was serious, opened the menu. Old habits insisted that she should ask for a plain cup of coffee, but a glance at Mark's face told her that he'd fling the request back at her. She read the menu from front to back, and said, "Can I have the phad Thai?"

She and Patty settled which meat it would have and how spicy it would be, and Brecken asked for a Thai iced tea. Mark ordered something called lamb chob yizang, which Brecken had never heard of, and another double espresso.

"Why?" Brecken asked him then.

He grinned. "Partly to see if you meant it. You want to give, you don't want to take, but you've got to do both to make this work. Partly—" The grin trickled away. "Do you have any idea what it means to get to do the very first production of the very first opera by one of the rising stars of the neoclassical movement? A hundred years from now people are going to remember Mark Tanabe as the guy who premiered Brecken Kendall's first opera." His voice went ragged. "A hundred years from now people are going to talk about this goddamn *lunch*."

Brecken opened her mouth to tell him not to be an idiot, shut it again. She knew enough about the history of music to realize that he might be right. The thought unnerved her, and she changed the subject. "How soon do you think you can get the budget to Mr. Chaudronnier?"

"It'll be on his desk first thing tomorrow morning," Mark told her. "Seriously. I've done this a few times, remember? A production this simple is extra easy—I don't have to include a big fudge factor in case the costumes or the sets or something else turns into a money sink." He cocked his head to one side again, regarding her. "You know, most of the time when somebody comes up with something new and innovative it costs a lot more than your ordinary production. It's kind of refreshing that you're doing the opposite."

"What I'm doing isn't new," Brecken said, "and it isn't innovative. It's just unfamiliar."

"Close enough," said Mark at once. "Nothing's actually original, you know. Whatever you come up with, you can be sure that somebody already did it in ancient Greek dramas or Japanese Noh plays or medieval European mystery plays or something. So—" With a grin: "Unfamiliar will certainly do."

A moment later the waitress brought their entrees. Once she'd headed to the door to welcome two newly arrived customers, Brecken looked at the flame-red sauce and uncertain shapes in his bowl and asked, "So what's chob yizang?"

"Peppers in pepper sauce," said Mark. When she started laughing: "No, seriously. There are some other vegetables in there and some rice noodles and a good bit of lamb, but it's mostly peppers." Then, grinning: "Mom grew up on the Yokohama waterfront and this is literally the only thing I've ever eaten that's hotter than her *tori kari*."

* * *

By the time she got back to June's house she had only a few minutes to rest before it was time to get dinner going. That was less of a difficulty than it might have been, since it kept her from brooding about what Mark had said about needing to take as well as give. For reasons she suspected she'd rather not know, his words stirred something cold and frightened in her deep places. No doubt she'd have to face up to it sooner or later, but just then it was easier to flee into familiar habits, fix a dinner even more elaborate than usual for June and Sho and the broodlings, read a cookbook while the shoggoths sprawled drowsily on the sofa, play her flute and chant the Vach-Viraj invocation and pray to the Dweller in Darkness, and then nestle under the quilts with a pseudopod embracing her and a scent like newly baked bread filling the air.

Days passed and Saturday came, wet and blustery, with great heaps of dark cloud marching across a high gray sky. Once Emily's lesson was over, Brecken headed for the lilac parlor, said the usual things to Charlotte, and talked companionably with her about music and Emily's progress and Charlotte's other children. It was an ordinary Saturday, another step in Emily's budding musicianship, another step likewise in the quiet friendship she and Charlotte seemed to be building between them. The one variation from the usual was that an envelope sat on the coffee table with her name on it, and Charlotte indicated it as soon as Brecken settled in the chair and Emily went to fetch Henrietta. "Father wanted to be sure you had the advance for the performance space," Charlotte said. "The Foundation's approved the budget your producer sent. Father said it was remarkably modest."

"Should I go thank him?" Brecken asked her.

A quick shake of her head dismissed the idea. "You'd just embarrass him."

"Well, please tell him that I'm very grateful." An idea occurred to her. "Are there other people in the Foundation I should thank?"

"You already have. I'm the vice president and secretary, he's the president and treasurer. If my cousin Jenny were home more, I'd try to talk her into becoming the vice president."

"Some friends of mine said she travels a lot," said Brecken.

"Oh, yes. She's in Honduras right now." Charlotte made a little helpless gesture. "She didn't grow up with the family, and these days she can rarely stay here for long."

Brecken considered asking why, but just then Henrietta came in. As tea and sandwiches and jam tarts made their appearance, the conversation veered elsewhere.

By the time she settled back against the seat of the Cadillac for the trip back to Arkham, she'd glanced into the envelope, and knew that she had a check for a thousand dollars in her shoulderbag. Even though it was made out to the Free Baptist Church of Arkham and presumably couldn't be cashed by anyone else, the thought of that much of someone else's money in her possession unnerved her. She tucked the envelope and check into the bottom drawer of her dresser, and tried not to think of the things that could go wrong.

Fortunately for her peace of mind, Leo Pistorius called back the next day. Brecken levered herself off the sofa and went to get it. "Hello, Satterlee residence."

"Miss Kendall." She recognized Pistorius' voice at once. "The contract is ready. Perhaps you can come to the church tomorrow."

"Sure," Brecken replied, and they settled on a time. "Use the same door as before," he said then. "I'll see to it that it's unlocked. I may be delayed. If that happens, perhaps you can occupy yourself with the organ." His laugh, dry as crackling leaves, startled her.

* * *

The door to the East Church opened easily, as he'd promised. Within, shadows hovered as Brecken found her way through the east chapel to the worship hall, where winter light filtered down through clerestory windows onto the long silent pews. Pipes glinted in the dimness above as she found her way to the organ, glanced around, wondered where Pistorius was. Finally she noticed the yellow sticky note above the upper keyboard:

I will be back at 11 am. Music is in the bench.

Brecken lifted the seat of the bench. In the usual way, the storage space under it had gathered up decades of musical odds and ends. She found two copies of what looked like a standard Baptist hymnal, one collection of pieces for weddings and another full of stickily sweet arrangements of Christmas carols, the third volume of an organ method from the middle of the previous century, sheet music for the themes of two movies she dimly remembered from childhood, and an arrangement of Pachelbel's famous Canon in D that left out all the difficult bits. Down at the bottom was what looked like another hymnal; she would have put it back with the rest, except for the title—*Songs of Our Elder Faith*—and the emblem on the cover: a golden ankh, the looped cross of ancient Egypt.

She opened it at random, recalling the hymnal she'd used when she'd played the organ on Sundays at the First Baptist Church in Partridgeville. The page before her had the music for a tune she knew well, set out in four-part harmony, but the words were unexpected:

```
Rise up, O thou great Cthulhu,
When the stars are right at last.
Casting off the mighty fetters
That for ages bound thee fast.
Dead yet dreaming, dead yet dreaming,
'Til the hour thou sleep'st no more,
'Til the hour thou sleep'st no more.
```

She read it a second time, wondered how a hymnal dedicated to the Great Old Ones had found its way into the church. Von Junz had written about worshipers of the Great Old One Cthulhu somewhere in *The Book of Nameless Cults*, she was sure of it, but she couldn't remember the details. With a mental shrug, she put the hymnal on the organ's music stand, set her volume of Bach organ pieces next to it, turned the switch that woke the organ, settled on the bench and pulled out a few stops for each manual. A dozen scales, backed with broken chords from her left hand and bass notes from the pedals, woke echoes in the worship hall and reminded her fingers of the differences between piano and organ technic.

She paused, found a hymn tune from *Songs of Our Elder Faith* that suited her fancy and played it, once with the spare and measured accompaniment common in American church music, once with a more orchestral arrangement of massed sounds, and then as a fantasia, with the hymn tune carried by the bass notes and both hands leaping and dancing over the manuals atop the foundation the pedals laid down. Despite its stark simplicity, the worship hall had good acoustics, neatly balanced between the dead sound that comes from too little reverberation and the muddy sound that comes from too much. When the hymn tune finally wound to its end, Brecken took in a deep breath, let it out again, and glanced back into the worship hall.

Leo Pistorius sat in the front row of pews, maybe a dozen feet away from her. He nodded a greeting, then got to his feet. "You were correct," he said. "The organ likes to be played." Before she could answer: "Mrs. Hirsland has the contract. If you're ready?" She turned off the blowers, put the hymnal back into the bench and followed him to the far end of the worship hall, where stairs spiraled up to the choir loft and down to whatever waited in the church basement.

What waited turned out to be familiar enough from the churches of her childhood and the First Baptist Church of Partridgeville: a social hall with tables and chairs, an upright piano in one corner, a kitchen at the far end of the hall, and a church office to the left—underneath the east chapel, Brecken realized after a moment. The church office was crowded with file cabinets and two large desks; a wooden office chair pushed up to one of those latter held a bird-boned old woman with faintly blue-tinted hair and keen gray eyes, who rose to greet Brecken.

"Anna Hirsland," Pistorius said. "Brecken Kendall."

Hands got shaken, and the old woman waved Brecken to a seat, then sat also. "Here you are," she said, handing two copies of the contract to Brecken. "Please review it carefully."

Brecken read through it, made sure that everything that should be there was there. "This is fine. I'll have the producer sign this and get it to you right away."

"Of course," she said. "The one thing we need to reserve the space is the advance."

Brecken aimed a silent prayer to whatever Great Old One had inspired Martin Chaudronnier to make sure she had the check. "We can take care of that right now," she said, and after a little digging found the envelope with the check in her purse. "Here you go."

Mrs. Hirsland opened the envelope and handed the check to Pistorius, who regarded it with an inscrutable expression and handed it back. "Excellent," said the old woman. "We can proceed, then." She nodded to Pistorius, who handed over two keys on a cheap metal ring and said, "Please let me know when you would like access to the church."

"For the rehearsals and the sets and things?" Brecken asked.

"And to play the organ." With a dismissive shrug: "It likes to be played."

Brecken managed, with an effort, to keep her reaction off her face. "Thank you."

"It will only be until the end of June," said Mrs. Hirsland. "You know the church is being sold, I imagine? After that—" A gesture scattered the future to the winds.

* * *

It took two more phone calls and a talk with June, but within a few days the contract was signed and Brecken had arranged to practice on the East Church organ Sunday mornings. It startled her that a church would be empty on that day, but the Free Baptist Church no longer met at the usual time, and the various groups and performances that rented the space occupied other days and times. The next Sunday, accordingly, Brecken left the house on Hyde Street in the gray light of morning and picked her way along salt-stained sidewalks to the East Church.

She had plenty to think about while she walked there. With the chamber opera done, she'd spent many hours on the instrumental piece for the Amberville wedding: a concerto in F for flute and piano, she'd decided. She'd written out the flute part over a few days, but the piano accompaniment was more challenging and needed work.

She'd gone to Kingsport the day before, worked with Emily on a slightly less simplified version of Beethoven's "Ode to Joy," and had a pleasant lunch with Charlotte and her husband. Alain d'Ursuras had come back from another business trip two days before, and Charlotte introduced them; dark-haired and dark-eyed, he spoke English with a noticeable French accent, and spoke and acted with the understated European courtliness that rich Americans had been trying and failing to copy for centuries. Brecken rode back to Arkham wondering once again whether Charlotte's apparent friendship could possibly be what it seemed. Then there was Fermata, who'd taken another turn for the worse in the days just past. Brecken didn't want to think about that, but she could hardly avoid it.

The door of the East Church was locked when she got there, but that was no surprise. She let herself in, locked the door behind her, and found her way to the worship hall. Sunlight half filtered through clouds came down from the clerestory windows, gleamed dim and heraldic off the soaring brass organ pipes. Brecken sat on the bench, got some of her favorite organ pieces out of her shoulderbag, and found the switches that woke the instrument.

They really do each have their own personality, she thought, as the blowers cycled and the organ woke up. She recalled the organ in the First Baptist Church in Partridgeville she'd played all too briefly five years back, the year her world changed forever: the sweep of its three great manuals, the genial hauteur with which the keys had responded to her touch. This one, she guessed, was less free with its secrets, less easy to win over, but it could be coaxed. She pulled knobs to rouse the pipes she wanted, played a series of scales and arpeggios to warm up, and then got to work on Bach's Fugue in G minor for organ, a favorite piece and not a difficult one. Once she'd played that to her satisfaction, she went on to other pieces from the Baroque organ repertoire, let herself sink into the ocean of sound the instrument could create.

She'd dreamed of spending many hours at the organ that first morning, but she had things to do and the day was slipping past, so an hour and a half had to suffice. Outside the sky was clearing and a brisk wind blew in from the Atlantic. She headed for Water Street and the Gilman Fish Market, a ramshackle place wedged between the street and a double row of abandoned railroad tracks. Pete Gilman, the big-bellied proprietor, said that he had the best seafood on the north coast, and far more often than not made good on the boast; he greeted Brecken with a broad grin, then got to work weighing and wrapping cod, haddock, and a big parcel of fish heads. "Somebody likes chowder," he said, teasing her, as he wrapped the latter. "You're just about the only customer I got under retirement age who knows what fish heads are for."

Brecken smiled, said something innocuous, paid up and left the store, wondering what Gilman would think if he knew what she really had in mind for the fish heads. A few of them would make fish stock, but her shoggoth family adored fish heads in cheese sauce, bones and all: the broodlings had delicate digestions compared to adult shoggoths, but they could ingest fish bones with ease and the calcium was good for them. Seeing the eyes staring up out of the cheese sauce as she served the heads had made her uncomfortable at first, but she'd gotten used to it.

She was most of the way to Hyde Street when a big gray SUV with tinted windows came past, headed the other way. She probably wouldn't have noticed it, but there was a long gap in the traffic to either side. Only when it was past did a stray memory surface and remind her why the sight left her feeling obscurely troubled.

Partridgeville, she thought. She'd seen SUVs like that in Partridgeville, prowling slowly up and down the streets of the neighborhood where she'd lived then, close to Hob's Hill, on the days when she had her first encounters with Sho—

The days right after Sho's people died.

A coincidence? Almost certainly, but she knew better than to think she could assume that. She huddled in her coat and hurried the rest of the way home.

* * *

Three days later, after another trip to Bolton and another chess club meeting at the library, she went to the East Church again. Mark Tanabe and Henry Blakeney were waiting for her on the sidewalk when she got there. She handed over one of the keys, unlocked the door, and led them in. The two of them went straight through the chapel into the worship hall and plunged into a conversation Brecken couldn't follow for more than a sentence at a time. A tape measure made its appearance;

Mark paced here and there, turning suddenly to look toward where Brecken guessed the stage would be, while Henry took what seemed like an endless sequence of notes. Brecken followed them up one of the narrow stairs in back to the choir loft, looked down at the worship hall from there, and then followed them all the way down to the social hall below.

"Sweet," Mark said to her once they'd arrived there. "This is going to work like a dream. You wanted the simplest possible staging, right? That's about the only option anyway, given the space and the limits in the contract, but the hall up there just begs for something really stark. We can use this space for music rehearsals while the stage crew puts the set together— well, if the piano's any good. Have you tried it?"

"No," Brecken admitted, "but I can." She crossed to it, settled on the bench, flipped up the cover to reveal the keys. Her fingers danced from one end of the keyboard to the other, playing every note, then ran through a series of chords, listening to the notes. A few of the keys had begun to drift noticeably out of tune, but on the whole the piano was in decent shape— good enough, certainly, for what Mark had in mind. "It'll do fine," she said, turning to face the others.

"Sweet," Mark said again. Then, considering her: "Can I talk you into playing a few bits from the score? I want to make sure Henry gets what you've done with the libretto."

"Sure." She got the music from her shoulderbag, turned back to the keyboard. "Here's the first act overture." The upright piano didn't have anything like the quality of the Chaudronniers' big Steinway, but she coaxed the music from it, let theme follow theme, until the discords that announced the King in Yellow rang out and the overture flowed down from there to its end. "And here's the finale from the second act," she said then, and played it: first the theme she'd given to the kingdom of Alar, then the theme of the King in Yellow; finally, rising up out of discords and resolving them, Cassilda's theme, bringing the opera to its end.

She turned to face them. Mark was grinning, but Henry's face was creased by a frown. "You don't like it," Brecken said to him.

"Musically it's solid," he replied, "but I'm wondering if we read the same play."

That got an unwilling smile from her. "You were expecting something more tragic?"

A shake of his head dismissed the last word. "No, something more disturbing. *The King in Yellow's* not your ordinary play. People get institutionalized after watching it. Your music makes it sound—" He stopped, searching for a word. "Not trite, exactly. Familiar, maybe. As though it makes perfect sense to you that Castaigne thinks the universe makes no sense at all."

"Well, it does," said Brecken. "What Castaigne was saying— that the universe is too big for us to understand, that it doesn't care what we think it should do, and if we get meaning or happiness out of it, that's our business, not something the universe is ever going to notice—that's common sense, or ought to be." Venturing a smile: "I know it's not that common."

Henry's frown deepened. "I hope you'll forgive me for saying this, but that seems like a really depressing way to look at life."

"I don't think it's depressing at all," Brecken said. "It's less of a burden than thinking that what you do matters to the universe."

Mark interrupted the conversation then with a laugh. "The two of you can argue about that some other time. Come on. I want to figure out how deep we need the stage to be, and I'll need both of you to help pace things out."

Another hour passed before Brecken said her goodbyes to Mark and Henry, settled her shoulderbag, and headed up Peabody Avenue toward home, brooding about Henry's words. Depressing? She knew that some people thought that way about the ideas she'd described to him as common sense, but she'd never been able to understand why. ♪*The world has no eyes♪*—once she'd understood what shoggoths meant by those words, something she'd always dimly known came into focus. Why the same insight was so hard for other humans to reach still puzzled her.

It occurred to her, as she turned onto Hyde Street, that the people who'd dressed Wotan and the other characters in Wagner's *The Ring of the Nibelung* as marshmallow animals might have been just as sure of their vision as she was of hers. A block later, it occurred to her that her vision might communicate just as poorly to her audience as marshmallow rabbits had to the dwindling audiences who attended opera at the New York Met.

She was still brooding about that when she let herself into June's house. June was napping, and so were Sho and the broodlings, though Sho roused herself long enough to whistle a greeting and lift up a pseudopod to be kissed. Brecken got dinner started, went back out into the parlor to find the broodlings back over on the waking-side. Five of them busied themselves with a game of stone-piling, four piping merrily to one another while Andante stayed mostly silent. Fermata slid over to a warm place near the parlor radiator and huddled there. Her mantle had gone entirely dull, and patches of it had turned very dark gray.

That night Fermata wanted only a little of her dinner. Later, when the broodlings were far on the dreaming-side, Brecken and Sho settled under the covers, and Sho clung tighter than usual, trembling. Neither of them had to say anything about why.

CHAPTER 11

LEAVES ON THE WIND

The next Saturday brought steady rain—another unseasonably warm and wet winter, the Arkham *Advertiser* said, though "unseasonably" meant next to nothing any more with the seasons so far out of joint. When Brecken got out of the car at the Chaudronnier mansion's carriage port, Emily came pelting out to greet her in a bright yellow dress, as though she'd made it her mission that day to put color into an otherwise gray world. They worked their way through an étude more difficult than anything Emily had yet tried, and the struggle to get fingers and breath to do what she wanted left the girl frustrated to the point of tears. Brecken had to spend part of the hour talking Emily out of her fretful mood, recalling times that Mrs. Macallan had done the same thing for her. They played the étude together one more time, slowly. Emily's performance was still awkward and unsteady, but she'd begun to make progress, and she'd recovered enough by the time she finished the piece to manage a fragile smile.

They talked over the next week of practice while Emily disassembled and cleaned her flute, and then Brecken went to the lilac parlor while the girl headed somewhere else. To Brecken's surprise, Mrs. Amberville was sitting across the low table from Charlotte, and tea for three had already been set out. "There you are," Mrs. Amberville said as Brecken came through the door; she didn't rise from her chair. "I want to find out whether you've done anything about the piece for my great-grandson's wedding."

"Good morning, Brecken," said Charlotte. "Please make yourself comfortable." Mrs. Amberville shot her an irritable look, which Charlotte pointedly didn't notice. Brecken said the appropriate things, then sat down in an armchair.

"I finished writing it last week," Brecken said to Mrs. Amberville then. "With your permission, I'd like to title it the Amberville Concerto."

Mrs. Amberville's eyebrows went up. "You've finished it." When Brecken nodded amiably: "Well, then, I want to hear it."

"I'll be in touch as soon as I can find a pianist," said Brecken.

Unexpectedly, Charlotte turned toward her, smiling. "You do know one of those."

Brecken's questioning glance got a quick nod in response, and she extracted a notebook from her shoulderbag, opened it to the right page and handed it across the table. Charlotte pondered each page, then smiled. "This is lovely. Let's play it."

"Of course." Brecken got to her feet and turned to Mrs. Amberville. "If you'll come with us, ma'am?" The old woman's expression went from cold to glacial, but she stood and followed Charlotte and Brecken out of the lilac parlor to the music room.

"Would you like to play the piano part through first?" Brecken asked.

Charlotte, as she raised the lid of the Steinway, smiled again and said, "I won't need to." Brecken suppressed her worries and got her flute assembled and ready while Charlotte settled on the bench. She was turning to ask for an A note to tune the flute when Charlotte sounded it, glanced up at her with another smile. A quick adjustment of the mouthpiece later, she was ready. Charlotte's gaze didn't turn away until Brecken nodded, one, two, three, four, setting the beat.

Then the first notes of the piano part sounded, introducing the theme, and Brecken allowed a smile of her own. It didn't surprise her that Charlotte could play well, but the deft phrasing and interpretation she managed on a piece she'd only glanced at spoke of more than ordinary skill. She spared a glance at Mrs. Amberville, saw the faint smile hiding behind the old woman's scowl, and had to stifle a laugh. Another measure, and then Brecken began playing the flute part, with high lilting notes that picked up the theme as the piano wove unexpected harmonies around it.

The first movement was an allegretto, light and quick, full of yearning; the second was a largo, suggesting a wedding procession with its slower pace. The final movement started out slow and triumphant on the piano, then leapt forward into allegro as Brecken's flute came in. Flute and piano danced around each other, setting out temporary discords and then resolving them, modulating up and then up and then up again, to end on a brilliant high F. Brecken held the note while Charlotte sent arpeggios cascading down from it, drawing out half a dozen subtle moods before the final F chord that brought them all together into one.

Silence, then. A flash of bright yellow caught Brecken's gaze momentarily; Emily had slipped into the music room and perched in a chair near the door. Then she faced Mrs. Amberville, hoping to judge her reaction.

Instead of saying anything to her, though, Mrs. Amberville turned to Charlotte and put on an edged smile. "My dear," she said, "I had no idea you played the piano so well. If your family ever loses its money I'm sure you'll do quite well for yourself."

Charlotte met the old woman's words with an unwavering smile. Brecken looked at Mrs. Amberville and hoped her face was as unexpressive as Charlotte's. Once again, a hint of amusement showed behind the old woman's scowl, but this time Brecken didn't find it funny.

Lift of an eyebrow told her that her reaction had been noticed and filed for reference. "That is quite acceptable," said Mrs. Amberville then. "Yes, you may call it the Amberville

Concerto if you like." The old woman got up from her chair. "I'll have my secretary contact you about the fee. She might ask you whether you have some other dates free; I have garden parties planned." Then, to both of them: "Well, I won't keep you longer."

A few moments later she was gone. Once the door closed behind her, Emily came over to Charlotte. "Mama," she said, "is the family going to lose its money?"

"No, dear. Your grandfather takes very good care of it." Then, because the girl's expression demanded some further reassurance: "Mrs. Amberville was making a joke."

"It wasn't very funny," said Emily.

"No, it wasn't," her mother agreed. She glanced up at Brecken, who hadn't yet trusted herself to speak, and said, "I think I need more than tea after that." To Emily: "Dear, could you have Henrietta come to the lilac parlor?"

* * *

The two of them were settled in their usual chairs around a lunch and a pair of glasses of brandy and water before Brecken let herself say, "Emily was right. That wasn't funny at all."

"No, it wasn't," Charlotte agreed. "But that's Leticia Amberville all over. I've thought more than once about looking up her family tree, to see how much of it's registered by the kennel club."

Brecken managed not to spill her brandy and water, but it was a near thing. Laughing, she set the glass down. "Thank you."

"You're welcome." Then, in a more tentative tone: "But there may also be something more serious behind it. May I ask a personal question?" Brecken motioned for her to go on. "Do you have any savings?"

"Not worth mentioning," Brecken answered, startled by the question. "Why?"

Her voice went low. "Father thinks there's going to be really serious trouble with the economy sometime soon. Not just the sort of thing we've seen over the last few years—something much worse. All the old families here have been talking about it, and bracing for it. Father's been moving our assets out of paper and into farmland for years now."

"I read something about that in the Arkham newspaper," said Brecken.

Unexpectedly, Charlotte smiled. "I talked him into letting the *Advertiser* do a story about it. We bought quite a few abandoned farms, and once that article appeared we had an easy time finding people who want to farm but can't afford land. It's worked out very well for us, and for them." The smile faded. "But what I meant to say is that if things turn out the way Father thinks and you end up needing help, let me know. Please."

Taken aback, Brecken opened her mouth, closed it again, and finally said, "Thank you, Charlotte. I—I will."

Charlotte nodded. To cover her embarrassment, Brecken sipped her brandy and water.

"I also wanted to say," Charlotte went on after a little while, "I really enjoyed playing the concerto with you. Partly, it's a lovely piece, and partly—well, I don't get a lot of chances to play music with other people. Our family has the habit of having children learn music but the Greniers and the Ambervilles don't."

"I'd be happy to have us play duets when I come down here," Brecken replied at once. Then, with a smile: "If we can agree on composers."

Charlotte laughed. "I'll trade you something by Bach for something by Brahms."

"You're on. Maybe we can compromise now and again on Mozart."

"Of course," said Charlotte. Then: "Or something by Brecken Kendall." Brecken blushed, but didn't refuse.

Once Brecken had settled in the Cadillac's back seat and Michaelmas steered it out onto Green Lane, though, Charlotte's warning about the economy circled in her thoughts, as unwelcome as it was inescapable. For the three years since her graduation, her job as June's caregiver had kept her and her shoggoth family fed and housed, and given her the freedom to pursue her career as a composer. All along she'd known that her refuge with June wouldn't last forever, and she kept an eye out for other jobs she could take, but those had become fewer and further between with each round of bad news in the paper—and what would a really bad economic crisis do to her chances of supporting herself, Sho, and the broodlings?

For a moment she wondered if Charlotte's offer of help might give her a way out, but she considered the idea and dismissed it. Any help the Chaudronniers might offer would be at most enough for Brecken, not for those on the other side of her divided life. Maybe, she thought, someday I can tell Charlotte about Sho—but the idea broke apart in her mind, went tumbling away into silence. There was no way she could take such a risk, she knew, until she knew where the Chaudronniers stood, and if there was a way to find that out she didn't know what it was.

* * *

Fermata was a little better the next day, but worse again Monday morning. After breakfast, Sho drew herself together and whistled to Brecken, ♪*I will try the thing I spoke of.*♪

♪*The healing?*♪

♪*Yes. Once the little ones have fed, will you take them below? It will be hard for them in any case, but if they can hear it will be harder still.*♪

Brecken gave her an uneasy look, but said, ♪*Of course I will.*♪

Half an hour later, accordingly, she shepherded five broodlings down the stairs, and tried to talk them into playing a game of tag in the parlor while she helped June get up for the day. The broodlings didn't feel like playing, though, and when Brecken left them they were huddled up in one corner of the sofa, as if bracing themselves for a blow.

June did most of the work of getting herself out of bed. She really is getting stronger, Brecken told herself, and it was true. Though the old woman still relied on the four-footed cane, her steps were less uneven and her grip on the cane was surer. Brecken warned her in a low voice about what was happening upstairs, and June nodded and headed for the door.

The broodlings were squabbling in shrill angry whistles when Brecken followed her into the parlor. Presto and Vivace had gotten into a fine quarrel, Allegro and Andante had taken their usual sides, and Adagio was trying to play her habitual role as peacemaker without much result. Brecken went over to them and whistled something reproving; Adagio looked upset and helpless while the others looked angry and ashamed. They lapsed into a sullen silence, then all at once, in perfect unison, flinched as though they'd been struck.

There was a bond among broodmates. Brecken had read that in the pages of Chalmers and von Junzt, and seen it herself many times: what one saw or smelled or felt, the others sensed also. She'd wondered many times what that could be like. Watching the broodlings huddle into the sofa again reminded her just how unpleasant it might be.

She got June settled at the table, got coffee started, and had to veer out into the parlor because the broodlings had resumed their quarrel. Making June's breakfast was more difficult than it had to be because of two more rounds of bickering. Once June had her meal, Brecken went back into the parlor to find the broodlings squabbling again. ♪I know you're unhappy,♪ she whistled in exasperation. ♪I know you can feel what's happening to Under a Quilt. It's not going to make things any better to fight. Will you please stop?♪

They fell silent, watching her with many eyes, but the moment she turned back to the kitchen the quarrel started up again.

Furious, Brecken rounded on them. "Stop it!" she snapped. "Just stop it. Presto, Vivace, get down off the sofa. Now!"

Wide-eyed, both of them plopped to the floor. She'd meant to send them to other rooms to sit alone for a while, but she happened to glance toward the entry and see dust along the walls, and inspiration struck. "If you've got enough energy to fight, you've got enough energy to do some cleaning. Come on, all of you." She stalked over to the entry, and the broodlings slid after her with an eagerness that surprised her.

"Vivace, you take this side," Brecken said, pointing. "Presto, you take the other side. Allegro, you follow Vivace and make sure she gets every single grain of dust. Andante, you do the same thing with Presto. Adagio, you go between them and make sure nobody cheats. Whoever gets to the door first wins the race. Okay?"

They made enthusiastic rippling motions that amounted to nods. At that moment Brecken understood: they desperately wanted something to distract them, and a quarrel was the best they could manage by themselves. "Okay," she said in a gentler tone. "Ready, set, go!"

They went. At first all was utter confusion, as Presto kept trying to leap ahead, passing up patches of dust she hadn't noticed, and Andante kept on calling her back to get them. Meanwhile Vivace veered from side to side, flinging out pseudopods at random, and Allegro kept on running into her, while Adagio brought up the rear, whistling helpful advice that none of the others noticed. Before they were more than a quarter of the way to the door, though, the five of them slid along the entry hall in a less erratic way, leaving the floor gleaming. Brecken turned, went back to the kitchen, and refilled June's coffee in relative peace.

She'd poured a cup for herself and gotten it fixed with creamer and sugar when five black shapes appeared in the doorway. "Can we do that somewhere else?" Allegro asked. Brecken, relieved, set down her cup and led them to June's bedroom. It took a little coaching to adapt the race to a square room, but in a few minutes she left them and ferried June's dishes to the sink. They raced through the back hall while June made her patient way back out to the parlor, and by then Presto and Vivace had ingested so much dust that they were sluggish and drowsy.

Brecken had to figure out how to divide the kitchen and the parlor among three broodlings, but managed it by pacing out the distances. Long before they finished, she and June were sitting on the sofa, June watching the proceedings with one eyebrow raised and a faint smile, Brecken too relieved to feel much amusement. Finally Allegro, Adagio, and Andante slid heavily over to where their sisters lay sprawled on the carpet, well over on the dreaming-side, and joined them in a comfortable heap.

Brecken pulled herself off the sofa and sat on the floor beside them. The talk she'd had with Adagio was much on her mind. ♪Another time,♪ she whistled, ♪if you're upset about Under a Quilt, will you tell me? We can find some way to make it easier.♪

Even the drowsiest of the broodlings was regarding her through at least three eyes as she spoke, and when she'd finished, they all slid into her lap and huddled there. She leaned forward and put her arms around them all. "Thank you, Mama Brecken," Adagio said quietly, and Brecken knew that she spoke for the others.

Half an hour later, maybe, a tapping came from the floor above, Sho's signal. Brecken roused the broodlings and shepherded them up the stair again. Sho had flowed up onto the sofa and lay there trembling with exertion. Fermata lay in the dog bed in the bedroom, her mantle still dull and opaque. The other broodlings slid over to her, and a few quiet whistles passed among them before they settled down around Fermata to make her feel more sheltered. Brecken, with much the same intention, sat down next to Sho and put an arm around the shoggoth.

A pale eye glanced up at her. "I don't think it helped," Sho said quietly. "I'll try again in a few days. Maybe it will work better then."

Brecken kissed her and then closed her eyes, thinking about the raw gaping wound that would be left in her life if Fermata died. When, the rain outside the window whispered to her. She shoved the thought away angrily but knew the rain was not listening.

That evening she took the bus as usual to Bolton. The evening was pleasant enough, and Brecken made an effort to flee from her worries into music and conversation. The one troubling note was the old National Guard armory on Central Avenue, where she'd seen signs of rebuilding. The last traces of construction were gone, and lights shone out into the evening from some of the windows. That wasn't what left Brecken's nerves on edge, though. Two things did that. The first was the continuing absence of any signage explaining who had bought the building and why they had put so much money into repairing it. The other was the row of identical gray SUVs with tinted windows in the parking lot behind the building, reminding her all too precisely of the one she'd seen in Arkham—or the others she'd seen years before in Partridgeville, prowling through the streets in the shadow of Hob's Hill.

* * *

The call from Mrs. Amberville's secretary came the next day. The woman on the other end of the line sounded pleasant and businesslike; she got Brecken's mailing address, made sure she was free the day of the wedding, and then inquired about four dates in the late spring and summer. Brecken, as she looked up the dates in her pocket calendar, tried to recall what Mrs. Amberville had said about them, and finally had to ask the secretary.

"I've been offered four gigs at garden parties in Kingsport later this year," Brecken said to June half an hour later. The two of them sat in the parlor, sipping coffee. June had her cup in both hands, and used both of them to raise it to her mouth. "What do I need to know?"

"The same family that's having you do the piece for the wedding?" said June, and when Brecken nodded: "Are they paying you well?"

Brecken looked slightly glazed. "More than twice what I'd usually ask."

"And none of them have asked you a thing about the old lore yet."

"No. Mrs. Amberville knows about the chamber opera—" Memory stirred. "She said something funny when I told her. I don't think it was English; it sounded like 'say crapo.'"

Both of June's eyebrows rose, though the left rose further than the right. She set her coffee cup down. "*Saint Crapaud*," she said.

"Yes!" Brecken answered. "Or something like that."

"That's 'Saint Toad' in French." When Brecken looked puzzled: "You haven't read von Junzt closely enough. That's one of the titles of the Great Old One Tsathoggua."

Brecken took that in, tried to make sense of it. "I wonder why she said that."

"You're not a Christian," June said then with a hint of a smile. "How many times since you moved here have I heard you say 'Oh dear God'?"

Brecken met her gaze. "There's something I'd rather say, but I don't think it's a good idea to talk about The Thing That Should Not Be—not around anybody but you or Sho."

June acknowledged that with a nod, then said, "That's why I think it was nothing more than habit. People who actually worship the Great Old Ones are more careful than that." Then: "Unless she was testing you, and seeing how you'd respond."

Brecken thought then of the time Charlotte had shown her the scores by Erik Satie. Had that been a test, too, to see if she would react to the Yellow Sign?

She left for the chess club meeting early, checked her post office box and her email. When she logged off the library computer and the clock showed quarter to six, she found the history of Kingsport where she'd looked up the Chaudronniers months earlier, turned to the index, and set out to learn as much as she could about the Ambervilles. They were another French family, as Brecken had already guessed, d'Amberville on the other side of the Atlantic. The tomb of Étienne d'Amberville, the first of the family to settle in the New World, was in the crypt of the oldest church in Kingsport. A little later, a footnote mentioned trials for witchcraft in 1692, and referred her to an earlier chapter; she paged back, and her breath caught:

```
One of the four, Jean-Louis Amberville, was
accused of worshiping Satan in the form
of a monstrous toad, and of consorting
with shapeless black devils in the hills
near Kingsport. All four were convicted of
witchcraft by the Court of Oyer and Termi-
ner and sentenced to death. Their execution
on April 11 on the gallows beside Kingsport
Green marked the end of a troubled chapter
in the town's history.
```

Shapeless black devils? Brecken thought she knew what that meant. A glance up at the clock showed that the meeting was about to begin, though, and she put the book away, headed for the event room, and tried to turn her thoughts to chess.

The next few minutes were a flurry of greetings and announcements, followed by the confusions involved in pairing up eighteen chess players so everyone was facing someone of roughly comparable skill. Brecken found herself facing a Miskatonic undergraduate who grinned every time he moved a piece. His style of play was quick and careless, and Brecken built up a methodical defense, took control of the center of the board, and then brought her queen and one of her rooks into play and forced a checkmate while half his pieces were still in their original places. He grinned then, too, but it was a different grin, more rueful and less brash.

Once Brecken left the library and headed home through the evening, her thoughts veered back to the passage she'd found in the history book. Shapeless black devils, she repeated to herself. In 1692, at least, there had been shoggoths in the hills near Kingsport. Were they still there? Had they fled to some more isolated region? Or—the thought twisted in her—had they suffered the same fate as Sho's people? She knew how small a chance she had of finding out.

* * *

For a change, the cold weather went somewhere else for the rest of the week, letting sunlight stream down from a blue sky like a preview of spring. "I've got a vision problem," Mark said on the phone Wednesday, as they planned a meeting the next day. "I just can't see staying indoors in this kind of weather." Brecken laughed, and arranged to meet him and Henry Blakeney at Upton Park at the foot of Hangman's Hill at one o'clock the next afternoon.

She got there early, after visiting the post office and depositing Mrs. Amberville's opulent check at the bank; her balance after the deposit was high enough that she would have treated herself to something from the little concession stand in the park gates if it wasn't still closed for the season. Further in, past groves of ginkgo trees with bare branches, she came to a dilapidated Japanese garden with little arched bridges crossing small ponds fed by Hangman's Brook, a fine old carousel that had been padlocked since long before Brecken moved to Arkham, and a pillared bandstand that had gotten a new coat of white paint sometime recently.

She turned away from the bandstand, caught sight of Mark and Henry outside the ginkgo grove, and went to join them. An unused picnic table under a bare ginkgo offered a place for Mark to spread out papers from his backpack and get Brecken's approval for the production. Not all the papers made sense to her—exactly what the set would look like, in particular, was far from clear from Mark's rough sketches—but all her questions got satisfactory answers, and by the time they'd finished she was feeling more than usually hopeful about the project.

"Okay," Mark said then. "Sean Howe's going to conduct, and I've already talked to some musicians—mostly the ones who played in *The Magic Flute*. I know pretty much everyone locally who can handle baroque music, but we can audition them if you like."

"If they know Mozart, they ought to be fine," Brecken said. "But I'd like to have them sight read a few passages each, to make sure they can handle the score."

"Yeah, we can do that. Now we're definitely going to want to audition for singers, and I want you there for that. I also want you to coach them and the musicians as we get things put together, so Sean doesn't have to start completely from scratch."

Brecken gave him a wry look. "I thought I was supposed to let them do their jobs."

"Sure, but first of all you've got to show them what you have in mind." He pulled out another sheaf of papers from his backpack. "Okay, then there's publicity. I've got a friend working on that. Not the easiest thing in the world, you know—I can get word out via local media and venues that cater to the theater crowd, but the art music scene doesn't want to hear about anything neoclassical these days."

"There are neoclassical forums and websites online," said Brecken.

"I know, and I'll be posting stuff to them, but it's still going to be a challenge. It always is for something new—" He grinned. "Or just unfamiliar. There's an audience for pretty much everything, but you've got to find your audience, and that doesn't always happen."

Brecken nodded. "Is that going to be a problem for you, if it doesn't happen?"

"Nah, I've planned for it. That's one of the reasons I went for a grant." He turned to the stage manager. "Anything you need to bring up?"

Henry shook his head. "Not at all. Producing this is going to be a piece of cake."

"I'm glad," said Brecken. "That was part of the point."

The wind picked up then, rattling dry leaves under the trees and putting some of the papers on the table into motion. Mark let out a squawk and lunged for them. Henry helped him, then turned to Brecken and said, "It's a sensible approach, especially the way things are these days. I hope you do more with it." Then: "But I'll also hope your next project's a little less ..." He stopped, hunting for a word.

"Depressing?" Brecken suggested.

He shook his head again. "Disturbing."

"But it's not disturbing to me," said Brecken. "That's just it."

"Castaigne's saying that nothing we do matters, nothing means anything, the kingdom of Alar—" Another gust of wind lofted a few of the leaves, sent them fluttering past. "Means no more than one of those," he said, motioning at the leaves with his head. "That's not disturbing?"

"But that's not what he's saying," Brecken said. "He's saying that nothing we do matters to the universe. Of course it matters to us." ♪*The world has no eyes, but we have eyes*♪: the words in the shoggoth language came easily to her mind. She wished she could whistle the sentence and have him understand it.

"And it matters to the characters. What everyone but Cassilda's forgotten is that the universe doesn't care what matters to them. They act as though it has to play along with their ideas, and because it doesn't, the kingdom of Alar falls."

"And that's not disturbing," he said.

"No, because you don't have to think that way—"

The wind surged again, sending dry leaves spinning into the air, and one of them—a ginkgo leaf, pale gold and fan-shaped—settled on the table. Brecken didn't have to force a smile. "You see? If I thought I could tell the wind not to blow leaves onto this table, I'd get upset. If I thought I could tell the wind what kind of leaf to put here, I'd be disappointed. If I know the wind's going to blow what it wants to, the way it wants to, I'm not going to get bent out of shape when it does that, and I might even notice that it's a really pretty leaf." All at once a metaphor she'd encountered in college occurred to her. "Did you ever read Arthur Machen?"

That got her a startled look. "Yes, I know his work fairly well."

"Do you remember the part of his story 'The White People' where the old man says something about talking cats and singing roses?"

"Well enough to quote it," Henry said. "'What would your feelings be, seriously, if your cat or your dog began to talk to you, and to dispute with you in human accents? You would be overwhelmed with horror. I am sure of it. And if the roses in your garden sang a weird song, you would go mad.' He was right, too."

"Why?" Brecken asked, baffled. "If a cat talked to you or a rosebush started singing, why wouldn't that be wonderful?"

"If the universe doesn't stick to its own natural laws, then everything's a crapshoot."

"But it is anyway," Brecken said. "That's just it. The universe does what it's going to do, and it doesn't care what laws you think it should follow. Why not learn to live with that instead of getting upset about it?"

Henry made a skeptical noise in his throat. Before he could say anything else, though, Mark laughed. "You two," he said.

"Well, what's your opinion?" Henry asked.

"That we're talking about an opera," Mark told him. "Lots of singing, lots of emoting, and then everybody dies. That's opera, right? I don't worry about the philosophy stuff, I just want to make sure the audience gets to see a really good show." Henry gave him an amused look, but Mark went on: "And we need to be in Boston in an hour and a half to see about some equipment rentals." To Brecken: "Unless there's something else you want to talk about—"

Brecken laughed and made a shooing motion with one hand. "Not a thing. Keep me posted." They said their good-byes and headed for the park entrance.

Brecken stood by the table for a little longer, and shook her head, wishing there was some way she could do a better job of explaining the thing that made such obvious sense to her. The wind stirred the ginkgo leaf on the table, and she picked it up. It really was pretty, she decided, and after a moment she tucked it into one of her notebooks for safekeeping.

She spent the way home brooding about Henry's words. Maybe that was why it wasn't until later that she thought about the men who looked like soldiers in civilian clothes who walked past her on West Street, glanced at her, and then looked away.

CHAPTER 12

WHISPERS FROM THE WORLD

That Saturday, when Emily came to greet Brecken in the carriage port, the child gave her a troubled look and said very little. Once they were alone in the music room, she turned to Brecken and said, "Grandfather pays you to teach me, doesn't he?"

Brecken managed to keep her surprise off her face. "Of course."

"Does he pay you enough?"

"Yes, he does," said Brecken, nonplussed. "In fact, he's really generous."

"Oh, good." Emily beamed and went to get her flute, and the rest of the lesson proceeded as though money had never been mentioned. Once the lesson was over and Brecken settled into a chair in the lilac parlor with Charlotte, she asked tentatively about Emily's questions.

Charlotte laughed ruefully. "I could wring Mrs. Amberville's neck," she said. "After you left last week, Emily wanted to know whether other families ever lost their money, and I had to explain to her that most families don't have any money to speak of and most people have to work for a living. We had a long talk about it. I know that probably seems strange, but I had that same talk with my great-aunt Sylvia when I was nine. I think most people who grow up in wealthy families

189

have it at some point. But—" She gestured with both hands. "Emily being Emily, of course she went to the cook and the maids and everyone else on the household staff and asked them if they had to work for a living and whether Father pays them enough."

Henrietta appeared with tea, chicken salad sandwiches, sliced winter pears, and wedges of Brie. When she left, Brecken said, "I hope the business with Emily wasn't too awkward."

"Fortunately, no. Most of the household staff have been with us for years. They're practically members of the family, and we make sure they're paid and treated well." Charlotte considered her, then said, "I've been wondering for a while now whether it's been uncomfortable for you to come here, with the mansion, the servants, all the rest of it."

Brecken knew her well enough by then to guess that an honest answer wouldn't be taken amiss. "I was a little flustered at first. This isn't anything like what I grew up with."

Charlotte opened her mouth, closed it, gathered up her courage, and said, "I know."

It took a moment for Brecken to realize what had to be behind the words. "Oh, of course," she said. "You ran a background check on me, didn't you?"

"We have to do that," said Charlotte, looking away.

"Of course you do," Brecken reassured her. Then, as the implication registered: "So you know about my mother." When Charlotte nodded: "I'm—I'm glad that wasn't a problem."

Charlotte closed her eyes, drew in an unsteady breath, and in a very quiet voice said, "My mother never went to prison. It might have been better if she had."

A silence came and went. It occurred to Brecken then that no one in the Chaudronnier mansion had so much as hinted that Martin had been married or that Charlotte had a mother. "I'm sorry," she said then. "That's got to be really hard for you."

The words seemed hopelessly inadequate, but Charlotte glanced up at her and managed a fragile smile. "Thank you.

It's not something we talk about, but—" She made herself go on. "I wanted that to be out in the open between us, and also the—the differences in our circumstances. It's so easy for things like that to—to get in the way ..."

Her voice faltered, but Brecken could guess the words she'd left unsaid. "Of friendship?" That got her a little tentative nod, and then a luminous smile when Brecken nodded in response.

They talked about little unimportant things while finishing up lunch, moved on to music once Henrietta took the dishes away—Brecken had brought a couple of Mozart pieces and her own Concerto in B flat, Charlotte had found half a dozen pieces for flute and piano in her family's music collection, and sorting out which of them they would play first was a pleasant task. Close to an hour of playing followed, and the afternoon was well under way before Brecken finally climbed into the Cadillac for the ride back to Arkham.

It wasn't until she got back to June's house and went in through the kitchen door that she let herself think about June's warnings and all the unknowns that surrounded Charlotte. She felt sure that Charlotte wasn't simply acting a part, that the two of them had become friends—or was that simply what she wanted to believe? The question stood before her, unanswerable.

That same question troubled her over the days that followed. Sunday's letter to her mother was haunted by it, though she penned a cheerful narrative about the chess club and the chamber opera and June's ongoing recovery. It loomed over her trip out to Bolton on Monday, and made her wonder whether her friends there might be guided by some unknown motive, too, though their friendliness was so unfeigned and their interests so straightforward that she felt ashamed of herself for considering the idea. On Tuesday at the chess club meeting she had to make an effort to push the question aside, though she managed it well enough not to lose too badly to Seth Ames, and ended up feeling winded and exultant.

The bulletin board in the vestibule hadn't had anything unusual on it when she'd come in, but on the way out she spotted a familiar shape: the image of Hastur from the cover of *The King in Yellow*. When she went to look at it, she found a photocopied flyer. A new chamber opera by Brecken Kendall, it said, open auditions for singers and musicians. The date it gave for the auditions was only a few days off, and Brecken found a notebook and wrote down the details at once. Flustered, she hurried home, only to find that the calendar on the wall of her parlor had AUDITIONS written on it in ink on that day. Sho and the broodlings greeted her pleasantly, and Fermata didn't seem quite as tired as she'd been the day before. Brecken made another effort to set aside her worries and managed it after a fashion.

* * *

She woke the next morning to find Sho stiff and sluggish, surrounded by an unfamiliar scent, harsh and stinging. ♪*I am not well,*♪ Sho answered Brecken's worried question. ♪*It is a thing that happens sometimes. In a day, maybe less, it will pass off. I need only to rest.*♪

♪*Rest, then, broodsister,*♪ Brecken replied, making herself smile with an effort. ♪*I will let the little ones know.*♪ Once she'd pulled quilts over Sho to make her feel sheltered, she put on bathrobe and slippers and left the bedroom, closing the door quietly behind her.

The broodlings huddled down and trembled when Brecken told them, and she wanted to do the same thing. In all the time she'd known Sho, she'd never known the shoggoth to display the least sign of illness, barring the week or so of sluggishness and hunger that ended with the arrival of the broodlings. Morning chores distracted her from her fears, but as she headed down stairs to help June it suddenly occurred to her that she had no idea how long shoggoths lived. The thought that

Sho might be near the end of her life struck Brecken hard enough to make her stop halfway down, tears stinging her eyes and a hard lump rising in her throat.

A scrap of shoggoth-lore she'd learned from Sho came to her rescue, gave her something to fight back with. What had her broodsister said? The memory surfaced: Sho's lineage normally budded twice, and Brecken knew already that with shoggoths, a second brood didn't come until the first had reached maturity. She started downward again, telling herself that she and Sho would be together for many years yet, but she still felt shaken when she got to the foot of the stairs and turned toward the parlor.

To her surprise, June was already in her armchair and had a cup of coffee sitting near her left hand, sending steam up into the cold air. Brecken glanced from her to the kitchen door and back, astonished, and June made a little sharp laugh. "Don't look so surprised," the old woman said. "I woke up early and didn't feel like waiting." The laugh softened. "And I somehow managed not to dump the whole cup on the kitchen floor."

"Thank you," Brecken said, laughing too. "The cleaning crew doesn't like coffee."

"Just as well. Can you imagine the broodlings on caffeine?"

Brecken choked, got herself a cup of coffee, fixed it with sugar and creamer, and settled on the sofa. "You made the New York *Times* again this morning, by the way," June went on.

"Quentin Crombie?"

June allowed a smile and gestured at the paper. Brecken picked it up off the coffee table, glanced over headlines about a rash of bankruptcies on Wall Street and bad news about glaciers in the Himalayas, found the right section after a moment's fumbling. The article wasn't by Quentin Crombie; it had been written by a reporter whose name she didn't recognize, and the occasion was a New York City performance of a chamber music group from Baltimore, the one that had written to Brecken a few months back. They'd played her Concerto in B flat, and the reporter praised it, though she referred to Brecken as "the reclusive neoclassical composer."

Brecken put down the paper, beaming anyway. June waited a little while and then asked, "Auditions this evening?"

It took Brecken a moment to extract her thoughts from the newspaper article and make sense of the words. "I'm not looking forward to those," she admitted. "I always hate having to decide who's not going to get a part."

The old woman allowed a half-smile. "No surprises there." Then, utterly serious: "Make sure you have an understudy for every part, and if somebody starts acting odd, get them counseling if you can. Not everyone can handle as much sanity as that play has to offer."

That thought circled over and over again through Brecken's mind as the day went on. She checked on Sho as afternoon shadows lengthened—the shoggoth was far over on the dreaming-side, and the unfamiliar scent had faded—and then got dressed for the walk to the church. Once she left June's house, though, other issues thrust those concerns aside for the moment. A cold wind flung scattered raindrops at her as she hurried through Arkham's streets; another takeout place that catered to university students, a pizza shop this time, had the usual handwritten sign on the glass door in front saying OUT OF BUSINESS; the traffic light at the intersection of Hyde and Garrison Streets had gone dark. A block further south on Garrison Street, she passed a burnt-out house with every window gone, the roof half collapsed, the clapboards on the outside walls charred black, and crime scene tape marking the ruin off limits. Hadn't the house been intact and lived in when she'd last walked by a few days before? Brecken thought so, but she couldn't recall for sure.

She got to the East Church a quarter hour or so early, just as Mark arrived. It took only a few moments to get the door open, the lights on in the chapel and the worship hall, and a few neatly handwritten signs posted to let singers know the audition was downstairs and how to get there. By then a couple of Mark's friends from the Miskatonic theater department had shown up and the first few singers were coming purposefully toward the door, so Brecken headed down to the social hall, turned on another set of lights, and started warming up on the piano. Hiring a pianist to accompany the auditioning singers was one of many expenses she and Mark had decided to forgo, and the decision still made sense, not least because they would have had to put in hours of rehearsal time to get the pianist up to speed for the sight readings from *The King in Yellow*. Sensible as it was, the thought of playing random musical pieces for strangers to sing to made her wish that the two of them had been less prudent.

Even so, the auditions turned out less difficult than she'd feared. The first two singers, young women with matching bottle-blonde hair and voices they'd trained too well to follow the current vagaries of pop-music fashion, went through their prepared routines, tried and failed to do anything interesting with Cassilda's song, and went their way. Mark rolled his eyes when the second one left. The third singer was a dark-haired Jewish woman in her twenties—the star of David necklace she wore would have given her religion away even if her name hadn't been Shelly Rosenbaum—who surprised them both with a beautiful soprano voice and a crisply handled aria from Mozart's *The Marriage of Figaro*. She managed a decent first pass through Cassilda's song, too. Mark made sure her contact information was correct before she left, and once she headed up the stairs, turned to Brecken and said, "Cassilda?" Brecken nodded enthusiastically, and his fingertips drummed briefly on his tablet.

That was the way the rest of the day went. Mark had already winnowed down the list, but even so, most of the singers who auditioned either didn't have the necessary skills or had trained their voices in ways that put operatic singing out of reach. After two or three singers who couldn't do what Brecken wanted, though, they would hear one who could: Shelly Rosenbaum, to start with; Sebastian Oliverão, the barrel-chested Miskatonic senior from Rhode Island who'd played Sarastro in *The Magic Flute* and gave one of Aldones' arias a solid try; Jacob Alpert, an amateur singer with a strong tenor, well suited for the Phantom's part; Janet Aichi, an alto with a background in dance who, Brecken decided maybe three notes into her prepared piece, would be perfect for the madwoman.

Then there was Phil Horvath, the last but one of the singers scheduled for that day. In his prepared piece, he gave a solid but undistinguished performance as a baritone, then suddenly soared up two octaves into the countertenor range and sang the rest of his piece there. Brecken kept playing the piano by sheer force of will, seeing a possibility she hadn't considered. When Phil was done, she handed him one of Naotalba's pieces scored for baritone and asked, "Can you sing this in countertenor instead?"

Phil grinned. "Any time." He drew in a breath, and sang the aria in a high cold tone that sounded like something of ice and metal rather than a human voice. Mark made sure to doublecheck his contact information, and when the singer headed back up the stairs, asked Brecken, "Is that going to be a problem?"

She didn't have to guess what he meant. "Not a bit. It'll take a little tinkering with the score, but it just means that the orchestra's going to take the low notes instead of the high ones."

Mark nodded, grinned, then said, "Okay. One more."

* * *

It took most of the next evening to finish casting, line up understudies, and make sure that two of Mark's actor friends, Sully McKendrick and Jean Berault, could handle the silent roles of Jasht and the King. After that, a few more evenings went into finding musicians who knew Baroque music well enough to play Brecken's score. Mark had been able to locate a good harpist and a big concert harp, but the player and the instrument weren't quite as well acquainted as Brecken would have liked—Fiona Matthews usually played folk harp, and needed some coaching and a few changes to the score before she could carry her end of the music.

The seven others had played alongside Brecken in *The Magic Flute*, and greeted her with enthusiasm when they gathered in the social hall of the East Church for the first time to go over the score with her, but six of them also needed help on certain passages. The exception was the cellist, Mike Ellison, who sight-read his parts with aplomb and grinned when Brecken gave him a startled look. "Emm Jay Ellison at Miskatonic dot edu," he said; it took her a moment to parse that as the email address of a regular purchaser of her music for strings.

It took a few more days and a flurry of emails to sort out a practice schedule, but for two solid weeks thereafter Brecken worked with the singers and the musicians one at a time or in small groups, getting them ready for the rehearsals Sean Howe would conduct. They talked now and then about the play— "Heavy stuff," Mike Ellison said, and the others agreed—but only one of them seemed unusually troubled by it. That was George Feldman, a thirty-something baritone that Brecken wanted as Thale. The morning after he got the script and score, he called Mark, said he couldn't do the part, and dropped off script and music at Mark's apartment fifteen minutes later. "I tried to get him to go see a counselor," Mark said that evening, shaking his head. "He wouldn't talk." Brecken winced, but agreed to pass the part to the understudy, a blocky young man named Brian Cray whose strong but imperfectly trained voice needed a good deal of coaching to accomplish what the role demanded.

The others seemed less troubled by the play than by Brecken's willingness to rework the score to fit their strengths and weaknesses. She reminded them that Mozart did the same thing when he was writing his operas, and that most Baroque composers had done it as a matter of course, but they were so used to treating scores as immovable objects to which they had to make themselves conform that it took a week or so before they got comfortable discussing possible changes. Fortunately the first violin—Marc Grenier, a distant cousin of the Kingsport Greniers, a spry middle-aged man with thinning gray hair and a habit of frowning where most people smiled—and the conductor adapted readily to Brecken's approach. By the second week of practices, she'd made all the necessary changes to the score, and thereafter the practices went as smoothly as such things ever do. Meanwhile Mark hurried from task to task, and kept her posted on ticket sales. They were better than he'd expected, he told her, grinning.

"Maybe I've found my audience," she said.

She'd meant it as a joke, but he didn't take it as one. "Maybe you have."

The rest of Brecken's life was less comforting. Sho seemed to recover promptly enough from whatever illness she'd had, and insisted she was fine, but every night she clung to Brecken as though something frightened her. Meanwhile Fermata's illness was getting worse. Brecken tried not to let those things upset her, but it took a constant effort.

It helped that the opera took up so much of her time. Evening after evening, Brecken and a group of cast members or musicians gathered around the piano downstairs at the East Church, working through this or that passage in the score. Those sessions made Brecken think of her Saturday mornings teaching Emily d'Ursuras, and reminded her even more of the dreams she'd had of teaching music to children. She told herself that if the chamber opera was a success, she'd be coaching musicians in other productions, and tried to believe that it was enough.

She did her best to stay out of the worship hall during those two weeks. Mark had a crew from Miskatonic's theater department busy with the set; from below in the social hall, it sounded as though they were taking the church apart one board at a time and putting it back together with the aid of two or three enthusiastic young elephants. More unsettling still were the trucks that pulled up on Powder Mill Street and the clatters and thumps as heavy things got hauled inside, over and over again, until Brecken wondered how much of the worship hall they'd filled and whether there was still room left for an audience.

The few times she heard Mark talking with the crew, every other word was in a jargon Brecken didn't know—rostra and battens were as much a mystery to her as parcans and gobos—and the unknowns simply added to her jittery nerves. Somehow the singers and musicians ignored the noise and rehearsed their parts without any sign of distraction. Brecken tried to do the same, but more than once she had to squelch an impulse to run up the stairs into the worship hall shouting, "No, no, it's supposed to have the simplest possible staging!"

One Thursday evening, a little more than halfway through a rehearsal of the duet between Cassilda and the Phantom of Truth in Act I, scene 2, the noise stopped. It took Brecken a little while to notice the silence, but when it sank in, she gave an uneasy glance up at the ceiling. The silence was more unsettling than the noise. Brecken forced her attention back to the score and the singers; Jacob and Shelly did one more pass through the entire duet, and then Brecken walked them through the score again and suggested details they could practice. She was finishing when footsteps sounded on the stair.

"Brecken?" It was Mark, looking more than usually rumpled in a t-shirt and jeans that were both liberally spattered with long-dried paint. "Got a moment?"

"Sure. What is it?"

"We're done." He glanced at Shelly, who grinned and hurried up the stair. "You want to see the set? I'm in the mood to show off a bit."

Brecken wasn't sure she was ready for that, but put on a smile and said, "Of course."

They climbed the stair to the worship hall. A few dim lights toward the back helped them find their way to the aisle, but the rest of the worship hall was in utter darkness. Mark led the way to the middle of the hall, just past the end of the choir loft, and called out, "Now."

The stage lights came up, bleak as a winter dawn, and Brecken let out a little cry. The stage was black, and behind it five tall banners in somber red and gold soared into the darkness above. That was all, barring lights on poles to either side. "That's perfect," she said aloud.

"Just you wait," Mark said, grinning. "Shelly, you can start whenever you want."

In the near-darkness, the first high notes of the prelude to Act II sounded on the organ. Brecken glanced that way, startled, to find Shelly sitting at the instrument. Eight measures passed, and then the bass line came in, patient and terrible—and at that moment the banners began to turn. It took them the whole length of the prelude to the second act to complete the turn, and when it was done the banners displayed the black of Carcosa and bore the Yellow Sign.

Brecken gazed up at them for a long moment, and swallowed. She had to remind herself that Mark didn't know the Sign was anything but a scrap of half-forgotten mythology.

"That's the only change in the set," Mark said then. "No flats, no curtains, no scenery, just lights and drapery. I think it's going to work like anything."

Brecken nodded. "I think you're right," she said. "It's really good." Above them, the Yellow Sign blazed in the dimness, like a trumpet sounding far off.

That image hovered in her mind's eye as she walked through the evening past empty buildings, rundown student housing, and newspaper vending boxes yelling about two men who'd been found strangled in their shared apartment in Arkham. She was glad to get back home and shut the world outside, but June startled her by glancing up from the sofa and saying, "We need to talk. It's about the Yellow Sign."

It took a moment for Brecken to process the fact that she didn't mean the set for the chamber opera. She perched on the other end of the sofa and said, "Okay."

"I got a message from the Fellowship while you were out," June told her. The old woman's gaze, intent and unsmiling, met hers squarely. "A warning. I was told that the other side has one of their negation teams in Arkham." Brecken drew in a sharp breath, but June went on. "I wasn't told why. I was also told that the Fellowship has moved some of its people here. I wasn't told why that was, either, though I can guess. The only other thing the message said was that there's going to be trouble, and to be ready."

"Ready how?" Brecken asked, once she'd processed the words.

June's shrug was almost as crisp as her motions had been before the stroke. "The message didn't say."

* * *

The last full week before opening night began in a flurry of familiar duties. Laundry kept Brecken busy Monday morning, though that had a disquieting element to it: for some reason the air in the basement smelled of freshly dug earth. She got a flashlight and shone it around the basement, but saw nothing out of the ordinary, just cobweb-draped boxes and fieldstone walls. By the time she went to catch the bus that evening she'd all but forgotten about it, and the Arkham *Advertiser* distracted her further with an ugly story about a car crash on the Aylesbury Pike: a SUV had gone skidding off the road into the Miskatonic River, no survivors. She spent the ride to Bolton trying not to think of that and failing.

She had to skip chess club on Tuesday so she could spend one more session working with Brian Cray and Rashid McDowell, but the practice went well. She was sure by the end of it that the two of them would be able to perform their duet in Act I, scene 2 with the furious energy it required. The next day, Wednesday,

Miriam Akeley had arranged to come over for coffee and gossip with June. Before she left for the East Church, Brecken got the coffeemaker going, set out a plate of ginger snaps, and then stopped on the way at the post office and the library.

The day was as ordinary as it could be, cloudy and damp with a chill wind hissing down half-empty streets, and she didn't see any of the men who looked like soldiers or any of the gray SUVs with tinted windows. Her post office box disgorged a welcome pair of checks, her email brought a note confirming the date of the April wedding she'd be playing, and she went over the shelf of new books near the door and ended up checking out an Indian cookbook—she knew next to nothing about the cuisine of that part of the world, but some of the recipes sounded delicious.

On the way out of the library, she stopped in her tracks, staring at a bright presence on the bulletin board she'd managed not to notice on the way in: a gorgeous full-color poster with Aubrey Beardsley's image of the King in Yellow on it. Alongside it, in an ornate art-nouveau script, were words she'd waited to see:

THE KING IN YELLOW
A Chamber Opera in Two Acts
Music by Brecken Kendall
Libretto by Oscar Wilde

She was flustered when she got to the church, thinking that she'd kept people waiting, but Mark had Brian and Rashid up on the stage, working through the blocking of the duel between Thale and Uoht. A quick question indicated that the rehearsal was stalled until that was over. Waiting for someone else to finish something, she'd already gathered, was a common experience in theater. The stage hands and lighting crew kept card decks in their pockets, and passed the time playing innumerable games of some complicated variety of poker Brecken didn't try to understand. The singers and musicians had their own ways of filling time, and she'd brought a notebook and a volume of Bach favorites and spent her spare minutes working on recorder arrangements. When she went down to the social hall, though, Henry Blakeney and Shelly Rosenbaum were bent over a folding chessboard and cheap plastic chess pieces.

"Might as well have a seat," Henry said. "They'll be at it for at least another hour."

Brecken settled into a nearby chair, considered the game. Shelly had already lost, she could see that at once, though it would take another two dozen moves or so on either side to settle the details. Watching those two dozen moves, Brecken could tell easily enough what had happened. Shelly's style of play was leisurely, too slow on the offense to leave Henry scrambling to hold onto his position and too yielding on the defense to force him to break off his attacks, while Henry built up a strong defense and then pressed her hard. The inevitable end arrived, and Shelly lay her king down on his side.

"Another?" Henry asked.

Shelly gave her head a rueful shake. "No, if I want to get beaten that badly again I'll go hire somebody with a stick." She got up from her chair.

Henry turned to Brecken. "Any chance you play?"

"Well, yes," Brecken admitted. Henry gestured, inviting, and she moved to the seat Shelly had vacated. He held out fists with a pawn in each of them; she indicated his left hand, and ended up with white. A few moments were enough to set the board, and Brecken moved her king's pawn two spaces and said, "Do you still think the music's not disturbing enough?"

His smile told her he knew exactly what she was doing. "I haven't changed my mind," he said, and moved his king's pawn to block hers. "But I suppose you didn't have much choice."

"How so?" She brought out a knight.

His queen's pawn moved up to defend the king's pawn. "You do Baroque music. That's got a lot of rules, a lot of formalities—everything has its place, everything means something. That doesn't leave much room for what Castaigne's play is saying."

Brecken thought of Miriam Akeley then, and the way she and Elias van Kauran had sparred at the reception. It wasn't a game she'd understood then, but the chessboard helped her grasp how it was played. Just then she felt ready to take risks, and moved her queen's pawn to threaten his king's pawn and the center of the board. "I think you've misunderstood what he's saying," she told Henry.

"It's pretty straightforward," he replied. "His whole theme is the futility of human life in a hostile cosmos." One of his bishops slid across the board to threaten her knight. It was a bold move, the sort she'd seen him use on Shelly, but she'd learned enough from June and the Arkham chess club to respond just as boldly. In quick succession, her pawn took his, his bishop took her knight, her queen took his bishop, and his pawn took hers, leaving two pawns facing each other again in the center of the board and her queen free to act.

"But the universe isn't hostile," she said then, bringing out a bishop. "It's indifferent. That's not the same thing."

"It might as well be." One of his knights went on the offensive.

She shook her head. "Not at all. An indifferent universe is as likely to throw something good your way as something bad— like the leaf I talked about in the park, or like Machen's talking cats and singing roses."

"If those actually existed," Henry said, "I bet they'd scare you silly."

Not at all, Brecken wanted to say, but caught herself. The things that would prove him wrong—her shoggoth family— were the things she could least risk mentioning. She contented

herself with a little laugh, and moved her queen to the far side
of the board.

* * *

Henry gave her a wry look, began building up a strong defense
around his king. "It's ironic," he said, "that you're saying this
while we're playing a game that's all about following rules.
If I started moving knights as though they were bishops, or
pawns as though they were rooks, there wouldn't be any point
in playing the game at all."

She moved another piece to the queen's side of the board,
considered his words. "This game isn't the universe," she said.
"It's just a game, and we could have played a different game
with different rules." He moved another piece to guard his
king, and she brought up a bishop to pin it down. "It's like
Baroque music. That's got order and structure and meaning, as
you said, and that's why people like it. It's not indifferent, the
way the universe is."

"It's friendly," he said. "Not hostile."

Brecken shook her head again. "The universe doesn't know
you exist. If it did know, it wouldn't care. That's not hostility."

Another clash followed, costing Brecken a knight and Henry
two pawns and control of a crucial section of the board. In the
aftermath, Brecken castled, getting her king in a safer position,
and Henry slid a rook over to prepare for the next skirmish.
"If you're trying to make something happen," he said, "something that matters more than pieces on a board or leaves on a
picnic table, and the universe keeps stopping you, it might as
well be hostile."

"But you don't have to do things that way," she said.
A memory from five years back surged up, edged with old
griefs: a conversation she'd had with her onetime lover Jay
Olmsted, where he'd talked about forcing the world to obey his
will and she'd tried to suggest a gentler way to face life. "You

don't have to try to make the universe do what you want. You can figure out where it's going and what it wants to do and you can work with that. You can find ways to fit what you want into what it wants. You can—" She tried to find a way to say what seemed so obvious. "You can—well, talk to it, in a sense."

He made a skeptical noise in his throat, moved his queen to a stronger position. "There won't be an answer. There never is."

All at once, as she glanced from the board to his face, understanding came. "That's what the characters in the play think," she said. "That's Castaigne's point. The universe is always answering, the way the heralds of the King in Yellow were always trying to talk to Aldones and the rest of them. It's because they won't listen to the message that the King has to come." All her pieces were finally in place for the attack she'd been preparing, and she slid one of her rooks straight across the board to take one of Henry's knights, cracking open the wall he'd built around his king.

He took the rook with his. "Don't try to tell me the King isn't hostile," he said.

"He didn't have to be." Her bishop took his rook and put his king in check, forcing his remaining knight to take the bishop even though that left his defensive position in tatters. "If they'd listened to his heralds or to the Stranger, it could have ended some other way."

He moved the knight. "Not any way Aldones would have wanted," he said.

"No," said Brecken. "No, but the universe is like that." There were many ways she could force the endgame, but only one that seemed appropriate just then. She moved her queen to the far side of the board, putting his king in check again. "It's like the leaf on that table in the park. You don't get to choose what happens to you, just what you do about it."

He had no choice but to take the queen with his knight, even though that left his king unguarded. "If you can do anything at all."

"I know. Sometimes you can't." Her remaining rook crossed the board to renew the check, and this time there was no other piece he could move to take it and nowhere for his king to hide. "Check," said Brecken then, "and mate."

Without a word, he nodded and laid his king down on its side. She was smiling when he glanced up again, but her smile faltered when his gaze met hers. Something haggard and hard showed behind his eyes, something she hadn't seen there before.

Before Brecken could say anything else, Mark came clattering down the stairs. "Brecken? Oh, good. I need you to play the music for the masked ball slower than snail snot, so we can get the blocking down. Shelly, I need you, too—everyone else is upstairs."

Brecken stood, aimed what she hoped would be taken as a friendly smile at Henry. He nodded, put on an answering smile that looked stiff and cold, and gathered up the board and the chess pieces as Brecken turned and hurried up the stair.

The rest of the rehearsal kept her too busy to think about the game or what she'd glimpsed so briefly in Henry's face. She fretted about it on the walk home, though, wondering if she'd accidentally said something hurtful. The wind rushed by, gave her no answers.

When she got back to the house on Hyde Street, June and Dr. Akeley were winding up their visit. "Someone called for you, Brecken," Miriam told her. "I left a note by the phone."

Brecken thanked her, went into the kitchen, and found the note. A blank moment passed as she wondered who Louise Conington might be. Then she remembered where she'd read the name before, and the world went silent and empty around her as she knew all at once what the message had to be.

She dialed, waited through three rings for the phone to be picked up. "Hi, Reverend Conington? It's Brecken Kendall." She listened in perfect silence to news she'd awaited for years, said "Okay" twice when it was expected of her, then "Thank you," and finally, "No, that's fine. But thank you for asking."

They made the appropriate sounds, and Brecken put the phone down again. She stood in the kitchen for a few minutes, seeing nothing, and then turned and went back into the parlor.

Dr. Akeley was gone. June, still on the sofa, sent a casual glance Brecken's way, then another, tautly focused. "Something's very wrong," she said.

"My mother's dead," said Brecken.

CHAPTER 13

WALLS OF SILENCE

June took that in. After a moment, she gestured at the other side of the sofa, and Brecken managed a nod, crossed to it and sat.

"What happened?"

Brecken clenched her eyes shut. "Another stupid fight. She was so angry, and once she went to prison she just stopped caring. They'd throw her in solitary for a month, and then they'd let her back in with the other prisoners and she'd just get in another fight."

"I remember," June said. "We talked about that."

Brecken went on as though she hadn't heard. "And this time she picked on the wrong person. By the time the guards got there she was bleeding inside, and they couldn't stop it in time. That's what the chaplain said. They couldn't stop the bleeding."

A silence came and went. "Will you have to make funeral arrangements?"

"No," Brecken said. "I told the chaplain they could bury her in the prison cemetery." Her eyes stayed clenched shut. "I know. I'm a horrible daughter."

June said nothing at all.

"I've hated her since I was a little girl," said Brecken then, in an ashen whisper: words she had never spoken to anyone else.

"And loved her longer than that," said June. "I know."

Brecken's eyes snapped open. The old woman was watching her with an unreadable look, but she recalled what she'd learned of June's mother and her strange destiny, and nodded slowly.

"Do you need to talk?" June asked then. "Or anything else?"

"Right now what I need is Sho," Brecken said, forcing a smile. "I'll—I'll be down to fix dinner at six. Later—" Her voice cracked. After a moment: "Maybe. There are things that Sho can't understand."

June said nothing in response, simply smiled fractionally and motioned for her to go. Brecken stood, got halfway to the stair, remembered the shoulderbag she'd left by the phone and went back for it. The Indian cookbook stuck out of the top. Well, that was a waste of time, she thought, and then stopped, baffled, wondering why she'd responded to the sight that way. She had too much else on her mind just then to follow the question to its roots, and set it aside as she trudged up the stairs.

♪*Broodsister?*♪ Sho said the moment Brecken stepped into the apartment. ♪*I think it is not at all well with you.*♪

♪*No,*♪ Brecken replied. ♪*But it's a thing that doesn't concern the little ones.*♪

The shoggoth language had at least a dozen polite ways to ask others to leave and not listen—sensible, Brecken had thought more than once, for a species that liked to live in a squirming communal heap. It accordingly took Sho only a brief whistled sentence to send the broodlings to the bedroom, where they closed the door and began to sing the day's lesson in ragged unison. Brecken sat down on the sofa next to Sho, let a pseudopod draw her close, and whistled in a quiet tone, ♪*My broodmother has died.*♪

A sudden tremor passed through Sho, and two more pseudopods flowed out to embrace Brecken. She tried to let herself sink into Sho's comforting shapelessness as she'd done so many times before, but it all felt distant and empty, as though it was happening to someone else far away. ♪*Did they stop feeding her?*♪ Sho asked then.

♪*No,*♪ Brecken whistled in return. ♪*No, it wasn't like that.*♪ She understood why Sho asked the question: the harshest punishment shoggoths knew, the penalty they set aside only for the most unforgivable deeds, was to wall the offender up in a tiny underground chamber and leave her there, perhaps to receive food and water at intervals, perhaps not. A moment later it occurred to Brecken that maybe it really was like that. The land mine that blew up beneath Corporal Jacob Kendall in a desolate valley in eastern Afghanistan had left Karen Kendall without hope and meaning rather than without food, but it had killed her just as surely.

She was shaking. She realized that suddenly, as though watching from outside. She was huddled into a ball, with Sho cradling her, but she felt nothing until Sho whistled ♪*Broodsister?*♪ again, and the numbness tore wide open. Then Brecken was crying hard, clinging to Sho as she sobbed, and Sho held her and spoke comforting words in English and the shoggoth language.

Later, when Brecken tried to recall the rest of that evening, all she could call to mind were brief fragmentary glimpses. She'd gone downstairs to fix June's dinner much later than she'd planned, and could never remember afterwards what it was that she had made. What she'd made for the shoggoths was another mystery—all she could recall was that every time she sat down, all the broodlings would settle in her lap, trying to comfort her the way they comforted each other. What else she did that evening left no trace in memory, except for a dim recollection of settling into bed, her eyes red and stinging, and Sho's cool black shapelessness flowing around her, shutting out a world that felt as desolate just then as the kingdom of Alar. Her own words circled through her mind: you don't get to choose what happens to you, just what you do about it. Then, Henry's: if you can do anything at all.

Sometimes you can't. Those words whispered themselves in the silence of the night, too. They reminded her of walls just then, walls of silence that surrounded her on every side and reached all the way up to the stars.

* * *

The next few days Mark had scheduled technical rehearsals for the lights and stage crew. Brecken had already arranged to miss those, and the news about her mother made any other choice unthinkable. Even aside from that, she had more than enough troubling news to keep her nerves on edge: Fermata's condition, the cryptic warning from the Yellow Sign, the signs of danger she'd watched all winter. She remembered to call a phone number she'd gotten from Mark and arrange for a complimentary ticket for June, and got her a seat at the last performance, which was the one she preferred—"A little more practice, a little less stress," the old woman had said, "so the last time's quite often better than the others"—but that was as much time as she put into her chamber opera or anything related to it.

Her trip down to Kingsport on Saturday was some solace. On the ride down and back, she could close her eyes and lean back into the soft leather seats and let the rest of the world go its own way for a time. The solemn intensity of Emily's focus on her instrument, the quiet companionship over tea and conversation that Charlotte offered Brecken afterward, and the delight she felt in their duets helped, at least for a while.

When she got back to June's house, though, the broodlings were in the middle of a dusting-race on the stair. From the way they bounded over to her once the race was done and huddled in her lap when she sat, she knew they were worried about their sister, and there was reason for that. ♪*She does not wish to feed,*♪ Sho said in a low whistle, once Brecken had gone upstairs and they were alone. ♪*You saw how little she fed on before you left.*

I tried to give her more while you were gone and she would not take it. She says feeding makes her feel ill.♪ The shoggoth paused, went on unwillingly. *♪I saw that happen with broodlings who died.♪*

Brecken clenched her eyes shut, put her arms around Sho, felt pseudopods flow in response. She could find no words, but then nothing needed to be said. If she and Sho had a future together, it would include another emptiness and that was all. Bitter though that prospect was, it was nothing new to either of them, and especially familiar to Brecken just then. In a moment of bleak clarity she glimpsed the whole trajectory: the days or weeks or months while Fermata's health failed, the shock of the loss, the grieving, the struggle back to something like ordinary life, the voice that would not be heard again and the absence that would always be felt.

The rest of the weekend crept by. Sunday, the day of the first dress rehearsal, she went to the East Church as dawn spread over Arkham, and picked her way through the dim silences of the east chapel and the worship hall. The banners behind the stage loomed up dark and cryptic. The only light she turned on was the little one that shone on the music shelf, leaving the rest of the church in darkness. That morning she'd brought a volume of Mozart arrangements and played some of his most tense and melancholy pieces, pushing herself and the organ equally hard, until she was as tired as though she'd run a race.

She started back for June's house not half an hour before the stage crew was scheduled to arrive at the church. Once back in the apartment, she started to look for paper and an envelope for the weekly letter to her mother, caught herself, and stood by the piano feeling wretched for a time, until a whistled question from Sho—*♪Broodsister, is there help I can give? The air tastes of your sadness♪*—sent her to throw her arms around the one reliable source of comfort she had.

Monday she went to Bolton as usual. She'd hoped that a pleasant evening of recorder music would help, but Hannah pelted her with question after question about the opera, ignoring Sarah's increasingly pointed glares and comments. Finally Brecken snapped, "Oh, for God's sake, can we please talk about something else?" Hannah jerked back wide-eyed, as though she'd been slapped, and apologized over and over again until Brecken wanted to scream at her to shut up. It was Danny who salvaged as much of the evening as could be saved, and he did it by pressing an extended index finger against Hannah's arm. Hannah turned to face him, obviously startled; he met her gaze with his own; what she read there, Brecken had no idea, but it made Hannah turn as red as her complexion allowed. She said scarcely another word thereafter.

The next two days, Tuesday and Wednesday, Brecken spent hours at a time sitting in a chair by one of the windows of the upstairs parlor, looking out at the gray wet landscape, not really seeing anything. The first shock of the news had passed off, and there were things she had to think about and a question she had to face. The book on Indian cooking sat on top of the piano, challenging her to understand why her first reaction had been what it was. Once asked, the question pointed straight to its own answer.

The thought circled through her mind, over and over again: I've spent my whole life trying to take care of people, the way I wanted to take care of Mom and I never could—

Each time, she had to make herself finish the thought: The way I wished she would take care of me, and she never did.

Between June's recovery and the frantic enthusiasm of the broodlings, she had little to do in the way of chores those two days except for cooking and serving meals. She kept her mind distracted the whole time while she was in the upstairs and downstairs kitchens, hiding from the fear that the delight she'd always felt in cooking for the people she cared about would vanish now that she'd glimpsed the misery at its root. That would have to be confronted sooner or later, she knew that in her bones, but she didn't have the courage to face it yet.

Wednesday night, as she settled down under the quilts with Sho and tried not to notice the faint but pervasive ammonia scent from Fermata, she faced a thought just as difficult. Her memory brought up people she'd known and cared about, one after another, from classmates in elementary school, through the boyfriends she'd had before Sho entered her life, all the way to June Satterlee. One after another, she saw how she'd tried to make them surrogates for her mother, people she could take care of in an attempt to fill the void in herself.

And Sho? The question couldn't be avoided, but she let out a long ragged breath as she realized that it wasn't the same thing at all. She'd started out taking care of Sho, but within weeks of their first meeting Sho had begun taking care of her as well: doing the cleaning chores a shoggoth could do so much more easily than any human, giving Brecken the unconditional friendship no one else in Partridgeville was willing to offer, wrapping her in comforting pseudopods when the events of that troubled year were too much for her to bear alone.

The broodlings were different in another way, and so was Emily d'Ursuras. There was a pact between the generations and Brecken knew it well. Though her mother had backed away from it, her grandparents were another matter, and Mrs. Macallan, her high school music teacher Mr. Krause, the flute and piano and composition teachers she'd had since then, all had accepted the pact and done their part so that Brecken could take their roles in due time. She thought next of Charlotte, then of Mark Tanabe, then all at once of her friends in Bolton and the chess club and all the people who were about to make her chamber opera something more than marks on paper, and knew that she could let the void she'd carried for so long be filled at last.

She slept hard that night. Toward morning, she dreamed. In the dream she was a child again, in the house in Woodfield where she'd spent the first fourteen years of her life. Her mother was somewhere inside, she was sure of it, but as she wandered from room to room she found all the furniture gone and no sign that anyone had lived there for years. Finally she went to the front door, which stood wide open.

Outside, the familiar suburban landscape stretched out beneath a sky dotted with puffy clouds. Wind rustled in the unmown grass of the yard. The front walk led to the sidewalk and the street, and the street curved away into unguessed distances. Brecken went through the door, closed it behind her, walked down to the sidewalk and kept on walking. She remembered the dream when she woke, and thought she could guess what it meant.

* * *

Thursday dawned at last, gray and cold, heralded by a pattering of rain on the windows of the apartment. Mark had called the evening before to let Brecken know that he'd arranged a ride for her at six-thirty, and Brecken clung to that detail as the day crept on and the sun's drowned desolate light slid westward behind a thick blanket of cloud. She spent most of the day with Sho, setting aside her grief for the past and her fears about the future in the shoggoth's comforting presence. As evening came on, she kissed Sho, put on her nicest dress, spent half an hour on her hair and makeup, wrapped herself in a ruana, and went down the stairs to June's parlor to wait.

Five minutes early a car pulled up on the street outside, and Brecken blinked and then started laughing when she recognized the car as Miriam Akeley's battered yellow Toyota. She hurried out into the evening, greeted the professor and settled into the passenger seat. Dr. Akeley wore a gorgeous pashmina shawl over a black dress, with a silver and moonstone shawl pin that Brecken let herself envy for a moment or two.

"June called and told me," Dr. Akeley said simply once they'd greeted each other. "I know there's not much anyone can say." Brecken thanked her, and as the car headed down Hyde

Street, the professor talked about things that didn't matter, and skillfully avoided any reference to the opera they were both about to see. Brecken was grateful for that, even though she knew just how temporary that respite would be. Soon enough, everyone she knew would be talking about *The King in Yellow*, and the rest of her career as a composer would be shaped by what they said. If what she'd done managed to communicate to them, that was one thing; if it meant no more to them than a display of marshmallow rabbits, that was another—and if the Radiance was watching as closely as she guessed it might be ...

She tried, without much success, to shut the thought out of her mind as Dr. Akeley pulled up along the sidewalk next to the East Church entry. "Go on in," she told Brecken. "I'll find a place to park. If you see Martin, tell him I'll be there in a few minutes." Brecken thanked her, got out and hurried up the walk to the familiar door.

Two volunteers Mark had parked at the door to take tickets greeted her with grins and waved her in. With the help of temporary curtains and racks, the far end of the east chapel had been turned into a cloakroom. Brecken checked her ruana there, went into the main hall. Close to a third of the pews already had people sitting in them, and conversation buzzed. She could sense the eyes that turned toward her, heard her name repeated in low tones over and over again. To her surprise, most of the people she saw weren't familiar to her from past performances in Arkham, and not all the voices seemed to be speaking a language she knew.

Before she could process that or find a seat in an inconspicuous corner, an usher—another of Mark's volunteers—hurried over to her, greeted her effusively, and led her up toward the front. Not many steps there, to her surprise, she saw a face she knew: Mrs. Eliot, the old woman she'd met at the Bolton Grange hall, who smiled in greeting. A little further on, amid a gaggle of expensively dressed old women, she spotted another: Mrs. Amberville, who gave her a sudden hard look softened by a faint smile, and then a nod. Brecken met her gaze with a precise smile and a nod of her own.

Finally she reached the front row of pews and a line of familiar faces. "Good evening, Brecken," said Martin Chaudronnier, rising to his feet. "You've met my niece Jenny, I think? Excellent." Brecken said the usual things, greeted Alain, Charlotte, Jenny, and Emily, whose face was alight with excitement. When they sat, Brecken was next to the aisle, in what was for all practical purposes the best seat in the house. Emily, sitting next to her, waited with barely concealed impatience. The first of the musicians took their places, Melinda Kress among them, and Brecken leaned toward her pupil and said, "Watch the way the flautist holds her flute, and how she fingers it. You can learn a lot from that." Emily sent a luminous smile her way, turned her attention toward Melinda and remained silent and focused until the opera began.

Miriam Akeley arrived when the hall was maybe half full, greeted everyone and sat next to Martin. The hall finished filling up, the musicians fell silent, and the buzz of talk rose and then suddenly dropped to nothing as the lights went down and Sean Howe went to the podium.

* * *

There would be other opening nights, other moments when Brecken watched her music lead the way to realms she'd only imagined before: in her second chamber opera, *The Call of Cthulhu*, as the basso-profundo voice of Cthulhu from offstage gave a ghostly reality to the magic-lantern images that provided the only scenery on the stage; in the most popular of her chamber operas, *The Great God Pan*, the night that Julie Mazzini premiered the role of Helen Vaughan and launched a legendary career as a soprano; in Brecken's one grand opera, *The Dream-Quest of Unknown Kadath*, when the Ballet of the Cats brought the audience to its feet, and ten minutes passed before the applause and cheering quieted enough for the performance to go on. When Brecken looked back in old age on her career as a composer, though, in a world that had changed utterly since that first performance, the words "opening night" always brought back to mind a raw spring evening in the East Church in Arkham, eight musicians waiting for Sean's baton to signal the beginning of the prelude, the stark simplicity of the stage, hanging banners wavering slowly in the unquiet air.

Then the baton came down, and the bassoon laid down a bass line over which the harp introduced the theme she'd given to Alar. The strings came in after eight measures, the rest of the instruments six measures after that, and thereafter the overture unfolded, setting out all the themes the rest of the opera would develop. Last of all, the terrible discords of the theme of the King sounded on the strings, echoed two measures later by the oboe and then by the flute. Then the overture wound down into quiet arpeggios on the harp over the bass line the bassoon played, and Ruth and Shelly came on stage in their simple costumes and ordinary theatrical makeup—or was it Camilla and Cassilda who strolled in the gardens of the kings of Alar, continuing a conversation they'd started long before, which just happened to be sung rather than spoken?

From there Act I, scene 1 unfolded its melodrama. Brecken risked glances at the audience from time to time, caught glimpses of their faces: not yet drawn into the story and the music the way she'd hoped, but interested and entertained, which counted for something. That continued until the final moments of scene 1, when Thale turned away in wretchedness and defeat, and then suddenly wheeled back toward the audience to embrace his doom and that of the kingdom of Alar. Brian's powerful voice rang out over a rising tide of music from the strings:

THALE: Let the red sun surmise what we will do,
When this blue starlight dies, and all is through.

Brecken had imagined those words bursting out in bitterness and defiance, Thale's pride and pain overwhelming his love for Cassilda and setting the tragedy in motion. The bitterness was in Brian's voice and so was the defiance, but so was something less easy to define: a hint of rueful foreknowledge, perhaps, as though Thale knew what he was doing and what would come of it, and accepted it as his destiny. In that moment Brecken grasped possibilities in opera she hadn't seen before, glimpsed the way a skillfully written score could make it easier for singers to find their own subtle reinterpretations, so that every performance could reveal something new. She pondered that, delighted, then suddenly realized that everyone else in the audience was applauding, and belatedly started clapping as well.

As the applause died down, Shelly came onto the stage to begin scene 2 with Cassilda's song. From the first achingly clear notes, Brecken knew the opera would be a success. Brian and Rashid made the duet between Thale and Uoht sound like the shouting match it represented, without ever straying from the taut harmonies of the music; the masked ball had exactly the air of desperate gaiety and looming disaster Brecken had tried to weave into it. Silence gripped the audience as the melodrama of the first act wound to its close, with Uoht kneeling by the dying Cassilda, offering words of consolation that not even he could believe any more, only to have Cassilda spurn them with her last breath:

UOHT: *And the lordship of all Alar shall descend—*
CASSILDA: *(bitterly) Not upon us, O King, not upon us!*
(She dies.)

Camilla shrieked in horror as her sister invoked the King and died, and fled through the empty streets of Alar, her screams fading as Sean led the orchestra in a crescendo. The coda rang out, summing up the catastrophe, and then the orchestra went silent, the stage went dark, and after a moment of silence the audience burst into another round of applause.

The great question in Brecken's mind as the intermission wound up was whether the music she'd written for the second act could help the drama do what Castaigne intended it to do, and transform the melodrama of the first into a glimpse into the heart of things. Sean's baton came down, the overture of the second act unfolded, Janet sang the madwoman's lines at the beginning of the act, and Brecken had her answer.

Utter silence gripped the audience. The King in Yellow appeared, gaunt as winter, and beneath the blank unyielding gaze of the Pallid Mask the melodrama of the first act unraveled thread by thread, revealing the emptiness that lay behind the grand facade of the court of Alar as it did behind all things human. Uoht and Thale fought to the death, Uoht won and then turned his blade on himself, and the King in Yellow took the blade and consigned it to a high and terrible destiny the music could only express in hints.

In the scene that followed, Naotalba died in stunned horror, Jasht in dread, Camilla in grief, the madwoman in an ecstasy of release, Aldones last of all in weary acceptance, and the King in Yellow stood in silence before the open tomb of Aldones to set the seal of the Yellow Sign on the doom of the kingdom of Alar. The lights dimmed and the finale began, first the theme of Alar, then the theme of the King in Yellow, and finally, beyond all hope, Cassilda's theme. Brecken had doubted up to that moment that the music could do what she wanted it it to do, and show the audience that in a world where all human things were passing shadows, Cassilda's failed and fragile dreams meant exactly as much as the immensity of Alar's fall. As the orchestra reached and held the final soaring chord, she knew that it had succeeded. Those dreams hung there in the night, luminous, as the performance ended.

* * *

Applause exploded from the pews. A few people stood, still clapping. Others followed, and then the whole audience was on its feet, applauding and shouting "Bravo!" in the grand operatic tradition. The singers came out for their curtain calls, one at a time since there were only eight of them, and Sully and Jean followed; all of them came out to bow together, and then Mark came pelting down from the stage to haul Brecken out of her seat and lead her, dazed and blinking, up onto the stage, where she and Sean and the musicians joined the cast in bow after bow as the audience clapped and cheered.

Finally the applause quieted and the lights came up. Mark said the expected words, thanking the Chaudronnier Foundation, thanking the audience. Another round of polite applause followed, and then the singers and the musicians headed for their dressing rooms. Brecken, still dazed, found her way down from the stage and into a crowd of well-wishers. Some of them were friends, some acquaintances, and some she was sure she'd never met, but all of them wanted to congratulate her. Michael Peaslee was among them; he gave her a look of utter seriousness and said, "That was really astonishingly good. I hope you're planning on writing more." She turned bright red, and had to work not to stammer as she thanked him. A little later, as the crowd had begun to thin, Elias van Kauran crossed to her and said, "Creditably done. The future of opera may not be quite as bleak as I'd anticipated." She beamed, and curtseyed to him; he executed a precise bow, and turned to go.

"Elias," said Miriam Akeley, from close by. When he turned: "I agree with you."

He drew himself up as though affronted, let out a derisive snort, and then turned and walked away. Brecken caught the little amused twist of his mouth, though, and laughed hard enough that she had to lean on the nearest pew.

When she'd recovered a little, Martin Chaudronnier approached her. "Brecken, I wonder if you'd be willing to join us for a late supper tonight."

Brecken glanced at him, uncertain. After the week she'd been through, the thought of a meal she didn't have to cook had a definite appeal, but old habits pulled her the other way.

"Please come," Charlotte said. "I'm sure you'll enjoy it."

That settled the matter. "Yes, please," Brecken said, "and thank you."

A brief discussion settled the matter of getting there. "I can take Brecken," said Dr. Akeley, "and—Jenny, do you mind my back seat?"

"I can take the back seat," Brecken protested.

"No, you can't," said Jenny. "You've got to be at least eight inches taller than I am, and if I was an inch taller it would be a tight fit." To Dr. Akeley: "Miriam, for heaven's sake, of course I don't mind. How many times have I ridden back there?"

Minutes later they were on the sidewalk in front of the church as the last of the audience streamed away. Martin and the other members of the family went one way, Dr. Akeley went the other, and Brecken and Jenny stood waiting for a time. The rain had stopped, but night gripped Arkham close, and the air was cold enough that Brecken was glad of the warmth of her ruana.

"Have you been to the Restaurant La Frenaie before?" Jenny asked her then.

Brecken recognized the name of Arkham's best restaurant. "No." Then, her insecurities surging up: "I hope I don't embarrass anyone. I'm not used to that kind of thing."

"Don't worry about it," Jenny told her. "Charlotte can coach you, the way she did for me the first time the family took me there."

Brecken gave her an uncertain look, and then a stray memory came to her aid. "Charlotte told me once," she ventured, "that you didn't grow up with the rest of the family."

"No, not at all. My mom ran away from home at eighteen, and I mostly grew up in trailer parks and homeless shelters. The first time I went to the Chaudronnier mansion—" She shook her head, laughed. "I felt hopelessly out of place."

"I felt the same way when I started teaching Emily," Brecken said, trying to process the idea of a scion of the second wealthiest family in Kingsport living in a trailer park.

"I bet." She glanced at Brecken. "It takes some getting used to."

Brecken nodded, and all at once thought of the graceful way that Charlotte had handled the differences in their social standing and guessed at what was behind it.

"By the way," Jenny said then in a quiet voice, "Miriam told us this afternoon about your mother. That's got to be really difficult. If there's anything we can do, please let us know."

Brecken thanked her, tried to think of something else to say, and failed completely. As the two of them stood there, for no reason that made any sense to her, there surged up in her the conviction that she could trust Jenny with the secret of her divided life. The impulse lasted only an instant before colder and more cautious thoughts stifled it. Not long after, Dr. Akeley drove up in her yellow Toyota and the two of them climbed in. The whole way to the Restaurant le Frenaie, though, she felt Jenny's gaze on her, and wondered absurdly if the woman could somehow read her mind and know what she was thinking.

* * *

The meal turned out less awkward than she expected. The Restaurant La Frenaie was a big Federal-era farmhouse in a part of Arkham Brecken didn't know well, all whitewashed stone walls, oaken beams, murmuring voices, delicious scents. She ended up sitting next to Charlotte and across from Jenny, which made it easy for her to keep a surreptitious eye on them and copy their actions. Servers brought rolls, butter, wine, and hors d'oeuvres, and after a decent interval, the meal. The food was even better than Brecken expected, and it made her want to find a good introduction to French provincial cooking.

That heartened her, made her feel as though the world might make sense to her again someday.

She'd worried about what she should or shouldn't say in so rarefied a setting, but Martin broke the ice by asking Emily what she thought of the opera, and the conversation flowed smoothly from there. The one embarrassing detail of the evening was that other people Martin knew came over at intervals and asked to be introduced to Brecken. Many of them, she gathered, were related to the Chaudronniers in one way or another, a good many of them were from France, and Brecken had to work hard to keep from getting flustered when it came out that all of them had come to attend the opening night of *The King in Yellow*.

She got back to June's house a little after midnight, sleepy and unsteady on her feet—she'd had only a few sips of each of the wines the waiters brought, and not even that much of the cognac that followed the meal, but those had conspired with the stresses of the week to leave her giddy. The house was dark and silent, and the way up the stairs required now and then a sudden grip on the railing. Finally, though, she let herself into her apartment, let out a ragged sigh of relief as she caught the familiar scent of shoggoths at rest.

The lamp clicked on a moment later as a pseudopod turned the switch. ♪*Broodsister,*♪ Sho piped. ♪*It is well with you?*♪

♪*It is very well,*♪ Brecken whistled back. Her ruana and purse found temporary places to be, and she went to join Sho on the sofa. ♪*And with you and the little ones?*♪

Sho made a little wavering tone: not good, not bad. ♪*We can speak of it when the light comes back. You are tired, I think, and should sleep.*♪

Brecken leaned over and kissed the shoggoth. ♪*You're right, of course.*♪

Soon after she nestled down next to Sho, closed her eyes, hoped that sleep would not hide from her, the way it did sometimes after a performance. To her surprise, she fell asleep at once and didn't wake until well into the morning. She had no plans for the day. *The King in Yellow* would be playing again that evening, but she pushed aside the sudden panic that tried to convince her to show up for the performance in case something went wrong.

Mark's right, she told herself. I can't take care of everybody. The thought made her feel small and vulnerable for a moment, but the moment passed, and she drew in a deep breath, and when she kissed Sho and climbed out of their bed she stood a little straighter than before.

June needed little help getting up for the day, and insisted on making the coffee herself. Sho stayed on the dreaming-side for more than an hour longer than usual and seemed tired when she finally slid out of the bedroom. Fermata was no better that morning but at least she was no worse, and the other broodlings were more than ready to be distracted by helping with the cleaning. Though it took a certain amount of ingenuity to turn each cleaning chore into a game, the apartment was spotless by the time Sho came out from the bedroom.

When Brecken went to help June with breakfast, five broodlings slid down the stairs with her and busied themselves ingesting dust, darting and bumping into each other until June laughed aloud. Brecken had to nerve herself up to read the day's Arkham *Advertiser*, but *The King in Yellow* somehow hadn't made the front page. The lead story was about the heavy rains and rising seas that were causing serious flooding in half a dozen nearby seacoast towns. Down below was a grim little story about a man who'd been found dead in his home with his neck broken; the police weren't sure whether or not the death was accidental. The only reference to Brecken's opera was a listing in the Local Events section, and if any of the opening night audience had to be taken away for psychiatric care, not a word of it found its way into the paper.

Later that afternoon, she made a first attempt to write a requiem for her mother, but what took shape instead was something gentle and wistful, stirring dim echoes of memory she couldn't yet track to their source. Saturday she went to Kingsport, to find Emily still giddy about the opera and Charlotte quiet and calm as always. Sunday was jarring at first, with no letter to write and no organ to play—the Sunday matinee was early enough that she knew the church would be full of people before she finished breakfast—and the Sunday *Advertiser* had a front page story about another car crash: a SUV had gone off the Old Kingsport Highway on Friday, plunged down a rocky slope and burst into flames. That left Brecken chilled, thinking about how often she'd ridden that route in the Chaudronniers' car.

The enthusiastic and mildly clueless review of her opera in the Local Events section did a certain amount to banish that shadow. Three hours over a notebook and another hour at the piano did more, as the first fragments of the not-requiem unfolded a few of their possibilities. The rest was still hidden from her. She kept working, knowing that it would come clear later on.

Monday and Tuesday followed, the first punctuated by a trip to Bolton and an evening playing recorder with her friends, the second by a shopping run to the First National grocery and an hour at the chess club, both by long hours mulling over the passages she'd written and beginning to weave them together into something that made sense to her. She fixed elaborate dinners both days, and found to her immense relief that the simple pleasures of cooking for friends hadn't deserted her. If anything, it was easier for her to enjoy the work of cooking and the enthusiastic responses of June, Sho, and the broodlings when she wasn't half-consciously weighing those against the miseries of her own childhood. That made it a little easier to face the rest of the uncertainties that surrounded her as the last performance came closer.

CHAPTER 14

WORDS OF RECKONING

When Wednesday came, Brecken had to remind herself more than once that *The King in Yellow* would finish its premiere run that night, that she'd agreed to be there for the last performance, and that June also had a ticket for that day. Mark called a little before noon to let her know he'd arranged for a ride for her and June, and she thanked him. Six-thirty came and their ride drove up: another of Mark's volunteers, a doctoral candidate named Will Bishop whose narrow chin and tuft of beard made him look oddly like a goat.

The three of them chatted amiably as he drove a well-aged Buick through Arkham's streets. He let June and Brecken off in front of the church entrance and drove away to find a parking place, and she went inside with June, checked her ruana, and searched for seats for the two of them. The hall was more than half full by the time they arrived and filled to capacity not long thereafter. Brecken remembered what Mark had said about the difficulties of finding an audience, and wondered how he'd managed to do it.

She knew what to expect from the opera that time, and when the lights went down, she could watch and listen with a calmer heart. Here and there, she glimpsed places where changes would have made the music just that little more perfect, but a moment's thought convinced her that rewriting the opera was the wrong choice. Unless the Radiance or something else stopped her, she knew for certain, she would compose more chamber operas, and the lessons she'd learned from *The King in Yellow* would flow into those in due time.

As the finale began, she closed her eyes, and let herself rest for a moment in the knowledge of what she'd accomplished, or what the music had accomplished through her. Whatever else happened, four audiences let her show them how Castaigne's vision could weave the world together instead of tearing it apart. Maybe those would be the only performances the chamber opera would ever have, but she guessed otherwise, and the enthusiastic applause that filled the space once the last note faded to silence encouraged her in that guess.

And the people who'd dressed Wotan as a marshmallow rabbit, she wondered then—how did they feel when they looked at empty seats and listened to sparse applause? How would she have felt if her opera had gotten the same response? Maybe—the thought couldn't be evaded—maybe, for all her efforts, it was sheer chance that her vision had communicated to the audience and theirs hadn't. Chance or not, she decided then and there, she would see if she could do as well, or better, with her next opera.

Once again the cast made their curtain calls, once again Mark came pelting down to lead Brecken up onto the stage and be applauded with the others, once again a crowd of well-wishers gathered to congratulate her when she left the stage. Her friends from Bolton were among them, and she blushed hard when Hannah said, "You've got to give us a score for Cassilda's song. I'm begging you." Danny, for his part, touched one of her hands and met her gaze squarely; in that moment she sensed, more clearly than words could communicate, his delight in the music and a sense of gratitude that left her baffled.

Twenty minutes later, after she'd seen June off with Will Bishop, she went down the stairs to the social hall, where Mark had arranged the traditional party for cast, crew, and musicians to celebrate a successful show. She settled into a chair, managed to fend off a proffered beer, let one of the stage hands talk her into accepting a daquiri he insisted was mostly strawberries. It wasn't, but she contented herself with little sips, let herself bask in the sense of belonging that filled the room and embraced everyone who had been part of the production.

Mark came down the stair last of all. "You ... *did* ... *GREAT!*" he shouted, and the others roared their response. After he'd gone to a table half covered with bottles and poured himself something complex, he made a beeline for Brecken, squeezed into a place at the table across from her, and said, "You remember what I said about how hard it is to find your audience? You must have looked behind the couch or something."

Brecken choked on the daquiri, laughing. "I figured you found them."

"I don't know who did it, but they turned up," he said. "We had a full house every night, or next thing to it. You know what that means? We're in the black. We really, seriously, honest to God, actually made a small profit on the show. All our bills are paid, everybody's got their paychecks, and the Chaudronnier Foundation's going to get their money back, which happens once in a blue moon with bright yellow spots. You know what else it means?" When Brecken shook her head: "My CV just turned into solid gold. I'll have zero problem finding a gig after graduation. One more production like this and I'll have theater companies falling all over each other trying to hire me." All at once he leaned forward and took her hands in his. "You've got to give me another opera. I'm begging you."

Partly because of the daquiri, partly because his words echoed Hannah's so precisely, she started laughing. "Okay," she said. "Let me see what I can come up with. It may take a while."

He let go of her hands, downed half his drink. "Take your time. I'll console myself with Mozart, Monteverdi, Wagner—"

"No marshmallow rabbits, I hope."

"I promise. Can you imagine *L'Orfeo* or *Parsifal* staged this same way, small orchestra, minimal staging, no gimmicks, just the music and the story?"

"Oh dear God, yes," said Brecken. "Please do it."

"I'll need somebody to arrange the score."

"We'll talk," she told him, and he grinned from ear to ear, downed the rest of his drink, raised his glass in salute, and went to congratulate someone else.

* * *

It was after midnight when Melinda Kress offered her a ride home, and she accepted gratefully. The party was still going when they left. Remembering stories she'd been told about cast parties, Brecken guessed that it might still be going when the sun lit the windows of the east chapel. It took all her concentration to walk in a mostly straight line to the kitchen door, let herself in, and get the door locked behind her. Once she was safe indoors, though, and Melinda drove away, she stood by the door for a long moment.

The Radiance hadn't done anything. That was the thought that circled through her mind as she stood there, looking out through the kitchen window at the dim lights of Arkham and the cold glory of the stars above. She'd written an opera about the king of the Great Old Ones, Mark had produced it, hundreds of people had watched it, and despite Brecken's fears and the Yellow Sign's warning and all the signs of danger she'd seen or sensed, the Radiance had done nothing to stop any of it. Had they somehow failed to notice? Or—the thought dazzled her, but it could not be avoided—did it somehow not concern them? The night offered her no answers. She wove her way to the stair, hauled herself a step at a time up to her apartment and to Sho.

The next day was a blur. She slept late, spent the morning yawning and blinking, lay down again after breakfast for what she thought would be a few minutes and didn't wake up again until the shadows on Hyde Street lengthened in the afternoon—and for the first time in months, that didn't make her think of the lengthening shadows over the kingdom of Alar. She was less groggy thereafter, and spent more time bent over her composition notebook, but when night came she nestled down gratefully next to Sho and slept straight through until morning.

The following day, Friday, she got everything that had been part of *The King in Yellow* cleaned out of her shoulderbag, and had just begun to wonder where her ruana had ended up when the phone rang. "Brecken? It's Henry," the familiar voice said when she answered. "Any chance you left something behind in the cloakroom Wednesday night?"

Memory returned all at once. "Yes," she said. "Yes, of course. I forgot to pick up my ruana before Melanie and I left."

"If you want to come down to the church this afternoon, I'll be here," Henry reassured her. "Better make it after five—say, five-thirty. We've still got to tear down the stage and the rest of the lights." Brecken glanced at the clock and agreed. All at once she remembered the way he'd looked after their chess game, the haggard thing that had showed briefly in his eyes, and wanted to say something about it, but he said his goodbyes and hung up before she had the chance to mention it.

She got to the church at five-thirty, as clouds alternately hid and revealed the westering sun and Peabody Avenue filled up with as much traffic as it ever saw. As she walked, she thought again of their chess game, the way the conversation had gone, the way he'd stiffened and turned brittle at the end of it. Had she accidentally brushed against some unmentioned grief of his? Or was something else involved?

The door was unlocked, and when she went inside she found the east chapel as it had been before the opera, with pews and lectern and bare wooden altar all in place. She'd expected to find stage hands still busy, but once the door closed behind her, an unexpected silence filled the space. "Henry?" she called out.

"In here." The voice came from the worship hall.

She went through the doors to the worship hall, didn't see him, looked around. The stage, the banners, the lights: all of it had been hauled away, leaving the East Church as it had been, dim and silent and empty. "Where are you?"

"Right here." The voice came from behind her, with an unfamiliar edge. She turned and stopped cold. He was standing not two feet from the door she'd just come through. His right hand was raised, and the dark shape in it could only be a gun.

"Don't try to scream or run," he said then. He took a few steps forward. "If you do I'll shoot you dead." A slow hard smile spread over his face. "The universe isn't giving you a pretty yellow leaf this time. Got it?"

After a frozen moment, she forced a nod.

"Good. This whole operation has been a disaster but you're going to help me salvage it right now. You're going to head out the door with me and get into a car, and I'm going to take you a long way from here. If you do exactly as you're told you won't be harmed."

All at once, the fears of the months just past crystallized into certainty. "You're with the Radiance, aren't you?"

That earned her narrowed eyes and a silence. "So you know that much," he said finally. "I wonder. Do you know what happened to the others who came to Arkham, the ones who would have shut down this misbegotten show of yours on opening night if things had gone the way they should have?" The haggard thing she'd glimpsed before showed again in his voice. "There were eighteen of them, good men, some of the best I've ever worked with. They're all dead now. Did you know that?"

Horrified, she shook her head. He considered that, said, "You know, I'm almost tempted to believe you. You really have no business getting involved in things like this. You haven't been anything like careful enough."

She drew in a breath, and said, "What—what do you want from me?"

"Don't be a fool," said Blakeney. "We know you've been associating with people on the other side—people and *things*." He said the last word as though it left a foul taste in his mouth. "We had a sniffer drone check the house where you live. We know what lives there with you. I don't know how you can tolerate living with those monsters, or what kind of hold they have over you, but that's done with. You're going to come with me to a safe place, and tell some people everything you know about them and about the people you've dealt with. Another team's going to come in and clean things out here, and then we'll get you settled in a different town where the other side doesn't have a presence and you can go on composing and playing music. If you cooperate with us, we can give your career a serious boost—we've got a lot of influence. All you have to do is come with me and tell us what we want to know."

She knew what she had to do then, and it was easier to do it than she'd expected, even though she felt sick with terror, even though she knew that it meant a sudden end to all her dreams. Maybe the fact that she was standing in the hall where Cassilda's song had filled the air a few nights earlier gave her the strength, maybe something else did that, but she drew in a ragged breath, and in a wavering voice said, "No."

"You'd better reconsider that," Blakeney said, his face hard.

"No," she said again, her voice steadier. "I'm not going to betray the ones I love."

A spasm of disbelief and disgust crossed his face an instant after she said the word "love"—and at that moment, something yanked the gun to one side.

It went off, but the shot plowed uselessly into a pew. An instant later Blakeney's feet went out from under him, and he landed hard. Quick as a viper, he twisted and tried to pull the gun free, but whatever had seized him was quicker still, and stronger. A darkness Brecken could barely see hit him hard, sending him sprawling, and something else just as difficult to follow tightened around the hand with the gun. Brecken

heard bones splinter, a hiss of agony out of his lips. Then the
gun dropped from what was left of the hand and both arms
twisted back. Yanked by the hair, his head went back also, as
whatever it was bent him like a bow.

"No, I don't think so," said a voice that sounded uncannily
like Brecken's.

* * *

Brecken had to reach for the back of a pew to keep from slump-
ing to the floor in astonishment and relief. ♪*Broodsister*,♪ she
whistled. ♪*I thank you.*♪

♪*Broodsister*,♪ a familiar piping voice replied. ♪*Forgive me.
This is for you—but it is not only for you.*♪

She was still trying to process that when Sho spoke again,
in English. "Your real name is Philip Heselton. Is that correct?"

The man Brecken knew as Henry Blakeney gritted his teeth
and said nothing.

"I can make this just as hard as it has to be," said Sho.
A pseudopod seized the mangled hand and twisted it, and
agony spasmed across the man's face. "You're Philip Heselton," she said. "Is that correct?"

"Yes." The word forced its way out.

"Thank you. A little over five years ago, you led a negation
team that destroyed a colony of shoggoths near Partridgeville,
New Jersey. Is that correct?"

The pseudopod closed on the mangled hand again. "Yes,"
he panted.

Horrified, Brecken stared at him as understanding came.

"Hunting shoggoths is a tricky business, Philip Heselton,"
Sho said then. "You really do have to make sure you kill them all.
If you don't, you know, they might have their own ideas about
what you did, and they might even decide to return the favor."

"Listen to me, Philip Heselton." Sho's voice had begun to
fray around the edges. "When I first realized who you were

and what you did, I thought about hunting down and destroying everyone and everything you ever cared about, and leaving you alive, all alone, to remember them and know what you'd lost. I very seriously considered that." With her voice shaking: "But I will not do to you what you did to me."

In the dim light, Brecken could barely see the upturned face, taut with agony and terror, but she thought that something stirred in those eyes, a knowledge as dreadful as the death he was about to suffer: the recognition that the monstrous shapes he'd killed had people inside them.

♪Close your eyes, broodsister,♪ Sho said then, and Brecken closed her eyes. What followed was mercifully brief: a muffled cry of agony, a hideous wet noise, and silence.

♪Turn away,♪ Sho said then. ♪You do not have to see.♪

♪No,♪ said Brecken. ♪There's supposed to be a witness, isn't there?♪

In a whistle that shook with grief: ♪I did not want it to be you—♪

Brecken opened her eyes.

She'd wondered for years, ever since she'd first read *The Secret Watcher* and taken from it her first lessons in shoggoth lore, about their way of formal vengeance, a tradition already immemorial before her ancestors first bore live young: the sudden crushing pressure on the body, the sudden tearing suction on the head, the acrid and venomous secretion that coated the corpse and spelled out words of reckoning nearby. She'd imagined the act and its consequences from time to time, too, when Sho told her broodlings tales of ages long past and the long bitter struggle against the beings the shoggoths remembered only as "those others."

The reality was nothing like what she'd imagined. Henry Blakeney's body sprawled awkwardly across the floor, like a doll that some careless child had broken and flung aside. A short distance away, his head lay where it had fallen; Brecken managed not to look at the red ruin of the neck and the things that dangled from it. The only things she'd envisioned correctly were the words of reckoning, which Sho had just finished writing in stinking black fluid on the side of a nearby pew. She didn't have to read the archaic pattern of dots to know that it spelt out the formal name of the colony of shoggoths beneath Hob's Hill.

♪*It is witnessed*,♪ she managed to say.

Pale eyes regarded her ruefully. ♪*I thank you*,♪ said Sho.

Brecken was shaking by then, with something more primal than fear. ♪*What are we going to do?*♪

♪*Leave*,♪ Sho whistled. ♪*That is what Nyogtha told me to say. We must leave at once.*♪

♪*But—*♪ She stared at Sho, at the broken corpse. ♪*Someone will find him.*♪

♪*I do not know. All I know is that we must go now.*♪ Sho motioned toward the stair that led down to the social hall. ♪*Nyogtha said there is no other way for either of us.*♪

Brecken nodded after a blank moment, let herself follow the shoggoth.

They hurried down the stair together, crossed the social hall in the faint light from dim high windows. Sho led the way into the kitchen, veered past elderly appliances, came to a door Brecken guessed led into a broom closet. The shoggoth flowed up against the door and did something to the doorknob; the lock clicked, and she pulled the door open.

♪*You will not be able to see*,♪ Sho said then. ♪*There are stairs going down. Let me take your arm and lead you.*♪ Brecken reached for her. A pseudopod flowed around her hand and lower arm, guided her into the doorway. The door swung shut, the last traces of light vanished, and another click sounded, soft and final.

The stair went down, and down, and down, and the air grew cold, damp, thick with nameless scents. Brecken let herself be guided through the darkness. A terrible suspicion had begun to stir in her, forcing its way past her horror at what had just happened and the rising spiral of dread about what would happen next, framed in words she didn't even want to think about. It was easier just then to turn all her attention to the uneven steps beneath her, the pseudopod wrapped around her arm, and the silent darkness all about them.

The stair ended, and they moved on the level for what seemed like a long time, through a lightless maze where her footfalls and the slow drip of water on stone made the only sounds. A sudden turn, then, and they began climbing a steep ragged tunnel. Finally Sho moved ahead and shoved something heavy out of the way, and they squeezed through a narrow gap into a cramped dark space that seemed somehow familiar.

♪*Where are we?*♪ Brecken asked.

♪*The basement of June's house,*♪ said Sho. ♪*We are home.*♪ She said the words as though accepting a sentence.

* * *

They slipped up the stairs to the first floor. The lights were off, and a trickle of dim shadows tinged with the last of the daylight filled the space. Faint piping sounds from above, reassuring, told of broodlings repeating a lesson. A moment passed before Brecken realized that the door to June's bedroom was open and June herself was nowhere to be seen.

♪*Where is she?*♪ Brecken asked, looking around frantically.

♪*I do not know.*♪

Familiar fears took on a sudden urgency. ♪*We must get the broodlings and leave at once.*♪ There was a word in the shoggoth language for the Radiance, but she could not remember it. ♪*The ones who hunt your people—*♪

♪*They will not come here,*♪ Sho said. Brecken gave her a baffled look, and the shoggoth went on: ♪*Nyogtha told me to say that also. He wishes us to stay here, where we will be safe.*♪

Brecken stared at her for a long moment, and then nodded, for want of anything better to do. After a moment she crossed the room, turned on the parlor lights, then went to the sofa and sat down. ♪*Then—then I think we need to talk,*♪ she said.

♪*Yes,*♪ said Sho, and flowed up onto the other side of the sofa. Pale eyes opened, waited.

A long moment passed as Brecken collected her thoughts. ♪*You know how to get to the church,*♪ she said then. ♪*You know about doors and tunnels I've never heard of, and they lead to the basement here. You've spoken with Nyogtha. And after what just happened and what the one who died said to me, I'm wondering*—♪ She made herself go on. ♪*If you had something to do with other humans who died.*♪

♪*Yes.*♪

♪*How many of them?*♪

♪*All of them.*♪

Brecken tried to process that.

"It might be better if I just tell you what happened," Sho said then. "In your language—it will be easier that way." Brecken nodded, and the shoggoth went on. "The Radiance sent one of its most experienced negation teams to Arkham last fall. Pure chance, maybe, but it was the same team that killed everyone but me under Hob's Hill."

"How—how did you find out?"

"Nyogtha told me, of course. He warned me months ago."

Brecken nodded again, slowly, beginning to understand.

"I didn't believe it," Sho burst out suddenly. "I didn't want to believe it. But Nyogtha had already showed me one of the ways to get into the tunnels, and he told me to go late at night to a house on Garrison Street—it was the one you told me about, the one that burned—and hide, and listen. There was a false ceiling in the parlor, so I hid there, and the two men below me talked, and one said that he was tired of all this waiting and watching, he wished they could just burn the bastards out the way they did that time at Partridgeville."

"Oh dear God," Brecken whispered.

Sho didn't seem to notice. "And I couldn't stand it. It wasn't even what they'd done. It was that he thought of it as—as the easy thing to do. The convenient thing. Go in, kill everyone with fire, drive away, just another day's work."

"I'm not exactly sure what happened after that. I was—blind, you would say, with anger and disgust. But a few moments later I was on top of them and they were dead. I think I broke their necks, but I'm not sure."

"Nyogtha came to me then. He told me that if I did as he asked, I would stop the Radiance from doing in Arkham what they did under Hob's Hill, and help him strike a blow against them from which they might never recover. He showed me what the negation team was there to do—please don't ask me about that now, I don't think I can bear to talk about it yet. I had horrible dreams about it for months. And all I had to do, to stop them, to save your life and many other lives, was to help Nyogtha kill them."

"I don't think I could have done it if I hadn't just killed those two men, but I was numb with horror and with the knowledge of what they'd done, and I let Nyogtha guide me. He had me soak the carpet with something that would burn and then light the house on fire."

"You did that?" Brecken said, astonished.

"I've never been more frightened," Sho admitted. "Not even when I first came to you in Partridgeville. But I did it, and after that, other things were easier. And now you know why I was so sick and wretched the next morning. I spent the rest of the night lying next to you, thinking about what you would think of me if you knew what I'd done and what I'd promised to do."

"I'm astonished that I didn't wake up when you came back," said Brecken.

Sho huddled down further into the corner of the sofa. "I did that too. Nyogtha showed me a way to make you sleep very deeply, so you wouldn't notice that I was going away at night."

After a moment, Brecken nodded. "Go on."

"There were thirty of them at Hob's Hill," said Sho. "I actually managed to read the mission report the team filed afterwards. Eleven of them died there. The report said that some of my people, while they were burning to death, flung themselves at the negation team and crushed and smothered some of them before they died. They did that much."

"Oh dear God," Brecken said again, staring in horror.

"But that left nineteen. I'd already killed four of them—there were two upstairs who burnt—and Nyogtha and I killed the rest." With a bleak little ripple of amusement: "Making the cars crash was the easiest part of it. If your people had any idea how easy that was, I don't think any of you would drive. A little something corrosive in a few places—but you know what happened. I won't go into the details unless you really want them."

"I don't," Brecken said. "Not now."

"But that left the negation team coordinator, Philip Heselton—the man who called himself Henry Blakeney, who came here a long time before the others to get things ready for them. I already knew who he was, and I wanted him to die last of all, and Nyogtha wanted the same thing, I don't know why. So after the last car crash, I waited and Nyogtha kept watch. He told me to hurry to the church as soon as you left, and he told me that Heselton needed to die there. I didn't know what Heselton had planned, so I hid among the pews and listened. I was going to kill him as soon as you went away—and you know the rest."

* * *

Silence settled into place in the parlor, edged with the faint piping of the broodlings above. "And now?" Brecken asked finally. Unwelcome futures hovered close around her in the fading light, but those would wait. Sho needed her first.

Pale eyes looked up at her, closed again. "I don't know," Sho said. "I don't know. I did what Nyogtha asked me to do, I did what my broodmother and my broodmates and all the others I knew under Hob's Hill would have wanted me to do, I hope I really did save you and everyone else from what the negation team planned—" Her voice began to shake. "But I don't know how I can feel clean or whole or happy ever again."

Brecken bit her lip and tried to think of something, anything, she could say. The answer that surfaced startled her enough that she wondered later whether Nyogtha might have put it in her mind. ♪*Winding To A Close,*♪ she whistled. ♪*I think you need me to offer judgment.*♪

Half a dozen eyes popped open, stared at her. ♪*Please,*♪ Sho said after a few moments. ♪*Maybe that would help.*♪

Brecken struggled to remember everything she'd learned of shoggoth customary law and the ways Sho had taught the broodlings. ♪*Is there anything else I need to know?*♪

♪*No. I—no.*♪

She drew in a long uneven breath, began. ♪*First, eight others depend on you, so the harshest punishments can't be considered. Do you accept that?*♪

♪*Yes,*♪ Sho said after a moment.

♪*Second—*♪ Brecken had to stop, think through the next part. ♪*You didn't choose to kill them without reason. Nyogtha called you to help him as your people have helped him for ages of ages. Your people's customs called you to kill them, and so did the need to protect me and others from them. You know much more of the ways of your people than I do, but I think even one of those reasons would be enough in their eyes to require forgiveness. Is that true?*♪

♪*It is true,*♪ Sho admitted.

♪*So—*♪ Then, all at once, Brecken saw what she needed to say. ♪*So the bitterness, the disharmony, isn't between you and anyone else. It's between you and yourself—and I think you've already punished yourself enough. Do you accept that?*♪

♪*No,*♪ Sho said at once.

Startled, Brecken piped, ♪*Why not?*♪

♪*Because it is not all between me and myself. It is also between me and you.*♪ Sho's whistle trembled again. ♪*I lied to you, I misled you, I made you sleep so you would not find out what I was doing. I will hate myself for a long time for that.*♪

The first faint trace of a smile stirred Brecken's lips. ♪*When someone's hurt, who knows what's enough to heal the hurt?*♪

♪*The one who is hurt,*♪ Sho admitted.

♪*This is what will heal the hurt for me,*♪ said Brecken. ♪*Broodsister, dearest one, I hope that nothing like this ever happens again, but if it does, promise me that you won't hide it from me. Bind yourself to tell me, no matter how little you want to. Will you do that?*♪

♪*I will. I bind myself, Cloud Before The Wind.*♪

♪*Then I am satisfied,*♪ Brecken said. She considered the huddled shape before her, and held out her arms. A little tentatively, Sho slid across the couch and nestled up against her, and she put her arms around the shoggoth, pressed her face against cool shapelessness as Sho began to tremble violently. "It's okay," she murmured, knowing that the sound of her voice just then mattered more than any words she said. "It really is okay."

It was not okay, and Brecken knew that with a clarity that hurt. Within days, maybe within hours, Leo Pistorius or one of the other people who worshiped at the East Church would find Blakeney's body; within days, maybe within hours, the Radiance would know that their plans had failed, and they would send in another negation team to finish the job. The future she'd dreaded for years was only hours away: she could find no way to deny that. She closed her eyes, forced her thoughts aside, tried to brace herself for the ordeal to come.

A few moments later the ordinary low sounds of traffic from outside drew together into a car coming closer. Brecken looked up, wary, as it turned and came to a stop in the driveway. Panic surged through her, but one of Sho's pseudopods took her arm again. ♪*No,*♪ said the shoggoth. ♪*We must stay here. This is the only place we will be safe.*♪

Brecken made herself nod, and settle back onto the sofa. A minute passed, maybe, before a key rattled in the kitchen door. The door opened and closed—and then she heard the familiar sound of June's four-footed cane on the linoleum.

A moment later June came into the parlor, glanced at them, and let out a ragged sigh. "Good," she said. "I was told one or both of you might not be around any more."

Brecken tried to process the words. "Who told you that?"

"Someone I never dreamed I'd meet face to face," said June as she settled on her usual end of the sofa. Brecken rejoined Sho on the other end. "Do either of you know who April Castaigne is?" When Brecken shook her head and Sho made a rippling motion that meant the same thing: "The commander of the Fellowship of the Yellow Sign."

Sho shifted suddenly in a way that radiated surprise. For her part, Brecken could only think to say, "Any relation to the playwright?"

"Why, yes," said June. "The Castaignes are descended from the King, and they've served him for I don't know how many centuries." Then: "She's—somewhere near Arkham right now; we can skip the details. She needed to know some things about what's been happening in Arkham, about your opera, and—" She shrugged. "About the two of you. I don't know why. I do know that we're all supposed to stay here indoors until we get word otherwise."

"Did she learn that from the Dweller in Darkness?" Sho asked her.

June seemed taken aback. "Nyogtha? No." In a low voice: "The message came from Carcosa—from my father."

Something had changed in the house when June finished speaking. Brecken knew that at once, but a moment passed before she realized what it was: the broodlings had stopped singing. She looked up suddenly, sensed Sho doing the same thing.

"Before both of you head upstairs," June said then, "I hope someone will tell me what happened to you."

"Sure," said Brecken. To Sho: ♪*I know you wish to see to the broodlings. Go, and I will speak to June, and then make food for us all.*♪ A pair of pseudopods embraced her, and then Sho slid off the couch and went to the stair. Brecken watched her go, then turned back to June and said, "It—it's kind of hard to talk about. Sho had to kill somebody."

The old woman nodded as though it was nothing unexpected. "April Castaigne thought it would come to that." Then, leaning forward with something close to her old decisiveness: "Tell me everything that happened, from the beginning."

Brecken managed an unsteady nod. "I can do that."

"Good," said June. "Because Castaigne isn't alone. The Fellowship's here, more of them than I've ever seen in one place. I need to know what's going on, because I think we're about to be in the middle of a war."

CHAPTER 15

SERVANTS OF THE KING

Half an hour later, Brecken was busy in the downstairs kitchen, trying not to think of Henry Blakeney's corpse sprawled in the silent church or the harrowing news June had brought. Outside the kitchen window, the last light had given way to darkness and a gibbous moon was rising. She had just finished mixing grated cheese into hot polenta when a low uneven knocking sounded at the door. "I'll get it," June said from the parlor.

"You don't have to," Brecken called back. "I can—"

The sofa creaked. "So can I," June said. "The nurse says I ought to get more exercise anyway." Soft footfalls and the clack of the cane's four feet against the floorboards faded as the old woman headed into the entry. Brecken glanced toward the parlor with a worried smile, then turned her attention to the polenta, sniffed a spoonful, added more salt.

She'd just set the polenta aside to cool and was gathering vegetables from the fridge for a salad when June called: "Brecken, you need to come here."

Startled, she put down the lettuce and headed into the parlor. June came back out of the entry and said, "There's a shoggoth at the door who wants to talk to you."

246

Brecken stopped, wondering if June was making a joke, but the expression on the old woman's face had no trace of levity. She hurried over to the entry.

There was indeed a shoggoth waiting for her there, just inside the door: only a little larger than Sho, drawn up into a compact trembling mass that spoke eloquently of exhaustion and fear. "Br'k'n K'nd'll," the shoggoth said, struggling to form the words.

♪That's my human name,♪ Brecken piped. ♪Today my name is Cloud Before The Wind.♪

The moment she began speaking in the shoggoth language, six eyes snapped open and stared at her. ♪I—I have no name today,♪ the shoggoth said. ♪The Dweller in Darkness asks me to give a thing to you, so that you may send it to another. I do not know that other. His name is this.♪ With a visible effort: "K'ng n Y'lo."

As soon as the name made sense to her, Brecken turned. "June—"

"I heard. I'll call the Fellowship." The old woman hurried to her study, closed the door.

♪She's gone to speak to the servants of that one,♪ Brecken said to the shoggoth. ♪The thing you have will go to him.♪

♪It—it must go quickly. Please—♪

♪It will. That one's servants don't delay.♪

The shoggoth hesitated a moment longer, then stretched and flowed. A space opened on the side toward Brecken, revealing something flat, a shape of gray metal. A pseudopod closed on it and held it out, and Brecken took it: an expensive laptop computer. ♪This is the thing,♪ said the shoggoth. ♪I—I killed to get it. It must go to the one I named—♪

Just then June came back out of her study. "They're on their way."

♪His servants have been called,♪ Brecken said to the shoggoth. ♪They'll be here soon, and this will go to him at once.♪

♪It—it is well,♪ said the shoggoth.

The creature crouched before her, trembling, and Brecken drew in an unsteady breath, pushed aside her worries. ♪*But I think you need shelter and food,*♪ she whistled to it. ♪*Will you come further in? Or perhaps there's another place you must go.*♪

♪*There is no other place,*♪ said the shoggoth. ♪*I do not know if there is a place for me anywhere.*♪

♪*You're welcome here,*♪ Brecken said. She would have said more, but suddenly the shoggoth was staring past her at the staircase, twelve pale eyes wide open.

"Mama Brecken!" cried a high piping voice. Brecken turned, to find Allegro bounding down the stairs toward her. The broodling stopped, seeing the newcomer. "Hi," she said, and then remembered her manners. ♪*My name today is Runs Ahead.*♪

♪*I—I have—no name,*♪ the shoggoth said in tones that wavered and shook. ♪*I have not had a name in—in—*♪

♪*There are other broodlings in this place, with their broodmother,*♪ Brecken said then. ♪*You're welcome to stay here also.*♪

♪*Then—then I will stay,*♪ the shoggoth said, in a whistle barely audible.

Brecken turned toward the stair. "Did your mother want you to tell me something?"

"She told me to find out whether you need help before dinner," Allegro said.

"Go straight back up to her," Brecken told the broodling. "Tell her that there's another of your people here, one who needs help, one who was sent by Nyogtha. Ask her to come down as soon as she can and bring all your sisters."

"I'll tell her," Allegro said, and bounded back up the stairs. Brecken watched her go, then realized that the shoggoth in the entry was watching the broodling too, staring after Allegro with a tremendous longing in her many eyes.

* * *

Shapes in motion, clatter of pots and mutter of boiling water as another pan of polenta got cooked the fast way, low voices as a lean woman with a wolf's eyes came to speak to June and left with the laptop, quiet piping sounds as Sho talked with the still nameless shoggoth, and then bowls of cheese polenta for all, with apricot jam on top for the eight shoggoths and salad on the side for the two humans: that was how the next hour or so went. Brecken managed to push her fears aside for the moment and enjoy the meal, the time with Sho and the others, the pleasures of the familiar. Afterward, while Vivace and Andante saw to the dishes, the newcomer settled in dazed satiety on one of the armchairs and promptly slid far onto the dreaming-side. Four broodlings nestled down on or around her. June, Brecken, and Sho sat on the sofa and talked.

"Her story started the same way mine did," Sho said. She huddled down, sheltered in the circle of Brecken's arms, staring with three eyes at nothing anyone else could see. "The negation team came for her people the way they came for mine, and Nyogtha led her to safety the way he led me. But she was like Traces A Line—" That was Fermata's name that day. "—and likes to be alone much of the time, and so Nyogtha guided her differently."

"He brought her to human servants of the Great Old Ones, and they took her to a place up in the mountains—its name is D'n'sh, or something like that. The humans there were very kind to her, they gave her shelter and saw to her needs. They knew some of our language, and their broodlings learned more of it, and so she was content for a while."

"But Nyogtha had something else he wished her to do, and so last summer he had her leave that place at night without saying anything to anyone. She went along the bank of a river for many nights, and then followed Nyogtha's guiding through hills and forests and then through one human town after another, until she came to a place where there were many buildings with no windows and many locked and guarded doors. That was where Nyogtha wanted her to be, and so she slipped into one of the buildings and found places to hide there, and learned the ways of the humans who worked in it. She was all alone, all she had for food was the garbage the humans left, and all she had for company was the hope of vengeance.

"She didn't say much about what happened to her when her people died, but I think ..." Sho's voice trickled away. "I think it was worse than what happened to me. Maybe much worse. The thing she wanted more than anything else was to hurt the ones who did it, hurt them so badly that the pain sat beside them night and day the way it sat beside her, and that was what the Dweller in Darkness promised her. So she stayed there and watched and waited. She said that Nyogtha warned her that the smallest mistake would betray her to a death worse than the one her people suffered."

"That's true enough," said June, who had listened to the tale with her left hand cupping her chin. "If they'd caught her, they'd have drugged her, put her on an operating table, and cut her apart while she was still alive, to find better ways to kill your people." Brecken winced.

"I don't know," Sho said. "But if she made mistakes they didn't betray her. She was waiting for a moment when a certain thing would be left unguarded, or have only one human guarding it. Finally that moment came. The thing was left with one human to watch it, and she dropped on the human and killed him, then hid the body and took the thing and left the place by the most secret way she could find. Nyogtha guided her, and he had one of his human servants wait for her in a certain place with a car, and the human drove her to Arkham and left her in a dark place she didn't know, and then Nyogtha guided her here. That's what she told me."

In the quiet that followed, the ticking of the kitchen clock seemed loud. Brecken looked down at the shoggoth beside her, caressed her, felt a soft fluttering in response.

No one spoke for a time. Andante and Vivace plopped to the kitchen floor, their chores finished, and came into the parlor. ♪Comfort the newcomer, little ones,♪ Sho told them. ♪She has need of that. She lived alone and unsheltered in great danger *for days of days.♪* They piped their assent, bounded over to the armchair, flowed up onto it and nestled down among their broodmates. The nameless shoggoth blinked a single eye open, made a faint unsteady whistle that reminded Brecken of sleepy mumbling, and slipped back over to the dreaming-side.

♪*You have also been in great danger,*♪ Brecken said to Sho.

♪*Not alone,*♪ Sho replied, ♪*or unsheltered.*♪ She flowed up close against Brecken's side, and Brecken tried to keep herself from worrying.

"D'n'sh," June said after a few moments had passed. "I wonder if that could be Dunwich. It's a little town west of here a good bit, up by Aylesbury, and I've heard enough odd stories about it to think that there might be worshipers of the Great Old Ones there." She frowned, considering. "It might be good to see if the Yellow Sign knows anything, and maybe send a message—"

A sudden rumbling boom like thunder set the air trembling. That's odd, Brecken thought, I didn't see any clouds earlier. An instant later the implications registered, and she untangled herself from Sho and got to her feet. The sound had come from the northwest, as near as she could tell. She went to one of the windows, pulled aside the curtains, tried to see past the shoulder of Meadow Hill and the roofs closer by.

Nothing but darkness met her gaze at first. A moment later she realized that something was blotting out the stars in part of the northwestern sky, something that climbed steadily upwards. Then red light flared in the distance, and a great fireball rolled up into the heavens, darkening into another great plume of smoke as it rose. Thunder followed moments later, low and hard, shaking the glass.

"Oh dear God," Brecken said aloud.

"That will be the Fellowship," said June.

Brecken turned to face her, appalled. "What was in the laptop?"

"I have no idea," the old woman said. "But if I had to guess, I'd say that Nyogtha kept his promise to our new friend—and the Radiance isn't going to forget tonight any time soon."

* * *

Months passed before Brecken heard the whole story of the night that followed: the commands from far Carcosa that sent the servants of the King in Yellow sprinting for their cars to meet shapeless allies from the deep places of the world, the explosions and gunfire heard in some places, the archaic weapons and sorceries wielded in others, and here and there, nameless forces that surged up out of the depths or plunged down out of the sky and left no traces that human minds could grasp or name. That night certain airplanes took off and never landed, certain buildings stood empty or had been blown apart when morning came, and certain ships were found drifting at sea, days or weeks later, with no signs of struggle and no one aboard.

At the time Brecken knew nothing of all that. The two great blasts north of Arkham were followed by silence and darkness, then by the dim howling of sirens in the distance as the fire department responded, and then by more silence. Eventually the three of them called it a night, June imperturbable, Sho exhausted, Brecken tense with dread.

Despite Sho's comforting presence pressed close against her, it took Brecken a long while to fall asleep. Worries chased themselves around her mind, and the image of Blakeney's headless corpse circled with them. A word that had been freighted with horror for Brecken for too many years coiled and knotted in her mind. They waked fears she'd faced again and again since a summer day in her fourteenth year, when she'd come back from an afternoon with friends to find her grandparents waiting for her with shocked solemn looks on their faces, bracing themselves to tell her that her mother had been arrested and charged with—

Murder. That was the word that writhed through Brecken's thoughts, tangled with her memories of Blakeney's death. It didn't matter, she knew, that Blakeney had been ready to kill her. The same thing had happened to her mother—a drug deal gone wrong, pistols yanked out of pockets, gunfire in an abandoned warehouse—and the tap of the judge's gavel and the thud of prison doors followed promptly. Once someone found Blakeney's corpse, and traced Brecken to it by any of a hundred clues, what else could happen, when no human in Arkham but Brecken and June knew that shoggoths were anything but a legend in old books?

Panic surged in her again, urging her to flee with Sho and the broodlings to a hiding place. No, she told herself. No. Nyogtha told us to stay, and I'll stay. Even if that means—

She wouldn't let herself complete the thought. She tried to fill her mind with music instead, and after a while she managed to drift off to sleep.

Somewhere in the hours that followed, she found herself standing by the bed, naked and just slightly transparent, looking down at herself and Sho lying under the quilts, brown skin and black iridescence all intertwined. Though it had been more than five years since the last time that had happened, she knew at once what it meant, and raised her eyes to see utter darkness where the walls of the bedroom should have been.

"Nyogtha," she said aloud. Her voice sounded faint and ghostlike in her own ears.

Yes. No voice answered her; instead, meanings seemed to condense out of the air. *It is well that you heeded the advice I gave my fosterlings. The game has not yet ended, and certain moves are still yours to make.*

"Tell me what I should do," Brecken said with an effort, "and I'll do it."

Go about your life in the days to come as though nothing has changed.

She stared at the darkness in horror. "But the Radiance ..."

The words trickled off into silence. She knew, without having to be told, that Nyogtha had already weighed her fate, Sho's, and the others', and measured that against whatever the Radiance could or would do to them. "Okay," she said finally. "I'll do it."

On each of the three days to come you will leave this house, Nyogtha said, *and while you are elsewhere, someone will speak to you of the Great Old Ones. In answer, you will show them the emblem of mine you were given in Partridgeville. You may then tell them anything they ask.*

The thought of speaking openly about her secret life to people she might not even know left Brecken shaken, but she made herself repeat, "Okay."

It is to be done three times, once on each day. Do you understand?

"No," Brecken told the darkness. "But I'll do it anyway."

It is well. Once that is done, I will speak to you again, and then the game will be over.

The blackness dissolved, and sleep swallowed Brecken instantly.

* * *

Morning came, casting gray light across a silent world. Once Brecken was sure she wouldn't get back to sleep, she slipped out from amid Sho's pseudopods, got the covers settled over the shoggoth, and turned to check on the broodlings. They lay in a comfortable heap in their dog bed, far on the dreaming-side; only Fermata lay apart, huddled into herself, and the dirty gray color in her mantle had become more visible overnight. Brecken winced, wished helplessly that there was something she could do, and left the bedroom.

The stair creaked beneath her as she slipped down to the first floor, went to the door of June's bedroom and opened it fractionally. June was sound asleep. Brecken found herself wondering how June would cope if her caregivers had to flee, turned her mind elsewhere with an effort. Three days, she thought. I've got to do as Nyogtha asked for three days, and then—

She closed the door, knowing she had no way of finishing the thought.

The shoggoth who'd arrived the night before was on the waking-side already, though still huddled beneath a spare blanket for comfort. A pseudopod slid out and produced a pale eye as Brecken came into the parlor. ♪*My name today is Beginning of Dusk,*♪ the shoggoth piped.

♪*My name today is Waiting for Spring,*♪ Brecken replied. ♪*It is well with you?*♪

♪*It is better with me than it has been for a long time of times.*♪

♪*I am glad.*♪

♪*And with you?*♪ the shoggoth asked.

Brecken knew better than to hide her worries, knowing that Beginning of Dusk could smell them. ♪*I'm troubled,*♪ she admitted. ♪*I don't know what those we fear are going to do now, and—and another thing happened.*♪

♪*Winding to a Close told me of it,*♪ said the shoggoth. ♪*I am glad that vengeance was done and witnessed in the old way, but I know there may be trouble because of it. The Dweller in Darkness spoke in my dreams in the dark just past, and told me that I should stay with you and Winding to a Close, wherever you go, and give you whatever help you wish.*♪

♪*I am very glad,*♪ Brecken said, and it was true; the thought of two adult shoggoths guarding her and the broodlings made their prospects seem a little less futile. ♪*I also dreamed of The Thing That Should Not Be, and he told me to abide here. I do not know why.*♪

♪*Who knows his reasons?*♪ Beginning of Dusk said. ♪*I do not know what dealings your people have had with him, but the elders taught me when I was a broodling that the Dweller in Darkness is subtle and wise beyond any other that has ever been.*♪

♪*I believe that,*♪ said Brecken.

The shoggoth pondered her, and then asked politely, ♪*Will there be food today?*♪

Brecken had heard enough stories about the shoggoth colony beneath Hob's Hill that this didn't surprise her. ♪*There is food here each day,*♪ she whistled. ♪*When the light grows, and then also when the light fades. It is my custom to sing on that thing—*♪ She indicated the piano. ♪*When I am done singing I will make food.*♪

♪*You are so very kind,*♪ said Beginning of Dusk. ♪*I will gladly listen to your singing.*♪

An hour of hard practice later, Brecken hauled herself off the piano bench, stretched her fingers, and headed into the kitchen. Once she'd gotten hot cereal going and started a pan full of water heating for poached eggs, she went out into the parlor and flopped onto the sofa.

♪*I thank you for singing,*♪ said the shoggoth. ♪*In the place I lived among humans before, another human sang on a thing like that. She also was kind to me, and she taught the human broodlings who gave me my human-name.*♪

♪*I didn't know that you had a human-name.*♪

♪*Yes. My human-name is this.*♪ She tensed, and then said, "Gya."

"Gya," Brecken repeated, puzzled.

♪*It is a word in the speech of the ones who live in the sea,*♪ Beginning of Dusk went on. ♪*It means* lost, *and the human broodlings gave it to me because I was lost before I came to them. I was very happy, because it was a true name.*♪

♪*I don't know anything about the ones who live in the sea,*♪ said Brecken. ♪*But if that's your human-name I'll call you that, and so will the other human who lives here.*♪

♪*You are kind to me,*♪ said Gya.

♪*You aren't the first shoggoth I've helped.*♪

♪*I know. Winding to a Close told me how you fed her and comforted her when she was alone and unsheltered.*♪ Then, tentatively: ♪*She says you are broodsisters, even though you did not bud together.*♪

♪*That is so,*♪ Brecken said, wondering how Gya would deal with something so shocking to shoggoth sensibilities.

♪*I am happy for her,*♪ said Gya, ♪*and for you. I do not wish a broodsister for myself, that is not my nature, but if I did, it would be good to know that such a thing can be, since all my broodmates are dead.*♪

♪*I am sad for you,*♪ said Brecken, and placed a tentative hand on the shoggoth's mantle.

♪*I thank you,*♪ said Gya, and just as tentatively flowed up against her.

* * *

Once breakfast was over, Brecken got ready for her weekly trip to Kingsport. *Go about your life in the days to come as though nothing has changed,* the Dweller in Darkness had said, and Brecken had resolved to do that, even though the thought left her weak with dread. One negation team was gone, and while the thought of their deaths sickened Brecken, part of her was glad of it, glad that those who'd brought fire and death to the shoggoths of Hob's Hill had paid a suitable price—but there would be others. She felt that in her bones.

The Cadillac stopped in front of the house on Hyde Street promptly at ten-thirty, though, and the ride down to Kingsport was almost unnervingly ordinary. Once Michaelmas pulled into the carriage port and Brecken got out of the car, Emily came trotting out to greet her as though it was any other Saturday. Inside, though, the Chaudronnier mansion was crowded in a way Brecken hadn't seen before—a low buzz of conversation in more than one language moved through the air, most of the rooms she passed had people in them, and some of those nodded and smiled at her as she passed. Brecken responded in kind, though she didn't recognize the faces, and only later guessed that they'd come to see her chamber opera.

Not long afterward, though, she and Emily were settled comfortably in the music room, and Emily picked her way slowly through two exercises she'd been assigned, listened attentively to Brecken's suggestions, then did a creditable job on an étude while Brecken played along with her on the piano. In the great scheme of things, the fact that Emily was showing signs of real talent meant little enough, but it left Brecken feeling better.

After the lesson was over, Emily gave her a hug and headed elsewhere, and Brecken went to the lilac parlor, wondering whether that would be full of people as well. It wasn't, but Martin Chaudronnier waited for her there as well as Charlotte. Cold sunlight slanted down through windows. Tea, watercress sandwiches, and thin crisp cookies made their appearance. After he'd taken a sip of his tea, Martin said, "I hope you don't mind my intruding on your time with Charlotte. Unless I'm very much mistaken, though, all three of us have been edging around a certain question for months now. Last night—" He paused. "I received some startling news, and one of the implications is that it's time that the question was asked."

Brecken kept her reaction off her face. She could sense moves reaching out in every direction from the next few moments, across a space far more complex than any chessboard could be. Far too many of those moves could lead to checkmate for her and the ones she loved, but she knew there was no way out. "Please go on," she said.

He met her gaze. "Are you by any chance a worshiper of the Great Old Ones?"

Nyogtha's words echoed in her memory, but even so it took an effort to push past the moment of surprise and the months of gathering fear behind it. She drew in a breath, said, "Not exactly." One finger slipped through the silver chain around her neck, pulled the medallion out and let it fall onto the front of her blouse.

Charlotte gave her an astonished look, then glanced at her father, who kept the same inscrutable gaze turned toward

Brecken for a moment longer. Then he allowed a trace of a smile, and nodded. "That wasn't something I expected," he said, "but it makes sense of a certain piece of news I've heard. Would you be willing to tell me what you know of the business last night?"

You may then tell them anything they ask, Nyogtha had said, but one question rose in her mind, imperative. "Is it okay if I ask," she ventured, "if you worship the Great Old Ones?"

"Yes," said Martin. "The family's done so since ancient times."

"Thank you," Brecken said. "Yes. Yesterday evening a shoggoth brought me a laptop and told me what to do with it, and about fifteen minutes later the laptop got taken by someone from the Fellowship of the Yellow Sign. This was about three hours before the explosions in Bolton. That's what I know."

"So that really was you," Charlotte said, then caught herself and reddened. "We heard a little about that," she went on after a moment.

"The family has certain connections," Martin observed, and sipped tea. "I'm impressed that you were able to talk with the shoggoth. That's an uncommon skill."

He was testing her, Brecken realized, and guessed that she could trust him with the truth. "I speak their language," she admitted.

Martin and Charlotte glanced at each other, and without a word Charlotte got up and left the room. "Would it be fair to ask how you learned it?"

"Sure." She drew in a breath. "There was a—a colony of shoggoths, the smallest kind, near Partridgeville when I lived there. The Radiance killed them, all but one, and she ended up hiding in the crawlspace under the place I rented. We—we became friends, and she came with me to Arkham. That's why I was able to talk to the shoggoth that Nyogtha sent."

He took that in, picked up the teapot. "More tea?" Brecken nodded again, uneasily, and took her cup back once he'd refilled it.

The door opened a moment later, and Martin said, "My granddaughter knows the shoggoth language tolerably well."

At that moment Emily came into the lilac parlor, her mother behind her. Brecken could think of nothing to do but whistle, ♪Do you understand what I'm saying?♪

Emily's face lit up. ♪Yes! I didn't know you could talk to shoggoths. Do you know any?♪

♪Yes, I do.♪ Then, habit taking over: ♪My name today is Waiting For Spring.♪

That got her a look of amazement and delight from Emily. ♪I haven't had a name in a long time.♪ She paused, then: ♪My name today is Talking Again.♪

"Thank you," Martin said then. "I hope you'll forgive me for doubting you." Before Brecken could respond: "So you have a shoggoth living with you. Did the one who brought you the laptop leave afterward?"

"No, she's staying with us too."

"Two shoggoths living in Arkham," Charlotte said, looking a little dazed. "I have friends who'll be surprised to hear that."

"Well," Brecken said, "actually, there are eight." Martin, Charlotte, and Emily all gave her startled looks, and she went on. "My shoggoth friend budded three years ago, and we're raising six broodlings together."

Emily grasped the essential point sooner than the others. "It's had *babies?*" When Brecken nodded, she went on: "Can—can I see them?"

Brcken glanced at Charlotte, who nodded her permission. "I'll have to talk to their mother," Brecken said to Emily, "but I'm sure she'll say yes." Then, as the obvious question occurred to her: "Do you know any shoggoths?"

"I did," said Emily, with a downcast look. "I've got friends in another town, and they used to have a shoggoth staying with them, and that's how I learned how to talk to them, but the shoggoth went away. I wish I knew where it—where she went."

An improbable suspicion surfaced in Brecken's mind. "Is it okay if you tell me what town that was?"

Emily glanced at her mother, who glanced at Martin, and a fractional nod went back the other way. "Dunwich," Emily said. "It's in the mountains. It's really pretty there."

D'n'sh? Brecken could think of only one way to find out. "Emily," she said, "the shoggoth you knew—is her human-name Gya?"

Emily's mouth fell open, and she stared at Brecken for a long moment. "Yes," she said finally. "Well, it's not really a *human* name." Then, all in a rush: "Do you know where it—where she is? Is—is she okay? My friend Sennie and I used to play with her, and she was so nice to both of us, and Sennie's been worried sick about her ever since she went away, and so have I, and ..." Her voice trickled away, and she turned a mute pleading face toward Brecken.

"There's a shoggoth staying with us in Arkham now," Brecken said, "and her human-name is Gya. I think she might be your friend. She had something she had to do, something secret, and she's been through a lot, but yes, she's okay."

"I want to see her," said Emily, with more resolve than Brecken had ever seen in an eight-year-old's face.

"We can arrange something soon, if you like," Charlotte said. "I met Gya in Dunwich, and I'm very glad to hear that she's safe. I don't know much of the shoggoth language but I learned this." Turning to face Brecken, she whistled: ♪*I thank you.*♪ Brecken blushed in response.

CHAPTER 16

SECRET LOYALTIES

Martin excused himself a moment later without explanation and went out into the corridor. Brecken caught his voice, low and intent, saying something in French, and just as the door closed other voices began to answer. Charlotte sent Emily away just afterwards—"you should write to Sennie right away and let her know that Gya's been found," she said, and Emily hurried off with that mission in mind—and then poured more tea for the two of them. "I hope you won't mind if I ask a few questions," she said. "First of all, are you in danger now?"

"I—I don't think so. I don't know." She glanced at Charlotte, but the question stirred too many unresolved fears, and she looked away again. "I almost got killed yesterday afternoon." She forced herself to go on, past Charlotte's sudden indrawn breath. "But my shoggoth friend was there. There was a negation team in Arkham."

"Do you need to go someplace safe?" Charlotte asked at once. "I can have Michaelmas take you to a hiding place right now if that's necessary."

"No," Brecken made herself say. "They're all dead now." That fielded her another sharp indrawn breath from Charlotte. Then, pushing through her own fears: "I'm supposed to stay in Arkham and go on as if nothing happened. That's what

Nyogtha told me to do." Tangled emotions strained at the limits of her self-control. "But—but it's not me that I'm worried about, it's Sho. I know what they'll do to her and the broodlings if they find them, and I'd rather die than let them hurt her, or—or any of them, and I—I can't—"

She hadn't wanted to cry, but tears were streaming down her face by then, and she couldn't go any further. Charlotte got her a handkerchief, made sympathetic noises while Brecken cried into it. Then, when she'd gotten her face imperfectly dry, Charlotte said, "Sho is your shoggoth friend?" Brecken managed a nod, and Charlotte visibly gathered up her courage and asked: "And—and am I right that she's more than a friend?"

All at once, the secret of Brecken's divided life hovered in the air between them. She could lie to Charlotte, Brecken knew. She might even be able to make Charlotte believe her. Eyes open, she chose otherwise. She'd declared her love the day before in front of Henry Blakeney's gun, and that made it easier to say to Charlotte: "Yes. Yes, a lot more."

Charlotte took that in. "I've wondered for months now if there was someone in your life you weren't talking about. It was—" Her gesture showed uncertainty. "How you reacted now and then when I said something about Alain, or the children. Of course I understand why you couldn't say anything before now."

Brecken blushed and nodded.

"The negation team, though," Charlotte said then, with a visible shudder. "I'm not sure what to say about that. I'll let Father know. If you need it, we can get all of you to safety—you and Sho and the rest. That's something we have to do now and then."

Raw relief left Brecken dizzied. "Thank you, Charlotte," she said. "Thank you."

"Just call us, or get a message to us in any way you can, and we'll have someone take you to a safe place." A silence came and went, then Charlotte went on: "If you don't mind my asking, how did you and Sho meet?"

The sheer ordinariness of the question called up a fragile smile. "I walked in on her when she was raiding my kitchen." She repeated the story she'd told to Martin, then: "So she stayed with me and I kept her hidden and fed, and she turned out to be a really sweet person. That was a really hard time for me, and she was always there for me when I needed someone, and—" A little helpless shrug ended the sentence.

"And you were there for her," Charlotte said. Brecken blushed, but nodded again. "Marriages between humans and the elder races happen," Charlotte went on. "With the people of the Great Old Ones, it's not any kind of issue. And if you're worried about me ..." She smiled. "When I met Gya I thought she was perfectly charming. I'll look forward to meeting your Sho."

"I'll look forward to introducing you," said Brecken. "Are—are there other shoggoths near Kingsport? I read something about one of the Ambervilles who was hanged for doing things with 'shapeless black devils.'"

That got another smile from Charlotte. "I know the book you read." The smile faltered. "Unfortunately not. There weren't many in the colony here, and the last of them died around 1800. When I was a girl I used to wish they were still here."

"Now they are," said Brecken. "Well, at Arkham, at least."

"That's close enough," Charlotte replied. "But there's another question I ought to ask. You said that Gya's been through a lot. Does she need medical care? There are witches who know how to treat shoggoths, and the family can certainly arrange for one to come by."

Witches? Brecken tried to make room in her world for those, too, and managed it after a fashion. "I don't know," she admitted. "It might be a good idea, though. I know she spent a long time living in ventilation ducts and eating lunchroom trash."

"The poor thing," said Charlotte, wincing. "She must be glad for the change."

"Oh, yes. Did you know that shoggoths adore cheese polenta?"

That got a delighted laugh from Charlotte. "No, I didn't! Still, our friends in Dunwich told me once that the shoggoths in the hills there will trade almost anything for the farmhouse cheese the Dunwich folk make." She shook her head, still laughing. "I'll call Martha Price and see if she can come by your house later today. Remember her name; I'll have her tell you that I sent her, so you'll know you can trust her."

Those last words circled through Brecken's mind as the visit wound down and she walked through the crowded mansion, past rooms where the tone of the low conversations had taken on a new ugency. They still filled her thoughts as she climbed into the Cadillac for the drive back to Arkham. Charlotte was used to secrets, Brecken guessed, and that emphasized the extent to which Brecken herself was not. Henry Blakeney's scornful words echoed in her mind: "You really have no business getting involved in things like this. You haven't been anything like careful enough." That Blakeney hadn't been careful enough either, and died because of it, didn't make things any easier.

And once someone found Blakeney's body—

She forced the thought away, watched the last farms give way to bare willows and twisted pines as the car drove on.

* * *

The house on Hyde Street offered her the shelter of familiar things and people. June was in the kitchen making a grilled cheese sandwich when Brecken got home, and waved aside her offer of help. Gya had gone upstairs and had been cajoled by the broodlings into singing a song neither they nor their broodmother knew, an ancient ballad of the wars against the Elder Things that made the broodlings shiver pleasurably. Sho herself, once Brecken shed her coat and shoulderbag and slumped onto the sofa, flowed over to her, threw pseudopods around her and clung to her, shuddering. Brecken put her arms around the shoggoth and stroked her mantle, murmuring words that didn't have to mean anything. The conversation she'd had with Charlotte circled in her head, leaving her dizzied, and she wondered how to explain it all to Sho once the two of them were alone together.

She was back downstairs, putting the finishing touches on a salad for dinner and trying not to think about the future, when a knock sounded at the door. The woman on the doorstep couldn't have looked less like the witches of Brecken's childhood imagination if she'd spent all day working at it. In place of warty green skin and a black pointed hat, she turned out to be a plain moon-faced woman in her forties with brown hair, a loud sweater, and a vast shoulderbag. "Martha Price," she said, introducing herself and shaking Brecken's hand. "Charlotte d'Ursuras asked me to come by. I hear you have a house guest who might need my help."

Upstairs in the apartment, introductions followed, and the witch started in surprise when Sho spoke to her in English. That turned out to be more than helpful, though, for Martha knew only a few words of the shoggoth language. Sho translated effortlessly while Brecken led the broodlings to the other end of the room, next to the kitchen, where she fed them cookies and got them talking about what they'd learned from Gya. Five of them engulfed the cookies and let out the scent of freshly washed mushrooms; Fermata said little and refused the cookies. The first faint traces of pale streaks could be made out on her mantle.

"Well, that's a blessing," Martha said finally. Brecken glanced up at the sound of her voice. "She's in better shape than I'd have expected. She needs plenty of food and plenty of rest, but other than that she's fine."

"I'm glad to hear that," said Sho. Then: "Please forgive me if this is rude, but could you look at one of my broodlings? She's not well."

"Of course. Have you had another witch in to see her?"

"No," Sho said. "I didn't know about witches." Martha gave her a startled look. From the other side of the room, Brecken said, "Neither did I. When Mrs. d'Ursuras told me she wanted to have a witch see Gya I wondered if you were going to come here on a broom."

Martha gave her a startled look, too, then allowed a wry smile and shook her head as she crossed the room. "I wish. I bet it would get me through traffic—" She stopped, staring at Fermata. "That broodling's seriously ill," she said in a very different tone.

"I know," Sho said.

"If one of you could translate—"

"She knows English," Brecken said. "They all do. Her human-name is Fermata."

Martha nodded, knelt by Fermata and started asking her questions in the kind of low soft voice that soothes children and animals. It had the same effect on Fermata, and after a few exchanges the broodling abandoned monosyllables and, in halting tones, answered the witch's questions. The other broodlings gathered around, watching in perfect silence with wide eyes.

All at once Martha stood up. "I'll be back within the hour. I need to get some herbs and some other things." In response to the question Sho hadn't asked: "If her channels aren't too badly blocked there's still a chance."

Forty minutes passed before she returned. "You've got a bathtub? Good," said the witch. "Run a lukewarm bath and put this in the water while it's filling." She handed Brecken a muslin bag that let out the sharp resinous scent of herbs. "When you handle that, wash your hands before you touch any shoggoth but Fermata, and rinse out the tub afterwards."

Brecken made some rough approximation of a suitable response and headed for the bathroom. Water splashed into the big clawfooted tub. She got the temperature right and dropped the bag into the swirling water. The water gradually turned the color of weak tea, and the resinous scent filled the bathroom.

"Ready? Good." Martha came in carrying the broodling in her arms. "Fermata," she said, "this isn't going to feel nice at all, but it'll help you. There's stuff that's stuck in you and it has to be gotten out. If you can stand it, drinking the water will help. Okay?"

"Okay," Fermata said in a small uneven voice.

"In you go." Martha lowered her into the bath.

The moment Fermata's mantle touched the water she let out a high shrill whistle, like a cry of pain. It trickled away a moment later, and the broodling lay there in the tawny water, trembling in misery. Brecken gave the witch a worried look. "At least fifteen minutes," said Martha, her face set. "The longer she stays in, the more likely we are to save her. I've never seen a case of this myself, but my grandmother treated it more than once, and I know some witches in Maine that help the shoggoths up there from time to time." With a little laugh: "This is a lot easier. They're used to treating broodlings that are bigger than they are."

Brecken nodded absently, only half processing the words.

"When she comes out she should be wrapped in towels and kept warm. If we're lucky some of the wastes will come out then."

"Okay." Brecken struggled to clear her thoughts. "And then?"

"Another bath with more of the herbs this evening, and another one tomorrow morning. After that, as often as she can stand it. We're in a race to get enough of the wastes out before they finish killing her." Before Brecken could think of anything to say to that, the witch turned and left the bathroom.

* * *

The rest of that day crept past. Martha Price went her way, leaving an ample supply of the herbs behind, promising to return in a few days, and leaving Brecken a phone number to call in case Fermata's condition changed. Fermata came out of the tub after half an hour, still trembling in misery. Brecken, who sat with her the whole time, bundled her up in towels and tucked her into a quiet corner of the bedroom. The water seemed murky when she drained the tub, and a gray deposit like soap scum had to be rinsed down after it, but were those the wastes the witch meant, or enough of them to matter? Brecken had no way to tell, and fled to the unfinished composition—not a requiem, she was sure of that, but she wasn't yet sure what it was—to drown her thoughts in music.

Faint gray patches marred the towels when Brecken took Fermata out of them for another bath that evening, and that seemed promising. The second bath was a little less equivocal; the water turned noticeably muddy and left more gray residue on the bottom of the tub, but Fermata didn't want her dinner and returned to the quiet corner, where she shuddered for a long while.

♪*I hope it helps her,*♪ Sho whistled quietly when the two of them finally nestled down together into the big four-poster bed. ♪*I have tried to make myself ready to say words of farewell to her, but it is not an easy thing.*♪

♪*Of course it isn't,*♪ said Brecken. ♪*When I think of being without her—without any of them—I know I would rather touch fire.*♪

Both of them were quiet for a time. "I need to tell you about something that happened," Brecken said then, and sketched out what had taken place at the Chaudronnier mansion that morning: the words Nyogtha had told her to watch for, the conversations that followed.

"I'm very glad," said Sho, when she was finished. "It's good to know that we have a way to escape if we have to." After a moment: "And it's good to know that another human knows about us. I want to meet her."

"She wants to meet you," Brecken replied. "I think you'll like each other a lot."

♪*I hope so,*♪ Sho said. ♪*I am glad to have Beginning of Dusk here, to hear more of the voices of my people, but I am also glad to speak with more humans.♪* In the softest of whistles: *♪And more than anything else to speak with you.♪*

♪Broodsister,♪ Brecken whistled back, and Sho flowed up against her.

Morning came, and with it the usual assortment of chores, made much easier by June's ongoing recovery and the assistance of Gya, who liked to leave the dreaming-side at first light. By the time Brecken went downstairs for the second time, June had the coffee maker going and sat defiantly at the piano, picking out a melody slowly but precisely with her right hand while her left danced through supple harmonies. She glanced up from the piano as Brecken appeared and said, "You made the New York *Times* again this morning."

Brecken gave her a dubious look, and the old woman said, "Exactly. Care to guess who?"

"Quentin Crombie?"

"Of course," June said. Brecken rolled her eyes, found the newspaper on the coffee table, tried to ignore the headlines about another sudden plunge in the stock market and the latest bad news from the Greenland ice sheet, and found the right section after a moment's fumbling. She had to turn to an inside page to find the brief waspish paragraph that mentioned her and her chamber opera, which Crombie hadn't seen and dismissed out of hand as an anachronism. Of course he referred to her as "the reclusive neoclassical composer," which had almost lost its sting, and of course he garbled the name of the chamber opera, calling it *The King of Yellow*. She shook her head, set the paper aside and went to the kitchen to start work on breakfast.

Gya, who had been listening to June's playing with every sign of attentiveness, slid out to the kitchen to help. To Brecken's astonishment, the shoggoth treated the stove with cool indifference, and responded to her surprise with the first ripple of amusement Brecken had seen her make, and a whistle: *♪I have seen and done too many things to be afraid of fire.♪*

♪Is there anything that frightens you?♪ Brecken asked.

♪*That those who have been kind to me might think me ungrateful.*♪

♪*When water drips upward and bubbles sink down,*♪ Brecken said; she'd learned the saying from Sho. A second ripple of amusement, more definite, fluttered through the shoggoth.

After the meal Brecken ran another lukewarm bath for Fermata. "I wish this didn't have to be so miserable for you," she said as she carried the broodling into the bathroom. Fermata said nothing. The faint pale streaks in her mantle were gone, but she was still more gray than black, and the ammonia scent of her illness hovered around her.

"If you can," Brecken said, remembering what the witch had said, "try to drink up some of the water. It'll help."

"Okay," said Fermata in a thin exhausted voice. Brecken put her in the water, and the broodling shuddered, then swelled as she drew in the water through her mantle pores.

All at once she began to shake violently. Brecken let out a low cry. The thought that Fermata was dying seized her. Over the moments that followed, though, the water around the broodling turned the color of fresh cement.

"Can you do that again?" Brecken asked, her heart pounding.

"Y-yes." Fermata swelled again, the spasms began, and the water turned a deeper gray. All at once, in a frantic whistle: ♪*The water's bad. The water's bad. Please—*♪

Brecken scooped her out of the water. Gray scum covered much of her mantle. With fumbling hands, Brecken got the shower head going and rinsed Fermata off. A few minutes later the broodling was wrapped in towels and tucked into the bedroom corner, trembling and sick but visibly darker, and Brecken went back into the bathroom and cleaned up the mess. The gray scum made a thick layer on the bottom of the tub, and it stank. She was glad when the last of it was off the porcelain, and happier still when the last traces were off her.

That done, she went back into the parlor, slumped on the couch. Sho and the others were downstairs, leaving the apartment silent for once. Brecken glanced at the clock, and winced.

Part of her wanted to hide in the silent room as long as she could, part of her wanted to run down the stairs and drown her thoughts in Sho's presence, but then she remembered Nyogtha's words: *On each of those days you will leave this house*—and there was only one place she'd planned to go on Sundays now that *The King in Yellow* had finished its premiere run.

To go to the East Church, though—that took an effort even to consider. The thought that Henry Blakeney's broken corpse might still be sprawled there appalled her in one way, the thought that it might already have been found and removed appalled her in another, and if there was a third option, she couldn't think of it. Fears chased each other around her mind, until finally she realized that those would be easier to bear if she knew what had happened. She hauled herself to her feet and went to change into something presentable.

Half an hour later, with her unfinished composition in her shoulderbag, she said her goodbyes and headed out into the morning. Wind keened over sagging gambrel roofs. A few scattered bursts of sunlight made their way through gaps in the clouds, turning roofs to silver and the Miskatonic to a rippled paving of light, as she followed the familiar route to the church. The uncompromising brown brick mass of the East Church rose up stark and square against distant hills as she neared the door.

The door was locked. That was the first sign, for she hadn't had a chance to lock it again when she'd gone there two days before. She paused there for a time, gathering her courage, then unlocked it and went inside.

Her ruana was folded neatly on a shelf in the vestibule. That was the second sign, and the air in the east chapel smelled faintly of floor polish and not at all of blood, which was the third. She made herself go into the worship hall. Where Blakeney's corpse had fallen, no trace of his presence remained. Shaken, she went further, and suddenly noticed the words of reckoning Sho had written, still perfectly legible on the side of the pew.

She stared at the words for a long while, thinking of the night the shoggoths beneath Hob's Hill had died, the long strange road she and Sho had traveled since then. After that, for want of anything else to do, she went further in, past the empty space where the kingdom of Alar had briefly risen and fallen again, to the soaring shape of the organ. One switch turned on the light over the manuals, another set the blowers cycling. She got out the old hymnal with the ankh on the cover, warmed up with three familiar hymn tunes, wondered briefly about the strange lyrics, and then opened her notebook and began playing her unfinished composition.

The opening notes sounded against a background of broken chords, shifting from minor to major and back again, a subtle texture of mingled emotions that seemed too familiar to belong to anyone else. She hadn't written it for her mother, she was sure of that as soon as the first notes sounded from the pipes, but she had to play most of the way through it before she knew for sure that it was her own childhood she was remembering, celebrating, and mourning.

The Woodfield Elegies, she thought, and knew as soon as the thought passed through her mind that there would be more than one. How many? She could not tell, not yet, but she sensed that the one she'd already begun would take all her skills as a composer to work out, and the ones to come would lead her into realms of music she hadn't yet begun to explore. That awareness flowed into the harmonies she improvised as the piece approached its end.

The last measures wound up with a final wistful chord. The chord finished, the echoes faded into silence—and in that silence came the quiet sound of a few hands softly applauding.

* * *

Startled, Brecken turned around on the bench. Five people she didn't recognize stood nearby, facing her. All of them wore clothes that looked vaguely rural and just as vaguely out of date. The two old women had white hair in curls, the younger woman wore hers in a ponytail. The old man had a thin line of white hair around a bald scalp, and the younger man, who was in his early forties and broad-shouldered, had sandy hair and a short beard. All five of them smiled at her, and the old man said, "Sorry for the interruption. That was really fine."

Brecken blushed, got up to greet them. "Thank you. I'm Brecken Kendall."

"Oh, we know," said the old man. "We got to see your opera Tuesday—really fine, really fine indeed." As Brecken fumbled with her thanks: "I'm George Bishop, and this is my wife Susan; Billie and Ruth Whateley, and Owen Merrill. Pleased to meet you."

Hands got shaken, and Susan Bishop said, "I reckon you know that this building's being sold. We're from the church that's buying it. Mr. Pistorius told us the organ's in fine condition. It's good of him to have someone play for us to prove it."

It took Brecken an instant to make sense of that. "I didn't know anyone but me would be here," she admitted. "I come here to practice on Sunday mornings."

"My word," said Billie Whateley behind her. Brecken turned, to find the old woman peering at the hymnal Brecken had left on the music shelf.

"What is it, Mom?" said Ruth, the woman with the ponytail.

"I do think that's one of ours," Billie told her.

"It was in the bench along with some other hymnals," Brecken said then. "I don't know where it came from. You're welcome to look at it."

Billie handed it to Ruth, and she passed it on to Owen Merrill, who turned to the front and then said, "Starry Wisdom Press, Providence, Rhode Island, nineteen oh-six. It's ours, all right. I wonder how it got here."

"Miss Kendall," Billie said then, "may I ask a great favor? If you'd be willing to humor an old woman, I'd like to ask you to play hymn number 54. That's such a favorite of mine."

"Sure," Brecken said. The hymnal found its way back to her. She opened it to Hymn 54, recognized it as the one she'd seen when she'd first played the East Church organ. The lyrics about Cthulhu stirred a sudden hope. She put that aside, called the familiar tune to mind, and set the registration to something a little more commonplace than she usually preferred.

Fingers poised over the keyboard, descended to wake the organ's many voices. Brecken improvised a brief prelude, and then started into the hymn itself, backing the melody with the kind of accompaniment she knew old-fashioned American churches liked to use: spare and dignified, with ample room for the voices of the choir. The great gleaming pipes sounded above her. As she finished the chorus, she glanced to one side and saw Billie Whateley beaming, eyes closed, recalling some memory from many years back. Brecken, delighted, improvised a brief bridge and then started the melody a second time.

Without opening her eyes, Billie began to sing quietly:

> "Rise up, O thou Great Cthulhu
> When the stars are right at last,
> Casting off the mighty fetters
> That for ages bound thee fast.
> Dead yet dreaming, dead yet dreaming,
> 'Til the hour thou sleep'st no more,
> 'Til the hour thou sleep'st no more."

Brecken managed to keep playing, but it took an effort. All at once, in an old woman's reedy voice, she caught some sense of the terrible history and the far faint hope that had guided the worshipers of the Great Old Ones down through the ages. The glimpse left her shaken.

The last chords faded into silence. "Mom," Ruth said, in a low tense tone.

Billie opened her eyes, revealing wetness. "I'm sorry. It's just that it's been so long."

"I don't think it's a problem," said George Bishop. With a glance toward Brecken: "I doubt someone who writes operas about the King in Yellow is going to get upset from hearing the name of one of the other Great Old Ones."

By then Brecken was waiting for those words, and relief washed through her. "Not at all," she said. As she turned to face them, she pulled the medallion out from hiding and let it fall on the front of her blouse, just as she'd done at the Chaudronnier mansion.

Susan Bishop recognized it instantly, Brecken could see that in her eyes, and so did Owen Merrill. The others looked baffled until Owen said, "You pray to Nyogtha."

Brecken nodded, uncertain what to say next.

That got her a wry smile. "Our teachings don't have a lot to say about him," said Owen, "just what he is and where he came from, and why you want to be very, very, *very* careful not to offend him or harm his servants."

"It's true," said Brecken. Then: "Do you pray to the Great Old Ones?"

They all nodded. "That's what our church teaches," said George Bishop. "The Starry Wisdom Church, that is. I don't know if you've heard of it."

"No," Brecken admitted. "Is it here in Arkham?"

"Not before now. A bunch of us are moving here, and opening a new church."

A possibility surfaced in Brecken's mind. "I wonder," she asked. "Do you think it would be okay for me to come here and practice on the organ sometimes, after you've bought the church? There aren't many organs here in Arkham, and this one is really fine." Thinking of an incentive: "I can show your organist some of its quirks."

"We don't have an organist yet," said Ruth Whateley.

For a moment no one spoke, and Brecken guessed that all five of them were thinking the same thing she was. "Miss Kendall," Susan Bishop said then, "once we're settled in here, we'll want to talk with you about that, and some other things too. In the meantime, I'll make sure that Mr. Pistorius knows that you're free to use the organ as often as you like."

"Thank you," Brecken said. "That's really nice of you."

She was saved further embarrassment by Leo's arrival. "Good morning," he said. "I see you and Miss Kendall have met. Mrs. Hirsland's in the church office with the papers. When you're ready, you can proceed to the signing."

They thanked Leo and Brecken alike and headed for the stair.

CHAPTER 17

UNSPOKEN PROMISES

Brecken, still trying to process it all, watched them go, and then glanced at Leo. He was regarding her with his usual calm gaze, but she realized after a moment that he was looking at Nyogtha's medallion. All at once she knew what was behind the gaze. "You know what it means, don't you?"

"Of course," he replied. "Do you?"

The question made her stop and think. "No," she admitted. "Just who it means."

His pale eyes regarded her, unreadable. "If I were to ask you where you were given that, Miss Kendall, would you tell me?"

"I don't know if I should," she admitted. "I really don't."

A moment passed, and then he nodded, the movement precise, measured, formal. "Not unreasonably," he said. "Perhaps you can help me with something." Before she could answer, he turned, climbed up onto the platform that filled most of the altar end of the worship hall, and crossed to the drab little door on the far end. Brecken got up from the organ bench and followed, uncertain.

Click of the lock sounded loud in the worship hall. The door swung open. A bare bulb inside lit up, revealed dim shapes on shelves, and what looked like hooded black robes hanging to one side. "Here," Leo said, indicating something wrapped in black cloth. "If you could take this to the east chapel."

278

He stepped out of the way, and Brecken slid the object off the shelf, leaving it wrapped. Flat and circular, it was maybe three feet across, and lighter than she expected. Leo led the way, and she carried it after him to the little bleak chapel.

"It hangs from the nail," he said then, indicating the heavy nail that protruded from the wall. She gave him an uncertain glance, carried it past the pews and the lectern. He folded back the cloth to reveal a hole on the back of the object; Brecken nodded, lifted it up, got the thing settled on the nail, still shrouded in its coverings.

Leo nodded once, and then reached up and tugged on the cloth. The coverings fell away to reveal a shape Brecken recognized at once: a disk of polished blackness, surrounded by delicate mosaic work in blue, green, and purple.

She stared at it, astonished, for a long moment, and then turned to Leo.

"It's traditional," he said, "for each new initiate of his to put that in its proper place. It's also traditional that none of them know what they've done until they've done it."

Brecken's mouth fell open. "You—" she began, then stopped, realizing what the old man had implied. After another silence: "You know all about him—about the Dweller in Darkness. You're—you're part of the witch-cult von Junzt talked about."

That got her a fractional smile. "Yes. We have records of his visit."

She drew in a breath and said, "There's a room with that symbol on the floor."

"Of course. You'll be taken there in due time."

She nodded slowly. "Is it going to be okay when you don't own the church any more?"

"The buyers are happy to let us keep meeting in the east chapel. We're happy to attend their services, as we did the Baptists', and to pursue our own work within the shelter of theirs. Unlike the Baptists, they know it, and the powers they worship approve it."

"The Great Old Ones."

"Yes. Certain things have changed." Before she could respond: "You needn't worry about what happened here Friday, by the way. What remained behind is gone, and a false trail laid—you'll see it in the paper soon."

Brecken stared at him, trying to process his words.

"Perhaps you would like to come here this Thursday evening at seven." He tilted his head, indicated the symbol on the wall. "This should be put away now."

"Of course," Brecken said, still dazed, and took it down. The two of them got it wrapped in its covering again and returned to the closet.

"Good," Leo said, as he closed and locked the door. "And please do hide the medallion. The Sign of Nyogtha shouldn't be shown to others without his permission."

He nodded again and walked away, leaving Brecken to stare after him in confusion.

* * *

She was a block from the church when the implications began to settle into place, and all at once she was fighting back tears. Part of it was knowing that Nyogtha had other worshipers close by, part of it was that she'd passed some test of his and would finally have the chance to take her gratitude further than a nightly prayer: "each new initiate," Leo had said, and she thought she could make sense of that. Then there was what Leo had said about the aftermath of Friday's confrontation. Gya's words about Nyogtha—♪he is subtle and wise beyond any other that has ever been♪—piped themselves in Brecken's mind, and she'd read enough strange lore to know that Gya was right. If The Thing That Should Not Be intended Blakeney's body to vanish, then it would vanish, and if he meant to lay a trail that led the authorities away from Brecken, that would happen too.

It was more than that, though. In her conversation with the people from the Starry Wisdom church, she could finally glimpse the shape of a future that had room for herself, Sho, the broodlings, and everything else that mattered to her. Working as a church organist wouldn't bring in enough to live on, she knew that well enough, but there would be weddings and funerals, maybe a choir to direct, maybe other possibilities. Those along with composing, teaching, performing, all the other ways a musician could earn a little money—that might cover rent on an apartment in one of Arkham's cheaper buildings, and the other necessities of life for her and Sho and the little ones, once it was time to leave the shelter of June's house.

She kept walking, tried without success to think about some other topic. Her thoughts were still a tangle of hope and dread when she got back to Hyde Street. That was when she saw an unfamiliar car parked in front of the house. She hurried to the kitchen door, went in, heard footsteps on the floor above and the whistling of shoggoth speech closer by.

♪Foster-mother,♪ Vivace called out as Brecken came into the parlor. Five of the broodlings perched on the couch with Gya. ♪The human who came yesterday is here now, doing something with the little one.♪ Fermata had been too sick that morning to choose a name. ♪Broodmother wishes you to know that.♪

Brecken thanked her, but her blood ran cold. The only thing she could think of that would have brought the witch back so soon was a worsening in Fermata's condition. She pelted up the stairs, dropped her shoulderbag inside the door and looked around for Sho.

♪Broodsister!♪ The shoggoth slid under the bedroom door. ♪It is well with you?♪

♪It is,♪ Brecken whistled back. ♪But is it well with you and the little one?♪

♪It is very well with all of us. Come and see.♪ She reached up with a pseudopod, took Brecken's hand, and led her to the kitchen.

There on the floor, gray shapes sprawled across the lino-leum. It took Brecken a long moment to recognize them as the towels she'd wrapped around Fermata earlier that morning, caked with the same gray sludge that had gone down the tub drain earlier. There was a lot of it—two or three cups altogether, Brecken guessed.

"That's all from Fermata," Sho said then, changing lan-guages. "I came back upstairs a little after you left and she was calling out, asking for water. I got her some, and the gray waste started coming out of her pores. She needed more water, so I brought her a big bowl to sip from and then went downstairs as fast as I could and called the witch."

Brecken gave her an astonished look. "You called her yourself?"

"June dialed for me." A ripple across Sho's mantle dismissed the detail. "I told her what was happening, and she said it was good news and she would be right over. They're in the bath-room now. I think it's very good news."

"Oh, I hope so," Brecken said. Sho gave her a grateful look.

When she stopped in the bathroom doorway, Brecken could see Martha Price bending over the tub, sleeves rolled up, lift-ing Fermata up out of water the color of winter stormclouds. The broodling still had grayish patches on her mantle but most of it was a healthy half-transparent black. "That's enough for now," Martha was saying to the broodling. "You should get some rest, and eat something as soon as you feel up to it."

"Please," Fermata said. "I'm hungry." Her voice sounded weak and drained, but the tone of exhaustion had gone from it.

"How about cheese polenta?" Brecken said. "A big bowl of it."

Six of Fermata's eyes popped open at once. ♪Foster-mother!♪ she whistled. ♪Please? You are so very kind to me.♪

♪How is it with you?♪

♪I—I think I'm better.♪

Brecken reached down to the nearest of Sho's pseudopods, gave it a squeeze, and then headed for the kitchen while Sho slid forward to take the broodling.

* * *

Later, Brecken settled on the sofa with Sho up close. Fermata lay sprawled on her lap, already well over on the dreaming-side, with a considerable mass of cheese polenta digesting inside her. Martha Price sat across from them and sorted through her shoulderbag.

"Sometimes you get lucky," the witch said. "The books I consulted last night said you never know whether the waste products are going to come out slow, or fast, or all at once— it depends on details of shoggoth physiology only the Elder Things knew. The faster the wastes come out, the better, and when they come out all at once like this, it's usually not too hard to keep the channels and pores clear after that, with the right herbal baths and incantations."

"So she'll be well," Sho said. She sounded dazed.

"More or less." The witch gestured her ambivalence. "She'll need to be treated for the rest of her life—there's no cure. She'll never be strong, and she almost certainly won't have broodlings of her own, but she can still have a long and happy life." Martha pulled a bottle from her bag and held it out; Sho extended a pseudopod and took it. "She'll need this for the next few weeks. Three drops in drinking water once a day."

"Thank you," Sho said. She was trembling hard, and Brecken put an arm around her to comfort her. "I suppose you know how much this means to me—to both of us."

"I think I can guess," said Martha, smiling.

Brecken had already thought of the one difficulty, and drew in a breath. "I should ask how much we owe you."

"Don't worry about it," Martha said; a motion of one hand dismissed the matter. "The Chaudronniers are covering it, and if they didn't, why, you could just sign for the credit."

"I don't have any credit cards," Brecken said.

Martha gave her a blank look, then a second look, perplexed. "That's not what I meant. Haven't you been in touch with anyone else on our side of things?"

"Just the woman who owns this house," said Brecken. "I don't think she knows anyone but me and the shoggoths and the Fellowship of the Yellow Sign."

That fielded them a third look, dumbfounded. Then Martha shook her head in evident astonishment. "And here in Arkham, of all places. Let me talk to some people, and then I can put you in touch with someone who can explain how it all works."

"Are there a lot of people on—on our side of things here?" Brecken asked.

"Some," Martha told her. "More in Kingsport and Bolton—and there's going to be a lot more after this summer." She stood up. "We'll get you taken care of." When Brecken made to get up and move Fermata onto the sofa: "For the Black Goat's sake, don't worry about it. I can let myself out. You keep that broodling nice and comfortable. She's earned it." She went to the door, closed it quietly behind her. Her footfalls faded into silence on the stair.

"Credit," Sho said after a long moment. "I suppose that's something like money."

"Probably. I don't know." With a shaken laugh: "What I do know is that I haven't been this happy in a very long time." She drew in a ragged breath, went on. "And something else happened while I was out, something you need to hear about."

"Something bad?"

"No, not at all." Fumbling with the words at first, Brecken told her about what had happened at the East Church. Sho listened in silence, then whistled, ♪*It is very good. I am glad you will be able to perform rites for the Dweller in Darkness—I know you have wished to do that. And June will wish to be alone again, once she is well enough.♪* Then, considering Brecken through three eyes: *♪Do you think the humans you met know about my people?♪*

♪I think so. They know about the Great Old Ones—and the ones who pray to Nyogtha, they will certainly know of your people.♪

♪I am glad. The church is full of dust, like a place left empty for a long time. I am thinking that as the little ones grow, we can talk to the humans and ask if they wish us to clean it. It is customary for my people to help humans who pray to the Dweller in Darkness, the work will help keep the little ones out of mischief, and—♪ A shudder moved though her mantle. *♪I am very grateful to them for keeping us safe, by hiding what—what was left there.♪*

♪So am I,♪ Brecken whistled. *♪Yes, I think they'll be happy to have you help them.♪*

♪I am glad. It is easy to go from here to the church.♪

♪I remember,♪ Brecken whistled. *♪The next time I sing at the church you can come and listen if you wish.♪* Sho did not answer, and huddled down into the sofa in a way that Brecken recognized at once. "Broodsister," she said, "you've done that already, haven't you?"

Sho glanced up at her. "Yes. Once Nyogtha taught me how to find my way into the tunnels, I went to the church and hid in the upper balcony every time you played, and I was there watching when they played your opera the first and last times. I—I just hadn't told you yet."

"It's okay," Brecken said. "I hope you enjoyed the music."

♪Broodsister,♪ Sho whistled, *♪I was very happy to hear your singing. The only thing that makes me happier than your singing is you.♪*

Brecken blushed and kissed the shoggoth. *♪And the only thing that makes me happier than my singing is you.♪* Then, in English: "I hope they do want you and the broodlings to clean the church. I want to see their faces the first time Presto and Vivace get into a dusting-race."

* * *

The next day would have been ordinary enough, except that Charlotte called the day before and arranged to come over at ten that morning. Emily would be with her, though not her other children: Sylvia was going through a phase of shyness around strangers, Charlotte explained with a hint of embarrassment, and Geoffrey was being very fussy just then. Brecken laughed and told her not to worry about it.

By morning the house was as clean as five broodlings could make it—they had been so excited by Fermata's recovery that only a ferocious round of dusting-races calmed them—and Brecken spent the evening baking cookies until the house was awash with the scent of vanilla and spices. Even so, she woke in a pointless panic, and couldn't concentrate on anything as ten o'clock drew closer and the last distracting chores got finished.

At quarter to ten, she glanced up at the clock, gave a little yelp, and got up from a chair in June's parlor, sure that she must have left something important undone. A glance around the parlor showed everything in place, and a moment later she asked herself: why am I frightened?

She stood there feeling small and scared for a while, until old memories rose up and gave her the answer. It feels like I'm still little, she thought then, and I'm not. It feels like Mom's going to come into the room and start screaming at me, and she's not—

Because she's gone.

Something heavy and ragged fell away from her then. She drew in a long deep breath, let it out, and settled back into the chair.

A little while later, a knock sounded at the door. Brecken went to answer it, and found Charlotte and Emily on the porch and Michaelmas in the Cadillac on the street. The usual words followed, Michaelmas drove away, and they all went into the parlor, where June greeted them in something very like her old precise manner.

An instant later a piercing cry of dismay and longing that could not have come from a human throat sounded from one of the chairs. Emily recognized it at once. ♪*Is it well with you?*♪ she whistled. ♪*My name today is Greeting Friends.*♪

♪*My—my name today is A Broken Circle,*♪ Gya said in answer. Then, in a sudden babble of notes so quick Brecken could scarcely make them out: ♪*Greeting Friends, Greeting Friends, do not hate me, if the Dweller in Darkness had not commanded me I would not have left without speaking to you, please do not hate me—*♪

Emily trotted over to her and flung her arms around the shoggoth. What she said to Gya, Brecken could not tell, for the child whistled in low tones that Gya alone could hear, but after a while the scent of freshly washed mushrooms filled the parlor. June directed a wry glance at the girl and the shoggoth, then turned back to Brecken and Charlotte and made conversation with effortless ease while Emily and Gya settled whatever it was they needed to settle between them.

Finally Emily came back over to them, beaming. "She wants to be alone now," she said. "She does that a lot." A few more words, and then Brecken and her guests climbed the stair to the apartment. As the door opened, Brecken glanced at Emily, saw the delighted look on the child's face as the almost-Brie scent of shoggoths at rest filled the air.

Inside, Sho sat on the sofa—she and Brecken had decided on that, though Brecken knew how many fears the shoggoth had to wrestle into silence to wait for a strange human in so vulnerable a place. The moment Charlotte saw her, though, she crossed the room and said, "You're Sho, aren't you? I'm Charlotte d'Ursuras. I'm so glad to be able to meet you."

"Thank you," said Sho. "Brecken told me about you." A pseudopod wrapped Charlotte's hand briefly—Brecken had taught Sho the gesture.

"And she's told me about you," Charlotte said. Brecken waved her to the sofa and then settled next to Sho, and Charlotte sat and proceeded to draw Sho into a lively conversation.

Emily found a nearby chair and sat, at first delighted and then disconsolate. At length, when the conversation paused, Emily said, "Ms. Kendall, is it okay if I meet the—the broodlings?"

Brecken got to her feet, contrite. "Of course." As she went toward the bedroom, five pseudopods slid out from under it, and each of them extruded a pale luminous eye. Just before she reached the door a sixth joined them, with the last faint traces of gray just visible.

♪Come,♪ Brecken whistled. ♪The human broodling I spoke of wishes to meet you.♪

Emily let out an incoherent cry, slid off the chair, and hurried over toward the door as the broodlings slid out from under it. Brecken stood watching for a while as Emily and the broodlings introduced themselves with shoggoth courtesies and settled down to talk, making sounds like the flute section in an orchestra warming up. Once she was sure they needed no further chaperoning, she turned to go back to the couch, then belatedly recalled the cookies she'd spent hours baking the day before, and veered toward the kitchen.

Not many minutes later, one big plate of cookies and one glass and six bowls of milk found their way to Emily and the broodlings. Another big plate of cookies, two cups of coffee, and a cup of hot chocolate made a similar pilgrimage to the coffee table, and Brecken settled on the sofa next to Sho and listened to Charlotte and the shoggoth. Their conversation reminded Brecken of every other time she'd heard mothers compare notes about their children.

A glance to the other side of the room showed that the Chinese checkers board had made an appearance. Fermata had sprawled on Emily's lap and gone over to the dreaming-side, while Emily and the other broodlings huddled over the board and chatted in quick flurries of high-pitched notes interspersed with sentences of English. It all seemed perfectly normal, and that was more than enough to make it perfectly strange.

All these years, Brecken thought, I've been sure that all the other humans would look at shoggoths and see only monsters. Maybe some of them would, or most of them, but maybe—

Emily laughed, and the broodlings rippled in response. Brecken sent a smile their way, saw Charlotte are doing the same thing and Sho watching with a comparable state of amused regard. Brecken beamed, refilled the cups, and let herself be drawn into the conversation.

* * *

Her thoughts were still a jumble of hopes and fears when she left for the bus station that evening. A flurry of APARTMENT FOR RENT signs and the burnt-out shell of the house on Garrison Street, still marked off with yellow tape, stirred unwelcome memories. When she got near the bus station she tried to find something else to think about, and made the mistake of looking at a newspaper vending machine with the latest issue of the Arkham *Advertiser*.

LOCAL MAN FEARED DROWNED, the headline on the front page yelled, right above a picture of Henry Blakeney. She stood facing it for a moment, then found change in her purse, bought a copy, and went to the bus station with it tucked into her shoulderbag.

The ten minutes or so before the bus came gave her ample time to read the article. According to the reporter, Blakeney had been reported missing on Saturday, and police had found his coat downstream from Arkham on the bank of Hangman's Brook Sunday afternoon. A search of the area had turned up no other trace of him, but marks on the muddy bank further up suggested that he'd slipped and fallen into the rain-swollen stream. The story finished up with a reference to half a dozen other accidental drownings in Hangman's Brook over the previous four decades or so, and cautioned parents not to let their children stray too close to the local watercourses.

Brecken stared at the article for a long while when she'd finished. In her mind, the image it set out—the coat lying on the streambank, the tracks of slippage in the mud, the body washed out to sea—warred with the memory of Blakeney's headless body sprawled on the floor of the East Church, smeared with the moisture-of-war, and the words of reckoning written nearby in the script the shoggoths had learned from the Elder Things far in the prehistoric past. She remembered what Leo had said about a false trail and the paper, and nodded slowly, trying to make herself believe that it was real.

The bus to Bolton arrived a few minutes late. Brecken climbed aboard, paid her fare, found a seat and tried to distract herself by reading the rest of the newspaper as the bus headed out Aylesbury Pike. That didn't help. The other front page article talked about tense meetings down in Washington that had something to do with the national debt, but nobody seemed to be willing to say exactly what. Inside, sandwiched between pieces about local happenings that didn't mention the explosions Brecken had heard, a two-page spread discussed the way changing sea levels would affect Massachusetts' north coast, described meltwater floods from the waning Greenland and Antarctic ice caps, and talked about towns already abandoned to the rising waters. One of the towns the article mentioned, Innsmouth, stirred a dim chord in her memory.

She nearly forgot about it all, though, when the bus swung past Briggs' Hill, turned onto Central Avenue and passed the old National Guard armory—or, more precisely, the place where the armory had been. Flame-blackened wreckage sprawled across the parking lots to either side, testament to the tremendous force that had flung the walls outward. As the bus rolled by the ruin of the building, she thought of the two great blasts she'd watched from the window of June's parlor and nodded slowly.

The great dark hulk of the Bolton Worsted Mills loomed up moments later, reminding her to pull the bell cord. A few moments later she was out in the open air, walking toward Pond Street. She fixed a smile on her face and tried yet again to shove away the things that perplexed her. Music, she told herself. This evening's about music, and the rest of it—

She tried to convince herself that the rest of it could be left until some other day.

Pond Street ended too soon. She climbed the stair, knocked on the cottage door. Matt opened it almost at once—had he been waiting? She said the usual things, shed coat and shoulderbag, followed him into the parlor. The others were waiting there, their recorders still in their cases. Tension coiled in the room. Only Danny, curled up as usual in his corner of the sofa, turned his usual half-smile on Brecken and seemed wholly at ease.

Once greetings were out of the way, Sarah waved her to a chair, gave her a bleak look, and said, "Before we get to anything else, we need to talk."

"Okay," Brecken said, mystified. "Is something wrong?"

"That's a good question," said Matt. "We're about to find out the answer." He glanced at Sarah, something wordless passed between them, and then he drew in a breath and asked, "If I mentioned the Great Old Ones, would you have any idea what I meant?"

"Yes," Brecken said, feeling a tremendous sense of relief. She extracted the medallion she wore, let it fall onto her blouse. "Yes, I would."

A moment of perfect silence passed. "I should know what that is," Matthew said then.

"It's the sign of Nyogtha," said Brecken.

Matthew said "Okay," Sarah said "Oh," and Hannah said "Wow," all at the same instant. They looked at each other and started laughing, and Brecken laughed with them.

"Okay," Matthew said again. "I wasn't expecting that. Do you know what we are?"

He didn't mean musicians, Brecken guessed that much. "What I know," she said, "is that Nyogtha told me that someone

would mention the Great Old Ones to me today, and I'm supposed to show them his sign and answer their questions. I'm
glad it's the four of you."

"I hope you still feel the same way ten minutes from now,"
Sarah said, looking grim. Brecken gave her an uncertain look.

"Here's the short version," Matthew said then. "The four of
us didn't put together a recorder consort for any of the reasons
we told you. We did it because we were told to. We belong to
a—an organization that worships the Great Old Ones."

"The Starry Wisdom Church?" Brecken guessed.

"You know about them? Good. No, the Esoteric Order of
Dagon, the people you met at the Grange hall on Black Friday."
He managed a smile. "We run with a lot of Starry Wisdom
people these days, so you're not entirely wrong." The smile
trickled away. "But Susannah Eliot—you met her too, she's the
Grand Priestess here in Bolton—asked us to form a recorder
consort and the order bought our instruments for us. Once we
could play well enough, she had us get in touch with you."
Meeting her shocked look: "Yeah. Our job was to spy on you."

"That's something we all have to do sometimes," said
Sarah. "We survive—the worship of the Great Old Ones survives—because we all keep our eyes and ears open and pass
on what we find out to the people who need to know it. Sometimes that means telling lies. This time it meant putting away
my fiddle for a couple of years so I could put all my practice
time into recorder, helping Matt and Hannah and Danny get
good enough that we could get paying gigs, and then getting
in touch with you and asking about recorder scores for your
Bourrée in B flat."

"Okay," Brecken said after a frozen moment.

"And the thing that hurt," Matt burst out, "is that you
turned out to be so friendly and so generous. We were ready
to do whatever it took to get into your confidence, when all we
had to do was enjoy your music and your company. Which we
didn't have to fake, by the way."

"Can I say something?" said Hannah. Before anyone else could answer: "We didn't have to fake any of it. You've been nice to me even when I've been kind of a jerk." Sarah opened her mouth to say something, thought better of it and closed her mouth. "And you didn't even get mad when I asked all those dumb questions about music theory last year."

"They weren't dumb questions," Brecken protested.

"See what I mean?" said Matt. "But that's the real story of what's been going on for the last two years—and if you decide that means you're going to get up and slam the door on your way out and never speak to us again, we won't blame you."

CHAPTER 18

FUTURES UNFOLDING

B recken tried to gather her thoughts. The others sat in silence, Danny serene, his cousins staring at the floor with worry written on their faces.

"Can I ask some questions?" Brecken said then. When Sarah and Matt both nodded: "Why are you telling me all this now?"

"Because Mrs. Eliot told us to," Sarah replied. "I don't know why."

"Okay," said Brecken. Reaching for the things that mattered: "What's going to happen to the Bolton Recorder Consort?"

"We've decided to keep it going," said Matt. "We talked about it, and it doesn't matter why it got started—it's worth doing."

"I'm glad," said Brecken. Then: "Do you have any idea why the grand priestess wanted you to—" She caught the words *spy on me* before they could slip out, and substituted something less offensive: "keep an eye on me?"

Sarah's expression told her that the original words hadn't gone unnoticed. "She told us a little about that. When you showed up in Arkham you had a lot of people on our side of things scratching their heads. You weren't part of any of the churches or orders or anything like that, but you obviously knew a lot about the old lore and weren't hiding the fact."

Brecken gave her a baffled look. "I don't understand. What made that obvious?"

"The shoggoth language you used in so many of your melodies," said Sarah.

An instant of blank incomprehension, and then Brecken brought her hands to her mouth, horrified. "Oh dear God," she forced out. A moment later the full implications struck her, and she lowered her face into her hands, feeling cold and miserable. *All along,* she thought, *while I thought I was being so careful, I was yelling "here's a shoggoth!" at the top of my lungs. Sho, broodsister, darling, what have I done—*

"It's okay," said Sarah, flustered. "That's how we found you, you know."

Brecken looked up, her face ashen. "It's not okay. You weren't the only people who recognized those."

"Do you need to get somewhere safe?" Matt said at once. "The car's right here, and I can get you out of danger and safe with friends of our side in under an hour. I mean that."

He did mean it, Brecken knew. "No. Thank you, but—but no." She lowered her hands, drew in a breath. "There's been a Radiance negation team in Arkham for a couple of months, but—but they're dead now." That got sudden shocked looks from the others; even Danny looked startled. "I may have to run for it at some point—" She made herself go on. "But it's not just me. There are others, and I'm waiting for word from Nyogtha." *I will speak to you again,* he'd said, *and then the game will be over.* What else might be over before that happened wasn't a question she wanted to think about.

"Okay," said Matthew. "The negation team—did they get taken out Friday night?"

"No, it was before then." Then, tentatively: "What happened Friday night? I saw the two explosions, and I know the Yellow Sign was involved, but that's all."

"You should ask Hannah about that," said Sarah. "She was part of it."

Hannah met Brecken's questioning glance with a grin. "Well, kind of. The King sent a whole bunch of members of the

Fellowship to New England a few weeks ago. One of their hep-
tads was staying with our people here in Bolton, and the Grand
Priestess sent me to help them once things got going. That
mostly meant riding in the passenger seat of a car and telling
the driver where to turn while the people in the back seat mon-
keyed around with high explosives." She grinned again. "Fun
times. But here's what they said. For some reason the other
side moved hundreds of their people to Essex County and the
areas close to it, not just negation teams but some of their top
adepts too. All the details were on a laptop—everything they
had anywhere in New England, bases and labs and weapons
dumps, who was where and how well they were guarded and
the rest. That got stolen by someone on our side of things and
it went straight to Carcosa—to the King—and all of the data
ended up in the hands of the Fellowship."

"I'm surprised it wasn't encrypted or something," said
Brecken.

"Oh, it was," Sarah told her. "A Great Old One can just look
at an encrypted file and see every possible decryption all at
once. Their brains are that much bigger than ours."

Brecken was still trying to fit her mind around that when
Hannah cut in. "So the Fellowship attacked them all at once.
I don't think they could have done it alone, but they had help.
You know more about shoggoths than just their language,
right?" When Brecken nodded: "They had help from shoggoths.
Big shoggoths. I've been up to Maine and seen the shoggoths
who live under the mountains there: good-sized ones, nine
or ten feet across. The two I saw made them look tiny. They
must have been fifteen-footers. I watched one pick up a car and
throw it through a bank of second story windows."

"The rest of us were down in the cellar while all that happened," said Sarah. "That's what we were told to do. We heard
the blasts, of course." With a nervous laugh: "And wondered if
the house was still going to be standing when we went back up
the stair. But I heard Saturday evening that the Yellow Sign and

the shoggoths made a clean sweep. Every target they wanted to destroy, they destroyed. The Radiance'll come back—they always do—but they got a good hard dose of their own medicine for a change."

Brecken nodded slowly, trying to process it all. It had been Nyogtha's doing, she was sure of that. He must have settled matters with the King in Yellow, then summoned the mighty Antarctic shoggoths and guided them under the sea to hiding places in North America, where they could wait until Gya's theft of the laptop gave them the knowledge they needed to strike. There was more involved, she guessed, and wondered whether she would ever know what part she had played in the plans of The Thing That Should Not Be.

* * *

"I wondered what was in the laptop," she said then. In response to their sudden startled looks: "I—I had it for a few minutes on Friday evening. A shoggoth brought it to me and somebody from the Yellow Sign took it away."

"You really do know about shoggoths," Hannah said, envious. Brecken nodded.

"Is it okay to ask how you know about them?" Sarah asked.

Brecken opened her mouth, stopped, remembered the way Charlotte had reacted when she'd found out about Sho, and decided to risk the same admission. "I live with shoggoths," she said, and watched the astonished looks as that registered. "Do you know about the colonies the Radiance destroyed five years ago?" Nods answered her. "I was living near one of the colonies then, and a shoggoth who got away hid under the floor in the place I was renting." Memories unfolded in her mind's eye: Sho crouched on the linoleum of the kichenette, shaking with fear; their first wary conversations; the unlikely bond that had grown and ripened between them. "I had a paper with some words in the shoggoth language—Nyogtha made sure I got that. So I could talk to her, and we became friends, and—well, we ended up falling in love."

A moment's silence went by as they processed that. Then, all at once, Matt said "Okay," and Sarah said "That's really sweet," and Hannah, grinning, said, "I want to see your kids."

Sarah rounded on her. "Hannah!"

"It's okay," Brecken said, with a luminous smile. "Sho and I— Sho is her human-name—we're raising six lovely broodlings, a little over three years old now." Then, having mercy on the perplexities written in their faces: "Biologically they're hers, of course, but that doesn't matter to me at all."

"That's really sweet," Sarah said again.

"Brecken," said Hannah. She had a look on her face that startled Brecken, uncertain and vulnerable. "Look, I know I really am a jerk, okay?" Before she could go on, Daniel leaned forward, pressed a finger against her forearm, and when Hannah gave him a startled glance, met her gaze. Hannah responded as though he'd shouted at her.

"He's right," said Brecken. "But go on."

Hannah blushed as red as her complexion allowed. "I want to meet your shoggoth friends. Seriously, I promise I'll be on my very best behavior."

"Of course you can meet them," said Brecken. "Let me check my schedule, and then I'll invite all four of you over for dinner and introduce you to Sho and the broodlings. They all speak English, so I won't even have to translate."

All at once she was trembling, and tears started in her eyes. "You have no idea what it means," she said, "that I can finally talk to you about my whole life. Thank you for being okay about—about me and Sho."

"Brecken," Sarah said, "of course we're okay with it. You haven't been around the people of the Great Old Ones much, have you? If you're entirely human, you're the only person in this room who is—yes, I mean that. People meet and fall in love all the time, even when they don't belong to the same species. I don't know anyone else who's married a shoggoth, but my mom's mom is a Deep One and so is my dad's mom's dad. Then there are the Great Old Ones—they're not even biological, but they've got half-human children."

"I know a daughter of the King in Yellow," Brecken admitted.

"You also know a son of Yog-Sothoth," said Hannah. When Brecken gave her a puzzled look, Hannah motioned at Danny, who simply smiled.

"The Black Goat of the Woods is my great-grandmother," said Matt. "That kind of thing happens all the time, so don't worry about anyone getting bent out of shape."

"Just wait 'til the Starry Wisdom people move down from Dunwich," Hannah said. "There are a lot of tentacles up that way."

"There are a lot of tentacles down this way," Sarah said pointedly.

"I met some of the Starry Wisdom people yesterday," Brecken admitted. "They're buying the church where my opera played."

"Is that the one they picked?" Sarah asked. "We knew they were looking for a church, the way the Esoteric Order of Dagon went looking for a lodge hall in Arkham."

"I hope they found one."

"Thank you," said Matt. "Yes, we did. There's an old Knights of Pythias hall on Peabody Avenue, a big place with everything we need. We're going to have a parochial school there for kids from the church and the order both." He considered Brecken. "I wonder. Have you ever thought about teaching music classes for children?"

"Yes. I've wanted to do that for a long time," Brecken said wistfully. "I don't have a music education degree, though."

His expression showed her how little that mattered. "You might want to talk to the Starry Wisdom elders and our priestesses, then. I know for a fact they don't have a music teacher lined up yet, and they want one. I'd bet money that they'd hire you."

Brecken stared at him for a long moment before she found words: "I—I'll do that. I hope you can tell me who to talk to."

Matt reassured her, but Hannah said, "I hope that won't take up all your time. I really want to see your next opera— and you've got to have your hands full already with six kids."

"Well, kind of," Brecken said. With a sudden smile: "Sho's a stay-at-home mom, of course. She takes care of the broodlings most of the time, I'm used to having a day job, and I'd really love to teach." Old fears surfaced, and she turned to Matt. "I hope they'll be okay with me teaching the way I want to teach, though."

The others gave her blank looks. "Well, of course," said Sarah. Then, catching herself: "I suppose outsiders don't do things that way, do they? All their plans and rules and theories." She shook her head. "As though our brains are big enough to make sense of the universe."

"The way we do things," said Matt, "is that you talk to the elders and the priestesses, and then you talk with the other teachers, and then you teach a lesson to some kids to show you know what you're doing, and unless the elders and priestesses decide that you can't do the job—and they won't—we all get ready for the start of the school year."

Brecken tried to process that, with the fraction of her mind that wasn't busy sorting through the ways she'd want to try teaching music to classes of children. Choral singing to begin with, she decided, and then a simple instrument with possibilities: recorders, maybe? Yes, plain inexpensive soprano recorders would work while the children figured out how much music they wanted in their lives and what they wanted to play—

Abruptly she realized that Matt had said something to her. Embarrassed, she apologized and asked him to repeat it. He grinned and said, "I'm about halfway through that right now. If everything goes well I'll be teaching math to the middle and upper classes come September."

"What kind of math do they teach in your parochial schools?" she asked.

Matt's grin broadened. "The arithmetic's pretty standard but the geometry's about as non-Euclidean as you can get. The lesson I'm going to teach Thursday after next is on five-dimensional solids." Brecken blinked, trying to process that, and he laughed and said, "Don't worry about it; kids love stuff like that. The thing is, teaching's an honest trade, and the credit you'll get for it goes a lot further than money does."

"A witch told me about the credit thing yesterday," said Brecken. "Maybe one of you can tell me how it works." Before he could answer: "But first, we should play. I've worked up an arrangement of Cassilda's song for recorders, and I want to see what you think of it."

That got a moment of silence. "You're really okay with what we did," said Sarah.

"If you're okay with me and Sho," Brecken said, "I'm okay with you." She pulled her recorder case out from her shoulder-bag, extracted the music, and smiled at them. "Besides, Monday evenings wouldn't be the same without recorder practice."

"True enough," said Matt, grinning, and started assembling his instrument.

* * *

June's house loomed up in the moonlight as Brecken neared it. She'd scarcely noticed the scenery on the bus ride home, and walked the two blocks from Derby Street deep in thought. After the practice session, they'd talked about how credit worked among the people of the Great Old Ones, and the changes in store for Arkham once the people from Dunwich moved to the old town. "The Esoteric Order of Dagon's buying up entire blocks of empty houses and leasing or selling them to their members and people in the Starry Wisdom Church," Sarah had said. "We're going to be getting a place there—it'll be more convenient once Matt starts teaching. You should look into it. The credit you'd get teaching at the parochial school ought to cover a big apartment or even a small house, with some left over."

We can do it. That was the thought that circled in Brecken's mind as she hurried home. We really can do it. Between teaching at the parochial school, playing organ in the church, lessons and music gigs and compositions and arrangements, she could keep herself and Sho and the broodlings fed and housed and comfortable. That would have been enough to leave her heart dizzy and dancing, but there was more to it, much more.

Martha Price hadn't exaggerated. Between Kingsport and Bolton and other nearby towns, more than a hundred worshipers of the Great Old Ones lived in that part of Massachusetts, and there would be many more once the Starry Wisdom people moved down from Dunwich over the summer. She'd already figured out that a great many of them had come to see *The King in Yellow*; the thought that she'd set out to find an audience and succeeded in finding a community made her laugh, but it also kindled something golden in her deep places, made her think of Grangers and Odd Fellows and other groups where helping one another was an ordinary part of life. Sitting on the bus as it lumbered toward Arkham, it occurred to her again that the help and comfort she liked to give to others was the help and comfort she'd spent her childhood longing for, and not getting. It doesn't matter, she thought. I like to be kind to people—but it did matter, because now she knew she could let others be kind to her.

That was the welcoming side of the future before her. There was also another side, and her friends in Bolton hadn't tried to conceal it. The Radiance was a constant threat, one that none of the worshipers of the Great Old Ones could afford to forget for a moment. The armed men they'd sent to Hob's Hill and Arkham were only the most obvious of their weapons. A phone call to Charlotte d'Ursuras or Matthew Waite would get her and Sho and the broodlings to safety if there was enough warning, but there might not be enough warning; there might not be any warning at all. The tunnels she'd learned about from Sho might help, and so might whatever unknown powers Leo Pistorius and Nyogtha's other human worshipers in Arkham could wield. Still, there were no certainties and Brecken knew it.

I've lived with that for five years, she told herself as she went up the driveway to June's house. Alone, too, except for Sho and June. Now that there are others—

She unlocked the kitchen door, drew in a breath, let it out again and went through. Inside, yellow light from the parlor spilled across the floor, and the only noises came from the refrigerator and the radiator pipes. Once she'd locked the door behind her, she went into the parlor. June was settled on the sofa, her reading glasses on, a hefty volume open in her lap and a glass of bourbon and water within easy reach of her left hand.

Brecken met her gaze with a bright smile. "I ought to nag you about getting to bed."

"Oh, probably."

Brecken paused. A dozen different excuses to put off the necessary conversation until the next day rose in her mind, but she pushed them aside. "Can we talk for just a bit?"

June gestured at the chairs and closed the book in her lap. Brecken went to the nearest chair, found Gya already there, far over to the dreaming-side. She smiled and went to the other, pulled it over close to the sofa, and sat.

"I was wondering," she said, "how you'd feel if Sho and I got a place of our own."

Even before she'd finished the words she could see the ambivalence in June's eyes. The old woman opened her mouth, closed it again, then said: "You will never, ever catch me being anything but grateful to the two of you."

"But you want your own life back," Brecken said.

June considered her for a moment, then looked away and nodded.

"It's okay," said Brecken. "Seriously, it's okay. I've been talking to people from the Starry Wisdom Church and the Esoteric Order of Dagon about teaching music and playing the organ for them, and I think we can work something out. Maybe as soon as this summer, if you're doing well enough to live by yourself again, Sho and I can move to our own place here in Arkham."

"Don't you dare become a stranger," June said.

"Not a chance," Brecken reassured her. "I'll be over as often as you can put up with me, and we'll be close by if you need anything. Besides, I want to see you wipe the smile off Seth Ames' face again."

That got her a sudden harsh laugh. "I'll keep that in mind," June said. A long moment passed. "If you can work it out," she said then, "that would be fine with me—but you'll have to give me your cheese polenta recipe."

"Sure. I didn't know you liked it that much."

"Oh, it's not for me. Gya and I have been talking, with Adagio doing translation duty—Gya's working on her English but she still needs lots of help. She's thinking about finding a quiet place to live, and I think I may just end up offering her one." With a shrug: "Sho was right, you know, when she said she thought Gya had been through a really bad time. Gya told me this evening that she'd budded about a year before the negation team came."

"Oh dear God," Brecken said, horrified.

June nodded. "Her lineage usually buds just once, and she's glad—the whole subject hurts too much. She's happy to see Sho's broodlings doing well, but sooner or later having them around is going to be more than she can handle. So I'm thinking that I can keep her safe and fed and teach her more English, and she can help me with the housework. Two maiden ladies setting up housekeeping together—what could be more New England than that?"

"Maiden?" Brecken asked, eyebrows going up. She'd heard stories about the way June had spent her teens and early twenties, before she'd settled down to pursue an academic career.

"Hush." June gave her a hard look, though the effect was spoiled by the smile that tugged at both ends of her mouth. Then, serious again: "But I think it could work. Shoggoths and humans don't have a lot in common, but somehow we seem to be able to get along."

Brecken thought about that as she said her goodnights to June, climbed the stair to her apartment, and greeted Sho and the broodlings. Fermata's movements were still stiff and she barely roused herself from the dreaming-side to whistle a greeting, but her mantle had turned all black again and was beginning to show patches of iridescence. The other broodlings bounced around Brecken as she sat down on the parlor floor, and Sho flowed up against her and wrapped two pseudopods around her. She considered telling them all about the evening's conversations, decided instead to talk to Sho privately first, and ended up misplacing the entire subject as the night deepened, the other broodlings joined Fermata on the dreaming-side, and Brecken and Sho settled under the covers in the big four-poster bed.

* * *

Somewhere toward dawn, as she more than half expected, she found herself standing beside the bed, glancing up from the quilts and the familiar shapes beneath them to the limitless darkness that replaced the bedroom walls. "Nyogtha," she said. "Is the game over?"

It is over and I have won, said a familiar not-voice. *Do you understand your part?*

"No," she admitted. "Not at all."

It is well for you to know. In the game the King's daughter plays with you, you have seen one of the smallest pieces, the pawns, moved into jeopardy, the bait for a trap.

"Yes. Yes, of course."

You were such a piece.

"I was the bait for your trap."

Exactly. Those I wished to destroy thought you were vulnerable. They hoped they could make you submit to their promises and threats, so they could use what they learned from you against the servants of the Great Old Ones. They thought I was too feeble to avenge my fosterlings. A trace of amusement tinged the not-voice. *I wished them to think those things, to distract themselves with those foolish hopes, while I moved other pieces into place around you—I, and the One in Yellow.*

We have been enemies in the past, he and I, but his servants aided my fosterlings in their time of need, and some of my fosterlings have been of assistance to his worshipers from time to time. What disagreements remained between us have been settled, and now our amity has been sealed in the blood of our mutual foes. He saw to it that you crafted the songs that lured them into our trap. I saw to it that those they sent here first perished, so that others would draw near and perish as well. You know the rest.

"Well, part of it," said Brecken. "I don't know everything that happened."

It is a simple thing. For each of my fosterlings they killed, five servants of the Radiance died. For each colony that was destroyed, five facilities of the Radiance ceased to be. Any harm that is done to me or my fosterlings, I repay in my own time and my own manner. I have had my servants communicate with the Radiance in five ways, to remind them of that fact. They will not trouble me or my fosterlings again.

"I hope they'll leave me alone too," Brecken said.

Amusement tinged the not-voice again. *They are foolish, but they will not be foolish enough to despise me a second time. When you come to their attention—and you will, I will see to that, when you use my fosterlings' speech in your music or tell the stories of the Great Old Ones in your operas—they will think I am tempting them again, seeking to lure them into repeating their folly, and they will fear me.*

Brecken swallowed. "Was—was that your idea? The shoggoth words in my music?"

No, it was your own thought. It was that act of yours that suggested to me the game that I have played. For that, I think, a gift is called for.

All at once Brecken recalled what Sarah and Matthew had said about the children of the Great Old Ones, and found herself wondering if that was the reward Nyogtha had in mind. Something too confused to be panic surged in her, and she thought: what if he wants me to have his child? Then, in a rush of pointless embarrassment: what if he doesn't?

No, the not-voice said. *I thank you, little one, but no. The ones who made me denied me that capacity.* A pause, then: *I am content with my fosterlings.*

Whether she was more relieved or more disappointed, Brecken could not have said. Through the confusion, she still managed to say, "So am I."

The infinite blackness of The Thing That Should Not Be regarded her for a moment. In that moment, as though reflected in Nyogtha's mind, she could see herself, all she had ever been and all she would ever be, a tiny and temporary shape poised against the aeonian immensity of the Dweller in Darkness. They were utterly different, she knew, and yet—

It is well, said the not-voice. *The gift I have in mind is also a task, and it concerns my fosterlings closely. I have pondered for some time now the fate of the smallest of their kinds. As you know well, they are vulnerable in ways the greater kinds are not, and since they were created to dwell in the houses of those who made them, they are also sociable and apt to the company of other species in ways the greater kinds are not.*

A little while ago—you would consider it a very long while—I began to consider that they might come to dwell with humans. I had not thought to put that to the test for another little while, but the actions of the Radiance forced the choice on me. Both those I sent to dwell with humans were treated very well, and for that reason I have decided to proceed.

From now onward I will lead more of the smallest kind to have dealings with humans. Many of them will come to Arkham, since they will wish to find humans who can speak their language. You will assist them. Another flicker of amusement stirred the not-voice. *I need not command you to do that, for it is your nature. Yet that is also the gift I give you, for they will protect you from those you fear. You know what my fosterlings can do, and you also know now of hidden places underground where you can be taken for your safety. They will guard you, and so will my human servants.*

"Thank you," Brecken managed to say. "Thank you."

The world is changing, little one. For an instant she could see just a little more deeply into the mind of The Thing That Should Not Be, and knew in a sudden dizzying rush that the universe had no eyes that could behold Nyogtha either, that it was as indifferent to the sentient darkness that surrounded her and the Great Old Ones themselves as it was to her, the shoggoths, or the dust mites in Mozart's wig. *The time of the Radiance draws toward its end,* Nyogtha went on, *and the hour comes when the Great Old Ones will resume their rule over this little world. What will happen before then, and what will survive to greet Cthulhu when he rises from the sea, not even the Great Old Ones can say. Yet their purposes and mine move along one path now, and I have made certain plans to protect my servants, shoggoth and human alike.*

She opened her mouth, but could find no words at all.

I count you among those latter, the not-voice said then, answering her unspoken question. *How should I not? I was made in imitation of the Great Old Ones. Like Tsathoggua, I dwell in darkness. Like Bokrug, I take vengeance in my own time. Like Cthulhu, I speak in dreams. Now I imitate Azathoth also. Has he his flute players? I have one of my own.*

* * *

Then Brecken was blinking awake in the familiar comfort of her bed, with Sho's sweet shapelessness wrapped half around her and the first gray light of a spring morning seeping around the edges of the curtain. She lay there for a long time, feeling the slow rippling pulse of Sho's body against hers, breathing the almost-Brie scent of a shoggoth at peace, while Nyogtha's words circled in her mind, luminous and dazzling. Finally she kissed Sho's mantle—gently, so as not to rouse her from the dreaming-side—and slipped out of bed.

The broodlings were heaped in their dog bed in the corner, all but motionless, though one drowsy eye rose from Andante's flank, looked more or less in Brecken's direction, sank again. Fermata lay a little to one side of the others, as usual, and her mantle was already tinged with broad patches of iridescence.

Brecken put on her bathrobe, left the bedroom and closed the door silently behind her. Chores waited, so did her instruments, and so did her composing notebooks, but the hour was early enough that none of those demanded her attention. She went to the nearest window instead, looked over the gambrel roofs and pallid lights of Arkham, the dark hills wreathed with mist further off, the sky poised between night's black and the first uncertain hues of the dawn.

Of all the things that could have come crowding into her mind just then—the deadly game in which she'd played so small a part, the future that she could begin to glimpse before her, the first stirrings of another chamber opera somewhere in the deep places of her mind, or the simple practicalities of the day ahead—Nyogtha's words about shoggoths and humans filled her thoughts. Something Sho had said about the Elder Things years before rose from memory: ♪*I think that things could have been different with those others. If they had said to us, we made you to do these things we need and wish, now tell us what you need and wish so we can live well together, we would have labored for them gladly, and praised them for giving us our lives.*♪ For some moments she wondered if human beings with all their faults and follies could succeed where the Elder Things had failed so miserably.

It's not the same, she told herself, and that was true. Humans didn't create shoggoths, after all: the distant ancestors of the human race still flopped aimlessly in brackish water when the first shoggoths slid out of the Elder Things' brooding-vats. Despite humanity's cocksure sense of its own importance, too—a common failing, von Junzt noted, of intelligent species in their clueless youth, before a few million more years in an indifferent world knocked some basic common sense into them—only now and again did humans rise or fall to the state of xenophobic arrogance that had been universal among the Elder Things.

She thought of the broodlings playing Chinese checkers with Emily, the ripening of her own relationship with Sho; thought also of tea with Charlotte and Sho, the way Gya had cried out when she'd greeted Emily, Hannah's longing to meet shoggoths. Maybe, she thought. Maybe we really can do it.

Then, unbidden—was it Nyogtha who put the images in her mind? She could not tell—her mind filled with brief fragmentary pictures of a distant time when the Great Old Ones had once again taken up their rule over the earth, when humans were not quite so young a race and not quite so brash and clueless. In those glimpses she saw shoggoths and humans dwelling together, the strengths of each making up for some of the other's limitations, weaving between them a society that was neither human nor shoggoth but somehow a little more than either. She saw human dwellings above ground and shoggoth tunnels below, intricate patterns of exchange and friendship and mutual loyalty binding the two species together, the Great Old Ones ruling over all in their incomprehensible majesty, Nyogtha pursuing his own subtle purposes from dark places far underground—and all at once, with an intensity that left her trembling, she saw the improbable life that she and Sho had made with each other as the seed from which that future would blossom in its proper time.

She clenched her eyes shut, blinded by the vision, and when she opened them again it had vanished. A first splash of sunlight spread across the sky, gilding the tips of the steeples. She spotted the East Church across the river, and turned away from the window, heading for the wall calendar to write down Thursday's appointment with Nyogtha's worshipers there. When she got there she found that she'd already made a note on that day. For once, her forgetfulness made her laugh, and she headed for the kitchen, got a pot of coffee started, then came back to the parlor and sat down on the sofa.

She reached for a notebook and opened it, found herself looking at some of the pieces she'd written toward winter's end. There on the last page, neatly pressed between sheets of paper, was the dry yellow ginkgo leaf she'd picked up at Upton Park.

Brecken pondered that for a long time. Henry Blakeney, she thought, and Philip Heselton: a retired middle-aged businessman leading a quiet life in a small New England town, and a hard-bitten officer of a paramilitary force who'd snuffed out a hundred lives under Hob's Hill and would have done the same to a hundred more in Arkham if he hadn't been stopped. One was the mask, one the reality—but was it that simple after all? She thought of their conversations, shook her head slowly, guessed she would never know for certain.

The ginkgo leaf remained, golden. I'll get this put in a frame as soon as I can afford to, she decided then and there. When Sho and I have a place of our own and I have a room for my books and music, it'll go on the wall over my desk. She could see it there against white plaster, challenging her the way she'd tried to challenge him: the one memorial, maybe, that Henry Blakeney would ever have.

She tucked the leaf back in its place, set the notebook aside. In the kitchen, the coffee maker murmured to itself. Outside, the day brightened and low sounds whispered up from Arkham's streets. The clock on the wall reminded her of the chores and challenges and delights of the day ahead, the rhythms of the life she and Sho had made together, the futures they and Nyogtha and so many others had set in motion. The rising sun touched the kitchen windows, splashed across old appliances and older linoleum. As if in answer, Brecken drew in a deep breath, rose from the sofa, and went to meet the morning.

ACKNOWLEDGMENTS

This fantasia on an eldritch theme is the second of two volumes. The first, *The Shoggoth Concerto*, began the story of Brecken and Sho, and spun the loose ends this second volume wove together. Readers of the series *The Weird of Hali* may find it helpful (or at least interesting) to know that *The Nyogtha Variations* takes place in the same fictive universe as that series, and ties into its characters and situations more extensively than *The Shoggoth Concerto* did, but touches only peripherally on the tale of the Weird of Hali and its fulfillment.

The events of this book take place some ten years after the events of *The Weird of Hali I: Innsmouth*, and the last chapter ends two months before the start of *The Weird of Hali V: Providence*. Much of the background to Brecken's interactions with the Chaudronnier family, including Charlotte's unmentionable mother and the complexities of Jenny's early life, are covered in *The Weird of Hali II: Kingsport*.

All my weird tales depend more than most fiction on the labors of previous writers, and this one fed even more enthusiastically than most on an eldritch banquet of sources from the golden age of the weird tale. Stories by H.P. Lovecraft, Clark Ashton Smith, Robert E. Howard, Henry Kuttner, Frank Belknap Long, and Arthur Machen all contributed raw material of various kinds to the story.

Certain more specialized debts also deserve mention. For the quote from Count Algarotti's 1755 *Essay on Opera* comparing operas to machines, I am indebted to Herbert Lindenberger's *Opera in History: From Monteverdi to Cage*. This and Joseph Kerman's epochal *Opera as Drama* provided some of the raw materials for the debates about opera, tradition, and creativity that structure certain parts of this novel. Thanks are due to the Seattle Opera, which introduced me to the opera as a musical form many years ago, and to the music department of the Providence Public Library in Providence, Rhode Island, which provided me with much of the background for Brecken Kendall's compositions. I also owe thanks to Edward Lasker's classic 1915 guide *Chess Strategy*, which helped me with another aspect of the story.

The hymn to Cthulhu on p. 163 is sung to the Welsh tune "Cwm Rhondda" ("Rhondda Valley"), better known to Protestants across the English-speaking world as "Guide Me, O Thou Great Jehovah." Nineteenth-century alternative religious movements in America, of which there were plenty, constantly took familiar hymn tunes and gave them new words. Since the Starry Wisdom Church, according to Lovecraft, was a nineteenth-century American alternative religious movement, I allowed them the same liberties as the Shakers, the Spiritualists, the Christian Scientists, and their many equivalents.

A more personal debt is owed to Sara Greer, who read and critiqued the manuscript. I hope it is unnecessary to remind the reader that none of the above are responsible in any way for the use I have made of their work.